Praise for Edward Willet's Worldshapers novels:

"This rollicking secondary-world contemporary fantasy opens with a bang. Karl, a portal traveler, bursts into a world where he doesn't know anyone or anything except that he must find the world's creator, Shawna. She's just opened a pottery studio and has no idea that she created the world she's in, until she unknowingly turns back time to save her own life from a man called the Adversary. He steals part of Shawna's shaping ability and forces her and Karl to go on the run and find a new way into the next world, learning more about her powers on a cross-country road trip. They grapple with the ethics of changing the world, the question of what makes people "real" when the worldshapers can change everything about them with nothing more than a thought, and the need to save the universe. . . . This novel sets up a fascinating, fluctuating universe with plenty of room for growth for the main characters, and readers will eagerly join their journey."
— *Publishers Weekly* (starred review)

"Highly amusing and fun. . . . This series is for fans of any piece or part of geek culture. With the infinite possible worlds in the Labyrinth, every book should be a new, enjoyable adventure." — *Booklist*

"Check it out if you like alternate world sci-fi/fantasy. It's a fun, quick read." — Game Vortex

"Edward Willett does an absolutely amazing job keeping the reader engaged in the plot and up-to-date with what exactly is going on." — The Book Dragon

"A splendid new cinematic novel. . . . All of the myriad aspects of Edward Willett's talent are obvious in this terrific blend of fantasy, references to great literature and history, and imagination proffered with a keen comedic sensitivity."
— San Francisco Review of Books

MASTER OF THE WORLD

OF THE

WORLD

Worldshapers: Book Two

EDWARD WILLETT

DAW BOOKS, INC.

DONALD A. WOLLHEIM, FOUNDER

1745 Broadway, New York, NY 10019

ELIZABETH R. WOLLHEIM

SHEILA E. GILBERT

PUBLISHERS

www.dawbooks.com

First Mass Market Printing, July 2020
1 2 3 4 5 6 7 8 9

For my daughter, Alice Laura Mae Willett, who is launching into university at the same time this book launches into the world.

ACKNOWLEDGMENTS

ANOTHER BOOK, ANOTHER round of acknowledgments! I always seem to thank the same people, and I'm going to again, but first, someone I've never thanked before: Jules Verne, without whose books this novel literally could not exist. Like Shawna Keys, I went through a Jules Verne phase as a young reader (my favorite, read multiple times, was *The Mysterious Island*), and it was a great pleasure to revisit his books and become reacquainted with his amazing imagination as I worked on *Master of the World*.

On more familiar ground, my thanks to my Hugo Award-winning editor at DAW Books, Sheila E. Gilbert. Her amazing ability to zero in on the things that need to be done to make any book the best it can be once again improved my tale immeasurably. Any remaining faults are entirely of my own doing.

Thanks to all the other fine folks at DAW Books. I'm always impressed by their skill and professionalism in the publishing of the finest science fiction and fantasy this world (and possibly a multiverse of other worlds) has to offer. I'm honored to be one of the authors in the service of whose work they bend their immense talents.

Thanks to my agent, Ethan Ellenberg, for all his work on my behalf.

Huge thanks to everyone who reads, not just my books, but *anyone*'s books. Writing is a solitary occupation most of the time, and yet in the end it is collaborative: the story does not live until it takes root in the mind of a reader. May this one blossom in yours.

And, finally, my thanks and love to my family: my wife, Margaret Anne Hodges, P.Eng., and our amazing daughter, Alice, who is entering her own new world—the world of higher education—just as this book appears. The Worldshapers of this series are fictional, but I am confident she will find her own ways to shape our world for the better in the years and decades to come.

May we all try to do the same.

ONE

BUFFETED BY SWIRLING winds, I clung to the rope ladder lifting me from the mysterious—and rapidly disintegrating—island in the ocean below toward the giant flying ship in the sky above and reflected on what a lousy week I was having.

Sunday night, I'd woken from a nightmare in which a stranger wearing a cowboy hat and a long black duster had been standing at the foot of my bed, only to look out my window and see a stranger in a cowboy hat and a long black duster looking up at my bedroom window.

Monday night, he'd been there again.

Tuesday, I'd officially opened my new shop, World-shaper Pottery, on trendy Blackthorne Avenue in Eagle River, Montana (hipster haven of the West)—although the store's opening had been overshadowed (literally) by the scaffolding covering the entrance (supporting two young men hanging the shop's sign) and the black storm clouds hanging over the Rockies to the west: clouds which, infuriatingly and bewilderingly, nobody but me seemed to find threatening.

Still, sinister strangers, scaffolding, and storm clouds aside, it had been shaping up to be a pretty good day. I'd had coffee with my boyfriend, Brent, at the Human Bean, the coffee shop down the street, and at lunch had headed back to the Bean with my best friend, Aesha Tripathi.

That was when things went literally to hell. Two van-loads of black-clad terrorists pulled up outside, charged into the coffee shop, and started shooting. Bullets tore Aesha's slight body apart, right in front of my eyes.

Then the leader of the terrorists walked over to where I sat stunned on the blood-slicked floor. "Hello, Shawna," he said. "And goodbye." He reached out and touched my forehead. I felt a weird shock. Then he drew his pistol and aimed it between my eyes. He was going to kill me.

This can't be happening, I thought, and then, "This isn't happening!" I screamed.

And just like that, it wasn't. It *hadn't.* Suddenly, it was three hours earlier—but Aesha was gone. So was everyone else who'd been killed in the attack. And the worst of it was, nobody remembered they'd ever even *existed.*

This, to put it mildly, freaked me out. The sudden appearance inside my shop, shortly thereafter, of the mysterious stranger who had been in both my nightmare and the street outside my window did nothing to soothe my nerves—especially not when he started spouting gibberish about me having Shaped the world in which I lived, and having an amazing amount of power, and being just one Shaper of many in a vast Labyrinth of Shaped worlds, and possibly the only one who could save the Shaped worlds from the Adversary who had just invaded my world (apparently he was the guy who'd pointed his pistol at my head), if I'd just follow him into all those other worlds and gather the knowledge of how they were Shaped, and then carry it to somebody named Ygrair, who . . .

Yeah, I pretty much stopped listening at that point, too. It was like "The Story Thus Far" at the start of an episode of a television series with a season-long story arc. When you're bingeing the show on StreamPix (and who watches TV any other way these days?), the minute you see that, you click the "Skip Intro" button.

But in the middle of this, "Previously, in made-up crap . . ." monologue, the storm broke . . . again. And then terrorists were shooting at me . . . again. Left without much choice, I fled with Karl Yatsar, as he called himself.

On the radio, we heard the mayor describe me as a

dangerous terrorist. Apparently, when the Adversary had touched me, he'd stolen my knowledge of how my world was Shaped, what Karl called the *hokhmah*. His power was somewhat limited by the fact I was still alive, which meant we were sharing the *hokhmah,* but he had enough to rewrite people's memories just by talking to them. He'd talked to the police, and the mayor, and . . . and then, I called Brent, and he didn't know who I was, and I knew the Adversary had reached him, too. I smashed my cellphone, not out of frustration (well, not *just* out of frustration), but because I realized it could be used to track me. Karl Yatsar and I holed up that night in a run-down closed-for-the-summer resort . . .

. . . and *that* was my very special Tuesday.

Wednesday had a lot to live down to, but it managed. First thing in the morning, I murdered a National Bureau of Investigation agent in a helicopter, just by imagining the pilot had to help me at all costs, so successfully the pilot pushed his partner out the door and onto the shore of the lake across which Karl and I, in a canoe, were paddling for our lives. The sound of the falling NBI agent hitting the wooden pier by the boatshed went a long way toward convincing me both that I really *could* Shape my world—and that maybe I really, really shouldn't.

Then we got into the helicopter, and the pilot cheerfully threw away his career by flying us up into the mountains before leading the pursuit away . . . though not as successfully as we might have hoped, since after Karl and I hiked off into the woods toward Snakebite Mine, the location of the Portal through which Karl had come from the previous world (already taken over by the Adversary), pursuers showed up at the fire camp where we'd landed. At Karl's urging to "do something," I hid our tracks by making it snow . . . or rather, by making it to have *already* snowed. Which also made for a cold, wet camp that night, but whatever.

Thursday, we woke to an unwanted visitor, a grizzly, which I convinced to go away just by thinking really hard that he *should* go away. After the snow and the grizzly, I *really* couldn't deny my ability to Shape my world, even though (much to Karl's consternation) I had no memory of his boss, the mysterious Ygrair, or being taught by her to be a Shaper at some weird school in some other version of reality, which Karl said was the *original* reality, the First World. Then we had to go around an avalanche that had resulted from the snow I'd caused to happen . . . I mean, caused to have *already* happened . . . and I had another reason to take Jeff Goldblum's advice in *Jurassic Park* and think about whether, even though I *could* Shape the world, I *should*. When it came to Shaping, it seemed clear, unintended consequences were a bitch.

This was reinforced later that night when we reached Snakebite Mine. After Karl cold-bloodedly shot two members of the Adversary's "cadre," who had been left there to guard the Portal, I Shaped the caretaker to let us into the mine. He blew himself up instead, burying the Portal under tons of rock . . . but I Shaped those, too, opening a path, and then helped Karl destroy the Portal, cutting the Adversary off from some of his power.

Then we drove off, and I Shaped an entire water-filled quarry into existence, into which we dropped the truck, and then I Shaped the caretakers of a dude ranch so we could take some horses, but I did it so badly they both ended up dead, as did a perfectly innocent horse, and then we rode all night long until *I* was practically dead in the saddle (I stayed awake only because I'm allergic to horses, and it's hard to doze while sneezing), and then we finally slept . . .

. . . and *that* was Thursday.

Friday, I Shaped a photographer to let us steal his car (at least I managed to avoid killing him in the process—well, as far as I know). Then I Shaped a pilot to fly us to Appleville, Oregon, my hometown . . .

. . . where I Shaped my mother to forget I'd ever existed. To forget she'd ever had a daughter. Of all the horrible things that had happened that week, that was the worst.

But it was only Friday.

Saturday, we stowed away on an apple truck to the coast. There, I Shaped a woman to let us onto her sailing yacht, the *Amazon,* because Karl said the only place he could make a Portal into the next world was out in the Pacific somewhere. Unfortunately, the Coast Guard found us (by then the Adversary had worked his way up to Shaping the President, so every branch of law enforcement and the military was looking for us). I managed to Shape our chunk of the ocean to bring up a fog (greatly impressing Karl), but in the process I also accidentally fashioned a typhoon, and that meant I spent Saturday night thinking really, *really* hard about the *Amazon* not sinking.

I guess I thought hard enough, because we were still afloat Sunday morning—*this* morning—which is when we found, right where the Portal had to be opened, a mysterious island that wasn't on any charts. The next thing we knew, there were helicopters and soldiers chasing us, and we were trying to find our way through tunnels infested with monsters, and then we were fighting for our lives on top of a human-sacrifice altar in an arena full of shadowy not-quite-real spectators. At one point a giant, naked David (Michelangelo's *David,* to be precise) smashed an equally naked (though not nearly as tall) soldier into bloody paste, then there was a fight, and then I stabbed a guy's foot, which spilled blood on the altar, and the Portal opened, and I went through it . . .

. . . and Karl didn't.

Which was how I had found myself on the almost-vanished island below, alone, only to be hauled aloft by a sailor hanging on to a rope ladder dangling from a giant flying ship both held aloft and propelled by . . . well, propellers.

In the bow, the strange craft flew a black flag with a golden sun in the center, one I'd recognized instantly, because I had gone through a Jules Verne kick when I was little girl (at least, that's how I remember it, although what in my past is real and what contrived, I can't tell): the flag of Robur the Conqueror, from the novel of the same name, which meant this impossible vessel had to be . . . yes, there it was, on the dark-blue bow in glistening gold script: *Albatross.*

The *Albatross*' hull might have come straight from a sailing ship, except for the absence of a keel—and except for the stubby biplane wings extending to port and starboard. These I presumed were primarily for steering purposes, not to provide lift, since the thing was currently hovering. What held it aloft were seventy-four whirling helicopter rotors, two on each of thirty-seven masts. The downdraft buffeted me as the man in an old-fashioned sailor's uniform who had pulled me onto the lowest rungs of the ladder looked down at me, jerked his thumb upward, then started to climb. For the first time, I saw he wore earplugs.

There is a knack to climbing a rope ladder, which I apparently didn't have. The thing swayed and bounced as I struggled upward, until I thought I'd either fall off or throw up, but eventually, panting, I reached the top. My rescuer, with the help of another man in an equally old-fashioned sailor's uniform—honestly, they looked like they'd stepped straight out of a community theater production of *HMS Pinafore*—hauled me onto the deck, through an opening in the wire trellis that ringed it in lieu of bulwarks, leaving me sprawled on my stomach. This gave me an unexpected opportunity to closely examine the deck. It wasn't made of wood; it was a smooth, unbroken expanse of dark-blue . . . something.

What *was* the *Albatross* made of? It had been nearly twenty years since I'd read *Robur the Conqueror*. For some reason "paper" came to mind, but that couldn't be right, could it . . . ?

The sailors—or maybe "aeronauts" was a better term—grabbed my arms and pulled me to my feet. I tried to tug free, but their grips tightened. They half-dragged me aft, beneath the howling rotors—making me wish I had earplugs, too—toward the cabins at the back. Atop the sternmost stood the helmsman, as *Pinafore*ishly clad as the rest of the crew, inside a glass wheelhouse. Behind him, as at the bow, hung two much larger propellers, vertical rather than horizontal, though only idling at the moment.

The whole flying monstrosity was impossible . . . or

was it? Verne had based his flights of fancy on what the engineers and scientists of his time knew or thought they knew. He'd certainly thought something like this was at least theoretically possible. And from what Karl had told me, the Shaper of this World could actually have altered the laws of physics enough to allow something like this to fly.

I'll ask the Shaper when I see him, I thought, as I stumbled toward the stern cabins (there were others at the bow) between my taciturn escorts, deafened and wind-blown. *Maybe I'm about to.* Clearly, whoever had Shaped this world had fancied himself master of it, and since this was the *Albatross,* the airship of Robur the Conqueror, aka Master of the World (the title of the second novel in which he'd appeared), he had surely set himself up as that Verneian character—supervillain or superhero, depending (like his better-known counterpart, Captain Nemo) on your point of view.

In a way, I was thrilled to be inside a world clearly modeled after Jules Verne's inventive tales. In another, I was terrified. Karl had not come through the Portal with me. I was alone, and while I knew in a *general* way what I was supposed to do to fulfill the quest I'd been unwillingly given—find the Shaper and get him/her to somehow give me his/her *hokhmah,* so that if/when the Adversary arrived, he could not steal that *hokhmah,* kill the Shaper, and then reShape this world into another copy of his preferred totalitarian "utopia"—there was one tiny little detail of that process Karl had never spelled out for me: exactly *how* one took the *hokhmah* of another Shaper, even if it were freely offered.

We reached the only door in the starboard side of the stern cabins. The aeronaut who had first hauled me onto the rope ladder pulled it open; the other propelled me through it.

I found myself in a short hallway, its walls the same strange, dark not-wood of the deck, with doors to left and right and another at the far end that presumably led to the port side of the vessel. Just past the right-hand door, stairs led up, probably to the glass wheelhouse over our heads; a little farther down the hall, stairs led down, beneath and parallel to those climbing up.

The noise had dropped precipitously. Very impressive soundproofing had clearly been built into this version of the *Albatross*. As I recalled, it hadn't been needed in the book version—the whirling of the blades had been soundless (Verne never having heard a real helicopter in action). Apparently, if the Shaper had bent the laws of physics, he hadn't bent them *that* much.

The man who had first grabbed me nodded to his companion. "Back to your post, Dardentor. I'll present her to the captain."

"Aye, aye, sir," said Dardentor. To my surprise, he actually tipped his cap to me. "Ma'am." He didn't go back out onto the deck. Instead, he went to the staircase and down. *Makes sense,* I thought. *The best way to get around the ship has to be belowdecks, where you don't have to fight the rotor wash.* "Very polite," I said out loud. "Now that we can hear ourselves talk, who are you?"

Apparently, politeness was limited to the lesser ranks. My guard ignored me, instead tugging me to the center of the corridor and tapping on the door that presumably led into the aft-most cabin.

"Enter," said a deep voice. My guard slid the door open, stepped back, and indicated I should go through. I took a deep breath, clenched hands suddenly inclined to tremble, and strode firmly around the corner and into the cabin beyond.

It looked . . . well, exactly like you might imagine the captain's cabin on one of Verne's science-fictional vessels *should* look: luxurious-late-19th-century-ship's-cabinish, with comfortable couches and chairs, hooded electric lamps illuminating sculptures and paintings (one of which looked like the *Mona Lisa*—how did *that* work, exactly?) and a sizable collection of leather-bound books in a floor-to-ceiling bookcase, which took up most of the bulkhead through which I'd entered. Four portholes, two to port and two to starboard, and big panes of glass in the windowed stern poured natural light into the cabin. The aft windows also showed a view of the sea—*no land in sight,* I noted—and the inner halves of the idling stern propellers.

The captain of the *Albatross* sat at a desk made of the same dark not-wood as the deck, the bright sea-reflected light streaming through the windows behind him turning him into a featureless silhouette. He stood as I hesitantly approached, and I abruptly revised my estimate of his size: the man was huge, easily as big as the guy Michelangelo's *David* had crushed back in my world, less than an hour ago by my inner clock. At least it appeared to be roughly the same time of day here as it had been on the island I'd just left, so maybe I'd be spared jet . . . er, Portal lag. Which totally had to be a thing.

My heart was pounding, but I wasn't going to let this giant, whose face I couldn't even see, put me on the defensive. "You must be Robur," I said, as boldly as I could manage.

"I am not," the man said, his voice a reasonable approximation of James Earl Jones' in Darth Vader mode. "But I know who you are."

"You do?" My heart leaped. *Karl got through after all!*

I realized that was impossible even before the captain of the *Albatross* dashed my momentary hope with his next words. "Your foolish assumption I am Robur proves my suspicion."

"It . . . does?" *This doesn't sound good.*

It wasn't.

"You are a spy for Prince Dakkar," the captain said, voice cold and hard as iron in January, "and you will answer my questions truthfully—or I'll have you tossed over the side to feed the sharks."

TWO

I BLINKED. "PRINCE who?" Although, to be honest, the name sounded vaguely familiar. Was he another Verneian character? It really had been a long time since I'd read the books . . .

"Do not play the fool with me," the captain said. "There is not a person alive who has not heard of Prince Dakkar, or his constant and evil machinations against the great Robur."

"Robur the Conqueror?"

His eyes narrowed. "Your own mouth betrays your guilt. Only the deluded followers of Dakkar call our Master by that slanderous name. Robur has conquered nothing. The lands under his sway welcome his benign rule, for he provides staunch protection from the vile depredations of *your* dark lord."

Dark lord. So, it's that *kind of world.* I felt like I'd just picked up a square in what was likely to be a rather large bingo card featuring Shaper stereotypes.

"Look," I said, "I know it's hard for you to believe, but I really don't know what you're talking about. I'm . . . a stranger. From . . . from far away." *Farther than you can imagine. Farther than* I *can imagine.* "I'm . . . looking for someone."

And until two minutes ago, I'd thought I knew who that someone had to be: Robur, who, even if he didn't want to be called "Conqueror," I was betting would answer to "Shaper."

The trouble was, this "Prince Dakkar" seemed an

equal-and-opposite force. I was willing to bet *his* followers saw *Robur* as the "dark lord" from whose "vile depredations" they needed to be protected. Could *he* be the Shaper, and Robur the Shaped adversary? (I flinched at my own choice of words: the Adversary who had chased me from my own world put any fictional dark lord to shame.)

Although "Prince Dakkar" would seem an odd persona for the Shaper to assume. The fact I couldn't remember a character by that name would seem to indicate he hadn't been a major figure in Verne's books. (The fact I couldn't simply pull out my phone and run an Internet search on the name was downright infuriating.) Why would a Shaper clearly enamored of all things Verne choose to play someone minor?

On the other hand, if he'd been *completely* enamored of Verne, everyone would be speaking French . . .

Maybe they are, a voice suggested. *Maybe there's a kind of universal translator at work . . . a TARDIS/Star Trek kind of thing.*

Dammit, you're my conscience, not the Doctor, I told myself. *Shut up.*

I realized the captain had asked me a question, mainly because his eyes narrowed and he snapped, "I asked you a question!"

"Um . . . could you repeat it?"

What was wrong with me, anyway? My mind was scattered, my thoughts buzzing around like flies disturbed from a dung heap, and that was a lovely metaphor, wasn't it, although probably appropriate considering how deep I seemed to be in sh . . .

"Who. Are. You. Looking. For."

The captain was clearly losing patience with me, and the side over which I could be hurled to the sharks—not that I'd survive the fall, so there was a small mercy—was not far away. I swallowed and tried to focus.

"I don't know," I said. "It could be Robur. It could be Dakkar." *Or it could be someone else entirely,* I added silently. But I didn't think so. Karl had said there must be a very powerful Shaper in this world, since his Shaping had leaked into my world and mingled with my Shaping to form the mysterious island . . . oh, hell, this was a Verneian world, let's capitalize it . . . the Mysterious Island as they had. And, unlike me, the Shaper in this world would *know* he was the Shaper and would not only know *how* to use his power but *enjoy* using it. An all-powerful someone in a world of his own creation was highly unlikely to role-play as, say, a blacksmith. *Unless he really liked hammering things and had a fondness for sparks . . .*

Focus.

The captain studied me for a moment. "Sit down," he finally said.

Figuring it would be harder for someone to grab me, haul me out of the cabin, and throw me over the side if I had a chair to hold on to, I gladly complied, sinking onto the plush red cushion of the nearest. (It was wicker, clearly a nod toward saving weight, although considering all those books in the bulkhead behind me, there were limits to how much weight the captain felt obliged to save.) My legs felt a bit wobbly, anyway.

The captain rounded his desk, pausing at a glass-fronted cabinet to pull out a crystal decanter containing a yellow liquid, and two rather large glasses. He sat down in the other chair that faced his desk, turned it so it faced me, put the glasses on the desk, pulled the stopper out of the decanter with his teeth, sloshed a sizable portion of liquid into each glass, reinserted the stopper with his teeth, took one glass, nodded at the other, and then sat back in his chair and studied me as he sipped from it.

I took mine with a hand that shook only a little—just enough to make the liquid break into tiny waves, echoing the waves of the ocean however many hundreds of feet below us, into which the captain had so recently threatened to throw me—sat back, and studied him in my turn, as I took a sip of . . .

Holy hell, what is this stuff? It had a million different herbal flavors, all tucked inside one god-almighty envelope of alcohol. I'd never tasted anything like it.

But did I mention the alcohol? That was what I really

wanted at that particular moment, and the fact the drink burned as it went down was only proof (about 80-proof, by my estimation) it contained that all-important ingredient.

I coughed only a very little, daintily putting the back of my hand to my lips as I did so, and kept looking at the captain. Like the crewmen, he wore an old-fashioned naval uniform though, of course, his was dark blue and featured gold braid and even those shoulder-pad things with tassels on them, whatever they're called. The fact he was dark-skinned and wore a large gold ring in each earlobe rather undercut the *HMS Pinafore* thing, though. All he needed was an eyepatch, and he would have made a great extra in a *Pirates of the Caribbean* movie.

"Thank you," I said. "What is it?"

"Strega," he said. "The witch, some call it."

Sounds Italian, I thought. *How does that work, exactly, in a Shaped world like this?* I took another sip, coughed a little more. "I can see why."

"I am wondering if that is what you are."

I carefully set the glass down. Much as I'd enjoyed my first couple of sips, much as I would have liked to drain it, it had suddenly occurred to me that keeping my wits about me was probably a better idea than getting pleasantly tipsy. Was "witch" better than "spy" in this world? That seemed an important thing to know. "Why would you wonder that?"

"We were ordered here by Robur to investigate the Mysterious Island . . ." (in his voice, I could hear the capital letters I had likewise decided to apply to the strange landmass) ". . . after ships reported its existence. We had barely arrived when it began to crumble—suspiciously fortunate for you.

"This part of the ocean is claimed by Dakkar. My theory was that Dakkar knew the Mysterious Island would attract us. Perhaps he knew it would disintegrate. Perhaps, using some infernal engine, he even *caused* it to disintegrate. Detecting our approach, he seized the opportunity to place you on the island, in the hope we would 'rescue' you and bring you aboard the *Albatross*. We know he has great interest in investigating this vessel, since no machine of his can match it. But you say you are not a spy, and, having spoken to you, I am now inclined to believe you. That being the case, what else could you be but a witch?"

Oh, there must be some *other possibilities,* I thought, but the truth was, I couldn't bring any to mind. "Shaper of the next world over" didn't seem likely to contribute anything useful to the conversation.

"Why . . . are you inclined to think I am not a spy? Not that I am," I added hastily, "but I'm not sure why you so abruptly changed your mind."

The captain took a sip of his own liqueur. "If you are a spy," he said as he lowered the glass, "you are the worst spy in history. You had no cover story prepared other than that you are a stranger from far away—as if that would explain your ignorance of the great war between Raj, evil domain of Prince Dakkar, and the free people led by the glorious Robur, Master of the World. There is no corner of this world where that conflict is not known, for the world is entirely shaped by it."

Interesting choice of words, I thought. "But . . . how do you go from that to 'witch'?"

"Witches," he said, "live in caves, away from all men. Everyone knows that. They dance naked around fires and engage in . . . unnatural acts . . . with each other and with the beasts who are their familiars."

Well, that's *a nasty little piece of folklore,* I thought. Whoever Shaped this world, Dakkar *or* Robur, I was beginning to take a serious dislike to them.

"I am not naked," I said, pointing out the obvious, "I do not have a familiar, and I was not in a cave."

"Not when we found you, true," he said. "But where else could you have come from? We had flown over the entire island, several times, and seen no one. All of a sudden, between one pass and another, you appeared, and the island began to vanish immediately thereafter. It looked like magic. You were there, and you are female. You must be a witch."

"You thought I was a spy at first," I said.

"I had to rule out the possibility," the captain said. "Also, I have orders telling me what to do about spies. I have no orders telling me what to do with witches."

Is that good or bad? I wondered, then wondered why I was asking myself, since I had no clue. "Is that good or bad?" I repeated out loud.

"It is good in that I have not been told to kill witches, whereas, if I believed you to be a spy, I would, as I stated, have you thrown over the side the moment I finished my interrogation." He shrugged. "Nothing personal, just orders."

"Despite leaving me with the impression you would not do that as long as I answered your questions?"

"Of course," he said. "It is permissible to lie to a spy who, by definition, is himself . . . or herself . . . a liar."

My dislike of the as-yet-unmet Shaper of this world deepened further.

"And is it bad in *any* way, this lack of orders concerning witches? For me, I mean? Not that I'm a witch," I quickly added. "I'm not." *Don't want him to think I'm confessing . . .*

"Not immediately," he said. "Drink more."

I looked at the strega, hesitated, then sighed and set down the glass, even though it was half full. "No, thank you."

He took another sip from his own. "Because I do not have orders concerning you, I will simply keep you prisoner and take you to Robur to do with as he wills. You will be safe until then."

"Gee," I said. "Thanks." I said it sarcastically, but I really was feeling hopeful. If Robur, and not Dakkar, were the Shaper, this captain would take me exactly where I needed to be . . .

. . . to do exactly what, I didn't know, since Karl Yatsar hadn't told me. But, with luck, it would take us a considerable amount of time to get to wherever Robur might be. With more luck, Karl would enter this world before then. He was able to sense Shapers. He'd go to wherever the Shaper was . . .

Which would be great if it was Robur. But if it wasn't, it would leave me at the mercy of some power-hungry conqueror type while Karl searched fruitlessly for me in the court of Prince Dakkar—if even *he* were the Shaper, since, though I thought it unlikely, it was still possible the real Shaper was making shoes in a small village somewhere.

Or throwing pots, I thought, and felt a wave of homesickness, for Eagle River, for my shop, for the Human Bean, for my boyfriend Brent, for my Mom in Appleville, for my best friend, Aesha.

Who was dead or, perhaps, had never existed. Mom, I had Shaped to forget me. Brent, the Adversary had Shaped to forget me (or else he'd been too cowardly to acknowledge knowing me when I'd called, in which case, good riddance).

"You can't go home again," the old saying has it. In my case, it was literally true. There was no going back, there was only going forward, and if I didn't have Karl to guide me, which for the moment I didn't, then all I could do was plunge forward myself, however blindly, in the hope of somehow getting closer to my goal. My head swam and I felt a little sick, and I didn't think it was from my two swallows of strega.

"You will be treated well," the captain said. "Though perhaps it would be best if you told none of the crew that you are being held as a suspected witch. Better they think you are a spy, perhaps one who has turned against her masters and has valuable information to share with Robur—that will explain why I have not executed you. If they think you are a witch, some of the more superstitious of the men might decide to throw you over the side, just to get you off the ship. It's bad enough you are a woman."

"Bad enough . . . ?" I blinked, then remembered something I'd read. "Crap. Sailors used to think women were bad luck on ships. Is that what you mean?"

"It is well-known."

"It is complete nonsense."

"So a woman . . . and a witch . . . would say." The captain tossed back the last of his strega. I looked longingly at what was left of mine, but womanfully refrained from finishing it off. "I will have you locked in one of the empty cabins," he continued, placing the empty glass bottom-up on the desk. It had the appearance of some kind of ritual or tradition. "You will be comfortable enough. You would not enjoy the deck, anyway, as we gain altitude and increase speed. We can fly at one hundred and twenty miles per hour. Between the rush of wind from our forward progress and the downburst of air from our airscrews, the deck is traversable only with the help of a stout tether. Generally, in flight, the crew remains belowdecks."

"I'll be fine in a cabin," I said. "Thank you." Then I thought of something else. "Will there be food? Soon?"

"I will arrange it," the captain said. He stood. "I will talk to you again, but I must inspect the vessel before we begin our return voyage. There were strange winds buffeting us as the island collapsed. I do not think we suffered damage, but it is even more important in a flying ship to be certain all things are in working order than it is in an ordinary ship."

I heartily agreed with that. I stood, too. "What is your name, captain?"

"Captain Nebuchadnezzar Harding-Smith, at your service," he said. He actually bowed his head and clicked his heels as an accompaniment to the introduction.

Nebuchadnezzar? Neb, the freed slave who was the faithful servant of Cyrus Harding in Verne's novel *The Mysterious Island*? (Come to think of it, that island also crumbled into the sea, although in its case it was due to a massive volcanic eruption.) I remembered the character Neb well, but this man was clearly not a servant. Also, where did that "Smith" come from? *Oh, Internet, how I miss you.*

"Do you know a man named Cyrus?" I ventured.

His eyes narrowed. "My foster father's name is Cyrus," he said. "Commodore Cyrus Harding-Smith, an aeronaut of some note himself, now retired. He introduced me to the Aeronautical Corps, and I am proud to be following in his footsteps in the service of the great Robur. But how could you know that?"

"A wild guess," I said.

"Or witchcraft." His frown deepened. "I warn you again, say nothing to the crew that might cause them to think of you in that way. Speak as little as possible, until you see Robur. Then speak the truth in detail, if you wish to live."

"Most definitely," I said.

Captain Harding-Smith went to the door of the cabin, opened it, and spoke in a low voice to the man who had brought me there. Then the captain turned to me. "Mr. Pencroff, my first mate, will show you to your quarters." He indicated the open door with a sweep of his arm. I took a deep breath, found I was gripping the back of the wicker chair so tightly the weave was impressing itself into my palm, forced myself to release it, and strode with what I hoped was an air of confidence to the door.

This time, Mr. Pencroff did not take me out onto the deck. Instead, he took me to the end of the hall, to the downward-leading steps. He indicated I should descend, so descend I did, finding myself in a hallway running fore and aft, with sliding doors every few feet. To my left— aft—the corridor ran, I guessed, about a third the length of the hull, ending in another door that presumably led to the hold.

Pencroff pointed to the right, however—fore—and so fore I went, toward the bow and the door at that end of the hall. "Passenger cabin," Pencroff said. He slid open the door. "Lucky for you it's empty. Otherwise you'd be locked in a storeroom."

"That's me," I said. "Lucky as they come." I pushed past him into the space beyond. Less than half the size of the captain's cabin overhead, it shared with it large glass windows aft. There were also portholes to port and starboard, with a cot beneath each. A table and two wicker chairs graced the space directly in front of the window. An ornately woven oval rug of red, blue, and gold covered the middle of the floor. Electric lamps, currently unilluminated, hung next to each of the portholes.

I turned to say "thank you" to Pencroff, but he was already sliding the door closed. It clicked shut, clicked again as he locked it . . . and then I was alone.

THREE

FOR A MOMENT I just stood there, surveying the cabin.
Then my legs gave way without warning, and I thudded
to my knees on that fancy rug. *Well, that's strange,* I
thought. *I should get up.*

But I couldn't. My shaking limbs wouldn't let me. Instead, I lay down, curled up, and bawled my eyes out.

Admittedly, this was not my finest moment of strong-
female-characterhood—and a fictional character was all
I was in this world, in a way, an unexpected one suddenly
popping up in the middle of a narrative crafted by an
author I had yet to meet. But look at it from my point of
view. It had been less than an hour since the struggle on
the altar and my stabbing of the foot of my attacker,
whose blood had opened the Portal through which I had
entered this world. And in the hour before that, there'd
been more blood—not to mention terror, explosions, and
a murderous Michelangelo's *David.* I'd been thrown out
of my world, and the only person who really seemed to
have a clue about what was going on hadn't come with
me. I'd been hauled aboard an impossible flying machine, and then promptly been threatened with being
tossed from it again, saved only because the captain had
decided I probably wasn't a spy, after all. No; he'd decided I might be a witch, instead.

And so I wept, in reaction to everything that had just
happened, and in reaction to everything that had happened before that, and for everyone and everything I had
lost. But you can't cry forever. After a while, sobbing just

seems kind of silly. Also, the carpet was thin, and the floor beneath it hard. Also . . .

Also, there was a knock on the door.

I scrambled up, wiped my face with my sleeve, and said, "Come in."

The door opened. It wasn't the first mate, Pencroff, but the other crewman who had taken me to the captain . . . Dardentor. He didn't come in. Instead, with both feet planted firmly in the corridor, he held out a covered pewter platter. "Food," he said.

I took two eager steps toward him, and he flinched back. I stopped. "I can't take it if you keep backing up."

He braced himself and stretched his arms out as far as they would go.

I approached more cautiously, so I wouldn't spook him again, took the platter, and then took three steps back. "Why are you scared of me?" The very idea seemed ludicrous. I wasn't even a Shaper in this world; just a woman, lost, alone, and now imprisoned.

"Are you . . . are you really a witch?" Dardentor said.

Of course not, I started to say; but then I stopped myself. Maybe that wasn't the right answer.

Instead, I narrowed my eyes. "What if I am? Would you throw me over the side?"

His eyes widened. "No, ma'am! Please don't think that, ma'am! Please!" He looked so frightened I took pity on him.

"I'm not a witch," I said. "I'm not a spy, either. Just a woman in . . . the wrong place at the wrong time." *Very, very literally.*

He didn't look much reassured. "If you were either, you would lie and say you weren't."

I couldn't argue with anything so self-evidently true. I sighed. "I can't make you believe me." The heavy tray dragged at my arms, and even though a metal dome covered it, such a savory smell emanated from it my mouth watered. "I'm going to put this down on the table," I said. I turned away from him. "You don't have to leave if you don't—"

The door closed, clicked, and locked behind me.

"Nice talking to you," I muttered, taking the tray to the table. *So much for seducing the door guard into letting me go.*

Not that I'd tried that, of course. But would I? If I had to?

Could I?

Now *there* was a question I'd never had to ask myself before and would rather not have asked myself now. But it certainly fell within what I knew of the parameters of standard operating procedures for spies.

Witches, I wasn't so sure about. Were witches real, in this world, real as in having actual magical power? As far as I knew, Verne had never used witches in a story. Admittedly, I'd only read his best-known—*20,000 Leagues Under the Sea, Journey to the Center of the Earth, The Mysterious Island,* and *From the Earth to the Moon*—and he'd written a lot more than that during his lifetime. Some of his books had also been published posthumously (albeit substantially rewritten, if I remembered right), all of which meant there were certainly some gaps in my Verneian knowledge.

As well, as Captain Harding-Smith proved, the Shaper of this world wasn't exactly treating Verne's stories as holy writ. I remembered the Mysterious Island as it had appeared in my world, its dark tunnels full of monsters and horrific statuary, nothing at all like the volcanic South Sea island of the novel. Karl Yatsar had thought it might be a mixture of my nightmares and the dark dreams of the Shaper of this one, although he'd also said he'd never seen anything like it forming around a potential Portal in any of the other worlds he'd visited, so what did he know?

Whatever it was, it hadn't been inspired by Verne, which meant the fact Verne hadn't mentioned witches didn't necessarily mean cave-dwelling witches weren't lurking literally beneath the steampunkish surface of this world. Cave-dwelling witches with a penchant for "unnatural acts" involving beasts would certainly explain some of those statues in the Mysterious Island's dark passageways. Requiring the shedding of human blood on an altar to open the Portal also fit in rather well.

All this time I'd been struggling with the cover on the pewter tray, which turned out to be held in place by four latches. I finally removed it, set it aside on the table, and looked down at the most mouthwatering meal I'd ever seen . . .

Well, no, not really. The repast consisted of a slab of gray meat, a pile of mashed turnips, a hunk of dark-brown bread with a skimpy swipe of butter across it, and a small cup of thin-looking red wine. But I had been on ridiculously short rations for days. To me, it was five-star dining.

I sat down at the table, facing the windows. I took a sip of the wine, grimacing at the taste—I'd recently poured a couple of bottles of homemade wine foisted on me by a "friend" down my sink, which it had cleaned out nicely, and it had tasted like a fine French Bordeaux compared to this. (The fact it was almost undrinkable was probably a good thing, since I'd decided I shouldn't be giving in to the completely understandable urge to drink.) Then I dug in, looking out over the ocean as I ate. In the distance, right at the horizon, I almost thought I saw land, although it could have just been a low cloud bank.

I was chewing (and it needed quite a bit of chewing) the last piece of my meat, pretty much as mindlessly as a cow chewing its cud, since my brain had apparently decided it had been doing too much thinking recently and had more-or-less shut down while I ate, when something caught my eye in the distance.

Multiple somethings, actually: nine glittering objects, airborne. While I stared at them, wondering what they could be, the *Albatross* shuddered as the aft propellers, of which I could see only the inner half, suddenly came to life, spinning up until their blades became a blur, though the noise was muffled by the thick glass of the windows. We were moving . . .

Something banged overhead, and I jumped. Smoke

swirled through the spinning propellers. And then, far to the stern, near where those shining sparks were swelling in size, a black puff of smoke materialized in midair.

We're shooting at whatever those things are, I thought. *We're under attack!*

But under attack by what? And by whom?

I leaned on the table and peered aft, shading my eyes with my hand. The things pursuing us were clearly gaining, despite the spinning to life of the propellers . . . and now I could see what they were.

Helicopters. Little, one-person helicopters, each looking a bit like an armchair with rotors.

Jules Verne never wrote about mini-helicopters, I thought.

Something dropped from the lead helicopter. Flame shot from it. It streaked toward us . . .

Toward me!

I ducked behind the table.

An instant later, the deck beneath me heaved, and the windows of my cabin shattered.

Glass sprayed the room, but safe behind the table, I wasn't cut. Cold air rushed in. I lifted my head above the tabletop and peered out into open space, past the spinning propellers, their roar earsplitting now the glass was gone. I could hear more thunderous chopping overhead as the deck rotors labored to pull the *Albatross* higher, away from the pursuers. Smoke now trailed from somewhere below me. I wondered what damage the rocket had done to the hull.

Another rocket dropped and ignited, from a different 'copter. I ducked again. Another explosion. Something hurtled into my cabin and smashed into the porthole to my right, driving it and a jagged chunk of the hull out into empty space. Wind howled in the opening. Raising my head, heart pounding, I saw that the starboard propeller, to my left as I looked out, had vanished. The smoke the *Albatross* trailed was now much thicker.

Bang! from overhead as the *Albatross* fired at her pursuers. A flash and a puff of black smoke between two of the oncoming 'copters upended them. Tumbling, they dropped like buckshot geese toward the water far below. If the pilots had parachutes, they didn't open within my sight.

I decided that close to the stern windows was *not* where I should be. In fact, on the *Albatross* was clearly not where I should be, but there wasn't much I could do about *that*.

Feet crunching on broken glass, I dashed to the door and pounded on it. "Let me out!" I shouted, to no avail.

I spun around again. Two more rockets sped toward us, aimed high . . .

Boom! Boom! over my head. Twin concussions knocked me to my hands and knees. Two objects fell past the stern, one a body trailing smoke (I hoped it wasn't Dardentor), the other long, black, and metallic—no doubt the gun that had been firing at the 'copters.

I'd developed a hatred of helicopters during my frantic efforts to escape the Adversary in my own world. That hate was clearly justified.

The *Albatross* was now shuddering violently, like a washing machine spinning a badly unbalanced load. One or both of the last two missiles must have taken out some of the topside rotors, a guess that seemed borne out a moment later as the *Albatross,* still circling due to the missing rear propeller, nosed down toward the ocean below.

Not good, I thought. *Not good at all . . .*

Flame spurted from guns mounted on both sides of the pilots of the oncoming 'copters. A bullet slammed into the wall above my head, right where I would have been standing if the last rocket explosions hadn't knocked me to the floor. Above, I heard the cracking sound of gunshots from our own crew, returning fire as the 'copters rushed toward us . . . and past us, roaring above and below and to both sides. I caught a glimpse of their pilots, dressed head to toe in leather, dark goggles and white scarfs obscuring their faces. Then my rectangle of sky, with its one spinning propeller, was empty.

We were now so nose-down I couldn't see the ocean. I scrambled up, turned, and pounded on the door again, to no more effect than the last time. Insanity is sometimes defined as doing the same thing over and over again and expecting different results, but I kept pounding anyway. It's not like I had a lot of other options.

Finally, I gave up, turned, and pressed my back against the door, which was easy to do with the angle of our descent increasing. I expected the 'copters to make another pass, to try to finish us off, but I didn't see them.

Maybe they've got nothing left to shoot, I thought.

Or maybe they just want to force us down. This thing floats. It's literally a flying ship.

Hm.

The fancy rug suddenly slid down the increasing slope into a heap at my feet, along with the shattered glass that had sprayed the room. I couldn't climb the smooth floor to the windows, so I worked my way to starboard and grabbed on to the cot to pull myself uphill. I'd just reached the top of the cot when the table suddenly broke loose of its constraints, slid downhill, turning as it went, and crashed corner-first into the forward bulkhead, with enough force to have snapped my spine had I still been standing there—and more than enough to smash open the door.

A minute ago, I'd wanted that door open, but now I was almost to the windows, which I was pretty sure was where I wanted to be if what I thought was about to happen happened. I just wished I could tell how close we were to . . .

The overhead rotors suddenly roared, and my heart leaped with hope—Captain Harding-Smith or Pencroff or whoever was still alive still had some control! We leveled out, so abruptly I toppled forward and fell full-length onto the floor. I grabbed the cot and pulled myself to my feet . . . just in time to be flung headfirst again as we hit the water.

Spray erupted outside my window and the jagged hole in the hull, though our forward momentum kept it from joining me on the floor. I picked myself up . . . again . . . and staggered to the windows. Hand against the frame—avoiding the daggerlike pieces of glass protruding from it—I looked down.

We were floating; though remembering the towering masts of our topside rotors, I wondered uneasily just how stable we were. There couldn't be a lot of ballast in a ship intended to fly. A sudden wave could flip us over, and I really didn't want to be aboard for that . . .

Wrong thing to worry about, I realized a moment later, because the water below me was rising rapidly. Between the first rocket, which had exploded somewhere below me and shattered my windows, and the one that had taken out the starboard propeller, it seemed unlikely the hull remained watertight. Once the water reached my cabin, it would pour in through the broken windows, the ship would start settling by the stern, more water would pour in, and in short order the deck that had sloped up to the windows would slope down instead, a literally slippery slope straight to Davy Jones' Locker . . . which, for all I knew, might be a real place in this Shaper's world.

The rotors still roared, perhaps to keep us from sinking. That might even work. But I wasn't going to just stand there and watch the rising water and hope for the best.

Originally, I'd wanted out the door. Then I'd thought I'd go out the stern, because I'd thought we'd hit the water nose-first and that might be my best hope for escaping the ship before it sank. Now the door suddenly became my first choice again. I hurried across the now-level deck, climbed over the table, scrambled over the wreckage of the door into the corridor, ran for the stairs, climbed . . .

. . . and stopped, three steps from the top, for a very good reason: the sudden appearance of a woman, all in red leather, tinted goggles hiding her eyes. In one hand she held a pistol.

It was pointed at my head.

FOUR

LIFE, SOMEONE ONCE said, is just one darn thing after another. Not a particularly profound observation, perhaps, but its truth was certainly being driven home to me this interminable day.

I sighed. "Hi," I said. "My name is Shawna Keys. I'm not a spy and I'm not a witch. Why are you pointing a gun at me?"

Without lowering her pistol, the woman pushed her goggles up onto her forehead, revealing bright blue eyes, narrowed by her frown. "Why would anyone think you a witch? Their land lies far from here."

"They're real, then?" Her frown deepened, and I added hastily, "I don't know why anyone would think that. Ask the captain." Then my own eyes narrowed. "Wait. Are you saying you think I'm a spy?"

"I do not know what you are," the woman said. "Except my prisoner." She stepped back and gestured with the pistol. "Up here."

I climbed the steps and emerged into the corridor. Captain Harding-Smith's cabin door stood open, and through it stepped a young man dressed in leather garb matching my captor's, except his was black instead of red. He was stuffing papers into a backpack. "I got everything I could find, ma'am," he said. Then he noticed me. "This is who they took from the island?"

"Shawna Keys," I said. "And you are . . . ?"

He ignored me. "Prince Dakkar will be pleased."

"I hope so," said the woman.

I heard a loud banging and muffled shouts from somewhere. The young man glanced at the stairs we'd just mounted. "Don't know how long those barricades we set up belowdecks will hold, ma'am."

"They'll hold long enough. They already have. 'Get on board, gather intelligence, grab whomever they lifted from the Island, get off,'" the woman said. "Mission accomplished. Time to go, Lieutenant Blackwell."

"Yes, ma'am." The man slung the backpack onto his back and hurried to the door at the starboard end of the hall.

The woman didn't follow him. "We're up here," she said, pointing up the next flight of stairs. "Move."

"Yes, ma'am," I said, echoing the lieutenant. I started up the steps. "I take it you're in command? What with the snazzy red leather and all?"

"Just climb," she snapped.

So much for feminist sisterhood, I thought. I climbed, emerging a moment later onto the windswept top of the captain's cabin. Aft, next to a twisted piece of metal I guessed had been the mount for the antiaircraft gun I'd seen twirling through the sky, accompanied by the smoking remains of its operator, stood one of the minihelicopters. Between me and it, a ship's wheel swung idly, untended . . .

Untended, I realized a moment later, because, to my right, the body of a man in one of the *Pinafore*sque uniforms of the *Albatross'* crew lay sprawled across the iron frame that held the shattered wheelhouse's glass—and impaled on the glass' jagged, swordlike remnants. Blood pooled beneath the corpse.

I swallowed hard and turned to look the length of the ship, toward the cabins at the bow, squinting into the blast of the rotors. About half appeared to still be operative. Others only spun idly in the wind from those that still worked. To my right, the shattered stumps of half a dozen masts surrounded two blackened holes in the deck, where rockets must have exploded. Three other masts had snapped off at the base but remained aboard, lying athwart the bulwarks.

The rotors that still worked spun frantically at full power, striving to keep us from sinking. Since our descent into the depths appeared to have halted, I guessed they were effective. *There must be pumps, keeping out just enough water to keep us in equilibrium,* I thought, taking refuge from the bloody scene behind us in analytical thought. Since the helmsman . . . I swallowed again . . . clearly wasn't at the throttle, there had to be a secondary control room somewhere, probably in the prow.

Only two 'copters had actually landed on the *Albatross:* the one behind me and another at the bow, which I guessed must belong to Lieutenant Blackwell, whom I'd momentarily met in the hallway outside the captain's cabin and whom I could now see picking his windblasted way along the deck. The others hovered, forming a circle around the forward cabins, guns—not machine guns, as far as I could tell, but single-shot firearms of some sort, mounted on the sides of the pilot's seats—trained at the forward cabins, but not firing.

Lieutenant Blackwell was in no danger of being shot as he made his way forward, for the simple reason there didn't appear to be any openings in the blank forward bulkhead, except for the closed door.

I remembered something from the Jules Verne version of the *Albatross,* something about Robur not installing any parachutes to safely lower the aircraft in the event of an accident because Robur did not believe in accidents. Apparently, this world's version of Robur didn't believe in accidents, either, or the possibility of being boarded. *Failure of imagination there, Robur,* I thought.

If Robur were also the Shaper, that oversight was a rather scary reminder that he didn't control everything that happened in his Shaped world any more than I had controlled everything that happened in mine—even though he, unlike me, presumably remembered Shaping his, and whatever training Ygrair had given him. Though this world might be Shaped, for the most part, the day-to-day events within it were not.

In other words, anything could happen.

More to the point, anything could happen to *me*.

Just like real life. It might feel like I was in some weird adventure story, but I could still end up dead . . . and in this world, the only person who would know or care would be Karl Yatsar, when and if he found his way into it.

My absolute aloneness hit me with renewed force. "Now what?" I said, turning to face the woman, still trying not to look at the dead helmsman.

"Now we get the hell off of here," she said, pistol aimed at my gut.

"How?" I looked around for a boat.

She laughed. "By helicopter, of course."

I was almost surprised to hear her use the word: it seemed too modern. But maybe it was older than I thought. I looked at her tiny version of one, then back at her. Twice. "That thing won't carry two," I said, very much afraid she would tell me I was wrong . . . which, of course, she did, in her own blunt way: she grabbed my arm and shoved me toward it.

"Look again," she snapped as I stumbled forward. I caught myself by grabbing the ship's wheel—and at the same moment spotted a complicated-looking leather harness hanging between the 'copter's landing skids, right where some of the hovering 'copters still carried rockets. Her 'copter, it appeared, had been specially modified to carry a prisoner . . . me.

I twisted around to look at her. "You've got to be kidding me!"

She didn't look like she was kidding. She didn't look like she knew *how* to kid. "You crawl in from the back," she said. "Arms through those loops. Tighten the belly belt. Stick your legs into the hoops at the back. Move."

I had no choice. I crawled into the harness as instructed and hung there like a trussed animal, prize of a successful hunt, about to be hauled back to camp in triumph . . . which was, of course, exactly what I was. I just hoped my head didn't end up adorning someone's basement wall.

The woman checked my straps, to make sure I was

secure. She left my hands free, which only surprised me for a moment: what was I going to do, unbuckle the waist strap, wriggle out of the rest of the harness, and throw myself into the ocean from a few hundred feet up? No, thanks.

She climbed into the seat over my head. The rotors started to whirl. Whatever powered them was itself silent. I'd seen two big black boxes as I'd struggled into my harness, one on either side of a silver cylinder from which protruded the shaft to which the blades were attached. *Batteries?* I thought. Even in my world, I didn't believe there were any batteries that could power a helicopter of this size.

But we aren't in my world, I reminded myself. (*Duh,* myself responded.) The entire *Albatross* was powered by impossible batteries. Of course, Prince Dakkar would have access to similar technology.

The chop-chop-chop of the blades increased, and then, without any fuss at all, we lifted from the *Albatross,* banked, and flew away over the ocean. I watched our shadow chase us over blue, whitecapped waves, speeding me on to my next adventure.

I was heartily, completely, thoroughly sick of new adventures.

A few minutes later, I was heartily, completely, thoroughly sick in a very different way, thanks to the up-and-down movement of the helicopter as it powered through the air, combined with the belly strap digging into the not-at-all-digested mass of food I had eaten . . . okay, overeaten, but dammit, I'd been starving . . . moments before the aerial attack had begun.

I deposited that food into the ocean to feed sharks or whatever else might be swimming down there, bending my head down as best I could in the hope that the airstream wouldn't spray the vomit the length of my body, and almost succeeding . . . although in those circumstances, "almost" really wasn't good enough.

I'm not going to make a very good impression when we finally land, I thought miserably . . . and then heaved again.

My stomach was, to reuse a perfectly good phrase, heartily, completely, thoroughly empty long before the flight ended, perhaps thirty minutes objectively—and about thirty hours subjectively—later.

In any event, after *some* miserable amount of time, our destination hove into sight: a vessel, much bigger than the *Albatross* but very much limited to the liquid rather than the atmospheric ocean—at least, as far as I could tell. A slender cigar shape, rounded at both ends, its smooth upper surface was broken only by a large oval bump with a glass window curving around the front of it, about a third of the way back from the bow, and a flat platform in the stern, revealed by two doors standing open like gull wings. Three concentric white circles marked the platform, which wasn't all that large, just large enough . . .

Ah. Just large enough for us to land on.

The strange-looking submarine . . . because that was clearly what it was . . . grew larger with alarming rapidity, as did the target platform. We swept up to it, tilting and slowing until we were hovering above it. Then we settled down toward it, down, down . . .

The platform's planks seemed to rush toward me. I found myself pushing against the harness with my body, not that I moved more than an inch. The skids on either side of my head banged against the platform. My body continued downward to the limits of the straps' elasticity, snapped upward again so much that the back of my head banged against the underside of the seat, and then sagged as the rotors quieted, leaving the tip of my nose no more than a foot above the platform's wood.

My pilot dismounted. I pulled my legs out of the harness, undid the waist belt, knelt as I pulled my arms free from the forward part of the harness, and finally backed out from under the helicopter on my hands and knees.

I looked up into the overly familiar barrel of my pilot's pistol. "Get up," she said. "The captain wants to see you."

That's not fair, my admittedly frazzled and overloaded brain said. *I didn't even get to say, "Take me to your leader."*

The platform started sinking into the submarine's

hull. Steel walls slid up on three sides while, in front, open space appeared. At the far end of it six bearded sailors waited by a closed hatch. To their left another mini-helicopter sat at rest, its rotors folded up and over themselves like a spindly tulip.

As our descent stopped, the sailors hurried forward onto the platform, giving me curious . . . and in a couple of cases, unmistakably salacious . . . looks as they brushed past me and my captor. As the red-leather-clad woman prodded me the length of the hold, I glanced back to see the sailors seize the mini-helicopter by its runners and lift it from the deck, presumably to tie it into place next to the helicopter I'd already seen. By my count, there were exactly enough empty spaces to accommodate all the helicopters I'd seen attacking the *Albatross*.

Two of those, though, wouldn't be coming back.

I stopped, not having much choice, when I reached the forward hatch. My guard stepped forward, holstered her pistol, undogged the hatch by spinning the wheel at its center, and then swung it open. She stepped to one side, drew her pistol again, and motioned me through.

Harpoons, spearguns, cutlasses, pistols, and rifles hung on the walls of the next chamber, above crates of ammunition. The chamber beyond that was a more ordinary storeroom.

We next passed a spiral staircase leading down. I saw nothing below us but a metal deck. Past that, we came to crew quarters, with sixty bunks lining the walls, stacked three deep. The top bunks were all occupied, snores coming from here and there, an arm dangling over the side of one.

Then came a spartan eating space and attached galley. There weren't enough tables to accommodate the number of crew the bunkroom implied, but then, as the bunkroom also implied, the crew must be divided into three watches, and there were certainly enough tables and benches to accommodate twenty.

We passed more spiral stairs. This time, one set led up and one down. Above, I saw natural light and glimpsed levers and mysterious control panels: the bridge, presumably, in the bulbous, glass-windowed protuberance I had noted from the air. Below, again, all I saw was metal deck. My guess was the lower levels contained the engine and electrical room—there had to be enormous batteries somewhere—plus the buoyancy tanks, freshwater tanks, storage holds, and maybe an underwater hatch for the use of divers.

What we passed through next, though, was a surprisingly sumptuous library: curved walls lined with books, thick sea-green carpet on the floor, leather armchairs and dark wooden tables scattered here and there. Beyond that was another eating area, which I guessed must be the officers' wardroom. We exited that into a long corridor with doors to either side and a closed hatch at the end, which, for the first time, my escort did not open herself. Instead, she pressed a button set in the bulkhead.

A moment later, the hatch opened of its own accord.

"Inside," my guard said, gesturing with the pistol. I stepped through, and for the second time in a couple of hours, found myself in a captain's cabin.

It was both similar to and different from Captain Harding-Smith's cabin aboard the *Albatross*. Similar in layout, with windows at the back and a table in front of them; different in size, and very different in that the windows at the back, rather than being wide, flat planes of glass, were hemispheres, like insect eyes. Blue sky showed at their tops, but mostly they showed the underside of the waves, and blue-green water darkening into the distance. A school of silver fish flicked silently past.

This captain was very different as well. Light- rather than dark-skinned, he had an unruly mop of black hair and an equally black beard . . . although, just like his aerial counterpart, if he'd only had an eyepatch and a parrot, he'd have made a fair pirate.

Seated behind the table, hands folded on its surface, he frowned at me as I entered, his face lit by a dozen electric lights in sconces spread equidistantly around the three non-glass walls of the cabin. (A rather grand chandelier,

something else Captain Harding-Smith's cabin had
lacked, hung from the ceiling but was not lit.)

I didn't wait for the captain to speak. *Seize the moment, keep them off guard,* I was thinking in some corner of my mind that was probably even more confused
than all the other corners of my confused mind. "Captain Nemo, I presume," I said, smiling what I hoped was
a cool, confident, knowledgeable smile. "Thank you for
welcoming me aboard the *Nautilus.*"

The effect was not what I hoped. The captain's slight
frown, of the puzzled-but-intrigued variety, collapsed
into a furious scowl. He leaped to his feet and slammed
both palms on the table. "Who are you, and how do you
know those names?" he demanded.

I gaped at him.

My guard grabbed my arm and poked her pistol barrel into the soft flesh of my neck, just below my jawline.
"Captain Hatteras," she snarled, "asked you a question."

I swallowed, which is harder to do than you might
think when there's a gun barrel at your throat. "I . . .
um . . . read them somewhere . . . ?" I said. (Okay,
squeaked.)

"Difficult to believe," Captain Hatteras rumbled,
"since neither name is permitted to be published in the
Principality of Raj and would be utterly unknown outside it."

"I . . ." I tried to pull my neck away from the gun,
without success. "I'm . . . not from around here," I said,
a little breathlessly. "I'm from . . . from the far side of the
world . . ."

"There is no corner of the world where that name is
permitted!" Captain Hatteras thrust a finger at the globe
that graced the corner of his desk to my right. "Can you
point to it?"

I blinked at the indicated sphere. It was all wrong.
The familiar continents weren't there. Landmasses were
shapes I'd never seen before, though the proportion of
water to land seemed about the same. *This Shaper re-
Shaped the whole planet.*

Presumably I could have, too . . . but from what Karl Yatsar had told me, I hadn't.

Well, why would I? I thought. I liked the world the way it was. I liked knowing there was a Paris in France and a Moscow in Russia and a Johannesburg in South Africa and an Ottawa in Canada and a Shanghai in China—even if they weren't, again according to Karl Yatsar, the real places, but merely copies of them from the First World.

"I . . . I can't," I said. "I've . . ." I pulled away from the pistol again. It followed me, digging into my neck harder than ever. "I've never seen that globe before. The place where I'm from isn't on it."

Captain Hatteras' eyes narrowed. "You are saying you are not from this world at all?"

"I . . . guess so?"

The pistol barrel jabbed me, so hard I winced. The captain's gaze flicked to my escort. He jerked his head to one side, and she pulled the gun back and took a step away.

I rubbed the place she'd been poking. "You believe me?"

"I believe it is not an impossibility. Some of our Dread Prince's scholars have speculated that this may not be the only world to host life. His Majesty is, in fact, currently working on a plan to send men to the Moon to see if there are Lunarians upon it."

"Ah." For a second, I'd thought some hint of the Labyrinth had penetrated this world, but, no, it was just more Verneian influence. *Also, Dread Prince? Is there a* Princess Bride *influence, too?* I hoped not—Rodents of Unusual Size were *not* something I wanted to encounter in real life.

Or whatever this was.

"Tell me," I said. "This mission to the Moon . . . it wouldn't happen to involve an enormous cannon, would it?"

The captain's eyes narrowed in renewed suspicion. "How could you know that?"

"Well . . . how do you think I got here?" I winced inwardly at the lie, but if it kept him thinking of me as whatever they called extraterrestrials in the nineteenth century, and not a spy for Robur . . .

"So, you claim to be from the Moon?"

"Um . . . no."

"Somewhere farther out? Mars, perhaps?"

The Shaper changed the world, but not the solar system, then. Or at least, I added, remembering something Karl had said, *not the lights in the sky that* look *like stars and planets.*

"I don't think I should say any more to you," I said. "I think you should take me to your leader." *There, I got to say it after all.* "What I have to tell him is for his ears alone." I tapped my own right ear with my finger, started to say something else, and then thought better of it. It was just possible I was laying it on a little thick.

Captain Hatteras pursed his lips. "Hm. Well, I will not press the matter. Whether you are telling the truth or not is not for me to determine. We will, indeed, take you to our leader . . . unless, once we are back in range of wireless communications, I am given other instructions."

Other instructions? That sounded ominous.

The captain glanced at the woman. "Lieutenant Commander, escort our guest to the brig."

The *brig*? That didn't sound comfortable. "Captain, I protest. I am an ambassador from another world. If you imprison me, you imperil relations between our two governments." If I'd been laying it on a little thick a moment ago, now I was ladling it on with a trowel.

Fortunately, it seemed to work. The captain rubbed his bearded chin. "Well," he said, at last, "you may have a point." He looked at the woman again. "She will share your quarters, Lieutenant Commander."

The woman stiffened. "Sir, I protest."

"Noted," the captain said. "But overruled. If she is not to be housed in the brig—and if she is indeed an ambassador, that would be a major diplomatic *faux pas*—then she must have quarters elsewhere. As you are the only other woman on the ship, and you have quarters of sufficient size, there is no other choice."

The only other woman on the ship? And commander of its air forces, as well? I glanced at the lieutenant commander. *Impressive.* I remembered what Captain Harding-Smith had said about women being bad luck aboard a vessel. Was Prince Dakkar more enlightened than Robur? Did that mean he was more likely to be the Shaper . . . or the other way around?

"Father!" burst out of the lieutenant commander at that moment.

Oh, I thought. *It's like that.* Nepotism, it seemed, was no respecter of worlds.

"Lieutenant Commander Hatteras," the captain said, his voice like ice, "you have your orders."

His daughter stiffened, then snapped a sharp salute. "Aye, aye, sir," she said, her voice every bit as cold and formal. She turned to me and waved the pistol toward the door. "Let's go."

" If she is an ambassador, holding her at gunpoint is both unnecessary and provocative," the captain said. "Treat her as a guest. *Your* guest."

Lieutenant Commander Hatteras' jaw worked, as if she were grinding her teeth. Then she jammed the pistol into its holder, bowed her head very stiffly in my direction, and said, "Please come with me, Ambassador."

"I would be honored, Lieutenant Commander," I said. I turned to the captain again. "My thanks," I said; then, to his daughter, "Lead on."

The lieutenant commander turned sharply on her heel and led me back to the door. As she opened it, I heard a tinny voice behind us say, "All surviving helicopters aboard, Captain."

"Then dive, Mr. Anderson," said the captain, apparently to thin air. "And take us home."

"Aye, aye, sir." A klaxon began to sound.

Lieutenant Commander Hatteras pulled the door shut behind us.

FIVE

LIEUTENANT COMMANDER HATTERAS' quarters lay behind the second door on the starboard side of the corridor we had followed to the captain's cabin. She pushed it open and stood aside. "After you . . . Ambassador." Her tone of voice conveyed her doubt the title should apply.

I stepped in. "Quarters of sufficient size" appeared to be a somewhat less accurate description of the space than "rodents of unusual size" had been for the creatures in *The Princess Bride,* though at least there were bunk beds. Hatteras clearly slept in the bottom one. It had a blue blanket covering it and a pillow at its head, while the upper one showed only a bare mattress.

The beds were so close to our right as we entered that the door banged up against them. To the left—but not very far to the left—were a table and two benches, each just wide enough for one person. Though they were folded down at the moment, hinges against the wall suggested they could be swung up out of the way at need. At the head of the beds, a smallish chest of blond wood bound in black iron rested in the room's corner, against the curving wall. In the other corner was a small sink, with a mirror above it.

"Cozy," I said, though "claustrophobic" would have been more accurate. It was also spartan enough to shame a Spartan. I saw absolutely nothing of a personal nature: no pictures, no books, no carelessly scattered clothing. Presumably, all items of that kind were in the chest, though

I'd seen much bigger bits of luggage stuffed into over-head bins on airliners in my world.

Between the chest and the sink, a bubble of thick glass, maybe eighteen inches in diameter, showed the bright blue of sky: but even as I looked at it, water swept over it, and the light changed to blue-green, the shade deepening by the moment. We were diving, and a moment later, the klaxon, muffled in here but still clearly audible, stopped.

"So," I said to my unwilling host, as she closed the door, "is this the *Nautilus*?"

She spun to face me, glaring from no more than a foot away. "I do not believe you are an ambassador. I still think it likely you are a spy for Robur. Why should I answer your questions?"

"I'm not asking for a military secret!" I said. "I'll see the name on the hull whenever we get where we're going anyway." *Unless I'm in chains and have a bag over my head,* I thought but did not say, not wanting to give her any ideas.

Her lips pressed together. "It is not the *Nautilus,*" she said after a moment. "The *Nautilus* is Prince Dakkar's private vessel. This is the *Narwhal.*"

That confirmed one suspicion: that Prince Dakkar and Captain Nemo were one and the same. That was probably from Verne, though I hadn't remembered it. So, in this world, Captain Nemo—Prince Dakkar—had a fleet of powerful submarines, not just the one. And no doubt Robur had more than one flying vessel.

Either, then, could be the Shaper, with the other his self-created nemesis. Although the whole setup still puzzled me. *Why would you go out of your way to make an enemy—literally?* I remembered again the altar built for human sacrifice, where blood had to be spilled to open the Portal between my world and this one, that stood on my world's version of the Mysterious Island—the island formed where this world's Shaping had somehow bled into mine.

Bled, I thought. *Such an apt word. Maybe too apt. Maybe the Shaper here* enjoys *bloodshed.* I didn't much like the thought, but why else would he Shape a world locked in perpetual war between two powerful forces?

All that flashed through my mind in an instant, as I turned toward the bunk beds. I patted the top one and glanced at my host. "I'll sleep up here?"

"Yes," Hatteras said. "I will have the quartermaster provide a pillow and blankets."

"Thank you . . . um . . ." I hesitated. "What's your first name?"

"Why?"

"Because it's really awkward having to call you Lieutenant Commander Hatteras."

Her eyes narrowed.

I sighed. "Maybe if you knew mine . . . ?" I held out my hand. "Shawna. Shawna Keys."

After a moment, reluctantly, she shook it, but only for an instant before letting it drop. "Lieutenant Commander Belinda Hatteras, commanding officer of the Seventh Flight of His Imperial Majesty's Flying Force, at your service." She clicked her heels and jerked a perfunctory head bow.

"Belinda," I said. "Nice name."

"It was my mother's."

"And your father is the captain?"

"I should not have let that slip," Belinda said.

Having to constantly defend myself from baseless accusations was getting old. "Belinda, honestly, I'm not a spy," I said tiredly. "I really am from another world. And I really do represent the . . . major power of that world." In fact, I had *been* that major power, though mostly without knowing it. I'd lost my world to the Adversary, of course, but the only way to explain *that* would have been to tell her my whole story, and she never would have believed it . . . even though it was no more unbelievable than me having been fired here from another planet by a giant cannon, and her father had been perfectly prepared to accept *that*.

Although, who knew? Maybe the Shaper had decreed that in this world, being shot into space inside a giant artillery shell would not turn you into a thin red paste on the back wall.

"It does not matter if I believe you or not," Belinda said stiffly. "I have been ordered to treat you as a guest, and I will do so. Is there anything you require? Food, or—"

"Yes," I said. "Please. Food." Very little of my dinner on the *Albatross* remained in me . . . though some of it remained *on* me. I looked down at my filthy clothing. "And . . . clean clothes? I reek."

Belinda's expression thawed a little. "You do," she said. She looked me up and down. "I think I can find you something. Wait here."

Where would I go? I thought but didn't say.

As Belinda exited, I went to the porthole and looked out. I could see little color in the water now, as we plunged to the dark depths where light barely penetrated. I winced. Shaped worlds seemed to have a knack for making metaphors literal: mentally, I, too, was plunging into dark depths where light barely penetrated. *Karl, where are you?*

Karl didn't answer, telepathy, alas, not working any better in this world than it had in mine . . . assuming he was even *in* this world and had not been captured or killed by the Adversary back in mine. He'd said the Adversary needed him alive, but accidents happen . . . as I knew all too well, having accidentally killed several people when my Shaping went awry.

Belinda returned, carrying clothing. "Ordinary seaman's attire," she said, putting it on the bottom bunk. "Feminine undergarments, I'm afraid, the quartermaster does *not* supply. Or other necessities. I bring my own."

"Can I wash what I'm wearing?"

"Yes."

"Can I get fresh underwear—and other 'necessities'—when we reach land?"

"Yes."

"How long until then?"

Belinda hesitated.

"Why keep *that* secret?" I said. "It's not like I can tell anyone."

She relaxed, and even smiled a little. "True enough. Our destination lies some 1,400 miles to the south. We should reach it in roughly two days."

Two days? I did some quick math in my head. That worked out to an underwater cruising speed of around thirty miles an hour. Pretty impressive from what I knew of submarines, which was, admittedly, not a heck of a lot.

"Where can I clean up?"

"There is a head reserved for officers, with a shower. It is unlikely to be in use this time of the watch." Her face turned grim. "And there are two fewer officers to use it. Goodbright and Comstock will not be returning. I must arrange their memorial ceremony for the morning."

I remembered the two helicopters I had seen tumbling to the ocean below. "I'm sorry," I said, and meant it. In this world, as in the last, people were dying because of me, although at least my Shaping hadn't caused *these* deaths.

"Not your fault," Belinda said. "The fault, as always, lies with the evil Robur." She took me out into the corridor and a short distance down it, opening another door to reveal a small compartment, divided into three parts. The front section held a sink with a cabinet under it, a mirror above it, and a clothes hook opposite it; the second part a toilet; the third a shower. "Behind the mirror, you will find shampoo and soap," Belinda said. "Beneath it, you will find towels. I will stand watch outside to ensure you are not disturbed."

"Thank you," I said.

"Water is distilled from seawater," she went on, "and must be conserved as much as possible."

"Which means what, shower-wise?"

"The water shuts itself off after fifteen seconds. Wet yourself and the soap, wash without the water running, then turn it on again to rinse."

I sighed, visions of a long, hot, luxurious shower vanishing as quickly as the steam from one would have, had I been allowed to have it. "All right."

Belinda went into the corridor and closed the door. I stripped out of the dirt-encrusted, dried-blood-and-vomit-splattered jeans, and plaid flannel shirt from my own world, hung them and my panties and bra on the clothes hook, used the saltwater toilet, and then stepped into the shower. It felt wonderful in the brief time I was allowed to enjoy it.

Clean at last, I toweled off (if you could call the thin and threadbare rectangle of cloth I found a towel). Leaving off my underwear and socks, so they could be washed, too, I donned the somewhat scratchy white shirt (complete with stereotypical sailor collar) and trousers (complete with stereotypical flared bottoms) I'd been given by Belinda, putting my hiking boots back on over my bare feet. The uniform, for all it made me look a bit like the Stay Puft Marshmallow Man from *Ghostbusters,* fit remarkably well. I'd been worried it would be loose enough around the waist to leave me at constant risk of embarrassment, but the trousers stayed put, and what more could you ask for in trousers?

I folded up my own clothes though I hated to even touch them. Holding them against me with my left arm, I opened the door. Belinda turned to look at me. "You wouldn't happen to have a hairbrush, would you?" I asked, running the fingers of my free hand through my wet, tangled hair.

She smiled. "Of course." She led me back to her cabin and retrieved a hairbrush—bone handle and some kind of animal bristles—from her chest. I put my old clothes on the table, then sat on the bottom bunk and pulled the brush through my hair. "Where do I wash those?" I said, pausing in my brushing to indicate the pile of my old clothes. My bra, panties, and socks lay on top, and possessed by who knows what, I sang, "I'm not wearing underwear today, no, I'm not wearing underwear today . . ."

Not surprisingly, Belinda looked at me as though I'd lost my mind, *Avenue Q* apparently not having been included in this version of reality by the local Shaper. *Hell, there might not be* any *musical theater in this world.* Now that was a horrifying thought.

"Sorry," I mumbled. "A song I heard . . ." I set aside the brush.

"I've heard worse in many a sailors' dive," Belinda said. "But I suggest you don't sing it in one." She smiled—for the third time, by my count, so I was definitely making progress. "And you do not have to wash your own clothes. The wardroom attendants will see to that. Benefit of being an officer. Just leave them there, and I will have someone retrieve them while we eat."

"But . . . I'm not an officer."

"I am." She opened the door. "Now, I believe you said something about wanting food . . . ?"

My stomach growled, and I leaped up. "Yes, please!"

Ten minutes later, we were seated in the officers' wardroom we had passed through on our way forward, a relatively spacious chamber maybe four times the size of Belinda's cabin. When we entered, she had spoken to the attendant, a boy who looked no more than fourteen, and bread, a selection of cheeses, slices of ham and beef, and a small pot of mustard had appeared in front of us moments later, along with a glass of wine for me and a glass of water for Belinda.

Having provided us with sustenance, the boy headed in the direction of Belinda's cabin, presumably to see to the washing of the clothes. I made a ham-and-cheese sandwich and pretty much inhaled it. Then I reached for my wineglass. Remembering what had passed for wine with my wasted dinner on the *Albatross,* I sipped it cautiously at first, then more deeply—it was actually decent. I closed my eyes and heaved a deep sigh, immediate hunger pangs sated and the wine warming me. I'd been running largely on adrenaline for hours, maybe days, and now that it was finally draining away, it was taking the last of my energy with it.

I belatedly realized Belinda had said something. I blinked at her. "What?"

"I said, what is it like, this place you come from, where Robur the Monster and our beloved Dread Prince do not exist?" She picked up a knife and smeared a soft, runny cheese onto a slice of brown, seed-encrusted bread.

"Assuming," she of course had to add, as she took a bite, "you are telling the truth."

Beloved Dread Prince? I thought. *Isn't that an oxymoron?* Out loud, I said, "Boring. Dull. Safe." Or at least it had been. I made myself a second sandwich. "I'm a potter, actually. I just opened my own shop."

"A potter?" Her eyes narrowed. "Why would your world send a potter?"

"I wasn't exactly sent," I said around a yawn. "It just kind of . . . happened."

"You just *happened* to fly to a new world as an ambassador?"

Crap. In my exhaustion, I'd momentarily forgotten I was pretending to be an ambassador. I picked up my wineglass to cover my confusion. *Sure,* I thought. *Alcohol is great at lessening confusion.* I sipped some anyway, but resolved, regretfully, not to finish the glass. "It's hard to explain." *Lame. Maybe a change of subject?* "What about you? How did a woman end up commanding a helicopter squadron?" I bit into my second sandwich.

"Flight," she corrected me. "The term 'squadron' is reserved for infantry and cavalry units."

"Flight, then. And how did you end up on a submarine? The captain of the *Albatross* told me women are considered bad luck aboard ship."

"It is unfortunately the same in the navy of our Dread Prince," Belinda said. "However, within the Prince's Flying Force, it is another matter. The inventor of the helicopter, and its first pilot, was a woman. Inspired by her, many women have advanced within the Force." She gave me a rather sharklike smile. "I assume there are sailors aboard the *Narwhal* who are offended by my presence . . . but I outrank them."

The second sandwich had vanished almost as quickly as the first. "It probably doesn't hurt that your father is the captain," I said after I'd swallowed the last bite, then instantly wished I hadn't as Belinda's face clouded. "I'm not saying you're not qualified . . ." I added hastily.

"Perhaps *you* are not, but many another has," Belinda said. She pushed the plate of bread and cheese away.

"My own mother among them. But my father being the captain has nothing to do with it. The *Narwhal* is the fleet's only aerial-supported submarine. Once I assumed command of Seventh Flight, it was only a matter of time before I was posted here, because every flight serves on *Narwhal* on a six-month rotating basis. It just happens to be my father's ship."

"In my world, submarines are called boats," I said, a useless fact which surfaced in my sleep-deprived brain like a bubble rising in a swamp.

Belinda blinked. "Why would something this size be called a boat?"

"I have no idea," I admitted.

"Your complete lack of knowledge about pretty much everything is the most compelling evidence of your truthfulness," she said thoughtfully.

"Um . . . thank you?" I risked another sip of wine. It was only half gone, but even those few swallows had gone to my head. I pushed the glass away regretfully. *No more.* "I'm sorry, I interrupted. You found yourself on your father's ship . . . ?"

"Yes. What consternation that may have caused here or elsewhere I do not know or care to know. I am pleased the Admiralty did not allow the coincidence to affect their decision to post my flight here on schedule. I am less pleased so many see, or pretend to see, some impropriety."

"I'm sorry," I said. "I only brought it up because of what they said on the *Albatross* about women being unlucky on ships. If it's any consolation," I rushed on, though *why would it be?* a part of me wondered, "in my world, women and men are treated equally within the armed forces, although of course there are physical requirements for some roles that mean either men or women are usually the best-qualified for them."

"It sounds a better world, then," Belinda said. "Can I visit it?"

"I'm afraid not," I said. "I can't even visit it." Tears flooded my eyes, as once again the realization I could never go home again struck my exhausted—and just slightly inebriated—brain like a hammer blow. I looked down at the table, swallowing hard. "I would very much like," I mumbled without looking up, "to sleep now."

"It is still early . . ."

"Not by my internal clock." In fact, I thought it was earlier here than it had been on the Mysterious Island in my own world, but for my overstressed body and mind, it was late indeed.

"Very well." Belinda glanced at her wrist, and I saw, for the first time, that there was a watch sewn into the red leather of her flying outfit. "I must debrief my flight in ten minutes, in any event, and I need to change out of these leathers."

She led me back to her cabin. The top bunk had been made, with sheets and a blue blanket, twin of the one on Belinda's. My dirty clothes had been taken away. I removed my boots, the only thing of my own I still wore, climbed barefoot up to the top bunk, lay down on top of the blanket without undressing, and turned my eyes to the bulkhead, listening without speaking to Belinda moving around, presumably removing her leathers in favor of whatever her shipboard attire looked like.

My slight curiosity as to the appearance of the uniform of His Imperial Majesty's Flying Force was not enough to convince my weary body to roll over.

I never heard her leave.

SIX

I WOKE FROM a dream of the Mysterious Island in which I was being pursued by Michelangelo's *David* down a corridor whose paving stones were turning to quicksand beneath my feet. Not surprisingly, I didn't have the slightest idea of where I was for a terrifying, disorienting minute or two, and bolted upright—banging my skull painfully on the steel ceiling not far above my head. Rubbing the bruised spot, I flopped back down again, swearing, but at least fully cognizant of my surroundings. The cabin was pitch-black. I was probably lucky I hadn't rolled out of bed and broken a leg or two on the deck plates six feet below.

"What's wrong?" said a muzzy voice.

I gave my forehead another rueful rub. "Bad dream," I said. "And I need to go to the bathroom."

"You need another bath? In the middle of the night?"

"The toilet, I mean. The . . . head."

"Oh. Just a second." I heard Belinda roll over, then a faint blue light suddenly illuminated the tiny cabin. "I'm sorry, I normally only turn it on if I have to get up. There's one above your bunk, too . . . can you see it?"

I looked up, then left, and spotted it: a glass tube, inset in the wall, with two buttons beside it. I pushed the top button, and the tube lit the same shade of blue as that spilling from Belinda's bunk below.

"You remember where the head is . . . ?" Belinda mumbled. The light from below switched off.

"Yes," I said. I carefully felt my way down the ladder.

Glad I hadn't taken off my borrowed sailor's clothes, since struggling into them again would have been a pain in the dark and the alternative of padding naked down the hallway of a submarine on which I was one of only two women seemed a bad idea, I eased open the door and looked down the corridor outside. Also lit by dim blue light, it looked deserted. Presumably the night watch was active in places other than officers' country ... wasn't that what they called it on a ship?

I used the toilet, washed my hands, and jerked open the door—to find myself face-to-face with a young man. He gaped at me, then blushed furiously (so furiously I could tell it was happening even in the blue light), probably because he, apparently not having had the same qualms I had, was stark naked. Fortunately, he was carrying a towel, which he immediately placed as strategically as he could. The blush extended all the way to his belly button, and possibly beyond. "Ma'am, I'm sorry, I didn't ..."

"It's all right ..." I suddenly recognized his face. "Lieutenant Blackwell, isn't it?"

"Yes, sir! I mean, ma'am. I mean ... I'm so sorry, ma'am, I didn't expect ..."

"It's really quite all right, Lieutenant. No offense taken." He was so earnest and embarrassed, it was cute. "Good night, Lieutenant." I turned right and walked back to Belinda's quarters, womanfully resisting the urge to look back as he ducked into the head. Grinning to myself in the dark, I lay down again, and fell asleep seconds later.

I woke to the clanging of a ship's bell. I rolled over to see Belinda already dressed. She wore a powder-blue, neatly tailored uniform, with red stripes down the legs of the pants, gold braid on the sleeves and shoulders, and a silver pin on her left breast in the shape of a stooping, screaming falcon, with two glittering emerald chips for eyes. From the right side of her white Sam Browne belt (though that probably wasn't what they called it in a world where Sam Browne had presumably never existed) hung a holstered pistol; from the left, a sword in a white scabbard, with a golden basket hilt. A red tassel dangled from the pommel.

As I sat up, she plucked a beret from her bunk, a pair of white gloves neatly folded inside it. "Good morning," I said. "That's a sharp uniform."

"Dress uniform," Belinda said shortly. "The memorial service."

"Of course." I was barely awake, but some impulse made me say, "I'd like to come if I may."

Belinda frowned at me. "Why?"

"I feel . . . responsible."

"You were a prisoner on the *Albatross*. You did not fire the airburst shell that killed Goodbright and Comstock."

"Nevertheless. If I may?"

Belinda flicked her left arm up to consult her wristwatch. "You have five minutes to get ready." She lowered her arm and nodded to the chest in the corner. "Your own clothing has been washed, if you prefer."

"I prefer," I said.

I slid out of the bunk and went to retrieve my clothing from atop the chest. Feeling self-conscious, I turned my back on Belinda and peeled off the borrowed sailor's uniform, then hurriedly donned my freshly laundered underwear, socks, jeans, and plaid shirt.

I sat on Belinda's bunk to pull on my boots, then stood. "Ready," I said. "It's not very formal attire, I'm afraid."

"No one would expect you to have any," Belinda said. "You are certain you want to attend?"

I nodded. "Absolutely."

"Very well." She opened the door. "Follow me."

I thought the service would be in the officers' mess where we had eaten the night before, but instead she took me through two more hatches, then through a door on the starboard side into a narrow chapel I hadn't seen before, its door having been closed when I'd been taken forward to Captain Hatteras' cabin. It had seating for no more than twenty, but it was not full. Everyone present—all men—wore a uniform the same color as Belinda's, though with less braid and, in some cases, neither Sam Browne belt, nor sword, nor stooping-falcon badge.

Belinda nodded to the pews. "Sit where you like," she said, then went to speak in a low voice to two others who wore emerald-eyed falcons. I guessed those with the badges were pilots, and the others support staff—mechanics and armorers, perhaps—though their uniforms marked them clearly as still part of the Flying Force, rather than the Navy.

I recognized Lieutenant Blackwell, seated in the front pew, and went to sit beside him. "Good morning," I said. He gave me a rather horrified look, and his ears turned bright red.

"Ma'am," he said. "Again, I must apologize for . . . last night was . . . I didn't . . ."

I waved my hand. "Forget about it. No harm done."

If he turned any redder, he'd self-combust. I changed the subject. "Did you know the . . . lost pilots?"

And then I could have kicked myself. There were no more than ten pilots on the sub, by the simple math of eight now in the room, two lost. Of course, he had known them.

"They were both in my class at the academy," he said in a subdued voice. "I've known them for . . ." He swallowed hard, and for a moment looked very, very young. "For . . . a long time."

"I'm sorry," I said, and meant it. Belinda was right, I hadn't fired the cannon, I'd been a prisoner belowdecks when they'd attacked the *Albatross* . . . but they wouldn't have attacked if they hadn't known I'd been pulled from the Mysterious Island, if they hadn't decided it was worth the risk to try to snatch me away from Robur's forces.

Why they thought it worth the risk, I still didn't know.

I didn't say anything more to Lieutenant Blackwell. I half expected him to get up and go sit somewhere else, but he didn't; and in a moment or two, as a few more blue-clad crewmen came into the chapel (though no more of the falcon-marked pilots), there was no place he could have moved to anyway.

I studied the chapel, wondering what religion would

be like in a world Shaped as much as this one. In my world, Christianity and Judaism and Buddhism and Confucianism and Islam and animism and many other religions existed, just as (presumably) they did in the First World. In my world, they all lived in harmony with each other, the religious wars of the past having burned themselves out ten years ago when the last of the jihadists had laid down their arms and suicide belts in the grand conference known as the Miracle at Mecca . . .

I paused. Ten years ago. Right when, according to Karl, I'd Shaped my world. Had I made that miracle happen? If so, yay me.

But this space was not decorated with any religious iconography I recognized. There was a backlit stained-glass window behind the rather plain pulpit of pale blond wood, but all it showed was the world—this world, with its strange oceans and continents, which I had seen depicted on the globe in the captain's cabin—cradled in a pair of hands. *He's got the whole world in his hands,* I thought, a line from a song I'd learned in Sunday School. That was a Christian song, but there were no crosses or saints or apostles or anything else that said "Christian" here.

In fact, the only other decorations were two banners hung on either side of the window. One was pale blue, with the screaming falcon symbol on it in red, while the other was white, with a green, stylized nautilus shell. I was pretty sure they delineated the two branches of Prince Dakkar's forces that manned . . . I glanced at Belinda . . . *crewed* this ship.

I expected Belinda to take charge of the ceremony, but instead she sat down on the front pew, on the other side of Lieutenant Blackwell from me. A bell rang, and the murmur of voices subsided. It rang again, and again, eight times in all . . . and as the sound of the last chime faded away, the door opened, and Captain Hatteras entered.

He wore a dress uniform of spotless white, sporting green stripes down the trouser legs and green tassels fringing the tails of the coat. He wore a pearl-handled cutlass rather than the straight swords of the flying officers, its scabbard hanging from a green sash, adorned with half a dozen impressive-looking medals, looped over his right shoulder.

Everyone in the chapel—including me, albeit a second late—rose to their feet. The captain stepped onto the dais and took his place behind the podium, solemnly surveying the silent Flying Force personnel assembled before him. "Bare your heads, gentlemen ... and ladies," he said. Hats came off all around me, and the captain removed his own, placing it under his left arm. "A moment of silence for Lieutenants Michael Elbert Comstock and Theodore James Goodbright."

The silence that followed was so profound I hardly dared breathe. It stretched on until I wanted to scream. Finally, the captain said, "Be seated."

All of us resumed our places on the pews. The captain turned and handed his hat to an adjutant who seemed to have appeared out of nowhere—I honestly hadn't noticed him until that moment—then took off his gloves and handed those over as well. The adjutant stepped down, turned, and sat straight-backed at the far end of the front pew, next to Belinda. The captain's eyes, perusing the tiny crowd, paused on me for a moment but then moved on.

"We who serve our Dread Prince," the captain said, "do so in the full knowledge that it may one day cost us our lives. We do not seek death, but we do not flinch from it.

"Lieutenants Comstock and Goodbright died doing their duty. They died in the service of their beloved prince. They died to protect their families and loved ones—*all* our families and loved ones—from the tyranny that would devour them, should Robur ever truly become the 'Master of the World' he styles himself.

"They died in the execution of a successful mission." Again, his eyes flicked to me. "Their names will be inscribed in the Chamber of Sacrifice and the Book of Remembrance. They will not be forgotten, and their families will want for nothing.

"Grieve their loss and their absence, but do not grieve their lives. They died for the greater good. They died heroes." He paused. "Let us pray."

Heads bowed all around me. I looked down at the toes of my boots.

"Almighty Shaper," the captain began, and I felt a jolt, like I'd stuck my finger in a wall socket. They were praying to the *Shaper*?

"Mystery at the Center of Existence," Captain Hatteras continued, "take unto yourself the souls of your faithful servants, Michael Elbert Comstock and Theodore James Goodbright. Their bodies are lost to us, but we know nothing is lost to you, neither body nor soul, for every hair of our heads is numbered, and nowhere we can go, in life or death, is outside the purview of your power.

"May our lost compatriots serve you in the heavenly realm as faithfully as they served you in this one. Shape them in that service, as you Shape all of us in your service. May all of us find and fulfill the great purposes you have set for us in this, your world, so that when, like Lieutenants Comstock and Goodbright, we leave this mortal realm, we may, like them, live for eternity in the warmth and light and love of you, our Shaper. Amen."

"Amen," said everyone around me.

I didn't join in. I felt ill.

The Shaper of this world . . . Prince Dakkar, Robur, or someone else entirely . . . had Shaped its inhabitants to *worship* him, to treat him as a god, complete with a lot of hooey about heavenly realms and eternal warmth and light and blah blah blah.

When I get his hokhmah, I thought to myself, *there'll be some changes made . . .*

And then I felt ill again, in a whole new way. Who was I to Shape this world? What gave me the right? If I started changing all the Shaped worlds into the worlds *I* would prefer them to be, how was I any better than the Adversary?

I might not be any better, but the worlds would be, I told myself. *Freer.*

Really? a part of me shot back. *You changed people at a whim so you could escape your own world. You re-wrote your own mother's memories. You saw the people of your world as playthings, just like the Shaper of this world, just like the Adversary.*

That's not fair.

Why not?

Because . . . because, shut up.

The truth was, I had no answer. Not yet.

The argument was moot, anyway. I still didn't know for certain who the Shaper of this world *was*. Until I figured that out, managed to get myself into his or her presence, and then got him or her to give me this world's *hokhmah* . . . however that worked . . . I wouldn't be Shaping squat.

Anyway, I told myself, *look on the bright side: you'll probably be dead long before you get anywhere near the Shaper. So, no need to worry about it!*

Karl had told me what he'd do in that case: grieve and then move on, searching for another Shaper with the power to do what he and Ygrair needed done. In fact, he'd thought, based on the way my Shaping and that of this world had mingled together to create the Mysterious Island, the Shaper of this world might be a possible alternate.

In other words, I was expendable to everyone but myself. Time enough to worry about misusing my godlike powers when and if I ever had them again.

"Those of you with personal memories of Goodbright and Comstock may now wish to share them," the captain said. "You have my deepest sympathy and respect." He nodded to his adjutant, who brought him his cap and gloves. The captain donned both, then went out.

Acting on an impulse, I followed him, catching the door as the adjutant turned to close it. "Excuse me," I said, then called, "Captain!"

Captain Hatteras turned. "Ambassador Keys," he said. "I was surprised to see you at the service. Why have you left it?"

"I didn't really know the . . . deceased," I said. "I just wanted to show my respect."

"I'm not sure leaving early really does that," he said

dryly, which stung, and was probably correct—although I figured Lieutenant Blackwell, at least, felt relieved I was no longer sitting beside him.

"I wanted to ask you something," I hurried on. "Well, two somethings."

"I'm rather busy," the captain said. He tapped the braid on his shoulders. "Captain, remember? I need to get out of this monkey suit and back to the bridge. So, please, keep it brief."

"I will," I promised. "First . . . have you been back in . . ." I hesitated; he hadn't used the word "radio," as I remembered. "Um, 'wireless communication' with your . . . superiors?"

"I have," he said. "We surfaced briefly overnight for that very purpose. They agreed with my decision to deliver you to the palace for further examination."

Well, that was a relief. I guessed. As long as "further examination" didn't involve thumbscrews and red-hot pokers.

"Your second question?" the captain prompted.

"I want to know more about your religious belief. About the Shaper."

"I am not a theologian, Ambassador."

"You just offered up a prayer."

"As may any man or woman. Is that not true in the world you come from?" He considered me for a moment, then looked at the adjutant. "Escort the ambassador to the library," he said, "and provide her with a copy of the *Word*."

"Yes, sir," said the adjutant. He indicated the corridor leading aft. "Ambassador?"

"Thank you—" I started to say to Captain Hatteras, but he was already striding toward his cabin in the bow. I turned back to the adjutant, an olive-skinned young man with remarkably high, finely chiseled cheekbones, and a pencil-thin mustache. "Lead on, Mr. . . . ?"

"Lieutenant," he said. "Lieutenant Ambergris. This way."

I remembered the library: its over-the-top opulence had been one reason I'd thought I must be on the *Nautilus*.

I was surprised to see half a dozen presumably off-duty sailors seated in the plush chairs, reading. If asked, I would have predicted it would be available to officers only.

They didn't react to Lieutenant Ambergris' entrance, or mine, other than glancing up momentarily. "Shouldn't they . . . salute you, or something?" I said.

He gave me a puzzled look. "In the library? What a strange notion. This way."

Rows of books covered both curving walls, with a rolling ladder providing access to the topmost shelves, but he led me instead to the aft bulkhead, where a single—and singularly large—book lay open atop a wooden lectern, illuminated by an electric light in a golden shade above it. Two giant carved hands, like those I had seen cradling the world in the stained-glass window of the chapel, cradled the top of the lectern, to moderately creepy effect.

"*The Word of the Shaper,*" Lieutenant Ambergris said, indicating the book. "Take as long as you like with it. You can find your way back to your quarters from here?"

"Uh . . . yeah," I said. Since my quarters lay in a straight line toward the bow, I wondered if he were joking, although there was nothing in his expression to indicate it.

"Very good," he said. "I must attend on the captain." Like Belinda when she'd introduced herself, he bowed his head and clicked his heels, then turned and strode back the way we had come.

I looked around at the crewmen, catching two of them staring at me. They promptly looked down at their books again. Then I looked at the book.

It was open about a third of the way from the front, the spot marked with a green silk bookmark. I leaned over it. *Blessed are those who faithfully serve those who govern over them, for that is the will of the Shaper,* I read. *Blessed are those who do not kick against the pricks, but pull calmly and steadily in the traces, for that is the will of the Shaper.* ("Kick against the pricks" might have confused me mightily if not for the aforementioned Sunday School attendance, in a church wherein the King James Version was the preferred version of the Bible. As the preacher used to joke, "If King James English was good enough for Jesus, it's good enough for us!")

The fact the Shaper had included that phrase in his (or her, I reminded myself; I *thought* either Prince Dakkar or Robur must be the Shaper, but it could still conceivably be someone else) holy book suggested a lot of the rest of the book might be borrowed; and sure enough, it contained a lot of Bible, a lot of it word for word: mostly the parts that dealt with morality and not being disobedient to parents and things like that.

Neither Jehovah nor Jesus made an appearance, however. Everything was presented as the Word of the Shaper: *Do unto others as you would have them do unto you, sayeth the Shaper.* (Notably missing from the Shaper's version of the Beatitudes was the blessing offered peacemakers in the Gospel of Matthew.) *The Word of the Shaper*'s core commandment was, clearly, *Fear the Shaper and keep his commandments, for this is the whole duty of man.* (At least the *Word* made it clear that the Shaper was male, narrowing the possibilities by half.)

The books of history in the Old Testament had, of course, vanished, but many of the Psalms and most of the Proverbs and some of the Prophets remained, albeit with "The Shaper" in place of the Lord. For example, Psalm 23 began, "The Shaper is my shepherd, I shall not want . . ." and ended with ". . . and I will dwell in the house of the Shaper forever."

And, of course, the *Word of the Shaper* began, "In the beginning, the Shaper Shaped the heavens and the earth . . ."

The more I read of it, the angrier I became at the unbridled display of unmitigated gall.

I remembered something Karl had said about the Adversary, after we had destroyed the Portal through which he and Karl had entered my world: how humans are hardwired for religious belief, and how the Adversary Shaped that innate inclination into a belief in him as a distant, unapproachable, perfect Deity—and an accompanying belief in the society he had set up as absolutely, unquestionably perfect.

The Shaper of this world had obviously taken the same approach. Such an approach would keep the world running as he wanted it to without him having to be constantly tweaking it, so he could focus on . . . what?

Amusing himself with an endless conflict between two powers armed with steampunk weapons, apparently.

The guy wasn't just a Jules Verne fan: I was willing to bet he was a wargamer, not just a computer gamer, but an old-school wargamer who'd refought the Battle of Waterloo with little tin soldiers on an elaborately landscaped board, or the First World War on a massive map covered with hexagons, working from a rule book only slightly thinner than a history of the war itself, and several times more complicated. (I'd once briefly dated . . . or, at least, *remembered* dating . . . a guy like that.)

I closed *The Word of the Shaper* with rather more force than was necessary, with a sound like a hand slapping a face, pretty much what I would have liked to do just then to the Shaper of the world in which I'd found myself. Ignoring both the raised eyebrows and annoyed frowns of the half-dozen crewmen, I turned and strode back toward the bow . . .

. . . and then paused, because as much as a grand exit in a mighty huff would have suited me right then, it occurred to me I had absolutely nothing to do in my quarters or the officers' wardroom, and I was in a library.

"Sorry," I said to the crewmen. I put my finger to my lips. "Shhhh," I said. That earned me a couple of grins, but more importantly, it turned everyone's attention back to books they were reading.

I went to the shelves and ran my fingers along the spines of the nearest books. They were familiar . . . but not quite right. *Evenhoe,* by Sir Wallace Scott. *Moby-Buck* by Hermione Melville, which, a quick perusal showed, was about an obsessed huntsman trekking the wilderness in pursuit of a great white stag. *Dr. Acula,* by Bram Striker, a horror story about a physician whose experiments with blood transfusions produced shambling, undead monsters with a thirst for even more blood . . .

Actually, that one sounded pretty good. I took it and looked around. There was no obvious way to check it out so, even though it made me feel oddly guilty, I simply walked out with it and headed back to Belinda's cabin.

My bad luck: the memorial service was letting out as I passed the chapel. Lieutenant Blackwell, of course, popped out just as I reached the door. "We have to stop meeting like this," I said as he registered my presence, just to see if I could make his ears turn red (I could). He hurried away without saying anything.

I waited to see Belinda emerge; she was the last. "I'm sorry I didn't stay to the end of the service," I said. "I needed to talk to the captain."

Her eyes flicked to the novel I carried.

"I wanted to know more about *The Word of the Shaper*," I said defensively. "I've been reading it in the library." I held up *Dr. Acula*. "This is just to pass the time."

"You had no obligation to attend at all," she said. "Thank you for doing so." She nodded at the book. "If you like that one, you should try the works of Ellen Elgar Poe. Her short stories are even better at inducing late-night shivers. 'The Rise of the House of Asher.' 'The White Dog.' 'The Overdue Burial.' 'The Musk of the Black Death.' 'The Husk of an Armadillo.'"

"They sound familiar," I said.

"She is well-known in our world," Belinda said. She cocked her head at me. "I begin to believe, Shawna Keys, that perhaps you are telling the truth, and you really are not from our world."

"I am beginning to believe it myself," I said, and, leaving that cryptic comment hanging between us, continued my way forward to our shared quarters.

SEVEN

ANOTHER NIGHT PASSED aboard the *Narwhal*—this time without my encountering a naked lieutenant in the corridor. Belinda's duties took her away before I awoke. I had eggs and bacon and coffee in the wardroom, then spent most of the day in the library, reading neither *Dr. Acula* nor *The Word of the Shaper,* but looking for history books and maps and anything else that could help me make sense of this strange world I'd literally fallen into.

I found several volumes of history, all pretty much the same, all describing the long-running war between the Principality of Raj and the Republic of Weldon. (The latter name almost made me laugh: in Jules Verne's *Robur the Conqueror,* the Weldon Institute was the organization of flight enthusiasts in Philadelphia to which Robur first made himself and his inventions known.) In every account, the Rajians, led by Prince Dakkar, represented everything that was good and right and beautiful, while the Weldonians, led by "Robur the Monster," were described as evil, depraved, and rapacious.

Before the war, there had apparently been a golden age, when Dakkar benevolently ruled a peaceable Principality described in such glowing terms I had the distinct impression lions and lambs had not only laid down together, they'd sneaked off into the woods for interspecies canoodling, and the land was awash, not with prosaic milk and honey, but sparkling wine and caviar.

Yet details of that golden era were extremely vague.

It was the setting of any number of novels and plays, but each began with the apparently legally mandated statement that they were works of fiction, no one really knew what had transpired in that long-ago utopian era, and nothing within them should be interpreted as a criticism of "our Dread Prince's beneficent reign." (Again, "Dread" and "beneficent" were not words I would have thought went together, but the writers and publishers, if they saw any contradiction, were very careful not to point it out.)

Even the descriptions of the key battles in the war (which all authorities agreed had begun when Robur had brutally invaded a peaceful province of the Principality with which his tyrannical state shared a border) had that same air of unreality about them, as if they had been concocted by fantasy writers out of thin air. There were no detailed accounts of the disposition of forces, casualties, territory gained or lost, or any of the other things one would expect to see in a military history: everything gave the impression of having happened "a long time ago, in a galaxy far, far away," only with fewer light sabers.

Another peculiarity: there was no indication that technology had advanced in the slightest since the war had begun. Both sides had land forces, including artillery and primitive tanks. Both sides had steamships, of the early "let's keep some masts and sails on them just in case" variety. Prince Dakkar had his submarines and his Flying Force of tiny helicopters. Robur had the *Albatross,* a fleet of smaller (and, from what I could tell, more ordinary, lighter-than-air) airships, and a secret weapon called the *Terror,* which the Rajian histories seemed to know little about but I thought I remembered from reading Verne. If memory served, it was a hybrid capable of driving on land, traversing water above or below the surface, and flying, too. What armament it carried in Verne's books I didn't remember, but, clearly, I couldn't expect everything to align perfectly with Verne—he'd never described one-person rocket-firing helicopters, for example.

But the most glaringly odd thing about the histories?

For all the fighting, the war remained a stalemate. Battles raged and forces advanced and retreated, but the overall effect seemed to be, effectively, nil.

By the end of my day's research, I was sure my original guess was correct: the Shaper of this World had created one vast, giant wargame, only instead of moving miniatures around on a papier-mâché landscape, or shoving cardboard counters from hexagon to hexagon, or blowing up pixels on a computer screen, he was using the inhabitants of his Shaped world as his pieces—and had Shaped them to not only accept the endless fighting, but to embrace it.

I've got nothing against wargames (I've enjoyed playing them myself) or wargamers (dated one, remember?) but to do it with real people, suffering real loss and real pain? I thought of the memorial service the day before for Goodbright and Comstock. As far as I was concerned, the Shaper of this world was one sick puppy . . . and yet, Ygrair had thought it perfectly all right to give him a world to play with.

So, what did that make Ygrair? And what did it make *me,* if I meekly followed instructions and tried to preserve all these worlds as they were, saving them from the depredations of the Adversary? Would the authoritarian world he would create here if he took control (if what Karl had told me about him was the truth) be any worse than this one already was? At least he wouldn't allow war.

I need to talk to Karl, I thought for the umpteenth time . . . but did I? I knew *his* priority: to do what Ygrair wanted done. He would not question her. For whatever reason, he was as loyal to her as the Adversary's cadre was to him—as the people of this world were to their respective leaders, arbitrarily assigned to them by the Shaper, and to the Shaper himself, self-established as their god.

Which raised an interesting . . . and uncomfortable . . . question. What if Karl was not, as he claimed, from the First World at all? What if he, too, were Shaped—Shaped by Ygrair to do her bidding? What if he only *thought* he was from the First World?

It would explain why his knowledge of it seemed so out of date . . . by about a century, as far as I could tell.

Although, to be fair, I suppose I couldn't really say I knew everything about the First World, because it could have changed drastically since I left it ten years ago. It could now be very different from my version of it. Did it have HiPhones and StreamPix? In it, had the long-delayed *Star Trek* musical finally made it to Broadway? (In my world, it was still in development hell, although one song from it, Scotty's big second-act number, "The Laws of Physics Break Dance," had made it to number sixty-seven on the Hot 100 chart.) Who was the president? Did she still live in the Emerald Palace?

She doesn't live there in my world anymore, I thought. *The Adversary controls everything by now.* And that, as much as anything, stiffened my resolve. The Adversary had killed my best friend and many others and had come close to killing me. Whatever Ygrair might really be, whatever Karl might really be, I had no doubt the Adversary was my enemy. And that meant, whatever might be wrong with this world—and this world's Shaper—my course remained set. Other worlds, after all, might be as free as mine had been, and letting the Adversary have this one would put them at risk. I had to try to do what I had been sent here to do . . .

. . . even though I had very little notion of how to do it.

Well, I thought, late in the day as, following the instructions on a discreet sign, I put the last of the history books on a designated table for later reshelving, *soon enough I'll be meeting Prince Dakkar. Maybe he's the Shaper. Maybe he knows how to give me his* hokhmah, *since presumably he remembers whatever Ygrair taught him. It may not stop the Adversary from coming into his world, but it will stop him from taking it over.*

Somehow. I wasn't entirely clear how. Karl had said that when I was given the *hokhmah* willingly by another Shaper, it would be mine "completely," so the Adversary couldn't get it. But wouldn't that leave the Shaper just an ordinary resident of his world? Why would anyone willingly give up that power?

Karl seemed to think they would cooperate due to their loyalty to Ygrair. I had my doubts.

He'd also said something about giving me "special technology," although I didn't know if that meant technology that would allow me to strip the *hokhmah* from another Shaper if they refused to cooperate, like the Adversary had done to me, or technology that would allow me to keep multiple *hokhmahs* inside me, or . . .

Maybe, by "completely," Karl had meant only that I would have the complete *hokhmah,* not that the Shaper wouldn't still keep it himself. After all, I'd kept mine when the Adversary had taken it from me. But if, after I left, the Shaper retained the power to Shape, did that mean the Adversary could just waltz in and take his *hokhmah* after all? Surely not.

Maybe there could only be one "original" of a *hokhmah* and one copy at a time? Maybe the version I would carry within me would serve to protect the original?

My brain was running around in circles. I couldn't answer any of my questions. Only Karl could. Whenever he finally made it into this world, he would surely head for the Shaper. I needed to try to do the same, so that we would finally reconnect.

I was lingering in the library, examining the works of Mark Tierce (*Gooseberry Flynn, The Adventures of Sam Carpenter, Prince Dakkar and the Pauper He Rescued from a Life of Poverty out of the Goodness of His Glorious Heart*), when the hatch into officer's country opened, and Lieutenant Ambergris, the captain's adjutant, entered. "Captain Hatteras' compliments," he said, "and would the ambassador please join him in his cabin?"

"Of course," I said. *Now what?*

I followed Ambergris forward, stepping into Captain Hatteras' cabin to discover that the dark water outside his windows had lightened. We were clearly moving up in the world, or at least in the ocean. Ahead of us, though, I saw an enormous dark bulk. *Land?* It had to be . . .

. . . and yet, just before we broke into the light of the

setting sun, which turned the sheets of water streaming down the captain's windows, for one glorious moment, into liquid gold, I thought I glimpsed enormous, spinning propellers attached to that bulk, bigger than anything on any ship I had ever heard of or dreamed of.

It was only a glimpse, and it made no sense a moment later, because once the water had cleared from the windows, what I saw ahead of us was, unmistakably, land: a harbor, with vessels at anchor, large buildings of wood and stone with red tile roofs, gulls swinging overhead, cannon-topped fortifications of white stone, and lots of greenery.

"The Island of Raj," said Captain Hatteras. "Jewel at the heart of the Principality of Raj, the realm of our glorious leader, Dread Prince Dakkar, long may he reign."

"It's beautiful," I said, and it certainly was, particularly right then, just before sunset, in what I'd heard photographers call "the Golden Hour."

Back on the surface, we sailed . . . steamed . . . what *was* the right word for forward progress in a battery-powered submarine? electricked? . . . slowly into the harbor. Our destination proved to be a pier isolated inside its own walls, just big enough to accommodate us. Before we entered our secretive slip, we passed two ships at anchor, a steel-clad steamer with towering masts to our right . . . starboard, I mean . . . and a smaller-but-still-substantial sailing vessel to port. The sailing vessel, which had the look of a merchant ship, had no weapons I could see, unlike the steamer, which bristled with gun turrets. In the distance bobbed smaller vessels—fishing boats, maybe, some with sails, a few which, since they lacked masts but were too large to row, I supposed to be powered by this world's ubiquitous batteries.

The vibration of the deck beneath my feet became rougher. We were slowing. The vibration increased still more, and then we stopped, next to the wooden pier. It ran straight ahead of us to an open gate in the inland wall of white stone (in shadow now, except for a fiery strip at its top, as the sun continued setting behind us), through which I saw only darkness.

I heard footsteps overhead; men on deck, presumably tying us to the dock. A moment later, a staticky voice said, "All lines secured, sir. Communications established." I looked up for the source of the voice, and spotted a box attached to the ceiling by a rod, with latticework sides: a speaker.

"Very well," said Captain Hatteras to thin air— apparently the thing hanging from the ceiling was a microphone, too. "Send the message dictated earlier. Top priority and secrecy."

"Aye, aye, sir."

Captain Hatteras turned to me. "We are telegraphing the palace with more extensive details of our mission, and your rescue, than we were able to provide via wireless."

Rescue, I thought. *A much nicer word than capture, or kidnap.* "And what will the palace do?"

"In the long run?" Captain Hatteras said. "I have no idea. I am not privy to the prince's decision-making. In the short run, though, I assume you will be questioned. On that basis, I have already arranged an escort to take you to the palace, once I have confirmation that is, indeed, your destination." He indicated one of the chairs on my side of his desk, in which I had not been invited to sit the last time I'd been in here, what with having Belinda's pistol stuck in my throat. "In the meantime, please make yourself comfortable."

I sat, but I can't say I was entirely comfortable. (Being told "you will be questioned" has that effect on me.) Captain Hatteras crossed to a cabinet to my left, took out a crystal decanter filled with a garnet-red liquid, and filled two small glasses with it. He handed one to me. I sniffed it. "Port?" I said.

The captain looked to my left, at the drink cabinet. "Yes, that's the port side."

"No, I mean the wine. Is it port?"

"Um . . . no, it's directly in front of you."

I sighed. "Is this wine *called* 'port'?"

He frowned. "No. Why would it be? It might just as well be called starboard. We call it forto."

"Forto?"

"For fortified wine."

"Ah." I sipped it. It was definitely port as far as I was concerned, but of course "port" in my world came from the fact this style of wine had originated in Portugal . . . and Portugal did not exist here. *Obviously asking for Scotch or champagne is out, then.* "It's lovely. Thank you."

"I trust you have been comfortable aboard our vessel, *Ambassador*," Captain Hatteras said, taking a seat across from me. I could tell from the emphasis he put on the last word that he was still not entirely convinced I deserved the title.

"Very," I said. "Your daughter has been most kind. As has the rest of the crew . . . the few members of it I have met."

"I am glad."

The captain sipped his forto. I took another sip of my port, then regretfully set it aside. With "questioning" apparently in the offing, clearheadedness again seemed something to conserve. We sat in silence. The captain showed no inclination to break it, so I did. "As we were approaching land, I thought I saw something strange."

"Indeed?" the captain said.

"Yes," I said. "Giant propellers, spinning in the distance. It looked as though they were actually attached to the coast."

"Why is that strange?"

"Propellers," I said again. "Attached to the coast. How is that *not* strange?"

The captain raised his eyebrows at me over his glass, as he took another sip of forto. Lowering the glass, he said, "You really don't know?"

"If I knew, I wouldn't ask, would I?" I probably let more exasperation into my voice than I should have, but not as much as I was feeling.

"Another point in support of your claim to be from another world, I suppose," the captain said, as he put the glass down on the table. "Although you could be feigning . . ."

"Just for one minute," I said, a little more exasperation seeping out, "pretend I've been telling you the truth all along—especially since I *have*—and tell me why there are giant propellers attached to the coast. Please?"

The captain shrugged. "Because Raj is an island like no other," he said, which wasn't much of answer, but it jogged another long-buried memory of a Jules Verne story.

"Oh!" I gasped. "The Standard Island!"

The captain frowned. "I just said Raj is an island like no other."

"Never mind the name," I said. "The point is, it floats, right? And has its own engines and rudders and propellers?"

"So, you *do* know what it is," the captain said. "Why, then, feign ignorance?"

"It wasn't feigned ignorance. It was genuine forgetfulness."

The captain looked dubious. "If you had ever once heard of it, how could you forget such a marvel? In our world, everyone, whether a free subject of the Principality of Raj or laboring under the tyranny of Robur the Monster, knows of Raj, the Floating Island, the land of plenty, which moves with the seasons from north to south so that it is always summer, the unassailable stronghold of our beloved Dread Prince Dakkar, the most glorious of his wondrous constructions, a beacon of light and beauty, of music and poetry and art, in a world darkened by Robur's depravity!"

His voice took on a tent-revival cadence as he spoke. I felt a (fortunately easily suppressed) urge to throw in "Amen! Hallelujah!" at the end. "What I heard . . . on my world . . . were mere rumors," I lied. "A fable, nothing more. I'm awed that it actually exists." That was true enough. I scoured my memories for more Verneian details. "The capital city is called . . . Milliard City, right?"

The captain looked at me strangely. "No, it is called Dakkarapolis. Of course."

Dakkarapolis? What an awful name. The Shaper at work again. Although I supposed he could have gone with Dakkarville, Dakkarburg, or, if he was feeling particularly Russian, Dakkargrad, all of which would have been worse.

"Of course," I said. "I must have misremembered. I don't suppose you have an ongoing religious conflict between the Larboardites and the Starboardites?"

"What?"

"Never mind." Just as well I could only remember fragments from my reading of Verne: clearly relying on it too much would get me into trouble.

The overhead speaker buzzed. The captain looked up at it. "Yes?"

"Message received from the palace, sir," said the tinny voice. "Message begins. 'Please escort the ambassador here immediately. Lapis Lazuli Gate.' Message ends."

"Thank you, Hollis," the captain said. He stood. "If you will finish your forto, Ambassador, I will take you to your escort."

"I'm finished." I stood. I wished the captain had offered me food, too—I'd skipped lunch, working in the library, and had been looking forward to supper in the wardroom—but no doubt the prince would provide something.

Or else throw me straight into the dungeon, I thought, but I pushed the notion aside. *The palace called me an ambassador. So, they're prepared to hear me out, at least. And if Prince Dakkar is the Shaper . . .*

But what if he isn't?

I'd know soon enough.

"Lead on, Captain," I said. Graciously, he took my arm and escorted me out of his cabin, to meet what my unhelpful brain insisted on calling "my doom."

EIGHT

I'D ENTERED THE *Narwhal* strapped to the belly of a tiny helicopter, rather like a deer roped to the hood of a four-by-four in rural Montana. I exited the submarine through the aft hatch of what I thought of as the conning tower, although I doubted they used that terminology here: the bulbous bump atop the vessel's spine wherein were located the helm and various much-more-mysterious devices of the brass-wheels-and-spinning-spheres variety, which I caught just a glimpse of before the captain ushered me out onto the deck.

A ramp sloped gently up from there to the wooden pier, where my escorts awaited me. Just beyond them, wooden steps zigzagged up the white stone wall.

One of my escorts turned out to be Belinda, which didn't surprise me; the captain's thinking seemed to be that, since his daughter had brought me to his submarine, she was responsible for me, which made me feel a bit like a stray cat.

The other escort was Lieutenant Blackwell . . . *Anthony,* I remembered, *his name is Anthony* . . . which did surprise me, because it seemed a little unfair to the young Flying Force officer, whose ears turned red the moment he saw me. I would have liked to have put him at ease, but it seemed unlikely that saying something like, "Cheer up, Lieutenant, I didn't really see much" would go very far toward reducing his embarrassment.

Instead, I just gave them both a smile. "Take me to your leader," I said, even though I'd already used that line with Captain Hatteras, because even if nobody else in this world knew why I thought it was funny, *I* thought it was funny.

"As she says," Captain Hatteras said, glancing at me. "She is expected at the palace. Lapis Lazuli Gate."

"And once we have delivered her, sir?" Belinda said.

"Place yourself at the palace's disposal," the captain said. "If they release you, return here. However, I think it likely they will wish you to report in detail on her capture."

"Aye, aye, sir," both escorts said, although Belinda's response trailed Anthony's by a fraction of a second. *It must be weird having your father as your commanding officer,* I thought.

Speaking of whom . . . "Thank you for your courtesy, Captain," I said. "I enjoyed my time aboard your vessel."

"You're most welcome . . . Ambassador." He clicked his heels, bowed slightly, then turned and went down the ramp and into the *Narwhal.*

I turned back to my escorts. "Lead on!"

Belinda, without a word, started along the pier toward the open gate in the stone wall, walking so briskly I had to jog a step to fall in behind her. Anthony fell in behind me—figuratively, not literally. Neither of us *actually* fell into the dark water of the harbor, which was now very dark indeed, since even the streak of sunlight that had lit the top of the stone wall ahead of us when we'd berthed had now vanished. Fortunately, all along the length of the pier, glass globes atop black steel posts began to flicker with bluish light, strengthening and steadying as we neared the gate.

I glanced up at one of the globes. Electrical, clearly, but without any sort of filament I could see, it looked like a will-o'-the-wisp imprisoned inside a transparent sphere. The lights continued on the other side of the gate, although there they were attached to ornate metal supports thrusting out from the smooth wall of a tunnel that stretched as far as I could see.

"Impressive," I said to my escorts. Neither responded. We kept to the right as we strode up the tunnel, because coming the other way was a long line of flat, broad, self-propelled multi-wheeled vehicles, each carrying multiple crates and barrels, some also bearing four or five workers, and all of them steered, at the front, by a driver standing at what looked like a ship's wheel. *Supplies to replenish the* Narwhal*'s stores,* I guessed. When I looked behind us, though, I didn't see any other crewmen from the submarine following us into the island's interior. Perhaps, had any been offered shore leave, they had climbed the wooden stairs I had seen, rather than following us into these subterranean depths.

We walked on in silence. After about a quarter of a mile, we reached a cross-tunnel. To our right, a closed steel-bound wooden gate, twin of the one that had stood open at the end of the pier, blocked the view; the stores-lugging vehicles had been emerging from the corridor to our left, although the last one in the train was now a hundred yards behind us. Looking down that side passage, I saw stacks of crates and barrels. Clearly, this was a main storehouse for Prince Dakkar's naval forces.

Beyond the crossroads, we passed through an archway, and the tunnel turned into a corridor, its gleaming white walls covered in what I, probably alone of everyone in this world (except, I guess, the Shaper) would have called subway tiles. The light globes now hung from the arched ceiling inside multipaned glass shades, casting rainbows here and there. A harried-looking man in an old-fashioned-looking black suit, carrying a clipboard, hurried past, not even glancing at us, heels clicking on the smooth stone floor; after that, we saw no one.

Thanks to the aforementioned Sunday School, I'd heard of lapis lazuli, and knew it was a semiprecious stone, but I honestly had no idea what it looked like. I also didn't understand why we'd been directed to the "Lapis Lazuli Gate," when it seemed obvious that the corridor would take us directly into the palace.

But it didn't.

A couple of hundred yards after we passed the hurrying functionary with the clipboard, we reached a set of stairs. After climbing those, I saw, still a long way off, the light at the end of the tunnel: an archway filled with the blue-gray of early evening.

Coming toward us were two more people, a man and a woman, both dark-skinned, walking briskly side by side. They paid us no more attention than the first man had. Instead of a clipboard, this man carried a briefcase that would not have looked out of place on the streets of any city in my world. He wore a very similar suit to the first man, though his was gray rather than black. In sharp contrast to his conservative appearance, the woman wore a sleek scarlet sheath, belted in gold, ankle-length but slit up the side almost to her waist, so that it revealed a flash of leg with every step she made. Ruby studs twinkled in her ears beneath her short, tightly curled hair; a ruby teardrop hung from a golden chain around her neck.

They passed. I stared after them, then skipped ahead a couple of steps to move up beside Belinda. Anthony closed the gap behind me, as if afraid I might make a run for it—to where, I couldn't imagine. "Who was that?" I asked Belinda.

Belinda frowned at me. "Who?"

"The woman we just passed."

Belinda glanced over her shoulder. I looked back, too, and saw the couple descending the stairs. "I have no idea." Belinda faced front again.

"But the way she was dressed . . . surely she's someone important."

"What was odd about the way she was dressed?"

A thought struck me. "Is she someone's wife? Someone on the ship?"

"Unlikely," Belinda said. "Spouses are not welcome on board. If she were married to an officer or crewman, they would meet in the town, or at their home, not in the stores tunnels."

"But . . . then why was she heading to the docks in that outfit?" *Could she be a high-class prostitute?* I wondered then, but if so, her most likely client would surely be Captain Hatteras, and since he was Belinda's father, I didn't voice the question. (I don't actually go out of my way to offend people if I can avoid it—believe it or not.)

Belinda gave me a puzzled look. "Again, what was odd about the way she was dressed?"

"Wasn't it a bit . . . fancy? For . . . whatever she might be doing in the stores tunnels?"

"I imagine she is a supervisor."

"And that was her business attire?"

"Presumably." She gave me a stern look. "We women of Raj do not believe in draping ourselves in drab homespun like the peasants of Robur's oppressed lands. Do not the women of your world enjoy fine clothing?"

"Yes, but . . ." *But, what?* I let it drop.

The twilight faded from the opening ahead of us even as we approached it, but as it did so, blue artificial light replaced it. When at last we emerged from the tunnel, night had fallen in earnest, but definitely not darkness—and the scene before us took my breath away.

The Palace of Prince Dakkar rose like an ornate layer cake from a vast circular courtyard, each layer narrower than the one below, each ringed by a wall with towers topped by flags, snapping in what appeared to be a brisk breeze, though no fingers of wind tugged at us in the sunken space in which we walked. All around the white wall through which we'd emerged were other open archways, presumably into other tunnels like the one we'd followed, which must spread out like strands of a spiderweb beneath the island's surface. Both the inner and the outer courtyard wall blazed with light, glowing globes marking each tunnel entrance, strings of lights hanging above us, running from wall to wall. Above it all, the palace sparkled, every window, it seemed, brightly illuminated.

Enormous slabs of white stone paved the courtyard, punctuated at regular intervals, perhaps fifty yards, with enormous metal lattices whose function I couldn't begin to guess. Fortunately, I didn't have to, since I had two knowledgeable escorts . . . assuming they'd answer my question. "Very impressive," I said honestly as Belinda led the way toward the inner wall of the courtyard and the towering palace beyond. We walked across one of the lattice-covered openings. Catching a whiff of the sea . . . a poetic way of saying "rotting seaweed and possibly fish" . . . rising from below, I looked down through the lattice into darkness. "What are these openings for?"

"The courtyard is a giant moat," Belinda said without looking around. "Should Robur ever invade the island and attack the palace—which will never happen, of course, since our forces would drive his army into the sea long before it could advance this far—hatches on the underside of the island, at the bottom of the lattice-covered shafts, can be opened, allowing seawater to flood upward, submerge the courtyard, and flow down the tunnels, washing away all attackers."

I stared around the vast space, my imagination providing appropriately apocalyptic images of such an event. "Has it ever been used?"

"No," Belinda said. "Though the hatches are tested regularly, they are always closed before the water rises to the courtyard, and then pumped dry once more."

That explains the smell, I thought. "Sounds dangerous," I said out loud. "What if they malfunction?"

"There are additional hatches, near the top of the shaft, which are closed during the tests and can also be closed in the event a bottom hatch fails."

The existence of a such a last-ditch defense, implying Dakkar wasn't entirely sure of his power, argued in favor of Robur being the Shaper, instead.

Then I saw something that argued the other way.

At first, I thought the courtyard deserted, but as we neared what I guessed was the Lapis Lazuli Gate, directly across from our tunnel—though the gate itself appeared to be made of iron, it was framed by dark-blue stone—I saw a group of men and women emerge from the next gate around the curve of the inner wall, laughing and talking. The men all wore versions of the conservative suits I had seen on the men in the tunnel—but the women, like the one we'd passed in the tunnel, were veritable popinjays in sleek, slinky dresses of brightly colored silk, glittering with gold-and-silver thread, jewels sparkling in earlobes and around necks.

Now I'd bet Dakkar is the Shaper, I thought, watching

a tall woman in a short skirt stride with remarkable confidence across the courtyard pavement on stiletto heels that boosted her into basketball-player territory, *because this reeks of male adolescent fantasy.*

Then I remembered what Belinda had said. *We women of Raj do not believe in draping ourselves in drab homespun like the peasants of Robur's oppressed lands.* Perhaps the people of Raj saw this style of dress as a defiant display of freedom. I remembered reading an account of someone who escaped from East Berlin to West at the height of the Cold War, and how overwhelmed she had been by the color and light and vibrancy on the west side of the Wall, so different from the drab conformity she was used to. Prince Dakkar might encourage women to dress attractively not for his own enjoyment (thought I'd be willing to bet that played into it at least a little) but to thumb his nose at Robur.

I was wondering how we'd get through the closed gate now towering above us when I saw, hanging to one side, a black rope. I looked up and saw that it turned on a pulley and disappeared into a hole in the wall. Belinda reached out and pulled it, and I heard the distant sound of a bell ringing.

Oh, please, please, I thought, *let a man with an enormous mustache and dressed all in green pop out and say, "Who rang that bell?"*

Apparently, however, the Shaper had not been a fan of *The Wizard of Oz.* All that happened was that a voice spoke from nowhere, with the tinny sound of the primitive speaker in Captain Hatteras' cabin aboard the *Narwhal.* "Name and business?"

"Lieutenant Commander Belinda Hatteras and Lieutenant Anthony Blackwell of the Seventh Flight of His Imperial Majesty's Flying Force, attached to HMS *Narwhal,* escorting Ambassador Shawna Keys, whose presence at the palace has been requested."

"One moment," said the voice.

We waited. To pass the time, I studied the Lapis Lazuli Gate. It was, I judged, about fifteen feet tall, and the wall of the palace extended another fifteen to twenty above that. I wondered how high the waters would reach if they ever flooded the moat . . . and really hoped I wouldn't be standing outside waiting to get in if that happened.

Although, if my theory were correct, and the Shaper of this world had set it up so there would be endless war . . . "always war, and never victory," with apologies to C. S. Lewis . . . then the kind of attack that would trigger such an apocalyptic defense would surely never come, because that would mean the war was almost over.

Without any further communication, the gate swung open. Dramatically speaking, it should have opened with a squeal of rusty hinges, but in fact it opened silently, revealing a short tunnel, brilliantly illuminated by the brightest light globes I'd yet seen, hung from the ceiling high above. At the far end of the tunnel, perhaps thirty feet away, rose another iron gate, twin of the one that had just opened.

As we walked to it, I took notice of gun ports to left and right, slits in the ceiling above us—perfectly placed for the defensive pouring of boiling oil and/or acid and/or something else I couldn't imagine and probably didn't want to—and some highly suspicious small, square openings in the floor beneath us. I didn't know what they were for, but I avoided standing directly over one as we waited for the inner gate to open.

It did, as silently as the outer one, and at last we entered the palace proper.

I thought we might find ourselves in an inner courtyard; instead, we were in another white, subway-tiled corridor. It stretched perhaps twenty yards ahead of us to a set of stairs, with closed, green-painted doors every five yards on both sides.

A woman awaited us. She wore what would have been called a sari in my world, made of rich red silk trimmed with gold, partially exposing her midriff. A ruby glowed in her navel. A golden tiara set with three rubies circled her black hair, and around her neck hung, on a golden chain, a round emblem embossed with the image of a nautilus shell in gold and silver. It had the look of an official symbol of office, and I remembered the nautilus shell on the banner in the chapel aboard the *Narwhal*. Clearly, the nautilus represented Raj, and just as clearly, this woman was someone important.

"Ambassador Keys," the woman said to me, her voice sharp, crisp, and professional. "I am Aouda Parsivalle, Private Secretary to His Dread Highness Prince Dakkar, Ruler of the Principality of Raj, Sovereign Knight, Grand Cross, of the Order of Ygrair."

That last name zapped me like I'd touched my tongue to a nine-volt battery. *Ygrair?*

"His Dread Highness welcomes you, Ambassador, and asks that you accompany me to his private receiving room, for conversation and refreshment." She paused expectantly.

Right, I thought. *Ambassador Keys. That's me.* I rummaged through my memory of . . . well, to be honest, medieval fantasy novels. "I . . . um . . . thank His . . . His Dread Highness . . . for the welcome. I am pleased to accept his most gracious invitation to . . . conversation and refreshment . . . and hope this will be the beginning of a . . . a long and prosperous relationship between our two realms."

Even though my realm has been taken over by an authoritarian monster, who could at any moment surface in yours, I thought, but did not say: I'd save that for the Shaper. Who I sincerely hoped was indeed His Dread Highness Prince Dakkar, lover of all things Jules Verneian.

"Then, Ambassador, if you will follow me?"

"I will indeed," I said, and I did.

NINE

CLIMBING THE STAIRS took us from clean-but-spartan subway-tiled subterranean hallway to Buckingham-Palace-has-nothing-on-this opulence. The bare paving stones gave way to thick, royal-blue carpeting, and the white wall tiles to pale-blue plaster with gilded pilasters every ten feet. Between the pilasters hung paintings of heroic, heavily armored warriors, either slaughtering other armored warriors astride even-more-heavily armored horses or kneeling humbly to receive dubbings or medallions or fur-lined scarlet coats or, in one painting, what looked like a basket of eels.

Although the Shaper might have launched this world long before I was thrust into mine, it could not possibly be older than a very few decades. So where had all this fake history come from?

Especially the basket of eels?

Not a question I could ask Aouda Parsivalle, or Belinda or Anthony, both of whom had now fallen in behind me as we followed our scarlet-clad guide.

More corridors, more stairs, more opulence, the latter increasing with each successively higher floor. In the end, Aouda ushered us into a room with so much gilding on walls, ceiling, fireplace, and furniture that a little subway tile would have been a welcome relief.

Two white-and-gold couches were arranged on either side of a low, white-marble-topped gilded-legged table, which itself stood on a gold carpet, the whole cheerily lit by a glittering gold-and-crystal electrically lit chandelier.

On the table rested a golden platter covered with a golden cloche in the shape of a dolphin leaping through ocean waves (the handle was its dorsal fin), two crystal goblets with stems of gold, and a crystal decanter in which glittered a wine of (of course) golden hue.

"Please be seated," Aouda said, with a gesture at one of the couches. She glanced at Belinda and Anthony, who without a word took up positions behind the couch, standing at parade rest. I sat on the indicated stretch of . . . I ran my hand over it . . . white, watered silk.

A fire burned in the hearth beneath the aforementioned gilded mantlepiece. Above it hung a painting, a head-and-shoulder portrait of a man wearing a golden cape trimmed with white fur, in sharp contrast to his dark-skinned, high-cheekboned face. He had long black hair, pulled tightly back into a ponytail that hung down his left shoulder, and piercing black eyes that stared down at me, cold and aloof. *Kahn Noonian Singh,* I thought.

"A reasonable likeness," said a voice from behind me, and I jumped, then twisted around to see a door I had not noticed (because it was disguised as a piece of the wall paneling) standing open, and the very man whose painted visage I had been staring up at smiling down at me.

He came forward. "Thank you, Aouda," he said to my guide. He indicated the table with his hand, palm up. "If you would do the honors?"

"Of course, Your Highness," said Aouda.

Prince Dakkar sat down opposite me. He studied me silently, still smiling . . . a very sardonic, knowing smile, just what I would expect from the Shaper . . . while Aouda filled our glasses with the golden wine. I glanced over my shoulder at Belinda and Anthony. "None for my escorts?" I said.

"They are on duty," said Dakkar. "It would not be appropriate to offer it, and they would not accept it if I did. Am I right, Lieutenant Commander Hatteras?"

"Yes, Your Highness," said Belinda, and somehow managed to convey, in those three words, her deep and total embarrassment that I had even asked such an inappropriate question, as though she were a teenager and I her clueless (is there any other kind?) mother.

I sighed, yet feeling slightly less guilty, lifted my glass—but didn't sip it. I didn't think the prince was likely to have drugged it, but on the other hand, I didn't know that he hadn't. In any event, it might very well be a horrible diplomatic faux pas to drink before my host.

The prince, if he noted my hesitation, didn't comment on it. Instead, he simply sipped from his glass. "A 2926 Brindaline from Volsinia," he said. "Just ten years old. An excellent vintage. I have several cases and look forward to seeing how it evolves over time."

His wine had come from the same bottle and the glasses were clear. I would have seen if anything had been dropped in mine. I took a cautious sip. "Delicious," I said honestly.

So, in the local calendar, it was 2936, presumably. Counting from when, I wondered, in this world I knew was truly of quite recent vintage? *There could be well-aged bottles of wine in the prince's cellar that are apparently older than the world itself is in reality,* I thought.

Aouda swept the dolphinesque cloche from the golden platter, revealing a selection of elaborate puff-pastry hors d'oeuvres in the shapes of animals and flowers. I picked up a cat and bit into it: it contained a savory fish paste that went extremely well with the "Brindaline," which I would have pegged as a Riesling in my own world.

I would have liked to have offered the platter to Belinda and Anthony, but no doubt they were as prohibited from snacking as they were from enjoying a glass of wine. I tried not to feel guilty—and mostly succeeded—as I bit into a second pastry, this one shaped like a daisy.

"How was your journey aboard the *Narwhal*?" the prince said. He had eaten only one pastry, a whale, in the time I'd eaten two . . . okay, three, now . . . and had done so in rather rabbitlike fashion, whittling away at it with his unusually white teeth. *Maybe he Shaped tooth decay right out of existence,* I thought.

"It was fine," I said. "How does it compare to the *Nautilus*?"

The prince showed no surprise I knew the name of his flagship—another indication he must be the Shaper: knowing I had come from another Shaped world, he would of course expect me to know of the *Nautilus,* whose origin lay in the First World. "Somewhat larger, but much less comfortable," he said easily. "The *Nautilus,* of course, was never intended to be a warship. The need for combat submarines was forced upon me by Robur's cowardly invasion of one of my protectorates, which precipitated this seemingly never-ending war." He took another sip of wine, then set the glass down again next to the golden platter. "I have several more helicopter-carrying *Narwhal*-class submarines under construction. The bulk of my fleet is made up of the smaller ship-killing *Swordfish* class. The *Nautilus* herself remains *sui generis.*"

"I'm surprised to hear a Latin phrase," I said. "Did you have ancient Rome in this world?"

"An intriguing question," the prince said.

"Is it?"

"Indeed." He picked up another pastry. "Intriguing because I don't understand it, which adds credence to your otherwise somewhat hard-to-believe claim of being an ambassador from another world."

I felt a surge of irritation. I was almost certain Dakkar was the Shaper, which meant in reality he knew *exactly* what I was talking about. Was he being coy because of the presence of the others, who were, after all, merely Shaped humans?

I actually thought that—"merely" Shaped humans—and immediately hated myself for it. Maybe that's why, suddenly fed up, I looked Dakkar square in the eye and said bluntly, "Are you the Shaper?"

His eyes narrowed, and he gave me a far more penetrating and focused look than he had yet favored me with. "Now that," he said, "is an even more intriguing question." He looked up at my escorts. "Captain Hatteras, Lieutenant Blackwell, that will be all for now. Aouda will show you to quarters. I will certainly want to hear your account of the rescue of the ambassador from Robur's airship, but first I believe I should have a conversation with the ambassador in private."

"Private, Your Highness?" Aouda said doubtfully. "Perhaps a single guard . . . ?"

"In private, Aouda," the prince said. "You may leave us."

Aouda looked from me to him. Clearly, she objected, but just as clearly, she knew she had already expressed as much of that objection as she dared. She gave a small formal bow, then turned and swept her arm toward the door of the audience chamber. "Lieutenant Commander Hatteras, Lieutenant Blackwell, this way if you please."

After bowing to the prince, they followed her out without a word. I watched them go, then turned, as the door closed, to find the prince standing. "Come with me," he said. He held out his right hand to help me to my feet. I hesitated, then took it with my left. Dakkar's grip was strong, his fingers warm. He released me and walked to the hidden door through which he had entered the room, opening it by pressing . . . something; even after watching him do it, I could not see anything that looked like a release. Still, the door swung open.

Rather than a hallway, it opened into another room: a far less ostentatious and far more comfortable-looking room, although a stereotypically masculine room, all dark wood paneling and leather-upholstered furniture. Hunting trophies and exotic weapons hung on the wall.

I use antlers in all my decorating, sang through my mind. "Gaston would be proud," I said.

Prince Dakkar glanced over his shoulder. "Who?"

I sighed. "Look," I said. "We're alone. So, admit it. You're the Shaper, aren't you?"

He kept his gaze on me for a moment, expressionless, then turned forward again. "Sit," he said, indicating one of two big leather-covered chairs, separated by a table, facing a fireplace that was merrily alight. I sat. It was comfortable. And warm. I'd left my wine in the other room. I rather regretted it, but again . . . wits, keeping them about me, etc.

The prince didn't sit immediately, instead busying

himself at a side table next to another door I suspected led to his sleeping quarters ... or possibly servants' quarters: the fire hadn't lit itself and I doubted the prince had started it. I couldn't see a third door, but that didn't mean there wasn't one, as the hidden exit we had just taken from the receiving room proved.

The prince returned to the fire with—I almost laughed at the sheer predictability of it—a brandy snifter in each hand. I took the brandy, sipped it, appreciated it, and set it down again. Starting with the port ... er, forto ... in Captain Hatteras' cabin, this was the third alcoholic beverage I had been offered within about an hour. Had I fully imbibed, I'd have been thoroughly tipsy. *"Now* will you answer my question?" I said.

Sipping his own brandy, Prince Dakkar narrowed his eyes at me over the rim of the snifter.

I belatedly added, "Your Highness."

His expression smoothed as he lowered the glass. "If you will answer mine," he said. "This other world you supposedly come from. Is it the moon, or one of the farther planets? Or have you perhaps ascended from the depths? There is a place in the north, within the crater of a volcano, where a cavern opens into the Earth. It has never been explored, but some say it goes all the way to the world's center, and that there could be entire unknown civilizations far beneath our feet ..."

More Verne, I thought irritably. "I am from none of those worlds," I snapped. "As I think you know. I am from the First World. The Original Reality, by way of my own Shaped world." There. That should convince him I was someone he could be open with about his ... Shaperhood? Shaperiness?

Or not. "Your words mean nothing to me," he said. "And yet, you do not appear to be mad. And Robur certainly wanted you ... which is, of course, why we took you from him. Clearly, you are searching, or pretend to be searching, for the Shaper.

"You understand how that puzzles me, since the Shaper is the One who brought our world into being, as detailed in *The Word of the Shaper* ... if you believe that book to be an accurate account of the world's creation, of course. I and many of the more scientifically minded of my realm believe it should be interpreted metaphorically at best, certainly not literally. However, we discuss such things only in private, since we do not wish to upset the common people, for whom belief in the Shaper and his Word are sacrosanct." He took another sip of brandy, then continued. "I am most honored and flattered you would ask me if I am the Shaper, but since I believe the concept of the 'Shaper' is merely a primitive attempt to understand the origin of the world, in the absence of scientific investigation and knowledge, I am also sorely puzzled . . . and I do not like being puzzled." He put down his glass, and his amiable demeanor transformed in an instant, cold sharpness replacing the warmth in his face and voice. "Who are you? What do you really want? *And what did Robur want with you?*"

Crap, I thought. *He's* not *the Shaper.*

Robur is.

Far from connecting with the Shaper, I'd connected with the very person the Shaper had, for whatever reason, crafted to be his implacable enemy.

Swell, I thought. *Just swell.*

TEN

I HAVE BEEN accused, from time to time, of speaking without thinking. This time, for a change, I thought without speaking . . . which did not please Prince Dakkar.

"I asked you a question," he said. "I expect an answer."

"It's not that I don't want to answer you," I said, which of course was a lie. "It's that I don't . . ." I paused.

Don't what? a small and somewhat panicky part of my brain asked.

"Don't what?" a large and increasingly unhappy prince echoed.

"I don't know what I should and shouldn't say."

"I am the Prince of Raj," Dakkar said. "*I* will decide what you should and shouldn't say."

Despite the fire, it was definitely getting colder in this otherwise comfortable room. "And I am an ambassador from another world," I said, trying to match his icy tone chill for chill, and doubly glad I'd refrained from drinking all I'd been offered. "I was sent to consult with Robur, who styles himself master of this world. You kidnapped me and are preventing me from carrying out my duty. This is not an excellent way to win friends and influence people within my government."

I paused, pleased with my own invention . . . but only for a moment.

"If you are truly an ambassador," the prince said, "you will be carrying credentials. May I see them?"

Crap. "Lost," I improvised. "When the island unexpectedly disintegrated."

"'Unexpectedly,'" the prince said. "You traveled from your world to our world—somehow—and managed to land on a mysterious island that 'unexpectedly' disintegrated. Not the greatest of planning by your government . . . if it exists."

"Are you questioning my honesty?" I said, with maximum huffiness.

"Yes," the prince said. "I am questioning everything about you and not getting answers." He leaned forward. "Let me be clear, Shawna Keys." I noticed he'd dropped the "Ambassador," which didn't strike me as a good sign. "I am prepared to believe you are from another world because of the manner of your inserting yourself into the affairs of this one: being rescued by the skin of your teeth from an island that should not have existed and which was literally dissolving beneath you does not seem to have any more reasonable explanation than that, however outlandish it might seem at first blush. I also believe you intended to be taken to Robur, because of where you appeared and the manner of your extraction. And the fact Robur's airship was there when you required it seems incontrovertible proof that he was expecting you.

"So, let us dispense with all dissembling. You came into this world from some other world, through some method I admit I cannot understand, with the express intention of contacting Robur. Tell me why. Tell me what advantage your presence gives him. Because Robur does nothing unless he believes it will work to his advantage. Do you have knowledge of new weapons? Are you offering an alliance of warriors from your own world? Has Robur promised that if you help him defeat me, he will grant you all my lands? Does an invasion force await your return?"

Stalling, I reached for my brandy snifter, but the prince moved it away from my hand. "I really must insist." He smiled. "If you do not answer, I will have no choice but to have you imprisoned and tortured." He said it lightly, as though he were joking . . . but there was nothing funny about that smile. It wouldn't have looked out of place on a shark.

This is all a version of good cop/bad cop, I thought, *with him playing both parts.* First, he'd given me a glimpse of how comfortable things could be for me if I cooperated. Now, he was pointing out just how uncomfortable things could be if I did not.

The trouble was, what could I tell him that would satisfy him? The truth? That the Shaper he doubted existed, but his common people worshipped, was, in fact Robur, his hated rival whom he was sworn to defeat? That . . . didn't seem wise.

"You're right," I said at last. "I'm not an ambassador. Nor am I really an explorer. I'm . . . a searcher." I spread my hands. "A . . ." (*think fast!*) ". . . theological spelunker." I winced inwardly but hurried on. "My world, too, had a Shaper, and like you and your scientific friends, there are those of us who are trying to find out the truth about her . . . in my world, the Shaper is thought to be a woman." *Damn straight, she is.* "When an island, different from yours, but every bit as mysterious, appeared in our world, we thought it must be her work. More than that, we thought it might provide a link to another world—because we have never believed that ours is the only world; we've always thought that, if the Shaper Shaped our world, she must surely have Shaped others, that if creativity on that scale were part of her very nature, she would never be satisfied Shaping just one." *Laying it on a bit thick, aren't you?* I thought, but I hurried on. "We . . . researchers at my . . . university . . . formed an expedition, of which I was a part, to explore the island, to learn from it whatever we could about the Shaper, and perhaps even to find a portal into another of her worlds . . . rather like the passageway into the interior of the Earth you believe exists within the crater of that northern volcano. Deep in the bowels of the caverns that honeycombed the island, I became separated from . . ." I paused. Time to be humble. "Oh, hell. The truth is, I got lost." I *wasn't* telling the truth, but never mind. "I stumbled through the tunnels, deeper and deeper, and finally found an exit. But it didn't lead into my world. It led into *this* world. And almost as soon as I emerged, the island began to disintegrate." I shrugged. "So, the truth is" (second time I'd said that; *methinks I do protest too much*) "I *didn't* come here to find Robur. I didn't know he existed. Or you, either. The *Albatross* was there when I arrived—so far as I know, simply to investigate the Mysterious Island—and pulled me to safety. Had it not been there, I would have drowned, and we wouldn't be having this conversation. Everything that has happened since, you know. I did *not* seek out Robur . . . it just happened."

"Then why lie to Captain Hatteras about being an ambassador?"

I spread my hands. "Can you blame me? Captain Harding-Smith on the *Albatross* thought I was either a spy or a witch, either of which he seemed fully prepared to toss overboard without bothering about a trial. Captain Hatteras was the second captain to question me within a couple of hours of my arrival, and I had no idea how he'd react! 'Ambassador' seemed my safest choice."

The prince snorted. "You are clearly not a witch. All witches have red hair and green eyes. Clearly, the captain of the *Albatross* is not a learned man."

Red hair and green eyes? Seriously? Robur decided what his Shaped world really needed was gingerphobia? Nothing I learned about the man inclined me to think better of him.

"You say you believe the Shaper of your world is female," the prince continued. "Why, then, did you ask me if I were the Shaper?"

"We *believe* it," I said. "We don't *know* it. You're a man of science. In science, one must always question one's assumptions. Perhaps she takes a different form in different worlds."

"You believe the Shaper created both your world and mine," the prince said.

"And potentially many more."

He leaned forward, eyes glinting in the firelight. "*How* many?"

"Perhaps as many as there are stars in the sky. No one knows."

He sat back. "You said when the island appeared in your world you thought it must be the work of the Shaper. Why, exactly?"

"Because it clearly did not form by any natural process. It appeared literally overnight. One day it was not there, the next it was. How else could such a thing happen if not by the work of the Shaper? If you believe she exists—and we do—then there is no other logical explanation."

"And your reasons for thinking it might link to another world, as opposed to simply being a new creation within your own?" The prince pushed the brandy snifter in my direction, once again more interested than threatening.

Making progress, I thought, but I did not take him up om the unspoken offer to have a drink. "It had certain . . . characteristics . . . that did not appear to belong in my . . . our . . . world." *You can say that again,* I thought, although I didn't. *Like obscenely horrific statuary and a human-sacrifice altar surrounded by ghostly spectators in Colosseum-like seating.* "We . . . my colleagues and I . . . hypothesized that it represented a mixture of the two worlds . . . that perhaps it was the result of a . . . leakage, for want of a better word . . . of Shaping energy from another world—this world—into ours." *That's what Karl thought, anyway.* "We further hypothesized that if that were the case, it might be a two-way street, and Shaping energy from our world might have leaked into this one, creating something similar here. And if *that* were true, it seemed to us, the two anomalous land masses might somehow connect, forming a bridge between the two worlds. That was what we set out to discover." I gave him a bright smile. "And, look, we were right!"

He didn't smile back, instead leaning forward again. "But why did the island dissolve?"

"That," I said, "I don't know." Which was true. It was nice to say *one* true thing, at least. "Maybe someone . . . i.e., me . . . moving from one world to the other broke the connection, and so the 'bridge' collapsed, taking both 'ends' with it. The same thing probably happened in our world." I said that without thinking (bad habits die hard), but the moment I said it, I realized with a shock it might very well be true. And if what had happened to the island on this side of the Portal had happened to the island on the *other* side of the Portal—*what had happened to Karl?* Had he found himself floundering in the middle of the ocean with no land in sight?

What if he'd drowned? What if he *wasn't* coming through another Portal after me? What if I were trapped in this world forever?

All the more reason to keep Prince Dakkar happy. I dredged up a smile from somewhere—I was aiming for demure, although I admit I've never been entirely sure what demure looks like, so I don't know if I succeeded or just looked like the hors d'oeuvres hadn't agree with me. "I am sorry for prevaricating," I said, giving myself a point for the polysyllabic substitution for "lying." I'd been trying really hard to sound erudite and . . . university-ish. Academic-ish? Whatever. "I have been feeling my way in this world, trying to figure out whom I could trust. Your force's attack on the airship was . . . a shock. It was my first intimation that this is not a world at peace."

"Is your world at peace?" said the prince.

I don't know my world anymore, I thought. *Though it probably is peaceful—the peace of a completely controlled society, under the thumb of the Adversary. But when it had still been mine . . .* "Yes," I said. "For the most part. But we have many more countries and kingdoms. Not just two, locked in perpetual conflict."

"Is that the impression we have given?" the prince said. "We have different countries and kingdoms as well. But almost all swear fealty to either the forces of light . . . that would be me," he said, with a surprisingly disarming grin, Prince Charming momentarily replacing Dread Prince Dakkar, "or to the forces of darkness."

"Robur?" *Duh.*

"Robur. He rules by tyranny. I rule justly."

"Then I am fortunate to have found myself by your side," I said. I meant it to sound ingratiating; it wasn't until the prince's smile somehow slipped over the edge from friendly to . . . a little too friendly . . . that I realized it could also sound flirtatious, or even seductive. Which was totally *not* what I was going for.

It seemed *I* was what the prince was going for, though. "I, too, feel fortunate to have found myself by your side," he said. He put his hand on my knee and I steeled myself not to flinch. "I apologize for my . . . ungentlemanly suggestion of incarceration and torture. I was worried your presence might represent a threat to my realm and my beloved subjects. Truly, I would never have harmed you." His hand tightened. "You fascinate me."

Urgh, I thought. But I didn't move my knee. I didn't think insulting him would help my cause. "As you fascinate me," I said. Then I pretended a huge, jaw-cracking yawn, covering my mouth with the back of my hand. "Oh," I said, lowering it again and, I admit, batting my eyelashes. *Urgh,* again. "I'm so sorry. I'm exhausted. It has been a very stressful two days."

The prince squeezed my knee again, but then, to my immense relief, leaned back. "Of course," he said. "Rest, and we will talk in detail in the morning." He turned toward the door next to the side table from which he had taken the brandy. "Eustasia," he called. "You're needed."

Ah. Not as alone as we seemed, I thought. Although Eustasia was an odd name for a manservant . . .

That was because the prince's personal servant wasn't a man. Instead, it was a woman—a girl, really, in her late teens, I judged—dressed in a uniform of the same red silk as Aouda's sari, though this struck me as more Chinese, with a gold-sashed tunic above loose trousers.

Apparently, all of his closest servants were female.

The knee where he had placed his hand suddenly felt a little . . . greasy. I resolved to wash it at the first opportunity.

"Eustasia, please show Ambassador Keys" (I noted the return of the honorific, entirely spurious though it was) "to the First Guest quarters. Make sure she has everything she needs, including food and drink, if required." He stood and held out his hand to help me to my feet. I had no choice but to take it, though I wished I could have refused. "Ambassador," he said. He lifted the hand he still held and kissed the back of it, with a little too much lingering of the lips for my taste. Then he lowered but did not release it. "I look forward to continuing our conversation in the morning."

"As do I," I murmured. I forced myself to leave my hand in his grasp until he let go. Then, fighting the urge to wipe the back of it on my jeans, I smiled at Eustasia. "Hello," I said.

"Ambassador," she said, inclining her head. "Please follow me."

I nodded, then glanced back at the prince. "Good night, Your Highness."

"Good night, Ambassador."

Eustasia led me back to the reception room, then out into the hall, down it, up another flight of stairs, down another hall to the right, and finally to a door at the end. She opened it, and I stepped into . . .

. . . well, the best description of it I can offer is that it reminded me of the inside of Barbara Eden's bottle in *I Dream of Jeannie,* the old sitcom I'd recently binge-watched with Aesha on StreamPix (accompanied by appropriately snarky comments from both of us). It featured pearlescent patterns and multicolored gems on the walls (except where long, wine-colored velvet drapes covered what I presumed to be windows), cushions everywhere, and no real furniture except for a large circular (!) bed, complete with canopy and bedspread in matching pale pink, and a small table of deep red wood, topped with what looked like mother-of-pearl, legs intricately carved into the shape of fish. Two red wood chairs, similarly carved, sat on either side of it. Behind it, fire already leaped in a large fireplace, the mantelpiece of white stone likewise carved with sea life—dolphins, squid, fish, gulls. "If you would like to refresh," Eustasia said courteously, leading me through the bedroom to the only other doorway, "through here you will find the water room."

I thought water room was just a euphemism for toilet, until I entered it. Yes, there was a toilet, more or less recognizable, in a discrete nook in the wall with its own door, and a sink—but rather than a tub, there was a pool, not quite big enough to swim laps in, but only just. Water poured into it from a spout studded with rounded rocks (painted—or possibly solid—gold), producing a cataract that looked very inviting to stand under, provided the water was warm enough.

I reached out and let it run over my fingers. It was.

The water in the pool swirled, hot-tub fashion, cycling out as quickly as it poured in, so that it was always fresh. The room's walls were covered in multicolored iridescent tiles, a cacophony of hues that should have clashed but didn't. Instead, the effect was . . . spectacular.

I couldn't wait to get into that pool. Especially after having been touched by the prince.

"You approve?" said Eustasia, with a smile.

"I do." I glanced at her. "How long have you been the prince's . . ." My voice trailed off.

"Bodyservant?" she supplied.

Ick! I thought. "Bodyservant," I repeated.

"Since I was sixteen," she said.

"How old are you now?"

"Eighteen."

"What . . . do you do?"

"Bathe him, dress him, feed him, clean his quarters, do whatever else he asks." She must have seen something in my face. To my surprise, she laughed. "No, not like *that*. He would never take advantage of me, or of anyone else. He is a perfect gentleman. He is the prince. He could not be otherwise."

"Of course," I said. *Aliam vitam, alio mores.* I reminded myself again that my quest was not to change this world to what I wanted it to be, but just to harvest the knowledge of how it was Shaped, its *hokhmah*, from the Shaper. I told myself that, even if I gained the power to change this world, doing so would make me no better than the Adversary. *Freedom,* I thought. *That's what Karl said Ygrair prizes above all else. She left Shapers free to express their individuality through their creations.*

But as I looked at this teenager whose job it was to bathe and dress a man old enough to be her father, I wondered if that "freedom" were the unmitigated good Karl had presented it as. And this could be a *mild* version of it. What could someone truly *evil* do with the power to Shape a world? Had Ygrair screened her Shapers in *any* way . . . or simply trained any and every person she discovered to have the power, no matter what they were like? And if the latter . . . what did that say about her?

Eustasia led me out of that Arabian fantasy of a bathing room into the equally haremesque bedroom. "Are you hungry?"

"Very," I said.

"I will have a meal prepared."

"Let me guess." I glanced at the mantel. "Fish?"

Eustasia laughed again. She had a very nice laugh. She certainly didn't *sound* like she had been traumatized by her duties as bodyservant to the prince. "It's true we have an abundance of seafood on the island . . . for obvious reasons . . . but there are also pastures for cows and sheep and pigs and fowl of various sorts. Beef, mutton, pork, chicken, goose . . . what is your pleasure?"

"Bacon," I said instantly. "Bacon and whatever else seems like an appropriate accompaniment."

"Bacon," said Eustasia, smiling broadly. "And to drink?"

Wine, I almost said, but stopped myself. Drinking because I was scared and alone and completely clueless did not seem like a good path to start down. "Water or juice," I said.

"Very good," Eustasia said. "I'll—" Her head turned as someone tapped lightly on the door. "One moment."

From where I stood, I couldn't see who was on the other side when she opened the door, but I recognized the voice that murmured something too low for me to catch: Lieutenant Anthony Blackwell.

Eustasia looked back to me. "Your escorts, Lieutenant Blackwell and Lieutenant Commander Hatteras, will stand watch and watch about, outside your door. This the prince has ordered, for your safety."

"My safety," I said, somehow managing (I hoped) to keep the sarcasm from my voice. "Of course."

Eustasia bowed gracefully. "Your meal will arrive shortly. I must return to my own duties at the prince's side. It has been a pleasure to meet you, Ambassador Keys."

"Likewise," I said, but as she closed the door behind her, I wasn't feeling nearly as much pleasure as I had been before it had been oh-so-subtly confirmed that I, ambassador, "theological spelunker," or what-have-you, was still a prisoner . . . and not the slightest bit closer to contacting the *real* Shaper of this world, Robur, self-styled Master of the World, and equally self-styled (since he had Shaped this world, it had to be by choice) mortal enemy of the prince who currently held my life and freedom in his hands.

For a moment I regretted not asking for wine with the meal. *A bottle of white. A bottle of red. Perhaps a bottle of rosé instead . . .*

But no. I glanced into the bathing room but decided to wait for my meal before I availed myself of it, not wanting to be caught severely underdressed by whoever brought it in—which could well be Anthony, and I'd embarrassed him enough already.

Instead, I went to the drapes, thinking I would look out the window at whatever view the palace afforded of the island . . . only to find the window shuttered, and the shutters locked. I rounded the bed and checked the other side. Equally shuttered, equally locked.

I flounced onto the bed, fuming, staring up at the elaborate chandelier, the electric light globes nestled among its crystal pendants casting rainbows and sparkles around the already rainbow-hued and rather sparkly room.

Rainbows and sparkles were about as far from appropriate for what I was feeling as could be imagined. It seemed clear that if I were going to find the real Shaper,

I had to convince the prince to let me go . . . or else escape.

Escape . . .

I thought of Anthony Blackwell again.

And then I felt awful . . . but I kept the thought of him in my mind.

ELEVEN

THE PROMISED SUPPER, delivered by a silent woman (dressed in a white version of Eustasia's silk servant's uniform) who vanished again without so much as acknowledging my thanks, was everything I'd hoped for: bacon and mashed potatoes, and bacon and asparagus, and bacon and a crisp green salad with a delectable blue-cheese dressing, and did I mention bacon?

The "water room" proved as wonderful as I'd hoped. Clean and relaxed and naked (no one had provided me with a nightgown or pajamas, and I wasn't about to sleep in my clothes), I fell deeply unconscious about two seconds after I put my head down on the pillow of that ridiculous-looking (and yet ridiculously comfortable) pink-shrouded circular bed.

I awoke to the sound of drapes being drawn, followed by a loud banging. As I swam up out of sleep and opened my eyes, the quality of the light in the room changed: daylight! I turned my head, blinking, and saw the same silent woman who had served my supper stepping back from the window she had just unshuttered. She started around the bed, presumably to do the same on the other side. "Good morning," I ventured, but she ignored me. She opened the drapes and unlocked and opened the shutters on that side of the bed, too, then pointed toward the fireplace. I raised my head and saw a covered tray waiting for me by a brand-new fire.

What was missing by the fireplace were the clothes I'd left draped over one of the chairs. "Where are my clothes?"

I asked, startled, and more than a little concerned, since I wasn't currently wearing any.

She pointed to the opposite side of the room, then bowed, and went out, momentarily revealing, as the door opened and closed, a uniformed back I recognized from having followed it most of the way from the *Narwhal* to the palace's Lapis Lazuli Gate: Belinda Hatteras.

I sat up, clutching the sheet to my chest, and looked where the woman had pointed. I didn't see my clothes. In fact, at first, I didn't see *any* clothes . . . then I picked it out, flowing pink silk that had been momentarily hidden among the similarly colored cushions: a sari, like the one Aouda had been wearing when she'd greeted us the previous evening.

"You've got to be kidding me," I muttered.

I stared around the room. No other clothes.

With a glance at the door, I got up and padded into the bathing room. No other clothes in there, either. *You'd think there'd at least be a bathrobe,* I thought sourly. *I should complain to the management.*

I used the toilet, washed my hands, came back into the bedroom, and made a careful circuit of it. No question: my clothes—the jeans and plaid shirt and boots and socks and underwear that had traveled with me through the Portal from my own world—had vanished. I could either wear the clothes provided or go naked.

Fuming, I examined them. Besides the sari—just a length of cloth maybe seven yards long and a yard wide—there were some pretty ordinary undergarments and a petticoat. Those I put on, but then stared helplessly at the sari. I'd seen them worn and admired them, but I'd never tried to don one myself. Where did you begin?

From the fact Aouda, his private secretary, had worn a sari, whereas Eustasia and the woman who had brought me dinner and awakened me this morning wore tunics and trousers, it would appear Prince Dakkar considered me equivalent in rank to a high-class employee rather than a mere palace servant.

Maybe I should have felt flattered. I didn't. *I'm not his employee, or his servant,* I thought angrily. *And when I see him, I'll tell him so. And demand my own clothes back!*

Don't overreact, a more cautious part of me urged. *They may have just taken your clothes for cleaning.*

Sure, I thought, as I picked up the sari. *Maybe.*

I stared at the sari. It seemed to me that it stared back.

I glanced at the door, hoping for help from the servant. It remained closed.

Fine, I thought. Tossing the sari back on the cushions, I stalked over to the table in bra and petticoat. *Time to eat breakfast. If the prince wants me in a sari, he can bloody well send someone to help me get into it.*

Breakfast proved to be as delicious as the supper had been, although sadly lacking in bacon, since apparently whoever was in charge of such things had decided serving bacon two meals in a row was too much (I disagree), and instead had provided me with sausage and eggs, toast and jam, a fruit cup, and a glass of orange juice. It was, in fact, a startlingly modern breakfast, which wouldn't have been out of place in any hotel restaurant in my world. Did it, too, reflect the Shaper's tastes? I wondered. How detailed had his Shaping been?

He'd clearly reworked the initial blank slate more than I had. As Karl had pointed out, I'd been content to copy the bulk of my world from the First World, only making a few changes here and there . . . and since I didn't remember Shaping my World, I wasn't even sure what changes they had been, for the most part.

The door opened just as I drained my juice glass and set it back on the pearlescent tabletop, with such perfect timing I was instantly suspicious I'd been under observation the whole time. Since much of that time I'd been naked, that was a disquieting thought. But it would certainly fit with the overall feel of this world . . .

At least if my guard had been spying on me through some hidden peephole, that guard was currently Belinda Hatteras. "Good morning, Ambassador," she said, and valiantly managed not to put her usual dollop of doubt on the word. "I am to escort you to the prince as soon as you have finished eating."

"I'm done eating," I said, standing, "but not exactly ready to see the prince. Did you take my clothes? Or was it that silent servant?"

"I have merely guarded your door," she said. "Do you object to the clothes provided?" She glanced at the sari. "Is that why you have not finished dressing?"

"I do object," I said. "I would prefer the tunic and trousers the servant who came in earlier wore."

"Unacceptable for one of your rank," Belinda said.

"Is there any other option beside the sari?"

"The what?"

I pointed at the length of cloth. "On my world, that is called a sari."

"How odd," Belinda said. "We call it a *penwahr*. It is a sign of high status. You should be honored."

"Penwahr" was a word I'd never heard, though it sounded vaguely French, which I guess made sense in a Verneian world.

"Well, whatever it is," I said, "I'd rather not wear it." I gestured at her uniform, indistinguishable, except for subtle tailoring of the chest and waist, from what the men of the Flying Force had worn aboard *Narwhal*. "You provided me with a sailor's uniform on the Narwhal . . . could you do so again?"

"Of course not," she said. "That was a matter of exigency. Here, it would be inappropriate and, when you next meet with the prince, disrespectful." She pointed at the sari . . . penwahr. "That is what you have been given to wear. You should wear it."

"Would you?" I snapped.

"Of course, I would," she said. "If my prince required it. As he requires it of you."

"Yes, but . . ." I bit off the rest of what I was going to say. *Arguing with a Shaped denizen of a Shaped world is like arguing with a non-player character in a videogame,* I thought. And immediately felt guilty again. The people here might have been Shaped, but they were still real people, flesh and blood: not programmed automatons.

But just get me within ranting distance of that Shaper . . .

Well, that was the goal, wasn't it? To get within ranting, and also *hokhmah*-obtaining, distance. And hopefully, whenever I did so, I'd find Karl Yatsar close at hand, waiting for me, ready to guide me once more. Because I was *really* wishing I had a guide right about then.

Other than the one waiting to take me to the prince, that is. I sighed. "Well," I said. "Help me put it on, then."

Belinda proved adept at the task, and in short order, with the cloth artfully wrapped around me, hung so that only a small portion of my midriff was exposed ("Without a jewel to adorn it, it is inappropriate to show your navel," Belinda explained, in a tone that implied I was remarkably dim for not already knowing that fact), and my feet tucked into the red-leather sandals that were the only footwear provided, I followed her from the room.

Today I was not taken to the receiving room outside the prince's quarters. Instead, Belinda led me down a couple of corridors to an open elevator, complete with an elevator operator—another silk-tunic-and-trousers-clad woman, of course, this one wearing blue. Belinda nodded at her without a word as we stepped into the car, the size of any typical hotel elevator anywhere on Earth, although rather more gaudily gilded than most, outside of, say Reno, Nevada. (I stayed in a resort there once. I know whereof I speak.) The elevator operator closed the (gilded, of course) accordion gates, then the inner (in a daring variation, silver) doors, then pushed a red-leather-handled lever forward. With a somewhat alarming amount of creaking and banging, we started upward.

"What, no Muzak?" I said, earning a slightly puzzled frown from Belinda. I didn't bother trying to explain. I was still seething over the loss of my clothes, annoyed at the way the prince had managed to maneuver me into dressing in the manner he preferred me to be dressed. Eustasia had claimed he was a perfect gentleman, but I remembered the way his hand had lingered on my knee.

The elevator stopped. The door opened, not into a corridor, but onto a landing, from which ascended a spiral staircase, its steps of golden filigree supported by silver shafts, entwined by golden vines laden with grapes of purple crystal. Belinda led me up those fairy-tale stairs. I looked up. High overhead, an elaborate gold-and-crystal chandelier hung from the center of a domed ceiling, from a representation of a blazing sun done in gold tiles. Concentric circles of blue and gold emanated from it.

We emerged into the center of the white-marble floor of a circular room, flooded with natural light, which poured in, along with a cool breeze, through open windows set in marble arches all around.

Directly in front of us stood the room's only piece of furniture: a throne, carved from the same red wood as the table at which I had just finished my breakfast, its arms and legs entwined in gold-and-silver octopus tentacles. The octopus' body, a golden crown on its bulbous head, topped the throne's high back. Below it was another crowned head, that of Prince Dakkar, seated on the chair's sea-green velvet upholstery.

Dakkar's crown, a simple golden circlet, gleamed in his black hair, which was again drawn back in a ponytail. Below that, he wore a golden doublet, white pants, golden shoes curled up at the toe, and a blue-green sash across his chest, bearing several elaborate medallions.

As I took my first step onto the marble floor behind Belinda, the prince stood, which surprised me: it could hardly be standard protocol for a reigning monarch to rise from his throne upon the arrival of someone he had summarily summoned, even an ambassador, and clearly, the elaborate octo-chair was his throne (which made this, presumably, his throne room, though evidently court was not in session).

The prince smiled at me. Then his eyes flicked to Belinda. "Leave us, Lieutenant Commander."

Belinda bowed. She turned and went back down the stairs, brushing past me, leaving me alone with the prince.

Dakkar looked me over slowly, appreciatively, from crown to toe and back again, and I felt myself blushing—and hated myself for doing so, but that's not exactly one of those reactions one can control, is it? "You look lovely, Shawna."

"I feel ridiculous," I snapped. (Actually, I was finding the sari/penwahr very comfortable, but I was determined to keep him off balance.) "Where are my own clothes?"

He made a dismissive gesture with his hand. "Gone. Burned. For your own safety."

"My safety?" The breeze from the open windows was cool enough that goose bumps erupted on my bare arms. "How do you figure that?"

"Those outlandish clothes," the prince said, "marked you as an outsider. Any spy of Robur's—and yes, there are such traitors among my people—would immediately spot you and know you were the one they have undoubtedly been told to watch for. Now, wearing the unremarkable clothing of a woman who works within the palace, you will be much harder to identify as an outsider."

"Since it appears I must wear this or go naked, I have little choice but to acquiesce," I snapped.

"Indeed," said the prince. A small smile played around his lip. "I would not have you naked."

I gave him a suspicious look. Was there an unspoken "yet" at the end of that sentence?

But the prince had turned away. "Come to the windows. I think you will find the view intriguing."

I was chilly enough that going to the windows wasn't as appealing a prospect as it might otherwise have been, but I followed him all the same, to a spot directly behind the throne. With an expansive wave of his hand, Prince Dakkar said, "Behold Raj, jewel of the Seven Seas, my Principality . . . and your new home."

Not for long, I thought defiantly, but I looked out all the same.

The throne room, atop the tall central tower I had seen from the courtyard far below, provided a stunning view. The city spread out around us in concentric circles, main thoroughfares arranged like the spokes of a wheel, side streets encircling the palace. All the buildings were made of white stone, roofed with red tile, glowing almost too brightly to look at in the morning sunshine from a cloudless sky. Outside the city, farm fields and forest stretched to the shore, miles distant, broken only by a low, barren hill, overgrown with trees, through which I glimpsed tumbled stone ruins. *Odd,* I thought.

The ocean sparkled all around. No other land was in sight.

The only bit of industrial blight on this scene of beauty was two towering smokestacks, one to our left . . . or perhaps "port" was the better word, since this floating island was really a giant ship . . . the other to starboard. A steady stream of smoke—not as black as coal smoke, but not not-black either—issued from each smokestack.

Ah-ha! I thought, more memories of Verne percolating up. *The island is powered by two massive generators burning . . .* what was it? Not coal. Something else.

I couldn't remember, but it didn't really matter. Dried seaweed, for all I knew. This was a Verne-inspired world, and a Verne-inspired self-propelled island, but it certainly wasn't a slavish copy, because Prince Dakkar— Captain Nemo—made no appearance in *Propeller Island* (or whatever it had been titled in French) that I recalled. The generators here might be burning something completely different from whatever fictitious energy source Verne had created for his book.

It struck me that my own thoughts and words from time to time took on a slightly convoluted, 19th-century, translated-from-the-French cast. Could that also be a function of the Shaper's will, I wondered? Or was it simply an unavoidable consequence of my current situation? For here I stood, within the improbable throne room of a most improbable prince, aboard an even more improbable artificial island of fantastically immense power and size. What could be more natural than that my cadences of speech, unmoored from my far-more-prosaic world, should lose their hitherto straightforward simplicity; should grow more complex; should tend toward the baroque; should, in short, become—

Stop that!

"Cool," I said, partly to break the Verneian prose-throes threatening to overtake me. "A little too cool, in the absence of proper clothing," I added, just to drive my annoyance home. I pointed out into the distance. "What are those ruins on the hill over there?"

The prince didn't even glance out the window. "Ancient remnants of some former civilization. They are of no importance."

Ancient civilization? I thought. *There's no such thing on a Shaped world.* Although, to be fair, my world had had the pyramids and Angkor Wat and Stonehenge and a bunch of other "ancient" stuff, copied from the First World, presumably. Maybe these ruins were something like that.

I turned toward the prince. "Why haul me all the way up here?" I said. "We could have talked just as privately and far more comfortably in the room we were in last night."

"I think you know the answer to that," said the prince, turning away from the view outside to the view inside— me, in all my goose-fleshed glory. "I brought you here to impress you with the grandeur of my realm . . ." He gave another of his disarming smiles. "And, I admit, in the hope I might also impress you with my *own* grandeur."

"Why?" I said. "Why try to impress me?" As if I didn't know. This whole scenario had "Hello, my name is Prince Dakkar, and I'll be your seducer today" written all over it. Flattering, in a way, but also . . . he barely knew me. What had brought this on? Was it just because I was someone new?

Probably. He's like a tomcat marking his territory. He's marking me as his.

Ick. Not the most pleasant of similes.

"I am hoping," said Prince Tomcat, "that I can help you find your way back to your own world . . . and that you can then convince your rulers to return to this world in force, and help me excise the deadly cancer that is Robur once and for all, giving all those who live here the freedom from war and its devastation they have so long been denied, giving them at last the opportunity to live life as it should be lived, unsullied by fear and heartbreak and violent death."

Oh, I thought. *Smooth.* For all his fine words, Dakkar's lingering gaze was not that—or at least not *just* that—of a benevolent ruler interested only in how relations with the country represented by an ambassador to whom he had granted an audience could benefit his people. He was interested in relations, all right, but not the international kind.

Then I wondered if I was being unfair. If the prince was as Shaped as everyone else—and he had to be, didn't he, since he wasn't the Shaper himself?—then he was simply acting according to the nature he had been assigned: playing a role set for him by someone else. Although that still didn't mean I had to play the role he had assigned me in *his* head.

In the books, Captain Nemo wasn't like this, I thought. Which was also interesting. Why hadn't Prince Dakkar been Shaped to be more like the character in the Jules Verne novels? Because Robur wanted to keep all the best bits for himself, and saw himself not only as Robur the Conqueror but Captain Nemo, too—even if he let this guy have the actual title?

Meanwhile, "this guy" was staring at me expectantly, awaiting my response.

"I can't promise that," I said. "Not actually an ambassador, remember? Just a . . ."

"'Theological spelunker,' yes, I remember." He dismissed that with an impatient wave of his hand. "Yet, when you return to your world, you will be an explorer of the first order. Feted, applauded, a sought-after guest by heads of state, asked to speak to learned societies . . . you will wield great influence. Others will follow in your footsteps, and when they do, I want to be the one who greets them, to impress upon them how necessary . . . how *absolutely necessary,* for the freedom and safety of all the people of this world . . . it is that they support me and help me to at last dethrone Robur from his unwarranted and oppressive perch of ruler of far too many unfortunate souls."

Quite the speech. Except I knew . . . or at least guessed . . . that Robur himself had Shaped the prince to be his almost-but-not-quite-equal eternal opponent, to give himself an opportunity to play steampunk warlord. Which made it quite likely that all the "unfortunate souls" currently within the realms ruled by Robur were every bit as loyal to Robur as those within the so-called enlightened realm of Raj and its satellite nations were to their Dread Prince Dakkar . . . unless he'd left those in conquered realms loyal to his counterpart, to spice up his game with a little rebellion, a soupçon of Maquis?

I gave myself a mental shake. None of that mattered, for the simple reason that, not only was I not an ambassador from my world, I was not a "theological spelunker," either. I could not return to my world, I could not bring others from my world into this one: Shaped people could not travel between the worlds . . . well, except for the Adversary's cadre. Apparently, he had the knack of it, but clearly the number of people to whom he could give the ability was limited. All of which meant I was the only member of my world who would ever enter this one . . . and I, by myself, could not change the power in this world in the slightest.

I had, in fact, only two choices: resign myself to becoming a permanent denizen of this world or try to fulfill the quest Karl Yatsar had saddled me with. Keeping my focus on getting to the real Shaper, Robur, would hopefully put me back in touch with Karl—vital, because only he could open a Portal from this world to the next, and the next, and the next after that, until finally I was face-to-face with Ygrair. Then, maybe, I could actually figure out what the hell was really going on, how I'd been landed in this Labyrinth of interlaced worlds in the first place . . . and why I couldn't remember any of it.

Put that way, it wasn't a difficult choice at all. I had to somehow reach Robur. That meant escaping Prince Dakkar. And that meant . . . humoring him.

He was staring at me again, frowning a little, perhaps wondering why it was taking me far too long to answer each of his questions. "The island has vanished," I said. "The cave through which I entered your world is gone."

"Are you saying you cannot return to your world?" the prince demanded.

"No," I said. "I think there may be a way." *Good beginning,* I thought. *But now what?* I felt like an author who hadn't planned out her story in enough detail, and now had to make things up on the fly. What was that called . . . ? Oh, right, "pantsing," because you were making things up by the seat of your pants. I figuratively hitched mine up (figuratively, since I wasn't wearing any) and forged bravely and blindly ahead. "Our . . . thinkers on this subject . . . believe that there are always two . . . call them Portals . . . on any world." *Just a spoonful of truth helps the make-believe go down,* I heard Julie Andrews warble in my head. "The one to my world has vanished, but that just means it has relocated." Also true. "I may be able to find it." I hoped that was true, but I had no proof it was. So far, in this world, I hadn't felt any of the kinds of mental tugs I'd felt near the Portals in my own world.

But then, this isn't my world, I reminded myself. And that naturally meant I wasn't attuned to the subtle sense of wrongness I'd felt near Portals in my own. To me, this whole world seemed wrong.

"Will it, too, be at sea?" The prince's face showed avid interest, which it had also shown when he'd first seen me in my new clothing, but now that interest was focused on my words rather than my . . . other assets.

"It might be," I said. "There's a theory, though, that . . ." I paused. "Perhaps a globe?"

"Of course," said the prince. "See to it," he added to the empty air, which confirmed my suspicion that, once again, we were not as unobserved as we appeared, as I no doubt would have found out in some uncomfortable and possibly fatal fashion had I attempted an act of violence on the prince . . . although I was pretty sure he could have attempted any kind of act on *me* with impunity.

Not if I aimed my knee right, I thought.

"While we wait," he went on, "perhaps you could tell me more of your world . . . ?"

I hesitated. *Well, why not?* I thought. *He'll never enter it, and the world I knew . . . the world I Shaped . . . is gone anyway.*

"I lived," I said, "in the small city of Eagle River, in

a place called Montana, a state within a larger country called the United States of America. It was a beautiful city, with a view of the mountains . . ."

Standing there overlooking the prince's self-propelled island, I went on in some detail, although I left out unnecessary details—you know, like me having been a potter rather than an academic, and seeing the Adversary and his cadre of utterly loyal followers attack the Human Bean and murder my best friend right in front of me, and how I'd somehow wished all that away, so that the corpses, the bullet holes, and the blood spattered on the walls and floor all vanished . . .

. . . but my best friend remained dead.

Instead of talking about any of *that,* I just talked in general terms about my lovely world, where peace had broken out in the past few years (coinciding with my Shaping of it, I knew now) after an admittedly violent history, where art and literature and music flourished, where there were colonies on the Moon . . .

"Really?" the prince interrupted. "Did they get there by giant cannon?"

"Um . . . no," I said. "Rockets."

"Rockets?" He blinked. "How extraordinary . . ."

I hurried on. I was describing New York City (and Broadway musicals, which seemed to fascinate the prince), when the ordered globe arrived, carried up the stairs by yet another silk-clad female servant. She handed it to the prince (who took it without a word of thanks), bowed, and departed.

The prince set the globe on the broad windowsill between us. "We are currently here," he said, pointing to a spot of ocean halfway between the two largest land masses, roughly equivalent to the Pacific Ocean, I guessed, even though nothing was shaped right.

"Where is Robur's capital?" I said. I needed to know that before I decided where I was going to predict the Portal might be located, although I couldn't be too obvious about it: I could hardly say the Portal was located right in the middle of Robur's capital city and the prince therefore had to somehow spirit me there.

"Quercus?"

"If you say so."

"It is here, on the northwest coast of Verne's Land." Prince Dakkar tapped what would have been South America if this really had been the Pacific Ocean.

"Verne's Land?" *Really?*

"Yes." His finger rested on a country marked in blue. "This is the Republic of Weldon."

"Weldon, yes," I said. The name still made me smile, lifted straight from *Robur the Conqueror* as it was. I didn't recognize "Quercus," but no doubt it was a Verneian reference as well, although the book version of Robur had his base on "X Island," the prototypical mad-scientist island hangout, ancestor to any number of subsequent mad-scientist island hangouts, from Crab Key in *Dr. No* to Buddy's island in *The Incredibles.* Located somewhere in the Pacific, X Island held everything Robur needed to construct his nefarious machines.

Huh. Come to think of it, that actually sounded more like Prince Dakkar's realm, except Propeller Island was taken from its own Verne book. (Verne loved his mysterious islands.) Well, as I'd already realized, Jules Verne's books were more inspiration than blueprint for this world. Perhaps the Shaper had simply combined the two.

The prince moved his finger out of the blue area, and over a series of smaller countries, delineated in a variety of colors. "And these are its vassal states—once-independent nations, conquered by Robur. Their borders are strictly controlled. It is very difficult for noncitizens to enter the Republic, which has made obtaining information about it challenging."

"But not impossible?" I guessed.

"No." He smiled. "My intelligence service is formidable."

All part of the game, I thought. It would be boring for Robur if Dakkar didn't have some successes in their never-ending war.

"So, Robur controls all of those countries," I said. "But you have . . . vassal states . . . as well, don't you?"

"Of course," the prince said. "Islands, for the most part, although there are a few coastal lands, as well." His finger moved from spot to spot in the ocean. "I rule the waves. Not a single island state gives fealty to Robur. He cannot conquer them by air, and his ships are almost defenseless against my submarines."

"When we first spoke, you said 'almost' all nations swear fealty to either you or Robur. Just 'almost'?" I was curious, but I was also buying time, trying to figure out how to get myself as close to Robur as I could before attempting to escape.

"Most," the prince said. "Only one of any significance remains neutral: the Free City of Phileas." He pointed to a narrow isthmus to the north of Verne's Land, where it narrowed before bulging out again. If Verne's Land had been South America, that isthmus would have been Central America, and the larger land mass to the north, North America.

I pointed to it. "There are no countries marked up here. Who lives there?"

The prince shrugged. "Primitive tribes. Some have built rather sizable villages, and even dwellings in cliffs, but most are nomadic. They fight among themselves. They are fortunate that Robur and I are engaged in a struggle for control of civilization. Once I have defeated him, I will turn my attention to subjugating and civilizing the savages, both there and elsewhere." He put his hand on the north pole of the globe. "So much of the world remains wild. I intend to tame it."

"I am sure the 'primitive tribes' will be . . . suitably grateful," I said, thinking of some Native American friends of mine who would have liked to have had a word with him and the Shaper about *that* proposed project. But most of my attention was on the green blob he had identified as the Free City of Phileas. "Where was the Mysterious Island located?"

"Here," said the prince, pointing to a spot considerably north our present location.

"Do you have a piece of string?"

"What?" He blinked. "No . . . oh, wait."

To my surprise, he reached up and undid his ponytail. Lustrous black hair fell around his shoulders. He grasped a strand, pulled hard, and then handed it to me. "Will this work?"

"Uh . . . yeah." I took it, a little gingerly; it still had its pale root at one end. "Is there a scale on the globe?"

He gave the globe a half-turn and pointed to a scale beneath an elaborate compass rose. Muttering under my breath (my phone number, my social security number, and some random directions) I marked out about four inches on the strand of hair between my fingers. "Turn it around again for me?"

He complied.

"Where was the island found again? I need you to be precise."

"I know the latitude and longitude by heart," he said. He carefully examined the globe, and then pointed once more at a spot in the ocean. "Here. Precisely."

I put my left thumb and forefinger, holding one end of the prince's hair, on the island's location, then carefully extended the hair, hoping I'd judged the distance about right . . .

I had.

"Here," I said, placing my right thumb and forefinger in the middle of that isthmus between North and South Verne's Land. "If . . . *if* . . . our experts' theory is correct, this will be the approximate location of the next Portal."

The prince leaned in for a closer look . . . and I suddenly felt shock, as though, impossibly, static had leaped between the ceramic globe and my thumb and finger. I jerked my hand back (dropping the hair in the process) and stared at it.

It tingled.

"Very close to the Free City of Phileas," said the prince thoughtfully. He glanced at me. "Why did you jump?"

"A . . . cramp," I said, but in fact, my mind was whirling.

Somehow . . . I didn't know how, but somehow . . . what I had thought I was making up on the spot was absolutely true.

I knew, beyond a shadow of doubt, that there *was* a potential Portal right where I had placed my thumb and forefinger. And if it was the way back into my world . . .

. . . then maybe, just maybe, Karl Yatsar was there, waiting for me.

TWELVE

"**YOU ARE CERTAIN** of that location?" said the prince, returning his gaze to the globe.

"No," I said, but, *Yes,* I was thinking, still stunned by my sudden epiphany. "As I said before, all I can say for sure is that, if the theories of our experts . . . who *were* right about the implications of the Mysterious Island's appearance in our world . . . are correct, then that is where it *should* be."

"Hm." The prince straightened. "Well, then. I suppose I should see about getting you there."

"Terrific," I said, albeit somewhat absentmindedly. I was flexing my tingling fingers, trying to figure out why the sensation was so familiar . . .

. . . and suddenly I had it: it was the same sensation I'd felt after accidentally'd putting my hand into Karl's blood on top of the sacrificial altar above which the Portal between my world and this had opened.

What did *that* mean?

I could think of only one possibility: somehow, when I'd touched Karl's blood, I'd absorbed the alien technology that gave him the ability to find potential Portals.

Which was also the technology that gave him the ability to open Portals. Did that mean . . . ?

I needed time to think, but I wasn't sure the prince was going to give me any. "Attend me," he said, again to thin air. I turned toward the stairs, expecting the woman who had brought the globe—but instead, the head that emerged from the hole in the floor, followed shortly by a slim teenaged body, belonged to Eustasia.

"Your Highness?" she said once she had stepped off the stairs onto the marble floor.

"Please send my compliments to Captain Hatteras of the *Narwhal* and ask him to attend me in the chart room at his earliest convenience. Same message to Colonel Everest. Have Ambassador Keys' escort proceed there as well. I will escort the ambassador personally."

"Yes, Your Highness." Eustasia descended the stairs.

The prince turned to me, crooked an arm, and smiled, teeth flashing white in his dark face in a somewhat predatory fashion. "Ambassador?"

I had little choice. I tucked my arm into his, and together we proceeded down the stairs to the elevator. Eustasia had vanished. I wondered if perhaps there were another elevator for her use, something less ornate and probably faster than the one the prince and I entered, which, under the guidance of the same elevator operator as before, began its leisurely descent.

The prince kept his arm in mine and stood a little closer than he needed to. I could smell a spicy, exotic scent. *Probably some cologne he had his scientists concoct in a laboratory just for him.* I could feel the warmth of his tall body next to mine, and I was chilly enough to enjoy it. In fact, from a warmth point of view I would gladly have snuggled up closer, but I didn't want to give him any more ideas than he clearly already had.

Except . . . I kind of did.

As noted, he smelled good. He was attractive. He was lean and fit. And, as princes go (not that I'd had a lot of exposure to princes . . . I winced; maybe exposure wasn't the best word, since I felt oddly exposed in my unfamiliar silk wrapping), he could be charming—rather odd, considering all his followers liked to refer to him as "Dread." There was some stupid part of my brain that wanted me to bat my eyelashes at him and maybe let out a girlish giggle, but I gave it a good mental kicking and it subsided. I was saving my girlish wiles for when they might do me some good.

The prince was sending me to Phileas. There was a Portal, or at least a potential Portal, there (though I still didn't know why I was so sure of that, or what that sudden shock of recognition and the tingling I could still feel meant). Karl Yatsar might be there. Even if he wasn't, it was a relatively short distance from there to . . . what had the prince called it? Oh, yeah. Quercus . . . capital city of the Republic of Weldon, ruled over by the Shaper, Robur. If Karl wasn't in Phileas, he would surely be in Quercus.

So, let the prince take me to Phileas. Once there, I would have to escape. I already had the inkling of a plan to do so.

It only made me feel *slightly* dirty.

Then I stiffened. *He's sniffing my hair!* "You smell delightful," he murmured. The elevator operator kept her eyes rigidly forward.

Even though I had been thinking much the same thing about him, I hadn't said it out loud and I wasn't about to admit it. "Thank you," I said, as primly as I knew how. I pulled my head away and turned it toward him. "Your Highness," I said gently, "I have a boyfriend."

"In this world?" he said. He didn't seem the slightest put off by my claim.

"No." *And not in mine anymore, either,* but I wasn't going to tell him *that.* "But that does not make a difference."

"Why not?" He turned toward me, slipping his arm from the crook of mine so he could take both of my hands in his. He looked down at me. "How can promises made in one world hold sway in another?"

"Promises are promises," I said. "If the mere fact of moving from one world to another means you don't have to keep them, then any promises I make to you in this world I can freely break when I return to my own."

His mouth tightened, and his eyes narrowed. *A hit, a palpable hit.* To my relief, he dropped my hands and stepped back. "A reasonable rebuttal," he said, his voice neutral yet, I thought, with a hint of anger in it. "But perhaps I will reason you out of that position and into one more to my liking." He gave me another predatory grin. "I think you will find, should that happen, that it is a position to your liking, as well."

I knew a double entendre when I heard it. I wanted to kick him, but instead I murmured, "There are many positions to my liking, so perhaps you are correct," and hated myself for it when his eyes widened, then narrowed thoughtfully. But, dammit, I needed him. And if he were busy trying to seduce me, and thought he was making progress, he might be less likely to consider the possibility my focus was on escaping him, not screwing him . . . although, by escaping him, come to think of it, I would also be screwing him. *English is such a weird language,* I thought, not for the first time in my life.

I can play his game, I assured myself, as the doors opened at last and he led me out past the stone-faced elevator operator. *I can even let him think he's winning. But in the end . . . I win, he loses.*

Well, provided he doesn't overturn the board and claim all the pieces.

He's a perfect gentleman, Eustasia said. *And he needs my help. I can play this game and not get burned. I can. I hope.*

This hallway was considerably more spartan than most of the others I had seen in the palace, presumably because it was where military types hung out. It seemed everyone in sight wore a uniform, men and women alike, although there were far more of the former than the latter. It made me feel even more self-conscious in my pen-wahr, although nobody gave me a second glance . . . or rather, *everybody* gave me a second glance, after they'd stopped and clicked their heels and bowed to the prince, but it wasn't because of what I was wearing, but of whom I was with.

The chart room, down one corridor, around a corner, and down another, proved to be a large room like I'd seen in movies about the London Blitz. In the middle, a huge table bore a map of the entire world. Flat wooden tiles like Scrabble pieces marked the locations of, I presumed, the forces on both sides of the Dakkar-Robur conflict. An island on which rested a miniature porcelain palace clearly marked us. Various ship/sub pieces were clustered around it, one of which, I guessed, represented the docked *Narwhal*. Other vessels were dotted around all the world's oceans. Nobody seemed to be frantically moving pieces around like you saw in those Blitz movies, but then, ships and submarines move much more slowly than airplanes and the scale of the table was enormously greater than a map just showing Europe.

As we got closer to the table, I realized something else: it was covered in a mesh of hexagons, and the wooden tiles were marked with obscure symbols in the middle and numbers at each corner. In some hexagons, multiple tiles, presumably representing multiple units, were stacked atop one another.

It was, literally, a giant wargame board. That gamer I used to date had had a thing for "classic" (his word) Avalon Hill wargames. They'd looked almost exactly like this. More than ever, I was certain Robur had Shaped his world so he could play wargames with real weapons . . . and real people.

I didn't much like Prince Dakkar, but increasingly, I thought I would like Robur even less. Yet, I still had to get to him if I could.

I was surprised to see Captain Hatteras of the *Narwhal* already there. I would have thought it would have taken him longer to reach the palace from the sub than it had taken us to descend from the tower, but perhaps he had already been in the building.

A tall, thin, tanned man with short gray hair, bushy gray eyebrows, and piercing blue eyes—not to mention a rather ridiculous amount of gold braid on his dark-green uniform—stood next to the captain. A few hangers-on—adjutants and lesser officers, I presumed—lined the walls, and Belinda and Anthony stood at stiff attention on either side of the door through which we entered. I nodded at Belinda, and then nodded and smiled at Anthony—coquettishly, I hoped, although I'm not sure I was any more successful at coquettish than I had been at demure, earlier. Still, he blushed, so perhaps I'd managed something close to what I was going for . . . and, I also noted with satisfaction, his eyes, ever so briefly, flicked the length of my body before returning to attention with the rest of him. (Well, hopefully, not *all* of him: I didn't want to engender quite *that* much of a physical reaction.)

Everyone saluted as the prince entered. He did not salute back. "Colonel Everest," he said to the braid-bedecked gentleman, as we approached the chart table, "May I present Ambassador Shawna Keys of . . ." He looked at me. "What should I call your world?"

"Montana," I said, because why not?

"Ambassador Shawna Keys of Montana," he said.

The colonel's right eyebrow rose in a credible imitation of Spock, of whom, of course, he would never have heard—any more than he would have heard of Montana. But clearly, he was not going to demand any more information from his Dread Prince than said Dread Prince was willing to supply. "Indeed," he said. "An honor, ma'am."

I curtsied. *Thanks, childhood dance classes!*

"Of course, you have met Captain Hatteras," the prince said to me.

"Of course," I said. "A pleasure to see you again, Captain."

"Ambassador," he said neutrally.

"Gentlemen," the prince said to the captain and colonel, "I have a mission for you. It is imperative that Ambassador Keys be conveyed to the Free City of Phileas. The *Narwhal* will transport her to the coast. You, Colonel, will assemble and lead the team that will escort her from there into Phileas."

The colonel frowned. "It will need to be a substantial escort, if she seeks to travel openly. Robur's troops infest the jungles around Phileas almost as thickly as the mosquitoes."

"She does not seek to travel openly," said the prince. "I am thinking in terms of a clandestine operation. A dozen men, perhaps, disguised as locals."

My cue. "May I request that Lieutenant Blackwell be

among them?" I said. "He has impressed me greatly in the short time I've known him."

The lieutenant's ears reddened, and I felt more than a little ashamed of myself, but I absolutely needed him among the members of my escort if my half-baked . . . hell, not even in the oven yet . . . escape plan were to have the slightest hope of succeeding.

"I'm sure that can be arranged," said the prince, looking from me to the lieutenant. "Captain Hatteras, Lieutenant Blackwell is assigned to your submarine. Will you release him for this duty?"

"He is stationed aboard my ship, but Lieutenant Commander Hatteras is his commanding officer," Captain Hatteras said. (I noted he did not refer to her as his daughter; keeping it professional, I guessed.) "I have no objection if she does not."

I saw the sharp look Belinda gave the lieutenant and me in quick succession, even if no one else did. I half expected her to refuse . . . but her prince had requested it, and whatever suspicions she might have had about my reasons for wanting the lieutenant on the mission or concerns about losing him for the duration from the flight she commanded, clearly did not outweigh her near-fanatical loyalty to the prince—a loyalty I was willing to bet had been engendered by the Shaper, Robur, just to make his global wargames more enjoyable . . . for him.

"I have no objection," she said.

The lieutenant himself, of course, was not asked.

Having made his request, and I having made mine, the prince handed me over to Belinda to escort me back to my quarters, leaving the lieutenant in the chart room, since he was now part of the mission to be planned. Apparently, the prince didn't believe I needed to trouble myself with the mundane details.

I thought about protesting, even demanding to stay, but I didn't. My priorities had changed. At this point, the more they thought of me as a frail female in need of manly protection, the better. What I *really* wanted was more information about this mysterious land we were heading to, with its jungles full of both mosquitoes and enemy troops, and its city, Phileas, that had somehow escaped falling under the dominion of either Prince Dakkar or the self-styled Master of the World.

"Have you ever been to Phileas?" I asked Belinda once the door to the chart room had closed behind us and she was leading me through the military-infested (in the colonel's evocative phrase) corridors of this wing of the palace . . . though on a different route than the one via which I'd arrived.

"Once," she said. She bit the word off in the abrupt way that's a sure sign one partner in the dance of conversation is ready to return to the punch table.

Nevertheless, I persisted. "What took you there?"

She led me through a doorway into a spiral stairwell, winding up and down what was presumably one of the towers, lit by medieval-ish slit windows on one side. "Orders," she said as we started down.

No point asking what those orders had been—she'd never tell me, and I didn't really care, anyway. What I wanted to know (and so what I asked next) was, "What was it like?"

She said nothing until we exited the tower, three floors down, into the more ornate corridors I remembered from outside my overwrought room. No more military uniforms here: the only people I saw were two female servants in white-silk tunics and trousers. They hurried past us with eyes downcast. One was carrying a bucket and mop, the other a tray with the remains of someone's breakfast.

"Come on, tell me," I urged as we started down the hall.

Belinda stopped so suddenly I almost ran into her, turned around, and fixed me in an icy glare. "Why are you asking me these things? I am your escort, not your personal tour guide."

"I thought . . . hoped . . . we were becoming friends."

Wrong tack. "I am not your friend," she said coldly. "Nor am I your enemy. I am an officer of the Flying Force of His Imperial Majesty Dakkar, Prince of Raj, commanding the Seventh Flight, attached to His Majesty's Submarine *Narwhal.* I was ordered to retrieve you from the Weldonian airship *Albatross,* which I did, in a raid which cost the lives of two of my flight members, and for whose deaths I will face an inquiry in short order. I was ordered to share my accommodations with you aboard the *Narwhal.* I obeyed. I engaged in polite conversation with you because I am an officer and a gentlewoman. I was ordered to escort you to the palace, whereupon I was to wait upon the prince's pleasure. I obeyed. I have now been ordered to escort you back to your quarters.

"But you have just, with a word, stripped me of another member of my flight, my second-in-command, no less. It is therefore my deepest wish that once I deliver you to your quarters, I will be released from this frivolous duty and allowed to deal with the pressing issues of my command: replacements, training, and answering to my superiors for the loss of two men. I do not wish to chat; I do not wish to tell you about my world. I do not wish to hear anything more of yours. I wish only to be rid of you." She took a step toward me, eyes locked on mine from inches away. "Have I made myself clear?"

I forced myself not to step back. I met her gaze squarely. "You have," I said. "But I'm sorry, Belinda. I would have been honored to have you as a friend."

"That means nothing to me," said Belinda. "Nor do you, except insofar as doing my duty requires me to interact with you. Which it does for the next two hundred yards of corridor—no more."

She turned on her heel. I swallowed, then followed her without speaking again.

Back in my ridiculous *I Dream of Jeannie* quarters, I went to the window and stared out over the capital of Raj, eyes lingering on the mysterious ruins atop the overgrown hill in the distance.

Belinda's complete rejection of my proffered friendship hurt more than it should have. My overtures, after all, had really been designed to help me achieve my goal of reaching the other leader of this divided world, the man I believed to be the Shaper. I had tried to use her for my own ends, as I still hoped to use Lieutenant Anthony Blackwell if the opportunity presented itself.

But all the same . . .

I could have really used a friend right about then.

THIRTEEN

AS A GENERAL rule, I try to limit feeling sorry for myself to half an hour at a time, tops. And anyway, sitting and sniffling while gift-wrapped in pink silk is as good a way as I've ever found (now that I've tried it) to start feeling silly in pretty short order.

I got up and pulled the cord to summon a servant, something I'd never done before, although I'd seen it often enough in movies. (Okay, really, I'd mostly seen it in *The Addams Family,* so I was almost disappointed when the servant who responded was neither seven feet tall nor obviously undead.)

The very-much-not-undead young woman who answered, wearing white silk tunic and trousers, wasn't one I'd seen before. Blonde, tall but a bit gangly, she looked about fifteen. "Yes, Ambassador?" she said, eyes on her sandaled feet. (Her toenails, I saw, were painted gold.)

"Three . . . no, four things," I said. "First, could you light my fire?"

"Yes, ma'am." Still no eye contact. "And the second thing?"

"Can you bring me a warm robe?"

"Yes, ma'am."

"Third thing. Can you bring me a book with information about the Free City of Phileas?"

"Yes, ma'am." She lifted her face a little, so I finally caught a glimpse of her eyes beneath her long lashes. "And the fourth thing?"

"Make some hot tea, and when the fire is lit, have a

cup beside it with me while you warm up and I ask you a few questions."

Her head shot up, then, like that of a startled deer. "Ma'am, I'm not supposed to . . ."

"You're supposed to do what I ask, aren't you?" I said. I didn't know that for certain, but it seemed a safe bet.

"Yes, ma'am, but . . ."

"If your superior has any concerns about it, have her talk to me," I said.

She actually smiled then. "Yes, ma'am! I'll do the fire first."

"Please," I said. "And . . . what's your name?"

"Aesha," she said, and my heart skipped a beat.

Aesha. The same name as my best friend, who had been killed in front of me . . . and then had never existed at all. For a moment I wondered if, despite everything I knew of Shaping (which, admittedly, was only what Karl Yatsar had told me), I had somehow conjured this teen-aged serving girl out of my own subconscious . . . but no. I had no power here. And in any event, this tall, blonde girl looked nothing like my East Indian friend.

Just sad coincidence, I thought.

I wrapped the bedspread more tightly around my shoulders and sat on the bed, watching Aesha quickly and efficiently light the kindling beneath the three logs someone had placed in the hearth while I was out, using matches she retrieved from a compartment hidden in the side of the mantelpiece. Then, as flames started to flicker, she gave me a quick curtsy, and almost ran from the room.

I moved over to the fire and warmed myself by it. Between the bedspread and the burning logs, I felt almost cozy for the first time since I'd put on that stupid outfit that morning.

I thought Aesha might be gone for a considerable amount of time, but she returned within fifteen minutes, a pink (of course) bathrobe draped over one arm. She also carried (somewhat precariously, due to the bulk of the bathrobe) a tray, bearing a teapot inside an incongruously domestic-looking cozy (knitted out of pink wool), two delicate china cups with gold rims and handles, a matching bowl of lump sugar, a matching pitcher of cream . . . and a book, bound in dark-green leather.

She put the tray on the table and first offered me the bathrobe. "Your robe, ma'am."

"Thank you." I stood up, tossed the bedspread back on the bed, took the robe, and pulled it on. "Much cozier."

Aesha reached down, took the book from the tray, and handed it to me. "I hope this will also serve your needs, ma'am."

I looked at the cover as I sat down in one of the redwood chairs by the fire. *The Reprobates Abroad,* proclaimed gilded, ornate letters. Block letters beneath that stated, "By Mark Tierce."

Of course, I thought, remembering all the books by this author I'd seen in the *Narwhal*'s library. *If there's a version of* Huckleberry Finn (*Gooseberry Flynn,* if I remembered right), *then there's also a version of* The Innocents Abroad. My assumption was that the *Huckleberry Finn* in my world was identical to the original in the First World . . . but I suddenly realized I couldn't be certain of that. For all I knew, Mark Tierce was the name of the author in the First World, and my world had come up with Mark Twain through whatever mysterious process the Labyrinth used when little details like that weren't specified by the Shaper.

It doesn't matter, I told myself firmly, before I got trapped in the never-ending chasing-my-own-mental-tail spiral such thoughts tended to lead me to. *All that matters is what* this *book can tell me about Phileas.*

A glance through the contents seemed proof enough that this tome could only exist in this world. There were numerous strangely named lands mentioned, through which the author and his disreputable companions had traveled over the course of some eighteen months, most of which came in for some kind of ridicule. Tierce also ranked the nations' various alcoholic beverages (apparently through a great deal of hands-on research), the drugs of choice (ditto), and the brothels (ditto ditto). Though written in florid prose, it was clearly as salacious

a book as some of the tawdrier bestsellers of my world—
and just as bestselling: it had been reprinted some twenty-
seven times in the last ten years, according to the title
page.

In the table of contents, the various countries the "reprobates" had visited appeared in two columns: "Dwelling
in the Glorious Light of Our Dread Prince Dakkar" on
the left, and "Suffering under the Lash of the Despotic
Robur" on the right.

All except for one: "The Free City of Phileas," which
had a place all its own in the center of the page, halfway
down.

I looked up at that point to see Aesha still standing
by the table, although she'd poured tea. "Please, sit down,"
I said. "Enjoy your tea."

Aesha sat, although not comfortably, perching on the
edge of her chair as though expecting to have to leap to
her feet and run out at any moment. Only after I took a
sip of my tea—which was very good—did she sip hers.

I tried to put her at ease. "So . . . how long have you
been in the prince's service?"

"One year, ma'am," she said. "I was apprenticed when
I turned fourteen."

Apparently, I'd guessed her age right. "And how do
you find the work?"

"I . . . don't have to find it, ma'am," she said, clearly
puzzled. "I'm told what to do."

I laughed. "I mean, do you enjoy it?"

"It is my job, ma'am," she said, brows still knit in
puzzlement. "It doesn't matter if I enjoy it or not."

I sighed. "Of course." I held up the book. "Have you
read this?"

"No, ma'am. I can't read."

I blinked. "You can't . . . ?"

"No, ma'am. It is discouraged in my family."

"Dis . . ." I felt a surge of outrage. "*Why?*"

"The most highly sought-after servants are those who
cannot read," she explained, in that special teenager
tone that implies, *you may be an adult, but you're not the
brightest bulb in the Christmas-lights string, are you?*

"Because they cannot accidentally discover things that they are not supposed to know."

"Then why not go all the way and render servants deaf and dumb?" I said angrily.

"Oh, that's done, ma'am," Aesha said earnestly. "But my family is not yet of that exalted class."

"Exalted . . ." I pressed my lips together and took a long, slow breath through my nose. *Not my world, not my problem,* I told myself again.

Aesha had barely touched her tea. I could tell that, though she might be physically comfortable seated by the fire, she was horribly *un*comfortable at being forced to have tea with the woman whom she'd been assigned to serve. I suspected her superior, whoever that might be, had ordered her to accept my invitation, despite her strong objections.

And so, I took pity. "You can go, Aesha," I said. "Thank you for the fire, and the robe, and the tea, and the book."

She popped up off her chair as though she'd been ejected from it. "Thank you, ma'am," she said. "I mean, you're welcome, ma'am." She blushed, dipped a quick curtsy, and hurried out. Somehow, she managed to imbue the sound of the door closing with a sense of deep relief. *Another teenager specialty,* I thought.

I sighed and picked up the book again.

Phileas, I gleaned (in between accounts of bar fights, a midnight escape from a brothel ahead of creditors, and a snide discussion of the shortcomings of a famous giant nude statue of a legendary hero, the masterwork of the Phileasian sculptor Michel Simoni), had, against all odds, maintained its independence from both the Principality of Raj and the Republic of Weldon, despite numerous attempts by both to forge an alliance. As a result, Tierce wrote, "You will never find a more wretched hive of scum and villainy." (Yes, I blinked at that, too.) "You must be cautious if you visit it. Keep your wits about you, and one hand on your purse. A pistol, dagger, and cudgel are also welcome companions. However, if you are wary, wily, and wise, you may find the wicked streets of this jungle town offer you delights you simply cannot find in the more 'civilized' cities of the world." After which, he went on to describe those delights in terms that made me want to wash my hands after turning the pages.

It became clear that I would find nothing more useful in the text, so I turned to the pictures—not photographs, of course, but line drawings—from which I finally learned the one thing I was most concerned about: what I'd be expected to wear to blend in with the natives.

In the Free City of Phileas, it appeared, clothing was mostly of the loose, flowing variety—clearly Phileas had a hot climate. Most women wore off-the-shoulder blouses and long, loose skirts, but I saw some women in the drawings wearing pantaloons like the men. Shirtless men wearing only loincloths were also common in the drawing: physical laborers, probably. Small children apparently ran around without worrying about clothing at all. Government officials wore uniforms appropriate to their positions. The Free City Guardsmen, who appeared in one drawing (with a typically snide caption mocking their sense of self-importance), wore fairly standard military-style uniforms, though perhaps a bit looser-fitting and made of lighter material than the uniforms I had seen on the prince's various forces.

Being of the pale persuasion, I had worried I might stand out because of skin color, but the citizens of Phileas, like those of the Principality of Raj (and, come to think of it, the crew of the *Albatross*) came in every shade of pigmentation, as far as I could tell from the drawings. Some looked Indian, some Asian, some African, some Native American, some Western European, some downright Scandinavian. It was pretty much the first thing I'd seen that made me think even slightly positively about the Shaper of this world, who had clearly decided he wanted a color-blind society . . . though I wondered what that meant to the world's "history." How could such a diverse range of external appearances exist in a world where cultures had never developed in isolation?

Maybe it's in The Word of the Shaper, I thought. *Maybe the Shaper simply said, "Let it be so," and it was so.*

It struck me that I still didn't know the limits on a

Shaper's power. I was beginning to think that, at least in the initial Shaping, there weren't many. So once again I had to ask myself, why had I changed *my* world so little from the original?

I closed the book and put it back on the tray, having turned the page to a "Very Special Appendix Included Only in this Limited Edition," and discovered some additional drawings of the adventures of Tierce and his male companions that put me in mind of the nasty statues in the hidden passages of the Mysterious Island on my world. My opinion of the Shaper, which had momentarily risen, dropped again precipitously, though perhaps that wasn't fair: Karl Yatsar had made it clear that much of a Shaped world organized itself spontaneously. It wasn't like *my* world hadn't still had a nasty underbelly.

In any event, the book could tell me nothing more about the Free City of Phileas. Now I had only to wait until my gallant escorts came to take me to the "hive of scum and villainy," into which, if all went well, I would escape.

Great, I thought. *And not a light saber to my name.*

Lunch (a delectable fish broth, crusty bread hot from the oven, a Brie-like cheese I would gladly have eaten an entire wheel of, and a chilled glass of a something within spitting distance of Chardonnay—not that I spat it; it was quite good) came and went. The afternoon dragged. I spent some time looking out the window at the bright, sunlit streets beyond the palace walls, bustling with traffic—some horse-drawn, some self-propelled.

Having nothing else to do, I finally returned to *The Reprobates Abroad* (avoiding the "Very Special Appendix") and read more about Mark Tierce and friends' debauched journeying. It turned out I was fortunate the prince preferred his female servants and associates clothed—alluringly, but clothed: there were southern islands were nudity was the norm (Tierce, naturally, highly approved).

Layer by layer, I was building up a mental image of the Shaper of this world, and layer by layer, I was becoming more disturbed by it. I thought again of Aesha's comment that the more "exalted" servants might be rendered deaf and dumb to serve Prince Dakkar better . . . a barbarity she seemed comfortable with, because, presumably, she had been *Shaped* to be comfortable with it.

Is this how it's going to be, world after world? Encountering the nasty work of other Shapers, and unable to do anything about it?

Except, maybe I *could*, once I had this world's *hokhmah*.

Supposing that were the case, should I use that power to bring this world more in alignment with how I thought it should be run . . . just like the Adversary had begun bringing *my* world into alignment with how he thought *it* should be run? The difference being, of course, that I would make this world better, not worse.

Don't you think the Adversary thought he was making your *world better?* my annoying inner Jiminy Cricket asked.

Based on what I'd seen here, maybe it *was* better than how some of the Shaped worlds were run. Which led to another heretical question. Even if I didn't change this world myself, why should I save it from the Adversary?

Another question for the absent Karl Yatsar: "Is diversity really better than uniformity, if uniformity provides stability and equality? If, among the many "diverse" Shaped worlds, there are worlds where injustice and sexism and racism and who-knows-what-other nasty isms are hardwired—might it not be better to allow the Adversary to establish his authoritarian uniformity?"

It occurred to me I didn't even really know what the Adversary's worlds were like—only what Karl had told me. I'd left mine before the Adversary had fully re-Shaped it, and while what I had seen hadn't been pleasant from *my* point of view, since the changes he'd implemented had largely been aimed at my capture and execution, for all I knew, my friends and acquaintances in Eagle River were better off now than they had been in my more chaotic, uncontrolled version of the world.

Then I took a mental hold of my virtual shoulders and

gave myself a mental shake. *And so what?* I thought fiercely. *The fact remains: the Adversary tried to kill you. He would have killed you had he caught you.*

If he had caught me here, or in another world, he would *still* try to kill me—to keep me from achieving the quest Karl had saddled me with (the increasingly impossible-seeming quest), to deliver the gathered *hokhmah* of as many worlds as I could to Ygrair, to protect the Labyrinth from ultimate destruction at the Adversary's hand.

Whatever the greater good might seem to some outside observer . . . some reader of this ridiculous fantasy novel I seemed to be trapped in . . . it didn't affect my decisions at all. I did not want to die. I wanted to stay ahead of the Adversary, reach Ygrair, and find out what was really behind this impossible extradimensional Labyrinth and the Shaped worlds that seemed to stud it like chocolate chips in a muffin from the Human Bean.

Where, let me remind you, your best friend, Aesha, was brutally murdered right in front of you by the aforementioned Adversary. Don't go soft. Whatever the faults of this world or any other world you might enter, preserving them is still better than letting the Adversary have them and continue to grow his power.

Maybe, I thought. *But that still leaves the central question: is preserving them better than trying to make them better?*

I knew what Karl would say. He'd yammer on about the importance of letting many different kinds of worlds flourish without interfering: the ultimate freedom of expression. But he wasn't a Shaper himself, as far as I could tell, so he'd never have to face this particular quandary. Supposing I ignored his advice and changed this world to more closely align with my vision of what it should be, what could he do about it?

Leave you here and go onto the next world without you, a part of me answered myself.

He won't, I answered back. *I'm too important to him. Are you?*

In the end, I came back to the same irresolute place I landed every time I thought about this: it was all moot.

I had yet to meet the Shaper. I didn't know how I'd get his *hokhmah*. I didn't know what I could do with it if I did get it.

One step at a time, I thought.

The next step, it turned out, was heralded by a knock on the door.

FOURTEEN

NO DOUBT TO her deep disappointment, my self-declared not-friend, Lieutenant Commander Belinda Hatteras of His Imperial Majesty's Flying Force, had been sent to collect me and escort me back out through the Lapus Lazuli Gate and down the long tunnel to the dock where her father's submarine, *Narwhal,* awaited us.

To her no doubt even deeper disappointment, she was once again ordered to share her quarters with me.

"Sorry," I said as we reached her cabin door.

"I have other duties," she said, and stalked off.

I went into her cabin, where I was pleased to discover new clothing on my bunk: a tunic-style blouse and pantaloons, both made of lightweight white cotton, like those I had seen some women wearing in the drawings in Mark Tierce's nasty book. There was a bright-red sash to go around my waist, and fresh undergarments. For footwear, I'd been provided with sandals like those I'd seen in pictures of ancient Roman soldiers, complete (I saw as I turned one over) with hobnails. I set those aside because I'd keep wearing the sandals that had come with my palace-issued penwahr while I was on the ship. (Hobnails seemed like a really bad idea on steel deck plates—on land, it would be a different matter.)

I'd just finished donning the new clothes when someone knocked on the door. I opened it to find Anthony Blackwell standing there at attention, stiff as a fencepost. Gazing somewhere over my left shoulder, he said, "Lieutenant Blackwell, reporting for duty."

I blinked. "To me?"

"Yes, ma'am. I have been assigned as your batman for the duration of this mission."

"My *what*?"

"Personal assistant, ma'am."

"Oh." Right . . . batman was a British military term. I'd seen it in books. I spared a thought for the much younger version of myself who would have been absolutely *thrilled* to have her own personal Batman, especially if Robin came along with him.

"Colonel Everest's compliments, ma'am," my new "batman" said. "He asks that you join us in the library to discuss the pending mission."

"You don't have to call me ma'am, Lieutenant," I said. "My name is Shawna." I gave him a bright smile. "And may I call you Anthony?"

"You may call me what you wish, ma'am . . ." His eyes flicked to my face, then away again. "Shawna."

Score one for me, I thought. "Then lead the way, Anthony."

I noted, as I followed him, that his ears had turned pink . . . again.

The library was far more crowded than the last time I'd been there. The chairs had been pushed back, rearranged around a large folding table set up in the room's center. Seated at the table were Colonel Everest, Captain Hatteras, and . . .

Crap. What's he *doing here?*

"Ambassador," Prince Dakkar greeted me as Anthony led me in.

Anthony faded away to stand with about a dozen men (and no women; Belinda was not part of this gathering) of lesser rank on the periphery. He alone wore a Flying Force uniform. The others wore dark-green uniforms like the colonel's, but with far less braid, far fewer stripes, and dark, rather than shiny, brass buttons.

"Your Highness, this is a pleasant surprise," I lied to the prince. "Are you accompanying us?"

He smiled. "I very much wish I could, Ambassador,

but duty demands I remain in the palace, to oversee our constant struggle against Robur's evil plans."

"Of course," I said. "That's too bad." Inside, I felt relief. Having the prince along might have made it impossible for me to escape—he'd never have let me out of his sight, day or (if he had his way . . . or at least had his way with *me*) night.

"I have come primarily to bid you farewell, once we have reviewed, one final time, the plan for your penetration"—he gave me a look I refused to respond to—"of the Free City of Phileas." He nodded to Colonel Everest. "You may begin, Colonel."

The plan the colonel set out, in dry, clipped, professional tones, wasn't exactly invasion-of-Normandy stuff. We would approach the coast aboard the *Narwhal,* submerged. Under cover of night, the submarine would take us as close in as Captain Hatteras dared, then surface. The boats we took to the shore would be manned by sailors who would then return the boats to the sub, leaving no evidence of our arrival.

"Sergeant Mokoum will guide us through the jungle to the Free City's border," the colonel said. He indicated a rather slender-looking soldier with dark skin and a gentle smile, about as far from the stereotypical infantry sergeant as you could imagine. "He grew up in the region and knows of a smuggler's trail that should be safe from the prying eyes of the forces Robur has patrolling the area."

"Why does Robur have forces there at all?" I said. Everyone turned to look at me, as though surprised I had spoken, or perhaps that I was capable of asking a question. (Did I mention I was the only woman in the room?) "It's a no man's land," I continued, ignoring their frowns. "Is he planning to invade?"

"I am not privy to Robur's thoughts, alas," Prince Dakkar answered. "Would that I were. However, recent intelligence indicates he may have found valuable mineral deposits in the mountains north of Phileas, which he seeks to secure for himself. Our mutual treaties with the Free City would not allow him to evict any Phileasians already there, but it appears they do not yet know about the find. That means, once he has occupied the site . . . well, finders, keepers, as children say."

I nodded and subsided, knowing the next question I wanted to ask I would not get an answer to: why was Phileas a Free City, and not a conquered one? It couldn't possibly stand against the forces of either Robur or Dakkar.

The only explanation I could think of was that, for some reason, the Shaper *wanted* the Free City to exist, that its independence was built into the very fabric of this world. But why?

Something else to ask when I finally meet him.

"Three days on the smuggler's trail will bring us to Palik, a village just inside the Free City's borders. After that, we may travel more openly, albeit still circumspectly, as ordinary traders. It is only a day's walk from Palik to the city itself." The colonel turned his gaze to me. "Once we are within its walls, Ambassador, we will look to you to guide us to this . . . Portal." His voice never changed inflection, but I was pretty sure he thought I was leading them all on a dangerous and pointless wild-goose chase.

The prince must have picked up on that, too. "That is correct, Colonel," he said, with a smile that definitely did not partake of the gentleness of Sergeant Mokoum's. "You will follow the ambassador's instructions to the letter. She carries a message from me to her rulers, which may turn the tide of the war in our favor and allow us to crush Robur once and for all. Do not fail me in this task."

The colonel had stiffened at the prince's first utterance. "I will not, Your Highness!"

"You have contact information for my operatives in Phileas," the prince continued. "They have a wireless communicator, which they will put at your disposal. I expect a report, relayed by the *Narwhal,* the moment you have succeeded."

"Yes, Your Highness."

The prince smiled again, with no more warmth than before, and rose. "Honors!" the colonel cried, and everyone in the room, including Captain Hatteras, snapped to attention and saluted . . . well, everyone except me. I stayed seated right where I was.

Prince Dakkar, who had turned to go out the aft door, paused and glanced at me. "I look forward to your return, Ambassador. I know you are a woman of honor and will hold to your promises, even across worlds. As I will hold to mine." Then he turned and was gone.

"At ease," said the colonel, and then, "Dismissed!"

The soldiers filed out in the wake of their prince, all but one, presumably the colonel's adjutant, who stood just behind the colonel's right shoulder, holding what I took to be a tightly rolled map. Other than Captain Hatteras, who stood at the foot of the table looking like he'd been sucking on a lemon, the only other person who remained in the library was my batman, Anthony. I gave him a quick smile; he almost returned it.

I'm getting there, I thought, and despite what I'd just thought . . . or maybe because of it . . . hated myself a little bit more.

"Ambassador," said Colonel Everest. He nodded to his adjutant, who promptly unrolled the map he carried on top of the one on which the colonel had been tracing the line of the smuggler's trail a moment before. The colonel indicated the new map with a wave of his hand. "Can you look at this and give me any better indication of our ultimate destination?"

Could I? I didn't know. "Let me see." I took a step forward and leaned down, resting my hands on the table. "The Free City of Phileas," proclaimed large, ornate lettering in one corner. Smaller (but still ornate) letters below that title informed me the map had been "crafted by the Master Cartographer Verinas as ordered by Kritarch Proth, Year 985 of the Founding."

The new map detailed a clearly ancient city, its winding streets suitable only for foot traffic or small carts or horses, a maze I could tell at a glance would be the easiest place in the world in which to get lost. *Perfect.*

And then, still staring down at the map, I felt another . . . flash, or jab, or shock; I didn't have a word for it. Whatever

it was, it suddenly told me *exactly* where in the city the
Portal either was or would be located: right. . . . *there,*
in the middle of a warren of alleys surrounding a courtyard. *Mogador Place,* read the courtyard's label. I stared
at it, memorizing it—and then tapped my finger on the
map as far from Mogador Place as I could and remain
within the walls. "I believe this is the most likely spot."

The colonel bent down to peer at it. "The Catacombs
of the Holy. Where priests and nuns of the Church of the
Shaper are interred." He straightened and gave me a
skeptical look. "You are certain?"

"I can't be *certain,*" I said. "But I think it is most likely."
I thought fast. "Portals are often attracted to tombs,
which are, after all, also doorways to another world . . ."
Not bad, I congratulated myself.

"It is holy ground," the colonel said slowly, still looking down at the map, "but access to it is not forbidden.
There are no guards, as far as I know, just a wall and an
unlocked gate. And we will not be disturbing any of the
sacred tombs . . ." He gave me a look. "Will we?"

"We will not," I said, completely honestly, since I had
no intention of ever setting foot in the place.

"Very well, then," said the colonel. "That is our target."

"How long will it take us to reach the coast?" I said.

The colonel looked to Captain Hatteras. "About five
days," he said. His expression hadn't sweetened.

Five days? I thought. *I'll be lucky if Belinda doesn't
smother me in my sleep.*

But, of course, she did no such thing. She followed
orders and did her duty with perfect politeness (albeit
mostly silently—I don't think we exchanged more than
a dozen words a day).

I spent most of my time in the library, reading up on
the world. I didn't pay much attention to the history,
which, after all, I knew to be entirely fictional, however
real it might seem to the Shaped individuals living here.
But the geography interested me.

Now that I looked more closely, I could see how the
world had been not so much changed beyond recognition as, well, Shaped. The continents that had looked so

unfamiliar on the globe, in fact, had recognizable geographical features—the Florida peninsula, Hudson Bay, Vancouver Island, the Great Lakes—just in unfamiliar places, as if the Shaper had had a giant jigsaw puzzle of the First World—or my world—and had jumbled all the pieces.

Of course, the changes in location of these features meant changes in everything else about them. The "Florida peninsula" extruded from this world's equivalent of Antarctica, although, except for the Florida bit, that southernmost continent looked more like Australia. "Hudson Bay" was actually on the far side of Verne's Land—roughly where Brazil would have been in my world. And the "Great Lakes" were disconnected and scattered across the continent to our west, more or less where Asia would have been in my world, except something that looked very much like England hung where Japan should have been, a completely unfamiliar large-island-or-small-continent occupied roughly the Easter Island position in the largest ocean . . . you get the idea.

Although there were a few cities and small countries along its coastlines, that Asia-like continent's interior was marked "Unexplored," as were many other areas of the map. That wasn't too surprising, considering this world, the same size as Earth, held, according to one book I stumbled across, a total population of no more than 100 million people.

Even that number gave me pause. Every one of those people had been Shaped out of nothing . . . or, rather, whatever the primeval matter of the Labyrinth was. It was a staggeringly large number, or would have been, if not for the fact my own world, a closer copy of the First World, held an incredible 7.5 billion people. . . . people who apparently had not existed until I called them into being. Oh, sure, they were based on originals in the First World, but their personal memories, ancestries, and histories all came from my world . . . even though, if Karl were to be believed, they hadn't existed until ten years ago.

At least I'd been letting them live their lives unShaped (not knowing I was the Shaper had made that easy, I admit). In this world, though their number was far smaller, all of those Shaped people apparently existed just so Robur could play games: 100 million people, living and dying, making babies, baking bread, working jobs, loving and hating and laughing and crying, as real to themselves as I was to myself.

One hundred million people, whom Robur could change in a moment, if he still had the power, into someone completely different, whose histories he could erase, whose memories he could edit, whose families he could disrupt or destroy, whose very lives he could snuff out on a whim . . .

It was the same power I had had, when I had Shaped my world, and had rediscovered when Karl entered it: the power I had used to preserve my own existence and further my own quest as I fled the Adversary, with little regard for the effect on those who were merely living their lives.

Karl had had little patience for my qualms. He clearly saw the Shaped denizens of these pocket universes tucked within the Labyrinth as not fully human: mere simulacrums of the real people of the First World, phantoms who could be used and abused as necessary. It seemed clear the Shaper of this world felt the same.

I couldn't. I felt guilt for every person I had harmed in my own world, guilt for the way I had already begun to manipulate those of this world—not with any power to Shape them, but just with old-fashioned human deceit. I had lied to Captain Harding-Smith. I had lied to Captain Hatteras. I had lied to Belinda. I had lied to the prince. I had lied to Colonel Everest. I had lied to everyone I had met here, to tell the truth (for once). I might not have the powers of a Shaper in this world, but I was still trying to twist things, to make the story come out the way I needed it to.

And yet . . .

And yet, I had to survive. Not just for myself—although, believe me, I'm all in favor of personal survival—but for the greater good of all the billions . . . maybe *trillions* . . . of Shaped humans in all the who-knew-how-many

Shaped worlds. In this case, the ends really did justify the means.

I'm the protagonist. The heroine. Whatever I do is, by definition, right. Right?

Right, I told myself firmly.

And so, the other thing I devoted my attention to during the long underwater trip to the coast near the Free City of Phileas was shameless flirting with my batman, Lieutenant Anthony Blackwell.

He had been ordered to wait on me, and so he was almost always nearby. He sat next to me in the officers' wardroom when I took my meals. He stood guard outside the head when I took my showers. He saw me to my room at night, took away my clothing for washing as required, brought me wine in the library if I asked for it. I chatted with him whenever I could.

After the first day, his ears stopped turning pink every time he saw me, and our conversation gradually become less one-sided. I learned about his growing up (youngest son of a family of four boys, in love with flying since he'd seen a helicopter buzz over their house at a low altitude, and the leather-clad pilot had waved to him). I laughed at his jokes: "Flying helicopters isn't dangerous. Crashing helicopters, now that's dangerous," and, "Flying is easy. Just stay in the middle of the air. Avoid the edges. You can recognize the edges by the appearance of ground, buildings, trees, and the sea," and, "The only reason helicopters can fly is because they make so much noise the ground won't let them sit on it." (I didn't say they were good jokes, I just said I laughed at them.)

I saw Belinda scowling in our direction from time to time; clearly, she still resented my having stolen away her second-in-command. But, well . . . tough.

If I could have figured out how to "accidentally" see Anthony naked in the hallway again, I would have. Even better would have been to allow him to "accidentally" see me naked, but I couldn't make that work, either. And yes, I was ashamed of both thoughts—but I had them, and if I could have worked out a way to do either, I would have, because . . . survival. Ends. Means.

I didn't have to *like* what I did to survive, but I *had* to survive, to find Karl, get to Robur, get his *hokhmah* (somehow), and get out of his world. And once I was out of this world, what would it matter what I had done here? *What happens in one Shaped world stays in that world . . .*

That thought was strangely freeing . . . almost dangerously so. Whatever horrible impulses I might give into here wouldn't matter in the slightest in the next world, or the one after that, or the one after that. All the embarrassing things I remembered from growing up in my own world mattered even less because I hadn't really grown up in my world, had I? I had no idea how many of those memories were real. Maybe none of them were.

What was I like in the First World? I wondered as I sat with Anthony in the wardroom, making sure my knee occasionally touched his beneath the table, smiling coquettishly (maybe) as he discoursed in learned fashion about the aerodynamical strengths and failings of their ridiculous little battery-powered one-person helicopters. *Maybe I was a horrible human being. Maybe that's why I'm willing to do whatever is necessary to survive.*

Oh, yes, to save the Labyrinth, blah blah blah, but mostly, to survive.

Two days later, as I clung to the gunwales of a tiny boat being rowed ashore into the teeth of a near-hurricane, photo-flashes of lightning revealing trees on the shore lashing like mad things, deafening salvos of thunder assaulting my ears, rain streaming horizontally into my face with the force of a firehose, it seemed I probably wouldn't.

FIFTEEN

THE *NARWHAL* HAD surfaced into the storm-tossed ocean perhaps half a mile offshore. I'd assumed, when I'd stepped onto the deck with Anthony and almost been blown back through the hatch by the gale, that we'd surely delay our landing, but Colonel Everest, who was there with the rest of my escort, shouted into my ear, "Terrific luck! No one could possibly see us in this."

I tried to grin, but I think it came out as more of a death's-head grimace.

A few minutes later I had found myself on the wind-racked sea in this ridiculously flimsy craft. If not for the lightning, we couldn't possibly have seen which way we needed to go, but the near-constant flashes of atmospheric electricity kept us from getting lost, although getting fried on the spot by a Jovian temper tantrum or capsized and drowned by a Neptunian twitch remained a distinct possibility.

But we made it to the shore in one piece, although not gracefully, because the boat did indeed capsize, throwing us into foaming, waist-deep water just when it looked like we might ground in neatly upright fashion. I scrambled ashore with everyone else, on hands and knees, sopping wet in my thin white cotton pantaloons and tunic, spitting salty water. The boat had righted once the landing party had been summarily expelled from it, and the two sailors aboard were already rowing back toward the *Narwhal*—not that we could see the waiting submarine through the rain and over the waves, even in the lightning glare.

I resisted the urge to take advantage of being on all fours to kiss the beach. But I also resisted the urge to scramble immediately to my feet. Instead, I stayed put, choking and coughing, as if I'd breathed in seawater (even though I hadn't). Unless I missed my guess . . .

I hadn't. Anthony knelt at my side a moment later. "Are you all right, Shawna?"

He used my first name! I exulted inwardly. But outwardly, though I hated myself for it, I said, as weakly, as I could, "I'm fine. If you can just . . . give me your hand?"

He gave me his hand. I let him help me to my feet. Then I staggered against him. He caught me, arms going around me. I nestled into his shoulder. "Thank you, Anthony," I whispered. Then (not wanting to overdo it) I straightened. "I'm so sorry," I said. I coughed again, just for effect. "I think I took on a little seawater, and my pumps don't seem to be working."

He patted me on the back solicitously. I gave him my best smile.

All this time, rain poured down, wind howled, and the sea thundered, but for a moment, we were in our own little bubble. I felt it, and I was sure Anthony did, too.

Which was exactly what I wanted.

Colonel Everest popped our bubble by suddenly appearing at our side. "We're right where we're supposed to be," he shouted above the howl of the wind. "Sergeant Mokoum says we should find shelter just a few dozen yards inside the trees. That rock at the forest's edge is the smugglers' signpost. Come on."

Sergeant Mokoum already stood by the rock in question. It looked like a raised finger, as though the shore were making an eternally rude gesture at the sea. I couldn't tell if it had been placed there, or if it was natural.

Is anything natural, in a Shaped world?

We entered the wind-whipped forest, branches lashing us as though trying to drive us out again. Navigating by lightning flash, I would have been hopelessly lost within a few feet, but Sergeant Mokoum seemed to know exactly what he was looking for. Sure enough, maybe thirty yards in from the forest's edge—not that I could see it anymore—we reached a steep, rocky slope. The lightning revealed a dark hole beneath a stone ledge. It looked like nothing more than an animal den, but Mokoum ducked into it, and one by one we followed, Colonel Everest bringing up the rear, behind me and Anthony.

By the time it was my turn, yellow light flickered in the underground space beyond the opening. When I straightened, after emerging from a short tunnel I'd had to bend double to navigate, I found myself in a dry, lantern-lit chamber, maybe thirty feet wide and twice that long. Stacked crates lined the back wall and half a dozen cots the right. Logs around a blackened firepit in the center served as rough benches. To my left, water, presumably from a natural spring, flowed out of a short length of pipe into a stone basin on a masonry pedestal. Constantly overflowing the basin, the water fell into the gravel surrounding the pedestal's base, where it vanished.

Two lanterns on each wall provided the light. Mokoum was already carrying wood from the back of the chamber and piling it in the firepit—clearly, the smugglers stockpiled it to ensure a dry supply. In a few moments Mokoum had a good-sized fire burning there, and the rest of us, eleven men and me, stood around it, wet clothes steaming. My gaze followed the smoke from the fire to the hole in the ceiling through which it disappeared. "Doesn't the smoke show above the hillside?" I asked the sergeant.

He laughed. "Yes, but it does not pour out in a steady stream; it dribbles out through a dozen tiny crevices, barely noticeable unless you are standing right on top of it. And anyway, who is there to see it tonight and in this weather?"

Food followed fire: dried meat, dried fruit, and thin, salty, crunchy sheets of what Mokoum identified as dried seaweed. To wash it down (and believe me, it needed washing down) there was some not-bad beer drawn from a barrel Mokoum found among the stores, although Colonel Everest limited each man to one small glass. "Water is for thirst," he said. "Of that, you can have as much as you want."

Not being under his command, and rather wanting to emphasize that fact, I was tempted to have *two* glasses, but keeping my wits about me continued to force me to minimize my consumption of alcohol. (Which makes it sound like I have a drinking problem. I don't, but there had certainly been a few times in this world when I would have enjoyed imbibing more than I'd allowed myself to . . .)

I made sure I sat next to Anthony on his log by the fire. I made sure our hips touched. He moved away. I waited a few minutes, not looking at him, just staring into the fire as I sipped my beer and my clothes slowly dried, then I stretched out my legs and rolled my shoulders—and somehow, once I had done that, our hips were touching again. This time, he didn't move away: he couldn't, without falling off the log. I could tell he was uncomfortable—but I pretended I wasn't aware of anything.

And hated myself a little more.

The plan had originally been to head inland immediately upon landing, but the storm precluded that. Even Mokoum couldn't guarantee we wouldn't get lost in these conditions. So, instead, we waited it out.

As an ambassador (and a woman), the escorting of whom to Phileas was the entire purpose of this mission, I of course rated one of the cots, without question. I wasn't about to argue. Anthony moved mine to the other side of the room from the others, close to the water basin, but of course there was no possibility of real privacy (although the small, smelly chamber in the back with a hole in the floor that served as a toilet at least had a curtain hung across it), so, much as I would have loved to have stripped out of my clothes and hung them by the fire to dry, I couldn't. It might have aided my flirt-with-Anthony efforts, but I didn't have any desire to titillate an entire squad of soldiers.

I slept fitfully, not too surprisingly, since the cots creaked whenever someone rolled over or changed places with one of the others, some men snored (and others made other noises I could have done without hearing), and every now and then a particularly violent gust from outside managed to make it through the short tunnel and cause an explosion of sparks from the fire. It wasn't until near the end of the interminable night that I slept soundly, only to wake with a start as someone cleared his throat above my head.

I blinked up at Colonel Everest.

"Morning, Ambassador," he said. I wasn't sure if he meant that as a greeting or a simple statement of fact. "The storm has subsided. We will now begin our journey inland."

I stretched and yawned and stood up, wishing, more than anything, for a hot shower and an even hotter cup of coffee. Instead, I got the aforementioned hole in the floor in the stinky alcove, the state of which by this time was best left to the imagination, and a piece of jerky that seemed likely to require as many calories to masticate as it would provide in nutrition.

Then it was out through the tunnel and back into the jungle. The sky remained cloudy, but that didn't seem to be doing much to alleviate the heat and humidity. My clothes had more or less dried overnight, but by the time I'd struggled up the slope in which the smugglers' hideout was set, they were soaked again, this time in my own sweat. The white cotton that had seemed far too thin in last night's storm now felt like wearing a bathrobe in a sauna. It was almost enough to make me wish I was on one of those islands Mark Tierce had written about where nudity was *de rigueur*.

Almost.

Without Mokoum, we would have lost the trail a dozen times in the first hour. I'd pictured something like a game trail, but there was no visible path through the underbrush. Instead, a series of signs pointed the way: the fork of a tree, a rock, a depression, an anthill—an endless series of markers Mokoum had miraculously managed to memorize. The only obvious indicators of a trail were occasional blazes in the trunks of trees, and most of those, Mokoum told me when I asked him, were actually red herrings, designed to send anyone unfamiliar with the trail off into the trackless forest.

I stayed as close to Anthony as I could during the march, but I was mostly too sweaty and struggling to even try to flirt. Colonel Everest, Anthony, and the rest of my escort (whose names I had made no effort to learn, since I hoped to be rid of them soon) seemed far less bothered by the heat and humidity and hilliness. *If I'd known I was going to be sent on a quest across multiple Shaped worlds through an extra-dimensional Labyrinth, I'd have signed up for a gym membership last year,* I thought, and managed to dredge up a small smile in response to my own witticism. If you could call it that.

The next two days were more of the same: heat, humidity, and (as the colonel had warned in the palace chart room) mosquitoes, swarms of them, in numbers that would have eaten us alive (or possibly simply picked us up and flown us away somewhere to suck dry later) if not for a liberal smearing on all exposed skin of something Mokoum concocted from leaves, berries, and . . . well, I know what it smelled like, but I hoped I was wrong and wasn't about to ask. The only break from the miserable slogging through miserable terrain (which, it occurred to me more than once, didn't even have to *exist* in a Shaped world), was an hour or so of sitting under an overhang in the ravine we were following, while a dozen armed men picked their agonizingly slow way along the edge of the gully above us. Whether they were Robur's men or an anti-smuggling patrol of Free City Guardsmen, no one told me before we were chivvied into our cramped and muddy hideout. I amused myself watching beetles the size of small dogs (only a *slight* exaggeration) crawling in and out of the countless holes in the back of the space, and imagining I could feel them crawling on me, too, although that was only actually the case half a dozen times, tops.

When, shuddering (at least, *I* was shuddering), we

emerged into the open, I asked Anthony who the men had been, endeavoring (very easily) to sound a little shaken by the encounter and in need of reassurance.

"A patrol of Robur's," he said. "Or that's what Mokoum reported."

"How could he tell? Were they actually in uniform?"

Anthony laughed. "No, of course not. No more than we. Mokoum recognized their weapons. Robur's men carry repeating rifles of a design no one else uses."

"More advanced than yours?"

I should have known better. Anthony bristled. "Different only. Definitely not more advanced. We are carrying the very latest Leniebroek Mark VIIs!"

Boys and their toys, I thought. "I'm so glad to hear it," I said. Then I turned my back to him and twisted my head around to look over my shoulder. I may have smiled coyly (again, not entirely sure). "Would you check my back and make sure there aren't any of those awful beetles on me anywhere?"

"Of course," he said gallantly. He stepped closer and ran his hands down my back. When he brushed—just brushed, as if by accident—my buttocks, I felt a surge of satisfaction . . . mixed, as always, with guilt.

I walked next to Anthony as we pushed on up the gully, Mokoum continuing to scout ahead of us on the right and a soldier by the unimaginative name of Smith to the left. Splashing through a shallow rivulet, I fretted I might have missed an opportunity. If I had known that we were hiding from Robur's men, I could have perhaps made my presence known . . .

. . . and sparked a firefight in which multiple people might have been killed, including Anthony, or even me, by mischance if not deliberately, and in which, after all, the colonel's men might have been victorious, thanks to their "Leniebroek Mark VIIs," after which, if I were still alive, the colonel would have been rightly peeved with me and possibly aborted the mission and hauled me back to the coast and the waiting *Narwhal.*

No. My original plan was the best. Get into Phileas, escape my escort with Anthony's help, and *then* find some way to make contact with Robur's followers and have myself taken to his capital.

"When will we reach the city border, Colonel?" I called to our leader, a few strides ahead.

He glanced back. "Tonight, if we are fortunate, we will rest in a proper inn within the Free City's territory."

"Wonderful," I said.

And it came to pass, as the King James Version of the Bible likes to put it, that everything foretold by the colonel happened just as he said, and lo! as darkness descended, I found myself in a bed, in an inn, in the village of Palik, which, just as Mokoum had promised, the smugglers' trail had led us to. Both inn and village clearly knew they were the terminus of a smugglers' trail, since there had been not the slightest concern exhibited by anyone at the sudden arrival of a party of armed men . . . and one woman.

The bed boasted a hay-stuffed mattress considerably more comfortable than either the cot in the cave or the ground of the jungle in our two overnight camps along the way. Better yet, mosquito netting hung all around it—and a good thing, too, since the windows were thrown open in the vain hope of cooling the room.

You would think, I thought as I lay there, stripped but still sweating—I slapped a mosquito that had infiltrated the bed space before the netting was properly arranged—*that the Shaper would have advanced the technology of his pocket world far enough to develop air-conditioning.*

Maybe he did, I thought, just before sleep finally claimed me (two days on the trail proving a rather effective sleeping potion despite the stickiness of . . . everything). *But based on what I've seen, probably only for himself.*

SIXTEEN

IN THE MORNING, feeling grungy (as well as not having air-conditioning, the inn offered neither shower nor bath, and about the toilet facilities, the less said the better), I walked beside Anthony again as we started toward the Free City, all weapons now out of sight, although the long cloth-wrapped bundles on the soldiers' backs, it seemed to me, could hardly be construed as anything else: a fact I noted to Anthony.

"It is not illegal to carry firearms," he said. "It is only illegal to carry them openly."

"And wrapping them in a sack counts as not carrying them openly?" I glanced at his waist. "And what about that big . . . sword . . . of yours?"

He was indeed wearing a sword, openly, as were the others, but I knew I'd delivered the question with just the right amount of double-entendreness by the pink that tinged his ears. He was remarkably easy to both tease and read. He was, in fact, so far as I could tell, the very model of a majorly nice guy, and again I felt bad about how I was using him.

Trying to, anyway: I wouldn't know if I'd succeeded until push came to shove.

Which could happen as early as this evening. I considered reaching out and taking his hand, but stopped myself. That would seem too forward, too obvious. He would immediately disengage if I did that and distance himself from me, and I didn't know when I might need him close. He might not help me even when the moment came, of course . . . but my plan, such as it was, depended on him doing so, and I couldn't risk jeopardizing the tenuous relationship I'd been building with him by making a wrong move at this late stage.

It had been dark when we'd reached the inn the night before, so I hadn't had an opportunity to look around at this new land. Now I could see that the omnipresent and oppressive jungle had given way to cleared land, although the windbreaks . . . if you called them that in this kind of farmland . . . were palms, instead of the alder, ash, poplars, and birch that were more common in Montana. (My Montana, anyway.) Also, of course, we didn't grow rice in Montana, and the water-soaked fields we were traveling between on the raised roadbed were clearly intended for nothing else.

The rice fields stretched on forever, it seemed, although there were mountains in the distance, to the north and east and south—every direction but west, directly behind us—where other things were presumably grown. Beans? Breadfruit? Bananas? Broccoli? Blueberries? Blackberries? Beets? Things that *didn't* start with a "B"?

This is a Shaped world, I reminded myself. *Maybe they're growing ambrosia or collecting the manna that falls from heaven every morning. Anyway, what does it matter? You're not here as a tourist!*

The landscape remained monotonously the same. We joined another road, which then joined another, each slightly busier than the last. Eventually, we were walking along what was clearly the Free City's equivalent of a major highway, crowded (relatively) with wagons and horses and people, whose dress, though it varied in detail, was close enough to what we wore that we blended into the stream without anyone giving us a second look. I even saw other men carrying covered weapons.

About three hours after that, as the sun sank behind us, we crested a ridge and saw the Free City of Phileas for the first time: high walls of black stone, topped with battlements; at the center, a fortress, roofed in black slate and flying blue-and-white banners from its many towers; between us and the walls, a drawbridge over an actual honest-to-God moat, leading to a portcullised gate. Phileas was the distillation of every medieval city in every medieval fantasy in every book, television show, or movie of the last fifty years.

Which meant, for me, it was sticking-out-like-a-dislocated-thumb *wrong* for a land that otherwise gave off Central American banana-republic vibes. Shaper's work for sure.

I didn't like the looks of those walls, and especially that moat. Even if I slipped away from my escorts, I'd be trapped in the city, with no way out except through gates, where they could easily post a watch. *Well, I'll cross that drawbridge when I come to it,* I told myself.

As a group, we came to it within another hour, as the setting sun stretched our shadows out in front of us like long black fingers clawing for purchase on the road. We crossed the foul-smelling, weed-choked moat, and passed through the gate beyond, without incident. The Free City Guardsman posted there, despite their city's medieval appearance, carried not only swords but carbines and pistols, and wore uniforms of nineteenth- rather than fourteenth-century cut, of the same shade of dark blue as the banners flapping from the towers. They looked a bit like Civil War reenactors on the Union side. They stared at us suspiciously, but they stared at everyone suspiciously.

The city was every bit as medieval fantasy inside as out. Looking up the road toward the central fortress, I recalled from my reading on the *Narwhal* that Phileas was ruled by a triumvirate of "kritarchs." None of the positions were hereditary: whenever a kritarch died, or became too ill to carry on, a council of electors, made up of the . . .

Not important, I told myself. I wasn't going to be around long enough to get caught up in the excitement of a Phileasian election.

Aside from the fortress, buildings over two stories were exceedingly rare. Although the main drag we were on ran straight, the adjoining narrow streets meandered, so that I could never see very far down them, catching, in the rapidly fading light, glimpses of cobblestones and lantern-lit windows, barred doors and barrels, and occasionally, shadowy individuals engaged in what always looked like suspicious activity, even though that was probably a function of the deepening shadows. All the same, it made me uneasy.

Along our street, still busy with wagons, though the number of pedestrians had lessened and the shops all seemed to be closed, lights began to spring to life as men moved down both sides, raising lit wicks on the ends of long poles to touch to lamps on black iron posts, first using a hook on the pole to open the glass housing. Like the carbines the Free City Guardsmen carried, the bright, hissing gas flames inside glass cages belied the otherwise medieval appearance of the city.

My escorts had arranged themselves in front of and behind me, with Anthony beside me and the colonel directly in front of us. I jogged a couple of steps to fall in next to him. "What's our plan?" I asked.

He glanced at me, his face pale in the gaslight. "The same plan it has been since we first discussed it. Escort you to the Catacombs of the Holy—on the far side of the city—so you can open this Portal of yours and travel back to your own world, from which our Dread Prince anticipates you will bring allies to help us defeat Robur. What part of that has been unclear to you until now?"

"I know that," I said, feeling a little stung. "But surely we aren't going straight to these Catacombs?"

"Why shouldn't we?"

Because if we do, I might not have a chance to escape. "Because I'm hungry, thirsty, and exhausted. Opening a Portal isn't like opening a door. It takes energy . . . energy I don't have right now. I doubt I could so much as sense the location of the potential Portal tonight—much less open it—even if I were standing right on top of it."

The colonel frowned. "You're saying you need a night's rest?"

"Yes," I said. "With some decent food, and a good

night's sleep, I can take us straight there in the morning and do what must be done."

"Every minute of delay adds to the risk," the colonel pointed out. "Robur has spies and men aplenty in the Free City. Someone may already have noted our arrival and think us worth investigating further."

"Would they attack us?"

"I don't know. The treaties both we and Robur have with the Free City prohibit it . . . but I believe Robur's men would violate a treaty in an instant if they thought it gave them an advantage. To think otherwise is to live in a fantasy world." (I womanfully didn't point out that from my perspective, he already *was* living in a fantasy world.) He gave me a sharp look, his blue eyes glinting in the gaslight beneath his bushy gray eyebrows. "You are certain you can't open a Portal tonight?"

"Absolutely," I said firmly. Since I couldn't open a Portal at *all*—only Karl could do that—it was even the truth.

He sighed. "Very well, then. I'll see what Mokoum can suggest." He raised a hand to call a halt. The men scattered, presumably in an attempt to be less conspicuous, standing in pairs and trios here and there on both sides of the street, talking. Wagons, now with headlamps lit, trundled by, the drivers giving the men suspicious glances. So few pedestrians were about now that the Rajians' attempt to look inconspicuous instead gave them the distinct air of a street gang waiting for a rumble with rivals. (Although that may have just been my fondness for *West Side Story* talking.)

Anthony, I was pleased to see, waited for me alone in the deep shadow beneath the awning of a closed shop. As I approached him, while my face was still gaslit, I tried to adopt an expression of dismay—successfully, apparently, because Anthony's first question when I reached him was, "What's wrong?"

"We need to talk," I said.

He blinked down at me. "We *are* talking."

He had me there. I looked around to make sure no one else was close enough to overhear us, then leaned in close and lowered my voice anyway. "It's Colonel Everest."

"What about him?"

"He scares me."

My eyes had adjusted to the shadows enough that I could tell Anthony was frowning. "Why? I admit he's a bit gruff, but I've never thought of him as scary."

"You're not a woman." I gave him a fleeting smile. "As I know very well."

He blushed. "I wish you'd quit bringing that up."

"Sorry," I said. "It's just . . . you're so easy to tease about it."

"What does you're being a woman have to do with . . ." His eyes widened. "You don't mean he . . ."

I pressed close to him. "Last night," I whispered. "In the inn. He came into my room."

I felt Anthony stiffen. "He *what?*"

"Not like that," I said hastily. I didn't want Anthony confronting the colonel in the street right here and now. "He knocked. He woke me up. He said it was vital he talk to me. I thought it was about the mission. I let him in. But he was . . . creepy." I paused. "It was hot, so I wasn't . . . I only had a sheet wrapped around my . . ." I took a deep breath. "He . . . leered at me. He clearly . . . wanted . . ." I let my voice trail off.

"Are you sure you're not imagining things?" Anthony said, his tone the coldest thing I'd experienced since landing in this steamy jungle land.

"I'm sure," I said. "Just now . . . you saw me go to him . . ."

"Yes."

"I told him I wanted to go straight on to the Catacombs *tonight,* to open the Portal as soon as I can and go home." I raised my head and met Anthony's eyes squarely, willing him to believe the lie. Unlike in my own world, here I didn't really have the power to do that. But there were other forces at work I hoped would prove just as persuasive. "He refused. He insisted we stay in an inn. I think . . . I think he thinks he can do whatever he wants now because I'll be leaving, and who's going to stop him?

Who will even know? He thinks I won't tell anyone because I'm desperate to get home, and he could keep that from happening. I could have an 'accident' . . ." I took a deep, shuddering breath, acting my little heart out. "I *have* to open that Portal, Anthony. For my own sake, and to keep the promises I made to Prince Dakkar. I can't risk failing, and that means I'm at Colonel Everest's mercy. If he comes into my room again tonight and wants me to . . . to do something . . . I may have to do it. *I have to find that Portal!*" That last sentence was close enough to the truth I had no difficulty making it come out with sudden fierceness.

"I'll guard your door," Anthony said, tone still cold and sharp as a frozen dagger.

Crap. "No," I said. "That would still leave him in control tomorrow. He could contrive an accident . . . for both of us." I turned my head, flicking my gaze around the others, scattered here and there. "These men—he hand-picked them. They're all loyal to him. And you . . . I *made* you come on this trip. You're Flying Force. There's bad blood between Flying Force and the Army." I didn't know that for sure, but rivalry between different branches of the armed forces had been a thing for as long as there had been different branches of armed forces, so it seemed a safe bet. "I don't want you hurt." I turned my eyes back to him. "What I need is to escape. To get out of the inn tonight without him knowing. I don't need *him* to get to the Portal, or to open it." True enough. "I will still keep my promise to the prince to the best of my ability." Also true, since I had *no* ability to keep that promise. "This has nothing to do with the prince."

Anthony kept his eyes locked on mine. I willed myself not to look away. It wasn't easy.

"You're asking me to disobey a superior officer," he said at last.

"He's Army, you're Flying Force."

"That changes nothing."

"Has he ordered you not to help me escape?"

Anthony frowned. "You are playing with words. My duty is—"

"Your duty is to help me get to the Portal so I can open it and, with luck, aid the prince in his prosecution of the war against Robur. Your orders were to serve as my batman—my personal guard and assistant. Well, I need your assistance, batman." Even in that moment, I almost smiled at that. "By helping me succeed in my mission, you're *obeying* your orders, not disobeying them." Inspiration struck, and I blurted, "Anthony . . . you know how, in fairy tales, unicorns will only come and lay their heads in the laps of virgins?" *At least, in the fairy tales in my world.* I hoped that was the kind of thing Robur had let copy over from the First World.

"Unicorns aren't real," Anthony said, an edge of annoyance in his voice that made me fear I was losing him.

"Virgins are."

He stared at me, still frowning; then he blinked, and his eyebrows lifted. "You're saying . . ."

"I'm a virgin," I said (okay, lied). "Only virgins can open the Portals. No one knows why. That's just the way the magic works. The way a lot of magic works."

"Magic," Anthony said.

It was my turn to let a little annoyance through. "Yes, magic! If you're going to believe I come from another world, Lieutenant Blackwell, and that I'm able to open a Portal to it, then you're also going to have to believe in magic. Magic, virgins, and the power of the latter to perform the former."

"You said if the colonel asked you to . . . do something . . . you would do it," he said. "But then you wouldn't be a virgin."

"There are things he could make me do that would leave me a virgin." *Ugh,* I thought, hating myself. But I didn't take it back.

Anthony looked away, up the street, to where Colonel Everest stood in deep conversation with Mokoum. In the dark, I couldn't tell if he was blushing, but I would have been willing to bet on it.

I followed his gaze, just in time to see the colonel nod, and Mokoum hurry away, presumably to obtain the lodging I had insisted on . . . and just told Anthony the *colonel* had insisted on. I hoped that lie didn't catch me out. (The lie about being me a virgin I figured I probably didn't have to worry about.)

"It is very hard for me to believe Colonel Everest would do such a thing," Anthony said, keeping his eyes on the man in question.

"Did you know him before this journey?" I thought I knew the answer to that, and hoped I was right.

"No. But he is an officer in our Dread Prince's Army."

"I don't know how things are in your world," I said, "but in my world merely being an officer in an army— *anybody*'s army—does not necessarily translate into being a perfect human being."

He snorted a little at that, and that sound of rather grim amusement told me I had him. "Very well," he said, looking back at me again. "Once we are in the inn . . . I will figure out what must be done to get you secretly away."

I felt a huge surge of relief . . . and a huge surge of guilt at the way I had manipulated him to reach this point. "Thank you," I whispered.

He bowed his head a little, a formal gesture, though at least he refrained from clicking his heels. He straightened. "We should rejoin the others."

"If the colonel suspects I've told you what I've told you . . ."

"He will detect nothing amiss," Anthony said. "I promise you."

I hoped he was right. I didn't know if they had poker in this world, but Anthony's tendency to blush and look flustered when I said something that embarrassed him did not fill me with confidence he could bluff effectively.

I just hoped *I* could. Because, in truth, I was the one gambling . . . and I'd just risked everything on one deal of the cards.

SEVENTEEN

"HE WILL DETECT nothing amiss," Anthony had promised me, but Colonel Everest took one look at his face when we rejoined the others and said, "What's wrong?"

"Nothing," Anthony said, with complete and total unbelievability.

The colonel raised an eyebrow at him, then at me, then snorted. "Lieutenant, I believe you've been shot down." He took a step toward Anthony, who stiffened into attention. "I trust I don't need to remind you that the ambassador is under our protection. My *personal* protection, in fact. You will comport yourself accordingly."

"Yes, sir!" said Anthony, staring straight ahead, face aflame.

Perfect, I thought—both the colonel's slapping down of Anthony with the insistence I was under his *personal* protection, and Anthony's flaming face. The colonel could not believe Anthony would dare to do anything against him, and how could Anthony take that "personal protection" bit except creepily, in light of what I'd told him? All that remained was to see what opportunities for surreptitious departure our lodgings provided.

If any.

Think positively, I told myself.

Mokoum returned within a few minutes and led us around a corner and down a narrow, dirty, and meandering side street, through a courtyard, down an even narrower, dirtier, and more meandering street, and finally through an open gate into yet *another* courtyard, paved in cobblestones. Empty horse stalls huddled beneath lean-to roofs attached to the walls to our left and right. Directly ahead lay an inn, a ramshackle wooden structure, at three stories one of the largest buildings I'd yet seen, though that was all it had going for it. Both its thatched roof and the broad portico facing us sagged. Yellow lantern light spilled into the courtyard through an open door and two big windows with cracked panes. Smoke drifted from a central chimney. Candlelight flickered behind only one of the upper-story windows. The rest were dark and shuttered, except for a couple where the shutters hung askew.

One might have expected raucous laughter to spill out into the courtyard, too, but the dark windows had already testified to the inn's remarkable underpopulation, as had the lack of horses in the aforementioned stalls. "Not a thriving establishment, I take it?" I said to the colonel.

He glanced at Mokoum, who answered, "I did not think you would want one. Although this is an inn, and can certainly put us up for the night, the rental of rooms and provision of victuals is really a . . . sideline."

"More of your smuggler connections?"

Mokoum grinned at me. "Does it matter, ma'am? It is a quiet place which is not troubled by the Free City Guardsmen . . ."

". . . because they've all been bribed," the colonel said. "Which makes it perfect for our purposes. Well done, Sergeant." He turned to the rest of us. "We will spend the night here, so that the ambassador may . . . recover her strength." He gave me a measuring look as he said it, and I hoped Anthony saw it and took it in exactly the wrong way. The colonel turned back to Mokoum. "Perhaps you should enter first, Sergeant."

"Perhaps I should, sir." He led us toward the open door.

What lay beyond was definitely a "common room" in the grand tradition of fantasy novels and *Dungeons and Dragons* campaigns: round tables, wooden chairs, a giant fireplace (unlit, fortunately, considering the heat) with the stuffed head of a hippopotamus over the mantel (okay, *that* was a bit weird), a bar, kegs of beer, a jolly innkeeper . . .

Scratch the last part. Our host proved to be a sallow-faced little man with only a few strands of graying hair crossing his liver-spotted pate. His hands shook as he took the money the colonel offered him, after Mokoum had murmured a few words of introduction. Then he disappeared into the back, to be replaced by a statuesque woman, both taller and considerably bustier than me, wearing a white blouse, a long black skirt, and a blue apron. Her black hair, streaked with gray, was drawn back into a severe bun. "Mr. Timmins says I'm to feed you lot," she said without preamble. "There's stew, or, if you prefer, you can have stew. There's bread, baked fresh this morning, so it's only a little crusty. If that's not good enough for you, I've got a few moldy biscuits you can have instead. Butter and honey. And to drink, ale or water—but if you drink the water, you should know the outhouse is a good forty feet out back of the inn, and you might not make it."

I blinked. And then I laughed.

Nobody else did, so the woman's brown eyes flicked to me. One corner of her mouth lifted in an almost-smile. "Sit yourselves, and I'll be about it," she said, and disappeared into the back after "Mr. Timmins"—boss, lover, or husband, I couldn't say.

We sorted ourselves at tables. I sat with Anthony, of course; the colonel joined us, which put me on edge. Maybe it did Anthony, too, but I couldn't tell. Maybe he would have made a poker player after all.

Not that it mattered—the colonel was only interested in talking to me. "What can we expect tomorrow?" he asked.

"I don't know," I said. "I have never been to the Catacombs of the Holy."

"Not that," he said impatiently. "When you open this . . . Portal. What will happen?"

"Oh," I said. I glanced at Anthony; he was studiously ignoring our conversation, instead looking at the bar as though trying to decide which of the beers to try. Since none of the kegs were labeled, it seemed a fruitless exercise. I looked back at the colonel. "Nothing dramatic," I said. "There will be a flash of light, perhaps, and then . . . a doorway. It might be inside an existing doorframe, or simply . . . hanging in the air."

The colonel frowned. "And then you will leave us."

"Yes," I said. With Anthony sitting there, I would have liked to have made that "yes" sound as if I were relieved, as if I couldn't wait to escape the colonel, but I also didn't want the colonel wondering what the hell was wrong with me—which, if I acted *too* weird, he very well might, perhaps to the point of putting a guard on my room.

"I will insist that your room be on the third floor tonight," the colonel said, "so that it cannot be accessed from outside, and I will place a sentry at your door." My heart skipped a beat. *Dammit, no!* "This is not the kind of establishment where I am comfortable leaving you unguarded."

"I will gladly volunteer," Anthony said, looking around from his perusal of the beer selection. "I am the ambassador's batman. It is my duty to—"

"Not tonight, Lieutenant," the colonel said. "The Flying Force is not as accustomed to long night watches as are we in the army."

That was so transparently stupid a thing to say that it suddenly occurred to me that Colonel Everest, having misconstrued my previous conversation with Anthony as having ended with me turning down his improper proposition, might be placing a guard on my door, and refusing Anthony's request to serve in that capacity, to protect me from my own batman. *He's being gallant,* I thought. *How annoying is that?*

The colonel's gaze returned to me. "Bishop will take first watch, I think; Crossman, second; Peacock, third." I still didn't know my escorts well enough to be able to put faces to those names. "Mokoum has been invaluable in our journey inland, so I will let him sleep, along with the others."

"I'm touched by your concern," I said. *Infuriated* would have been a better word, but I kept it to myself.

"It is my duty to be concerned for you and about you," said the colonel, "until you open the Portal and leave us for your own world." He twisted around at the sound of footsteps as the woman returned, carrying a platter bearing three bowls of stew, three mugs of beer, three spoons, and a plate with a loaf of bread, a blob of butter, a pot of honey, and a knife. She placed the platter on our table, gave me a wink (which I took as a symbol of female solidarity), and then departed to get the food for Mokoum and the others.

Female solidarity, I thought again, watching her disappear into the kitchen. *I wonder . . .*

We ate in silence, both Anthony and the colonel seemingly disinterested in saying more. Mokoum and the others only talked in low voices, taking their cue from the colonel's silence, I guessed. As for me, I kept my head down and ate mechanically—the stew, by the way, was excellent—hoping Anthony would take it as a sign of my discomfort in the colonel's presence.

Colonel Everest finished first. Draining the last of his mug of ale, he stood, said, "I will assign your sentries. Have a good night. I look forward to the conclusion of our mission on the morrow," and then strode over to the other tables.

Anthony leaned close. "He's setting a guard," he murmured. "Do you really think he will pay you an unwelcome visit?"

"Do you really think that among the men he hand-picked for this mission aren't those he has enlisted *before* to help him with this kind of thing?" I said softly. "At least the three he named to be my guards? Anthony, all I know is what happened in the last inn. And . . . call it feminine intuition. That man scares me. Even if I tell him only a virgin can open the Portal, he might not care, might not leave me . . . intact. He doesn't believe I'll come back with help for the prince, anyway. He might just take what he wants from me, then have me killed, and lie to the prince about what happened. He might say

I escaped—or he might even say I succeeded and vanished into thin air, confident none of his men will tell the prince the truth. The prince would wait for me to come back, I never would, and he'd just decide I was a liar from the beginning. Whether Everest rapes me or kills me, the result is the same: I will never leave this world, and the help my world could provide your Dread Prince will never materialize."

"I would tell the prince the truth," Anthony said.

"So, the colonel kills you, too, and tells the prince you couldn't bear to leave me and chose to follow me into my world, instead." Which was all but impossible for a Shaped individual, of course, but nobody but me knew that.

Anthony's right hand, resting on the table, clenched into a fist. "Then I must get you away tonight. The guards will make that difficult . . ."

I nodded in the direction of the woman, who had taken up a position behind the bar, polishing mugs that, so far as I could see, needed no polishing. Probably she was really keeping an eye on the strange men who had so suddenly invaded her common room. "I have an idea," I said. "You should join the others. If you can make them believe you tried to proposition me and got shot down, like the colonel suggested . . ."

Anthony's ears turned pink again. "Of course," he said.

"I'll go over to look at the hippopotamus after I've spoken to our hostess," I said. "Come over and I'll tell you what's what—and then slap your face."

"What? Oh. I understand." He nodded once, then got up—rather abruptly, as if I'd said something that offended him—grabbed his chair, dragged it over to one of the other tables, and sat down. Colonel Everest, who was heading toward the archway that led into the wing of the inn to our left, glanced back at him, then at me, but didn't slacken his stride. In a moment, he had vanished down the hallway.

I got up from the table at which I had been left in solitary splendor, and walked over to the bar, plunking myself down on one of the stools of black wood that fronted it. "Hi," I said to the woman.

"Hello," she said. She held up the mug she'd been polishing, checked it for spots in the light of the two lanterns hung in reflectors behind the bar, then put it back on its shelf behind her.

"I'm Shawna," I volunteered.

She raised an eyebrow at me as she turned around again. "Jovita," she replied.

I glanced over my shoulder at the men, then leaned forward and lowered my voice. "I need your help," I murmured.

Jovita glanced at the men, too, then took down the same mug she'd just polished and started polishing it again. "I'm listening."

"I fell in with these men by accident," I said. "I'm from a village near the border . . ." *What was the name of that place? Oh, right.* "Palik. Have you heard of it?"

"I have," said Jovita.

"My husband . . . departed unexpectedly with another woman, leaving me destitute. I have family here in Phileas, but the journey from Palik seemed far too hazardous for an unaccompanied woman to undertake." I knew I was talking like a character from a nineteenth-century novel . . . originally in French, translated into English, no doubt . . . but I couldn't stop now I'd begun.

"I met the leader of these men, who styles himself a 'colonel,' by chance, and he, learning of my plight, offered to conduct me safely to Phileas." I lowered my voice still further. "But he would not let me separate myself from him and his disreputable followers when we reached the city, instead insisting I come with them to this inn. And now, he insists I spend the night here, with guards posted at my door for my own 'safety.'"

"I take it you don't think safety is really what's on his mind," Jovita said.

I shook my head. "No. Last night, he came into my room when I was . . . not properly dressed . . . and I felt he had . . . designs on me."

"Fucking bastard," said Jovita conversationally. "Didn't like the looks of him the moment I saw him. Want him knifed overnight?"

That caught me by surprise. I looked for the flicker of a smile Jovita had showed me earlier when I'd laughed at what she'd said, but the look she gave me this time held no levity. "No," I said hastily. "No, I don't want him *killed*."

"Don't see why not," Jovita said. She put the mug back on the shelf, pulled down one every bit as clean, and began polishing it. "He certainly wouldn't be the first to check in but never leave."

I blinked at that turn of phrase but managed to forestall myself asking if one of the rooms had mirrors on the ceiling and pink champagne on ice. "I just want to get away."

"And that young man you were sitting with after the old guy left is going to help you?"

I nodded. "He . . . interrupted . . . the colonel last night, or things might have gone badly."

"You mean you'd invited him into your room, but the colonel showed up first?" Jovita said. She raised an eyebrow. "Over the shocking departure of your husband so quickly?"

I opened my mouth, then closed it again.

This time Jovita *did* laugh. "I'm not judging, dear, I heartily approve. If your husband ran out on you, I say you cuckold him at the first opportunity, and as often as you can. Get yourself pregnant right away. Then you can claim the brat is your husband's and sue him for child support."

That was such a modern-sounding notion I gaped at her. Then I closed my mouth. "I'll . . . take that under advisement," I finally said.

"You do that," Jovita said cheerfully. "All right, here's the plan . . ."

Half an hour later, I stood by the window of a third-floor room that overlooked the enclosed backyard of the inn. The room boasted (if that's the right word), a narrow bed, a hard, wooden chair, and a table, on which burned a single candle. Jovita had brought in a hip bath and had just finished filling it with hot water. The first of the evening's door guards, Bishop, stood watching as she opened the shutters, letting in a flood of marginally cooler air. "Too hot to get into right now," she said to me. "The breeze will help it cool faster."

Then she shooed Bishop into the corridor. "Out," she said. "Keep your prying eyes to yourself." She glanced at me. "Best cover the keyhole, miss."

Bishop reddened and started to splutter an indignant denial, but I only heard the first couple of words before the door closed. I went to it, closed it, and locked it with the key I'd been given—and as I did so, saw that, indeed, the keyhole could be blocked by a little swinging plate. I made sure it was in place, then went back to the bath.

Jovita was right: the water was too hot for me to get into right away, but within a few minutes it was just right. I stripped and took the most enjoyable—and probably the most-needed—bath of my life. (Oh, the water room off my quarters in the prince's palace had been far more luxurious, but for pure satisfaction, nothing beat this one: the dirtier you are, the more you appreciate clean, hot water.) Jovita had provided me with a bar of soap, scented with lilacs, that did adequate double duty as shampoo. She'd also left a surprisingly soft towel. Unfortunately, I had to put my dirty clothes back on, but I still felt more human than I had for a couple of days.

Then I blew out the candle and, fully dressed, lay on the bed and waited.

I didn't mean to sleep, but the bed was comfortable, and it had been another long, hot day of hiking. Despite the warmth, I soon dozed off.

I jerked awake to a noise outside my window. I rolled out of bed and crept across the floor to the window, trying (without much success) to keep the rickety wooden floor from creaking. Sticking my head out, I found myself looking down the length of a collapsible wooden ladder to a dark form climbing my way, barely visible in the dim light of the moon and stars—Anthony (I hoped).

Jovita had told me where the ladder could be found, in a shed out back of the vegetable garden, and provided me other suggestions for our escape. I had passed the plan on to Anthony as we stood in front of the mounted hippopotamus head, just before I slapped him (Anthony, not the hippopotamus), to solidify our cover story.

Jovita had assigned Anthony a special room on the ground floor, through the window of which he could slip out, without fear of being observed from anywhere else in the inn or its grounds. (The fact this inn had such a room told me a lot about its usual clientele.) She had also provided him with a disguise (the fact she had a disguise handy told me even more). Anthony was to don the disguise, sneak into the backyard, and retrieve the ladder from the shed. If the colonel had placed a guard outside, Anthony would have to incapacitate him. The guard might glimpse his attacker, though—hence the disguise.

Once the way was clear, Anthony was to raise the ladder to my window. I'd climb out and down, we'd put the ladder back where it belonged, and then Anthony would unlock the gate in the back wall of the yard with a key Jovita had also provided. I'd slip into the alley and hurry off to my supposed Portal opening. Anthony would lock the gate, sneak back into his room, remove his disguise, hide it under his mattress for Jovita to retrieve later, and be in bed ready to be shocked when my absence was discovered, and the alarm raised. If all went well, Colonel Everest and his men would never know what had happened to me, or that Lieutenant Anthony Blackwell of His Imperial Majesty's Flying Force had had anything to do with it.

It should have been the slickest and lowest-drama escape in history—but it wasn't.

As I looked down at Anthony, wearing what looked like a monk's robe, climbing up the ladder, shouts rang out from the front courtyard—shouts, and then, a moment later, shots. I heard the sound of splintering wood. A woman screamed—Jovita!

Footsteps pounded down the hallway toward my room. I spun as the door crashed open. The lantern light in the hall silhouetted Colonel Everest, wearing only trousers, barefoot and bare-chested, a pistol in his hand.

"The inn is under attack!" he snapped. "We have to get you out of—"

A flash lit the room, accompanied by an impossibly loud sound that made me gasp and clap my hands over my ringing ears—and then over my mouth, stomach heaving, as the colonel, with a neat round hole in the middle of his forehead, toppled forward and crumpled to the floor, revealing a much larger and bloodier hole in the back of his skull, the contents of which were sprayed, wet and glistening, on the wall on the far side of the hall. The smell of burned gunpowder tickled my nose, and the unmistakable scent of voided bowels.

Bishop burst around the corner, gun drawn, then froze, staring, not at me, but over my shoulder. I twisted my head around to see Anthony in the window, his still-smoking pistol now aimed at Bishop. "Leave it, Samuel," he said quietly. "My quarrel is not with you. Go help your mates."

More shouting and shooting and crashing noises came from downstairs. I looked back at Bishop as, face contorted with rage or fear—I couldn't tell which—he swore, turned, and ran down the hall.

"We'd best be on our way, Shawna," said Anthony.

I spun to face him, shocked by what had just happened. "Why . . . ?"

"For you," he said. "For your honor. For the mission. For my prince." He held out his hand. "Come. Hurry. Someone has attacked the inn. Robur's men, Free City Guardsmen, criminals, it doesn't matter. This is our chance to escape."

I took one more horrified look at the blood, black as pitch in the dim light, spreading beneath Colonel Everest's shattered skull, then let Anthony guide me out the window and onto the ladder. It bounced precariously under us as we descended but didn't fall or collapse. Once on the ground, Anthony stripped off the voluminous robe of his disguise, dropping it at the base of the ladder, and we dashed between the vegetable garden and the outhouse to the gate in the back wall of the yard. Anthony pulled a key from the pocket of the black civilian coat he wore beneath the robe, struggled to get it into the keyhole, finally managed it, unlocked the gate, pushed it open . . .

"Hey!" someone shouted behind us.

Anthony grabbed my arm and threw me through the gate, so hard I ended up on my hands and knees in the alley beyond, then snatched his pistol from its holster, turned, and fired back at the inn. I'd fallen in such a way I could see through the gate. I glimpsed two men standing in the inn's open back door, silhouetted against the light inside. They ducked out of sight as Anthony's bullets tore splintering chunks from the head of the door: he'd aimed high, presumably in case the men were part of our escort, not our mysterious attackers. Then he slammed the gate shut.

"Anthony, I'm so sorry," I said, staring up at him as he turned back to me, though I couldn't see his face in the dark alley. "I didn't mean for . . . for you to . . ."

But you always knew it was a possibility, didn't you? a coldly rational part of me pointed out. *Even if he hadn't killed anyone for you, helping you escape would have destroyed his career. Yet you seduced him into helping you, just the same . . .*

I'm trying to save billions of lives in countless worlds, I reminded myself fiercely. But I still felt awful, for him, and for the gallant colonel. "I'm so sorry," I said out loud again. "But also . . . very glad for the company."

I reached out my hand. Anthony took it and pulled me to my feet. I *was* glad for the company, though not in the way I knew Anthony would likely take it. I hated myself again for leading him on . . . but I did it anyway, because now, everything was about survival, and having Anthony with me seemed like my best hope for staying alive.

Anthony squeezed my hand. "Thank you," he said. "And now?"

"We run," I said.

EIGHTEEN

RUNNING FULL TILT at midnight down pitch-black alleys in an unfamiliar city with sketchy ideas of trash removal is an . . . interesting . . . experience. I tripped over something within twenty feet and would have fallen headlong if Anthony hadn't held me up. Clearly, running wasn't conducive to long-term good health, but neither was stopping. We'd only run fifty paces before the gate banged open behind us and footsteps raced after us.

The next thing I tripped over sat up, swearing. I sensed rather than saw whoever it was reach for me, but I kicked, and he swore some more, and then we were past him. "Hey!" he bellowed after us, not very originally. Then our pursuers must have tripped over him, too, because I heard a lot more swearing, and what sounded like a fist meeting flesh, and a moan. It sounded like our pursuers hadn't been gentle about removing the obstacle from their path, but maybe it had bought us a few strides.

I banged my shoulder against a rough stone wall, then the alley took a sharp turn to the right. We rounded the corner. Gaslight glowed ahead of us—one of the major streets. We charged forward . . .

. . . but then I tripped, and crashed into Anthony, and both of us went down into a puddle of I-didn't-want-to-know-what. I got to my hands and knees, scrambled to my feet, turned to help Anthony up—and stopped, because, in the light spilling from that gaslit street, now at my back, I could see the shadowy figures of two men, presumably the ones we had seen silhouetted in the inn's back door, walking toward us, pistols drawn.

Anthony had only made it to one knee. He'd fallen on his back, so he was already looking at the approaching men. His own pistol was still in his hand, but he very carefully did not raise it.

"There's the woman," said the man on my right. I could see now they were dressed pretty much the same as we were, in the drab clothes favored by the locals, but I didn't recognize either. They weren't part of my escort. "Think it's her?"

"Don't know," said the man on my left. "Who are you?" he said to me.

"Who are *you*?" I demanded, rather than answer.

"We surrender," said Anthony. He dropped his pistol and raised his hands. Reluctantly, I followed suit.

"Orders?" said the first man to the second.

"Kill every man," said the second. "If we find a woman, take her to the boss."

I've watched a lot of movies, read a lot of adventure stories. I know when someone says something like, "Kill him, keep her," you're supposed to scream out, "Wait!" and those threatening you will change their minds and take you to their leader and conveniently make it possible for both of you to escape in order to continue your adventures.

I screamed, "Wait!"

The man on the left fired.

The pistol flash stabbed my dark-adapted eyes. The sound wasn't as loud as when Anthony had shot the colonel over my shoulder, but my ears rang just the same. Something warm splattered my cheek. I raised my hand to it, turned toward Anthony . . .

. . . and saw him topple forward and splash face-first into the noxious puddle in which we had fallen.

The back of his head was missing. Just like the colonel's.

The breath whooshed out of me like I'd been punched in the stomach. I dropped to my knees.

The man who had shot Anthony holstered his gun. He started forward.

Anthony's pistol lay between his body and me. White-hot fury flooded me. Barely thinking, I snatched up the pistol in both hands.

"Don't—" the man on the right started to say. He didn't finish, because my first bullet tore through his throat and the base of his skull in a spray of blood, bone, and brain. I snapped my aim to the left, too fast: my second shot only ripped a hole in that man's upper arm, shattering the bone, even as he reached for his pistol again. Clutching the wound, he staggered back, then turned and ran, so that my third shot struck shards of brick from the corner of the wall behind which he'd vanished.

I staggered to my feet. I wanted to throw up. I wanted to weep.

I wanted, more than anything, to go home.

Instead, I turned and ran toward the light at the end of the alley.

My first impulse was to fling the pistol away, but some part of me retained a level of rationality despite the horror and panic threatening to engulf me. I pushed the pistol into the red sash belting my waist, instead, and slowed to a walk as I emerged into the well-lit street—which I recognized immediately as the one we had been walking along before we'd headed to the inn—trying to look nonchalant and undoubtedly failing, since my heart was pounding, I was gasping for breath, and I dripped sweat. Fortunately, there was no one to see me. Glancing back toward the city gate, which lay slightly downhill, I saw distant figures in the street. I remembered passing theaters and restaurants and bars down there. Up here, though, where the shops were long-closed, the city seemed deserted.

Ahead of me, perhaps a hundred yards away, I recognized the shop awning under which I had told Anthony of my distrust of the colonel. My mind immediately shied away from that memory: there were nightmares regarding the colonel and Anthony waiting for me the next time I slept.

I focused instead on the men who had chased us. From what they'd said, they clearly weren't Robur's: they'd seemed to be local toughs, enlisted to keep an eye out for suspicious groups traveling with a woman—which had to mean Robur had a spy in Prince Dakkar's palace, someone who had known about this mission and managed to send word ahead to the Free City.

What had happened back at the inn? Had this local gang wiped out the whole escort? Or had these two seen us and left that battle before it was decided?

I felt something on my cheek, touched it, looked at it, and saw it was blood. Anthony's blood. Remembering the warm spray hitting me when he was shot, I looked down.

Blood had spattered my entire front, mingled with black filth from the puddle into which we'd fallen just before we were caught. I did not look like a respectable woman of the Free City, I looked like I'd just murdered someone (*you did,* an inner voice said coldly) and here I was, walking down a bright-lit street. If a Free City Guardsman saw me . . . or another member of that gang . . . or one of Robur's men . . .

Over there—the mouth of a dark alley. I dashed across the cobblestones and into that dim promise of hiding. It led, after a short distance, into a small courtyard, holding multiple plots of land planted with vegetables and herbs. Doors opened onto it from the backs of the surrounding buildings. *It must be a communal garden,* I thought. A narrow space between two of the buildings led to another a street, not as wide as the one I'd left, and not gaslit, either. In the darkness between the buildings, before I stepped into that street, I stopped, and gulped air, and tried to think.

Those men would have taken me to Robur's forces. All I had to do was let them take me prisoner and, eventually, I would have reached the Shaper. Instead, I had killed one, shot the other, and run. So much for being devoted to my quest.

It had been an instinctive action, an unthinking lashing out at the man who had killed my friend. And Anthony *had* been my friend. Maybe not as much of a friend, or the kind of friend, I had led him to believe he could be, but a friend, nonetheless.

And what had I done? Manipulated him, seduced him, swayed him to my side, to the point he had murdered Colonel Everest to protect my not-at-all-threatened honor, fled with me, and died in an alley in a puddle of blood and sewage.

The nausea I'd successfully fought off in that alley suddenly caught up with me. I twisted, bent over, and vomited onto the dirt behind me. A shuttered window loomed over me, but if anyone inside heard me, they sensibly did not look out.

Usually, throwing up makes you feel better, even though it's horrible while it's going on—but not this time. The poison I needed to expel was in my mind, not my stomach. All I'd done was leave a bad taste in my mouth.

I hawked and spat, then straightened and swiped my sleeve across my mouth. I had to keep going. Staying in one place was sure to get me caught. The man I'd winged would have reported back to his gang by now, maybe even to Robur's forces. They knew where I'd been. The farther I ran from where we'd been attacked, the larger the area they'd have to search . . .

Yet I still didn't move. Facing the street again, leaning against the brick wall to my left, I tried to think past what had just happened to what needed to happen next.

Somewhere in this city, there was either a Portal, created by Karl Yatsar, or the potential for a Portal, which Karl would eventually open. If the former, Karl could be in the Free City right now. If the latter, he could arrive at any moment.

So, how did I find him, or where he would appear?

The answer was clear: find the Portal.

But how?

I'd felt it, back in the *Narwhal*'s library, looking at the map of the Free City that Colonel Everest had spread out before me. Surely, I could I feel it again, now I was actually in the city that map had depicted?

I closed my eyes and put my head against the rough

bricks, trying to concentrate, trying to shut out all the fear and anger and shame and guilt roiling my mind. It wasn't easy, but I kept at it, breathing deeply, focusing, looking for that indescribable sensation, that sense that there was a weak place in this world, a crack in its reality . . .

. . . and suddenly, there it was. Like an itch I couldn't scratch.

I raised my head. My cheeks were wet with tears I didn't remember shedding. I wiped them away with the back of my filthy sleeve.

The Portal, or potential Portal, was *that* way, off to my right, though at an angle I couldn't walk directly, since the street didn't run that way. I fixed the point in my mind, clung to it. It was the only goal I had and offered what I felt was my only hope: the hope that I might soon be reunited with Karl Yatsar.

I've never liked stories where the terrified heroine has to be rescued by a man—but if Karl was at the Portal and up for a little rescuing, I decided, I'd be more than happy to be the damsel in distress, just this once.

Out into the street, and to the right. The spark of the Portal lay at an angle off to the left. I found an alley going in the right direction . . . almost. Soon the spark seemed off to the right, so I angled that way . . . then straight ahead . . . right . . . left . . .

Through streets and alleys and courtyards I passed almost in a trance, like a ghost. I saw few people—all furtive phantoms who, like me, ducked in and out of alleys, in and out of shadows. I kept one hand on the pistol in my sash at all times. Perhaps because of that, no one approached me. I neither heard nor saw any sign of pursuit.

The spark of the Portal became a candle flame, then a bonfire. It drew me like a moth. A new thought grew. If this *were* the Portal Karl had come through, or soon would come through, then *I could go back to my world.* Not to stay—too dangerous, with the Adversary now in charge—but just for a little while, just until Robur's men decided they'd lost me and the prince's men (if any were left alive) had returned to the *Narwhal.* Depending on where I found myself, I could . . . eat a hot dog. Watch a movie. Have a Coke. Enjoy one last moment of normalcy before, once more teamed with Karl, my quest began in earnest . . .

The Portal was close now. Ahead, the alley I followed led into another well-lit street. The Portal, I knew, lay somewhere not far beyond it, down the matching alley on the other side. Without thinking, I stepped into the gaslight—

"There she is!" someone shouted.

My heart leaped into my throat. I spun to the left and saw six men in the street, maybe a hundred yards away, running toward me. One of them was Mokoum.

My Rajian escorts!

Then another shout, from my right. I turned. More men, coming from that direction.

The two groups saw each other. The Rajians carried their rifles openly now; the men to my right were also armed. Both sides scattered for cover: rain barrels, overturned benches, entryways to the narrow two-story dwellings lining the street. I took my chance and dashed across the street into the facing alley. Both groups of men shouted.

Then the shooting started.

There'd been no signs of the Free City Guardsmen at the inn, despite the gunfight. *Probably bribed,* I thought, remembering what the colonel had said. But we were in a different part of the city now, a wealthier part, judging by the houses and the gaslight. An open gun battle here would surely draw Guardsmen, confusing the situation further. Everyone's focus would be on whatever happened behind me, which meant I still had a chance to escape, if only I could disappear from the streets. I had to . . .

That's when I found the Portal's location, a surge of sensation slamming into me so suddenly I skidded to a halt, clinging to the bricks of an archway into a passageway, at the end of which stood a wooden door. Wiping sweat from my forehead, I walked to the door and frowned at it. It looked completely ordinary. I reached for its latch, intending to see if it was locked, but the moment I touched the handle, I jerked my hand away again, as though it had shocked me.

Which it had—except it hadn't been an electrical shock. It hadn't even been an *external* shock. It had come from inside me, as though . . . as though something had switched on.

Something had, I realized an instant later. It must have, because, suddenly, I knew that what I had found was not an open Portal, but a potential Portal, one that had never been opened . . .

. . . and that I had the ability to open it.

I hadn't learned it. Nobody had taught it to me. I just *knew* it, in a blinding flash of inspiration, as if God Himself had reached down and put the knowledge into my mind.

I was still thinking this must be the new Portal linking Robur's world to mine, still thinking I could slip through it and see my own world one last time, even hide out in it briefly (if I was careful), still thinking Karl couldn't be far away, and so I stepped forward. My hands, of their own volition, made gestures in front of the door—gestures I recognized as the twin of those Karl had made in front of the Portal above the altar on the Mysterious Island.

The air began to glow, blue lines forming in the wake of my moving fingers. I stepped back. The lines not only remained in place, they burned more brightly, shifting from blue to eye-hurting white . . .

. . . . and then, with a soundless flash, they vanished.

The door looked the same, but a strange breeze, deliciously cool and yet at the same time damp, dank, and, most disturbingly, redolent of decaying flesh, seeped through the cracks between its planks and the gap beneath.

What the hell?

I reached for the latch. If the door *had* been locked, it didn't matter to the Portal: it swung inward.

On the other side, a path paved in crushed white stone, pale in the light of a full moon, wound down the steep slope of a valley before disappearing into the deep shadows of the pine forest that filled the valley floor.

On the far side of the valley, that forest broke like an ocean wave against the base of a tall, glimmering crag of pale stone. Atop that crag brooded a castle, a single light glowing in its highest tower. Things with wings flitted around that tower, just visible in the bright moonlight.

Somewhere in the distance, a wolf howled.

It looked like something out of an old black-and-white horror movie from my world—but it was *not* my world. I could *feel* it wasn't my world, had *never* been my world. It belonged to another Shaper: not me, not the Adversary, not Robur.

And then I realized two more things.

First, I had just found and opened—solo, with no help from Karl Yatsar at all—a Portal into another Shaped world, the next world my quest would take me to if I survived this one. That had to mean that somehow, when I'd touched his blood on the altar in my world, I had indeed absorbed the alien technology he carried within him.

It also meant, second, there was no reason for Karl to be anywhere near.

The crackle of gunfire behind me had stopped. Someone would be on my heels again in a moment.

I had to hide. I started forward, thinking I could duck into this new world until it was safe to return to this one, but the wolf howled again, and this time it was much closer—and then I saw it, running toward me along the white stone path, no ordinary wolf, but a giant creature almost as tall at the shoulder as I stood on two feet. Its eyes were fixed on me . . . and those eyes glowed red, not with reflected light, but with their own internal hellfire.

I stared, frozen, as the thing galloped up the hill. It gathered its haunches beneath it and leaped. I saw white fangs glimmering in the moonlight—

And then I slammed the door shut. It shuddered as the thing flung itself against it. Claws scraped against the wood. In terror, driven by some impulse I didn't really understand, I slapped my palms against the wood. Blue light flared, my hands and arms tingled, and the scratching of claws ended in the space of a heartbeat.

I knew without question that the Portal had closed, that all that lay behind this door now was whatever had lain behind it before I had approached it.

I also knew that whenever I wanted, I could open this Portal again and enter the next Shaped world of the Labyrinth . . . although, unless that thing on the other side had moved on, the prospect wasn't exactly appealing. In fact, that whole *world* seemed unlikely to be appealing. Had that been a *werewolf*?

But that was a problem for a later date. First, I had to save the world I was in now.

Starting with myself.

NINETEEN

THE PASSAGEWAY TO the Portal was one of several short passages opening off the winding alley I had run down, each of which ended in a door. Other doors opened here and there directly into the alley from the dark buildings looming overhead. I tried them in turn, moving farther and farther down the alley, ducking quickly through the pools of light cast by occasional—very occasional—lanterns. Shouts continued to sound from the direction of the street—but who was doing the shouting?

I didn't think the men I'd seen in the street had been Robur's. They hadn't moved with military precision as they sought cover, unlike Mokoum's small force. Even in the brief glimpse I'd had of each, I'd noted the difference. That probably meant they were members of the gang that had attacked the inn, working for Robur, sure, but not actually his forces.

Maybe I should just surrender to them, I thought, even as I tried yet another locked door. *They'll take me to Robur's men, and then they'll take me to Robur.*

Except, one of the members of that gang had killed Anthony and seen me kill his companion. They might have been sent to look for me by Robur's men, but now that I'd shot two of their number, killing one, they might not care what shape I was in when they handed me over to Robur's forces. They *probably* wouldn't kill me, since presumably they wanted to get paid . . . but "probably" and "presumably" aren't very satisfactory words in a context like that.

I wondered if more of my Rajian escort had been killed in the firefight in the street. The gentle Mokoum, perhaps? Other men who had done me no harm, who had simply done their duty to help me get where I now was, based on the lies I had told the prince?

I couldn't turn myself over. I had to find my own way to Robur and confront him, Shaper to Shaper. And then . . .

And then, I had no idea. One thing at a time.

Another shout. I twisted around and saw someone in the alley, standing beneath one of rare lanterns, a rifle in his hands.

Had he seen me?

I couldn't tell. He turned and shouted back up the alley. Though I couldn't make out the words, he was clearly calling for reinforcements. Maybe he couldn't see me, but he knew I'd come this way. If I could only get through one of these damned doors and lock it again behind me, he and his friends might go right by, assuming I'd simply panicked and was once again running for my life through the Free City's back streets.

If I could only get through . . .

Aha! *This* "damned door," set in a long section of brick wall between two crumbling buildings, wasn't locked!

Unlike the Portal door, it swung outward. I jerked it toward me, then yelped and froze, suddenly finding myself face-to-face with a woman, dressed all in black, whose hand was still outstretched to open the door from her side. By the light of a lamp hung on her side of the wall, we stared at each other in shocked silence for a moment, then I gathered (or, at least, half gathered) my wits and said, "Uh, hi. Mind if I come in?"

Shouts, getting closer.

"Like, right now?" Without waiting for an answer, I hurried through, shoving the other woman aside in my haste, then spun and pulled the door shut. It had a bolt: I slammed it into place.

I turned, only to find a dagger at my throat and dark

eyes staring at me suspiciously from the other side of the hand that held the hilt. I held very still. Even swallowing seemed a bad idea.

"Who are you?" the woman snapped. She was several years my senior, judging by the lines in her face. Before, I'd only registered that she wore black. Now I saw she wore trousers, a tunic, and a hooded cloak, though the hood was thrown back, showing long black hair, tied back in a practical ponytail much like my own.

"Shawna Keys," I said. Shouts seeped through the door behind me, still some distance down the alley, but nearing. "I'll be happy to answer your questions, but could we perhaps, you know, hide first?"

The woman's eyes flicked to the door. "Who is chasing you? Free City Guardsmen?"

I gave her my best guess. "Thugs hired by men belonging to Robur."

To my surprise, her mouth quirked in unmistakable amusement. "Indeed? Well, I have no love for either the local gangs or the dregs Robur sends to haunt the environs of the Free City. I will hide you. This way."

She turned and led me toward a cluster of wagons, each with a lantern glowing by its door, nestled against a stone wall. Those lanterns, the lantern above the door I'd come through, and two more hanging on either side of large double doors across from my smaller entrance, provided enough illumination for me to get a sense of the space around us: a large, enclosed courtyard. Weeds grew up through the cracked cobblestones beneath my feet. Off to my right I saw a pool of darkness, a rectangular pit with scattered stones around it—the basement of a large, long-gone building. Animals must have pulled the wagons into the courtyard, but there was no sign of them. Certainly, they weren't in the tumbled-down ruins that might once have been stables on the far side of the hole in the ground that must once have been an inn.

The wagons consisted of six small ones that made me think "Gypsy" (were there Romany, or people like them, in this world?), plus one much larger one, with a furled awning along the top of the side facing us, which made me think that entire side could be either lifted or lowered.

I could see writing on the wagon's flank, but the flowery script was too ornate for me to read in the dim light until we were almost on top of it—and then it stopped me dead.

"Worldshapers Theatrical Troupe," read the biggest letters, silver against a dark-blue background spangled with stars and comets and planets. Smaller letters on a floating red banner near the bottom added, "Music, Comedy, Drama, and Tragedy."

I didn't believe in signs and portents, which was too bad, because if anything pointed to me being in the right place, it was this: a theater company of almost the same name as my pottery studio, the name I had subconsciously chosen because it was also the name of the unusual individuals of whom I, apparently, was one.

Loud bangs echoed off the courtyard walls: someone was pounding on the door I'd come through with a rifle butt or sword hilt. "Open up!" a voice shouted. "We know you're in there. We saw the light."

"Shit," I said.

"Aptly put," the woman replied. "Hurry. That door is strong, but they'll get through it eventually." She led me to the door at the end of the wagon, pulled down a little three-step staircase that had been folded against it, clambered up it, and took the lantern off the hook beside it. Then she pulled the door open and squeezed to one side. "In here."

I brushed past her and found myself on a darkened stage, curtains hanging at either end, half-glimpsed flats with painted trees and stars against the wall to my left. The woman came in behind me, knelt down, and pulled aside a carpet. Then she pushed something on the floor, and a trapdoor dropped open. "Get in," she said, pointing into the dark space beneath the stage.

I hesitated. There came an ominous crash from the courtyard, then another. That door was going to give way any minute. Taking a deep breath, I sat down, swung my legs over the side of the trap, and dropped into the darkness—not far; my feet thudded against a padded surface, leaving my head above the stage floor. "Get down, and push the trap closed," the woman ordered. "Hurry!"

I obeyed. I crouched low, then reached up and pushed the door back into place. It clicked as it latched. The glimmer of lantern light around its edges vanished as the woman threw the rug over it again. The light shifted, shining through cracks in the floor planks as she hurried to the door and out, closing it behind her . . . and then, it was absolutely black.

In the pitch darkness, I had no good sense of the space around me. Presumably, there was some way to crawl through the under-stage area and emerge out of sight of the audience, but since the thugs chasing me would be the only audience, and unlikely to stay out front where the audience belonged, attempting an exit didn't seem like a good idea.

I sat down on the padding, made myself as comfortable as I could—which wasn't very—and listened.

The wagon muffled the sound from the courtyard, but I heard more bangs; silence for a moment; and then a particularly loud, crashing, splintering sound. Angry men's voices, a quieter woman's voice: my benefactress'. The voices came closer. More bangs and new voices added to the mix, angry voices, including more women— the other actors of the troupe, disturbed from their sleep, I guessed.

Then my heart skipped a beat as the wagon shifted. The door banged open. Light shone again through cracks in the planking overhead. The woman or one of the thugs?

The latter, I thought. *And if he's smart enough to realize stages often have trapdoors and decides to take a look . . .*

Fortunately, he apparently wasn't a connoisseur of the theater. He stumped around and then went out, closing the door again. "All clear!" I heard him shout.

Another male voice answered him. With some more back and forth, the two voices receded into the distance. I heard the murmur of the voices I thought belonged to the actors, but they, too, faded as wagon doors banged shut.

In deathly silence that stretched out for roughly an eternity—perhaps a bit longer—I stayed right where I was. Then the wagon shifted again, light shone through the cracks above me, footsteps approached—and the rug hiding the trapdoor was pulled back. "Mind your head!" the woman called through the planking. "Hold the door up while I release it."

I knelt, reached up, and put my palms against the trap as she pressed the catch she had pressed before, then maneuvered myself to the side and let the door swing down. The woman, on her knees, lantern on the floor beside her, looked down at me. "Come out," she said. "They're gone."

I stood and, not without some difficulty, managed to pull myself out through the trap. I rolled over on my back and sat up. "What happened?"

She grinned as though she'd just had the time of her life. "Before they smashed through the back door, I ran over to the main courtyard gate, unbarred it, and swung it open a little. I got back to the smaller door as they broke through, so they found me right where you did, just this side of it. I demanded to know who they were and what they wanted. They told me who they were was none of my business, but what they wanted was a particular woman. They gave a pretty good description of you and demanded to know if I'd seen you.

"I said I had seen you come in, and had tried to confront you, but you were armed," her eyes flicked to the pistol still stuck into my sash, "and threatened to shoot me if I didn't show you a way out. Not having a choice, I opened the wagon-gate for you, and you slipped away.

"There were five of them. The one who seemed to be in charge told two men to search the wagons and then catch up. The other three ran out through the gate.

"My troupe was not pleased to be rousted out of bed. I sent them back into their wagons as soon as the men were gone. Of course, they wanted to know what's going on, but I told them I'd explain everything in the morning. For now, I don't want them to see you."

"All of the men are gone now?"

"Gone, and the wagon-gate barred again. The latch on the back door is smashed, of course, but I've jammed it closed with a plank of wood from our set-building stores. People worse than that lot might come through otherwise." She stood then, gracefully, in one easy movement from kneeling to upright, and held out her hand to help me to my feet. "My name is Athelia Richelot. And you, Shawna Keys, owe me a story—a true one."

"I do," I said. "But first . . . thank you."

She bowed her head in acknowledgment of my gratitude, then picked up her lantern from the stage floor and led me back out into the warm night air. No one moved in the courtyard. Her actors were clearly doing just what she'd told them to. *Well,* I thought, *if they're like most actors I've known, they're so happy to have a job they won't do anything to jeopardize it. And she is their director, presumably.*

Athelia put the stage wagon's lantern back on its hook beside the door, then took me to the last wagon, closest to the closed wagon-gate. She went up the little fold-down steps, lifted down the wagon's lantern, opened the door, stepped in, and then motioned me to follow her.

I entered as she hung the lantern on a hook in the middle of the ceiling. The wagon's interior looked exactly like I might have imagined such a thing: like a hobbit hole on wheels. It had rounded walls, and a ceiling just high enough to allow me to stand upright, as long as I avoided the lantern.

At the far end, a raised platform held a mattress covered in a red blanket, with green-and-blue pillows with gold tassels stacked at one end. On the front of the platform, the gilded handles of multiple drawers glinted in the lamplight.

Red-cushioned benches lined the walls, except for immediately to my left, where a tiny stove held a single copper pot and a copper kettle, and immediately to my right, where a cabinet held a water basin. I saw myself in the mirror behind the basin and quickly looked away again. I'd seen enough stuff likely to give me nightmares that day without looking at *that*.

A red-and-black rug bearing an intricate geometric pattern of interlocking circles covered the wooden floor. Around the edges of the rug, the floor, like everything else in the wagon that could be polished, gleamed in the warm light of the lantern.

"Have a seat," Athelia said, indicating the bench past the cabinet with the water basin on it. "Would you like some tea?"

"I would kill for some," I said, then instantly regretted my choice of words as it came back to me with sudden forcefulness that I *had* killed someone that night: not the first person I had killed, since my clumsiness as a Shaper had resulted in several deaths in my own World, but the first person I had killed directly and with intent. I remembered the explosion of blood as my bullet tore through the man's throat, and suddenly I really *needed* to have a seat. Shakily, I dropped onto the bench.

I expected Athelia to have to light a wood fire in the stove, but instead she simply turned a knob and blue flames erupted beneath the kettle. "Gas?" I said, startled.

She glanced at me, one eyebrow raised, Spock-style. "You sound surprised."

"I didn't know you could use it in a . . ." I'd been calling it a wagon in my head but realized that wasn't really the right word. ". . . caravan."

"There is a tank beneath the floorboards," she said. "Within the city, we can use gas freely, because it is easy to obtain. On the road, we usually burn wood to conserve the gas for when it's really needed. Do the caravans where you are from not have gas stoves?"

One again, I'd made an unwarranted assumption about the technological level of this world. *That sort of thing could get you killed, Shawna,* I told myself.

Well, that, and getting chased by angry, heavily armed men.

"I'm sorry," I said.

"For what?" Athelia sat on the bench across from me. "Turn your head," she said. "To left, then right."

I did.

"You have dried blood all over your face, and in your hair, and on your clothes. Is any of it yours? Are you hurt?"

"No," I said. "It's all . . . someone else's." *Anthony* . . . Tears stung my eyes.

Athelia indicated the basin on the cabinet to my left. "The water is cold, but there is soap and a washcloth in the top drawer beneath it, if you wish to clean yourself."

I suddenly did, very much. "Thank you!" I stood, but my legs were still shaky; I would have fallen if Athelia hadn't jumped up and grabbed my arm. "Thank you," I said again. I took a deep breath, then managed to turn to the basin.

The water wasn't really cold—nothing ever seemed to be really cold in this sweltering place—and the fact it was cool seemed more refreshing than anything else. By the time I had washed my face, turning the water pink and the washcloth pinker, the kettle was singing. As I sat down again, Athelia got up, put tea from a pouch at the back of the stove into a teapot, and poured in the water. A moment later, she handed me a steaming mug. I sipped it, expecting something herbal, but it tasted like good, strong, black tea—and I didn't think I'd ever tasted anything so wonderful. *I guess that tells me at least one thing they grow in those mountains I saw as we approached the city.*

We. I might be the only one of those "we" still alive. Anthony had killed the colonel because of the lies I had told him. Some local thug had killed Anthony. Some of my escorts might have died in the attack on the inn or in the street battle.

The death count associated with the quest I had been drafted into by Karl Yatsar already exceeded my ability to tally reliably. And this was the *first* world outside of my own I had visited. Would my efforts to save the Shaped worlds ultimately resemble instead the bloody swath of murder and mayhem cut through multiple universes by some uncaring alien force in a straight-to-video sci-fi flick?

Athelia held her own mug in both hands as she took a sip. She lowered it again. "Now," she said. "Will you tell me your story?"

I could have lied, or told only half-truths, leaving out anything about other worlds and Portals and quests and all the rest of it. But Athelia's simple request, and her willingness to help me escape my pursuers before she'd heard a word of explanation, opened the floodgates. The truth was, I desperately *wanted* to tell someone everything that had happened to me: who I was, where I had come from, the life I had lost, the impossible quest I had been saddled with, my guilt and horror and fears. And so, rather than dissimilate, I began at the beginning and spilled it all out.

Athelia, to her credit and my growing surprise, simply listened. She didn't laugh, call me crazy, or yell for help. She just sat quietly, refilling our tea mugs as required, until, at last, I reached the present.

"So that's it," I said, a little hoarse—I'd been talking for more than half an hour, I guessed. "All of my escorts have been killed, wounded, or scattered. I lied to Prince Dakkar to get him to send me here, so I can't go back to him, even if I wanted to—which I don't. I'm convinced Robur is the Shaper, and I'm convinced the men chasing me were hired by his forces here in the city—but surrendering to them seems like a really bad idea. At this point, I don't think they'd treat me gently."

"I agree," said Athelia. "Whatever they were told about you, it cannot even approximate the truth. I suspect they simply think you are a Rajian spy. They might not kill you, but by the time they delivered you to Robur's forces, you might wish they had." She snorted. "And even then, Robur's commander here . . . I have heard . . . is as stupid and sadistic as they come. Not a man into whose hands I'd willingly place *my* life."

I swallowed. "Good call on my part, then. But it doesn't change the fact I have to get to Robur, and I have no idea where he is. I also have no money and no allies and know almost nothing of this world."

I stopped before I started crying. There was only one swallow of tea left: I drank it down, lukewarm though it was, and then just sat, slumped, feeling drained and defeated, helpless and hopeless. I'd thought telling someone everything would make me feel better, empower me to get up and go after my goals, as though I'd been to a good self-help lecture. Instead, all I seemed to have accomplished was to bring myself to the end of my rope.

Where do I go from here?

Athelia touched my knee, startling me. I looked up into her dark-brown eyes.

"Tell me," she said. "Can you sing?"

TWENTY

WHEN I WAS twelve years old, I played Maria in Apple-ville Middle School's production of *The Sound of Music,* an avant-garde minimalist version in which the mountain scenery, the grand von Trapp mansion, the abbey, and every other set was rendered in poster paint on cardboard. This perfectly matched our level of characterization.

Did any of that really happen? I thought, not for the first time. *Are those real memories from the First World, or are they somehow fake? And if they're fake, where did they come from?*

Another question I had no answer for. Karl had been of no help on that score, since he professed to be flummoxed as to why I had no memory of being taught by Ygrair to be a Shaper, and then of Shaping my own world.

All I knew was, if there was one song I could sing, it was "The Sound of Music."

And so, "Yes," I told Athelia.

"Let's hear you, then," she said.

I sat up straight, took a deep breath, and launched into the chorus (figuring the verse wasn't needed for an audition, any more than it had been when I'd auditioned for Miss Ellingsworth all those years ago). "The hills are alive . . ." I sang, and so on, right through to the end.

Athelia nodded approvingly. "Adequate. I've never heard the song, but it's pleasant enough. Can you act?"

"I've been pretending to be something I'm not the

entire time I've been in this world," I pointed out, which actually elicited a chuckle.

"Fair point," she said. "Your roles will not be challenging, in any event. I think we can make it work."

"Make what work?"

"You," she said, "are the newest member of the world-renowned Worldshapers Theatrical Troupe."

"Uh . . . thanks," I said. "But how does that help me, exactly?"

"First," said Athelia, "it will allow you to hide in plain sight of Robur's men, Dakkar's men, Phileasian gangs, or anyone else looking for you. Theater, remember? We have an extremely talented makeup artist."

"Who?"

"Me," Athelia said. "Second, it offers you a way to safely escape the Free City. We are about to pull up stakes and head to our next destination."

"Very kind," I said, "but once we're out of the City, I'll need to . . ."

"And third," said Athelia, over my protestation, "our next destination is Quercus."

I stared at her.

"The capital of—" she began helpfully.

"I know," I said. "The Republic of Weldon. You'll actually take me there?"

"We're going anyway. Very appreciative audiences in Quercus. It's like a second home to us."

"And we'll find Robur there?"

"Unless he's abroad. But even if he is, I'm sure they will summon him back quickly."

I examined the offer from all sides. It seemed too good to be true. It was also too good to turn down. "Well then," I said. "I'm *thrilled* to be part of the Worldshapers." I paused. "Um . . . where did that name come from, anyway?"

"It came with the troupe when I took it over. Is it not apt?"

"A little too apt," I said. *Curiouser and curiouser.* Another question struck me. "You were going somewhere when I burst through your back door. And you're all dressed in black, as if wherever you were going, you didn't want to be seen. Can I ask where you were headed?"

"You can ask." Athelia gave me a brief smile, but no more. "Now, about your appearance . . . a wig to change your hair, lines to age you. Perhaps a scar. Also, a darker skin color."

I yawned. "Now?" I heard the plaintiveness in my own voice. I sounded like a whining six-year-old who needed a nap—but I didn't care, because I *did* need a nap. A good long one, say, ten to twelve hours. A nice, stiff drink would have been welcome, too, but I hadn't been offered one. Instead I'd had tea, which had caffeine in it and wasn't conducive to relaxation—but with exhaustion dragging me down like a lead blanket, I didn't think it was likely to keep me awake.

Athelia took pity on me. "No, not now. You should rest." She pointed to the bed. "You can sleep in here. I still have to do what I was heading out to do when you made your unexpected appearance."

"That thing I can ask you about . . . but you won't explain."

"That's the thing."

"Won't that mean leaving the back door open?"

"I'll chain it and padlock it on the other side once I'm out."

I nodded and yawned again. "When will you be back?"

"Not until morning. Stay in here until I return. Then I'll introduce you to the rest of the troupe." She looked me up and down. "We're not the same size, so I can't offer you any of my clothes. But . . ."

She stood up, turned, and lifted the hinged top of the bench she'd been sitting on, revealing stacks of neatly folded clothing. "These are garments we've picked up here and there for costume use. You should be able to find something that fits. What you're wearing," her nose wrinkled as she straightened, "should probably be burned. Now, I must go—I'm very late. The others know you're in here, so they won't come crashing in if they hear strange noises." She went to the door, opened it, and glanced back. "Oh, yes," she said. "Chamber pot in the top drawer beneath the bed, should you need it. But you're responsible for emptying it in the morning if you do."

"Of course," I said.

Without another word, she went out. And without another word, I took off my shoes and lay down on the bed. I wasn't about to get undressed—I didn't want to be that vulnerable. I left the lantern burning, too, but neither the light nor the tea I'd drunk, nor even the horrible events of the night, kept me awake. Within a minute or two, I was dead to that world . . . or any other.

I woke to voices outside. The lantern had burned out, but morning light streamed through the high, narrow windows. I felt rested for having slept—but also, having slept in my clothes, as grungy as a rag doll I once saw lying in a road, black tire marks across its back. The metaphor of having been run over seemed to match my general mental state, after the horrors of the previous day.

Anthony's blood still stained my filthy clothing. Suddenly revolted, I rolled out of bed and opened the bench Athelia had been sitting on the night before. I found a knee-length tunic in blue cotton and some loose trousers in green that looked like they would fit, and even some clean underwear in a bag at the bottom. I stripped, bundled my dirty clothes together and put them on top of the bench I'd taken the clean ones from, and after a brief clumsy interval to use the chamber pot, put on the fresh clothes and a pair of ankle-high boots of near-enough my size I'd also found, glad to be rid of the hobnailed Roman-soldier sandals I'd worn since *Narwhal*. Then, as instructed, I waited for Athelia to return.

I didn't have to wait long. Perhaps she'd heard me moving around: within five minutes the door opened, and my hostess entered, carrying a steaming pitcher. "Good morning," she said.

"Good morning," I returned politely.

She put the pitcher on the cabinet beside the basin in

which I had washed the blood from my face the night before, then picked up the basin. She glanced at the covered chamber pot by the bed. "Full?" she said laconically.

"Yes," I said. "Where do I empty it?"

"You don't," she said. "I've changed my mind. I don't want you going outside yet. I'll take care of it." She frowned at my discarded clothes. "I don't want anyone to see those. Blood-covered clothing tends to attract attention. We'll burn our trash before we leave—I'll make sure they're in with it." She turned back to the cabinet, took the full washbasin, and went out. She brought it back in empty a moment later, poured hot water into it from the pitcher, and pulled a fresh towel from the drawers beneath the basin. "Wash up," she said, then bent over and hefted the chamber pot. By the time she came back with it emptied and cleaned, I'd washed my face and arms and hands and felt much more human.

Alethia returned the chamber pot to its place beneath the bed, then turned toward me, hands on hips. She still wore the black-on-black outfit she'd worn in the night, not too surprising, considering I'd been occupying her living space since then. "Now to disguise you," she said. "As I suggested last night: darker skin, some aging, a wig—and also, I think, a distinctive, but not horribly unattractive, scar. I'd suggest a limp, but it's too easy to forget which leg is supposed to be injured."

I blinked. "You can do all that?"

"I," she said, "am the mistress of the Worldshapers Theatrical Troupe. I can do many, many things."

Which she then proceeded to prove. By the time she was finished, I was olive-skinned, had a mass of black curls instead of my usual straight-hair-pulled-back-into-a-ponytail, thicker eyebrows and eyelashes and, indeed, a distinctive-but-not-horribly-unattractive scar, a thin, pale line running from just below my right eye to the corner of my mouth. "The result," she said as she carefully crafted it, "of an accident."

"Involving a mechanical rice-picker?" I offered.

She frowned. "There is no such device."

I sighed. The worst thing about talking to people from different worlds was that no one got my *Star Trek* jokes.

"Once your clothes are burned, there will be nothing to connect you to the search for the mysterious woman who, according to what the Free City Guardsmen are putting about today, murdered several people in cold blood last night and was indirectly responsible for a gun battle on Artigas Street."

"They're not wrong," I said, guilt seizing me again. "None of those men would have died if not for me."

"Did you kill them?"

"One of them," I said miserably. "The one who killed my friend."

"Then he is the only one whose death you are truly responsible for, and it sounds like he deserved it." Athelia shrugged. "You can't change what happened. You can only press onward. You say you must go to Robur. We can take you there. Focus on that, not the past." She smiled a little. "In any event, today you will be too busy to feel guilt."

"Why?"

"You are now a member of the Worldshapers Theatrical Troupe. Tomorrow morning, we leave the city. Tomorrow night, we have a village performance. Which means, today, you rehearse."

First, though, she introduced me to the rest of the troupe. By not allowing me to leave her caravan before she'd completed my disguise, she explained, everyone could truthfully say they had not seen anyone meeting the description the Guardsmen were circulating.

There were eight members of the troupe in all, counting Athelia. They ranged in age from a girl and boy in their mid-teens (Caroline "Kitty" Kemble and Colly Chatterley) to a married couple in their late sixties (Lacy and Cinnabar Quibber). Somewhere in the middle, age-wise, were the handsome leading man, Barton Bullock, Athelia herself, and the identical twins, Zanda and Zinta Vilks, beautiful, slender, and of indeterminate gender.

"Kitty," who was indeed cute as a kitten, looked Japanese to me. Colly had ebony skin. Lacy Quibber had an Inuit look, but her husband Cinnabar looked Scottish: burly, red-haired, and bearded. Barton, meanwhile, looked Arabian, and the twins were pale, skinny, blonde-haired, and green-eyed. As I'd noted before, there seemed to be, in this world, absolutely no connection between physical appearance and nationality, or anything else, more confirmation the Shaper had decided he wanted a truly color-blind world. *One point in his favor.*

Introductions out of the way, Athelia asked me to sing "The Sound of Music" for the Vilks twins, who, she explained, provided all musical accompaniment. Somewhat self-consciously, I *a cappella*-ed my way through it. The twins proved adept indeed: Zanda (or possibly Zinta) took up a sort-of guitar with eight strings, Zinta (or possibly Zanda) chose a flute, and the resulting accompaniment was more than satisfactory. I worried about my voice among these professional performers, but everyone applauded, although they also expressed bewilderment that they had never heard the song before.

"It's a local favorite where I come from," I said, eyeing Athelia, who gave a small nod of approval.

"Now," she said briskly, turning all attention back to herself, "we must also work you in here and there in at least a couple of our longer pieces. I'm thinking the maid in *Love's Neighbors Tossed,* and of course we can always use another noisemaker in *Cymbalella.* You're tall enough to play one of the draft animals, too."

"Oh . . . kay," I said, completely at sea.

It turned out I was *literally* at sea in another of the pieces in their repertoire, *Twelve Angry Sailors,* in which I played, if that's the word, the great green whale who destroyed the titular sailors' ship (represented by a made-to-be-broken model) in the opening scene, and returned later to gobble down one unfortunate member of the crew (represented by a small gingerbread figure—quite tasty he was, too). Suffice it to say, my thespianism was not severely tested: no doubt Athelia was worried I'd screw up their well-oiled productions if given *too* much responsibility. Nevertheless, I appeared on stage, at least briefly, in everything, as might be expected of a new member of the troupe—particularly one with an unfortunate scar that made beautiful-leading-lady roles problematic.

By the end of the day I had been integrated into the troupe pretty well, I thought. That night, I slept in the stores wagon, on a cot reserved for guests, tucked in among barrels and crates. It was a bit stuffy, but I didn't mind. Once again, I fell asleep in minutes.

The next morning, at first light, Athelia came in and touched up my makeup. Then I "helped"—mostly by staying out of the way—as the troupe loaded its wagons and hitched them up to the horses, retrieved by Barton and Cinnabar from the stables where they'd been boarded. By the time the sun rose above the city walls, we were rolling toward the gate.

Athelia insisted I remain seated beside her on the lead wagon as we trundled along. "If you were observed rehearsing with us yesterday, it would look suspicious for you not to be visible today. We want it to appear that you have always been a member of our troupe. It's unlikely anyone took much note of us upon our arrival, so it's even more unlikely they will have noted you are new."

"Unlikely" wasn't the same as "certain," but I did my best to look unconcerned as we rattled over the cobblestones. The wagon seat wasn't nearly as comfortable as the plush black-leather upholstery of my sadly departed Fjord Model Z, and the wagon's jerky motion threw me from side to side so much I had to hold on to the edge of the seat with both hands, but I tried to school my face into a look of boredom, and not to swivel my head nervously—as every fiber of my being was screaming at me to do—to see if Free City Guardsmen were closing in.

In the end, nobody attacked us, yelled at us, tried to stop the wagon, or—to be honest—paid any attention to us at all. The gate had opened at sunrise, only minutes before we arrived there, and as a result there was a huge flow of pent-up traffic in and out. The only non-animal-drawn vehicle I saw was a puffing steam-powered tri-wheeler steered by a leather-clad and goggle-wearing man using a tiller, such a perfect cliché of steampunk vehicular transportation I almost giggled. He looked even more uncomfortable than I did, though, since the wind, whipping straight down the boulevard, blew the steam regularly whistling from his boiler's safety valve straight into his face, so that his head and shoulders glistened wetly in the morning sunshine.

Our providers of locomotion, on the other hand, trotted placidly onward, emitting nothing . . . well, okay, occasionally emitting *something,* but it could mostly be ignored, since we weren't the ones who had to clean it up.

I couldn't help but tense a bit as we rolled through the gates. It looked to me like there were more Guardsmen than when I'd entered with the Rajians. They were scanning each face, and occasionally stopping wagons to search beneath cabbages or under the wagon bed. I tensed more as an officer stepped forward, walking alongside as we rumbled over the drawbridge, the stench of the moat rising around us thick enough to slice with a cheese knife. I forced myself to ignore him and hoped he'd return the favor.

He did. Instead, he grinned up at Athelia, placing a hand on the edge of her seat to steady himself. "Great show the other night," he said. "When will you be back this way?"

Athelia smiled down at him. "Hello, Captain Bjarne. Look for us in six weeks, I should think. Same place. We'll be premiering our production of *Astound the World in Eighty Ways.*"

"I love that one!" said Captain Bjarne. "Wouldn't miss it." He released the wagon seat and waved as we pulled away. "Safe travels and big crowds!" he called.

"Thank you, Captain!" Athelia called back.

Then we were across the drawbridge. The road I and my Rajian escorts had followed to the city carried on straight ahead, but after a short distance my new escort turned her wagon left, onto a broad macadam road running south through the open fields. There was no way to tell if we were being watched, or even followed, since early though it still was, with mist rising off the rice fields, turning the sun into a pale disk in the eastern sky, many people were already headed to and fro. I didn't relax until, late in the morning, as the main road angled east, we turned off it onto a much narrower dirt track, rutted and dusty, heading due south.

The rice fields had earlier given way to wheat fields. Ahead rose hills clad in dark jungle. "This road is little used except by local farmers," Athelia explained to me as we bounced off the macadam. "Impassable when it rains, but there seems little danger of that at the moment. We have used it before, so any observers should think nothing of us using it now."

I swiped sweat from my forehead—the sun was now blazing down at us from a clear blue sky—and nodded my agreement.

"We will take no chances, however," she continued. "It will take us all of two days, and part of a third, to reach the river that marks the Free City's border with the Republic of Weldon. We will spend each night in a village, where we will perform, exactly as we would whether you were with us or not. Once we cross the river, we will be in Robur's territory, though still far from Quercus. At that point you can, of course, surrender to any of his forces we happen to come across . . ."

"No," I said. "I will not be dragged to Robur like a prisoner. I'll arrive as an equal. I'm a Shaper, like him." *Apparently, every bit as egotistical as him,* a sardonic corner of my mind remarked. "Thank you again for your assistance. I don't understand why you're being so helpful, but . . . I'd be lost without it." *There,* I told myself. *See? Humility. Not egotistical at all.*

Athelia smiled. "Suffice it to say I am enjoying the challenge of spiriting you to Quercus without Robur's forces knowing anything about it."

I frowned. "An odd sort of challenge for a theatrical impresario to enjoy."

Her smile broadened. "I am many things. Theatrical impresario is only one of them."

And with that, since she refused to answer any more questions, I had to be content.

Singing "The Sound of Music" to a couple of dozen

ill-dressed peasants in the dusty commons of a village of thatch-roofed mud huts is surprisingly stressful. My heart pounded as I waited backstage (literally, since the wagon-stage had no wings). Athelia introduced me, as I'd requested, as Maria von Trapp. Zanda (I'd figured out how to tell the twins apart over the past two days) began the haunting flute solo, and I mounted the stairs to the stage (fortunately without tripping), opened my mouth, and this time began at the beginning (a very good place to start). "My day in the hills . . ."

The nerves went away pretty quickly, and the villagers, for all their grubby appearance, listened attentively (which gave them the edge over the audience at the matinee performance for local elementary schools we'd given at Appleville Middle School) and applauded enthusiastically.

After that, I was fine, and, at the climax of *Cymbalella,* still wearing the donkey-head and tail from my earlier appearance as the ass made to walk upright and serve as a waiter, clattered enthusiastically with my tambourine once the princess discovered the scullery maid was her long-lost sister, the curse was broken, and the evil witch's tower came tumbling down.

The villagers repaid us with meat and bread and ale and wine, and the next morning we trundled away down the dirt road, with half-naked children cavorting alongside us for the first half a mile or so.

The day clouded as we continued, and I looked uneasily at the lowering sky, remembering what Athelia had said about the road being impassible if it rained, but the precipitation held off, allowing us to give our second show at the even tinier and grubbier village we came to next—we did *Twelve Angry Sailors* this time, and I do believe my ship-destroying, sailor-gobbling whale was the hit of the evening, at least among the smaller members of the audience.

Overnight, it *did* start to rain but only a miserable drizzle, and although the road grew increasingly muddy, we reached the river without getting stuck.

There was no bridge. ("This isn't exactly an *official*

border crossing," Athelia said.) Instead, our horses and wagons splashed across a shallow ford. On the other side, another short stretch of muddy road led to a barbed-wire fence with a chained, locked gate blocking the way. Beyond that, the road stretched maybe a hundred yards before intersecting a much broader road, whose black glisten promised pavement of some fashion.

I was sitting, wet and miserable, in my usual place beside Athelia as we rolled up to the chained gate. She hadn't reapplied my makeup that morning, so I figured I looked a streaked and blotched horror. I felt about the same. The supposedly waterproof poncho-like cape I wore in fact leaked, so that water kept running down my back. I peered out from under the dripping hood at the obstacle in our path. "Now what?" I said grumpily.

Athelia didn't answer. She simply jumped down from the wagon, walked past the horses (who seemed unconcerned by the rain, barring the occasional flick of ear or tail), reached beneath her own poncho, drew out a key, unlocked the lock, pulled away the chain, and pushed the gate open. She came back, mounted the wagon, and flicked the reins. We rolled through.

"Why do you have a key to the gate?" I said, puzzled. "An arrangement with the local farmer?"

"I'll tell you in a minute," she replied.

Once all the wagons were through, she went back and chained and padlocked the gate again. Then she climbed up beside me once more and drove onto the paved road.

I stared down at it. Rather than the crude macadam of the road leading out of the Free City, this looked like modern asphalt, smooth, black, and unbroken, as if it had been laid yesterday. *Shaper's work,* I thought.

We turned right, the direction, presumably, of Quercus.

"Well?" I said, when Athelia remained silent.

She glanced at me, eyebrow raised. "Well, what?"

"You said you'd tell me why you had a key to the gate."

"Oh, that." She laughed. "I honestly thought you'd have figured it out by now."

"Figured out what?"

She leaned in conspiratorially. "Worldshapers Theatrical Troupe is a cover, Shawna," she said in a stage whisper. "We are actually special agents of the Secret Service of the Republic of Weldon, answering directly to Robur, Master of the World. He sent us to the Free City specifically to find you and bring you to him." She leaned back, grinning. "Thank you for making it so easy."

TWENTY-ONE

IN AN EMBARRASSINGLY clichéd fashion, I gaped at Athelia, open-mouthed.

She laughed. "Excellent whale-face. You should use that next time we do *Twelve Angry Sailors*."

I closed my mouth. Then I opened it again. "You're a spy?"

"If you like. Although spies gather information. We were sent to gather *you*."

"But . . . then . . . why didn't you just hand me over to Robur's men in the Free City?"

Her smile faded into a moue of distaste. "The men Master Robur sends to the Free City are the dregs of his forces. The scum of the city streets. They serve their purpose—keeping Dakkar's men on their toes—and occasionally carry out some assassination or sabotage at Master Robur's command, but mostly they are there so that they do not cause trouble anywhere else. They were only supposed to watch for your arrival, and then report to me. But Captain Zoof—soon-to-be ex-Captain Zoof, I suspect, once I report to Master Robur—thought he would capture you himself and then simply hand you over to me, in the hope of reward. Without authorization, he hired the Phileasian street gang that attacked your inn, killed your friend, and battled your escorts—and stirred up a hornets' nest in the process. The Free City Guardsmen overlook the games the Rajians and Weldonians play in their streets and environs, for the most part, as long as they don't endanger civilians. But by now they must know Zoof hired that gang. A gun battle on a main thoroughfare? They'll be cracking down, and that may play havoc with . . . other long-term plans."

I remembered what Colonel Everest had told me about the mineral deposits the Weldonians wanted, north of the city.

"Zoof has always been a fool," Athelia continued. She sighed. "I've never understood why Master Robur put him in command of the Free City detachment."

Before she had revealed who she was, she'd just called Robur "Robur." Now, I noted, he was "Master Robur" every time.

Damned if I'll call him that, I thought. "Robur must have a spy in Dakkar's palace, too, since he knew I was heading this way."

"I am not at liberty to say," Athelia replied. "But in this case, I do not think he needed one. He is the Shaper . . . a fact I knew long before you told me your story."

That startled me all over again. "What? How?"

"He told me himself: about the Labyrinth, the Shaped worlds, Ygrair . . . all of it."

I blinked. "I guess that explains why you didn't run screaming from the room when I told you my version of it."

She chuckled. "Robur knew the Mysterious Island might be the result of a passageway opening between this world and the next. He sent the *Albatross* to investigate. He was most displeased with Captain Harding-Smith for letting you get kidnapped by Dakkar's men. When he realized you were heading to the Free City—however he knew—he sent orders to Captain Zoof to watch for you and sent us to retrieve you."

I glanced over my shoulder, though I couldn't see the other wagons following us along the blacktop. "Do the others know . . . about the Shapers, I mean?"

"Oh, no," she said. "They know only that you were our intended target and that I successfully found you." She laughed again. "You asked where I was headed, dressed in black in the middle of the night? To my nightly meeting with Zoof. When I finally got there, I tore a strip off him—and told him to get out of the Free City before the Guardsmen came calling. I hope he's miserable, camping in the sodden jungle. I also made use of his wireless communicator to report to Master Robur. I cannot carry one in our wagons—they are not small, and so there is too much chance of it being discovered, and who would believe a traveling group of players would have such a rare and valuable thing?"

A sudden thought struck me. "Worldshapers Theatrical Troupe. Robur named it, didn't he?"

Athelia smiled. "Of course. It should have been a clue to you."

"You're the only person Robur has told the truth?"

"As far as I know." Her smile broadened. "And I know . . . quite a lot . . . about what goes on in the Republic of Weldon."

That pretty much confirmed a suspicion that had been growing in my mind. "You're not just a spy, are you?" I said. "You're the commander of Robur's intelligence agency!"

She bowed. "At your service. Technically, my rank is General, but for obvious reasons, I'd rather you didn't use it."

I sat back on the wagon bench. The rain had intensified, and I was still wet and uncomfortable . . . but I also felt a sense of great relief. "Does this mean I don't have to wear this ridiculous makeup anymore?"

Athelia grinned. "You're hardly wearing it now. But, yes, you can remove its remnants completely at the first opportunity."

The "first opportunity" came at the next town, altogether more prosperous looking than the grubby villages on the other side of the border, boasting paved roads, more three- (and a few four-) wheeled steam-powered vehicles, and a neat and tidy inn in whose courtyard we set up for the evening's performance.

Meanwhile, we had proper rooms, which even had proper running water and proper bathtubs. I emerged from the bath clean and looking myself again (as I confirmed in the mirror), got dressed, went downstairs, had a lovely meal in the lovely dining room, sang and "acted" my little heart out that night onstage, and in general had a completely satisfying, and therefore in narrative terms (had I been living a story) utterly boring, evening.

Which made a nice change.

And so it continued for three more nights. Smooth roads, nice inns, appreciative audiences. I asked Athelia to tell me more about Robur; she refused. I asked her to tell me more about the Republic of Weldon. That she was happy to do, at great length. The Republic, as I'd noted on the globe Dakkar had shown me, covered a large swath of Verne's Land. ("Who was Verne?" I asked Athelia. "Early explorer," she explained.) There were ten Districts, each with its own elected governor and council, but the democracy (and the resemblance to a true republic) ended there. In Quercus, Robur ruled supreme. He could overrule any decision by a district governor or council.

"And no one complains about it when he does?" I said.

Athelia gave me a puzzled look. "Why would they? He is Master of the World. His decisions are final, and his rule benevolent."

And that was all she had to say on *that* subject. Robur, clearly, had Shaped those in his inner circle to be as unquestionably loyal to him as he had Shaped Dakkar's closest followers to be unquestionably loyal to their Dread Prince. *All the better to play his wargames,* I thought sourly.

On our second day, we rolled, in the space of a minute, out of lush forest and into a region of blasted, blackened trees. On a hill in the middle distance, broken walls thrust up, like jagged teeth of stone.

I stared around, astonished. "What happened here?"

"No one knows," Athelia said indifferently. "Ancient history. Nothing to do with us."

Ancient? The trees had been destroyed recently enough that the undergrowth was only now beginning to grow up around the trunks. In this semitropical climate, no more than a few months could possibly have passed.

I said as much to Athelia. She shrugged. "I know it

seems odd, but it's looked the same for as long as anyone can remember. These ruins long predate the founding of the Republic."

I didn't argue. But it did occur to me that "as long as anyone could remember," in a world with an active Shaper, might be no longer than the day before yesterday . . . literally. *But why would he Shape ruins?*

We left the ruins behind and didn't see anything similar for the rest of the journey into Quercus. Despite the relative comfort of our nightly lodgings and the continued appreciation of the evening crowds for my song stylings and animal impersonations, my unease began to grow. I didn't have a clue what to expect when at last I came face-to-face with Robur. He was expecting me . . . but did that mean he would welcome me? Would he believe me when I told him of the threat posed by the Adversary? Would he remember Ygrair?

Would he know where Karl Yatsar was?

Maybe Karl's in Quercus, I thought. *Maybe that's one reason Robur sent the Worldshapers Theatrical Troupe into the Free City. Maybe Karl told him how important it was that I be brought to him.*

Maybe. But Athelia, when I asked her one day (as we crossed a massive iron bridge over a Mississippi-sized river), told me she had never heard of anyone named Karl. Nor, to her knowledge—and as head of Robur's Secret Service, she had a lot of knowledge—had any strangers recently come to Robur's palace.

That didn't *prove* Karl wasn't there . . . but it didn't give me much hope that he was, even though I tried to tell myself he could have arrived after Athelia had left for the Free City, rather than having been a reason for her being sent.

Traffic grew heavier as we rolled deeper and deeper into the interior of the Republic of Weldon, with more and more of it mechanized. Robur, in his supposedly infinite and benevolent wisdom, had apparently never bothered to introduce the concept of stripes, or even rules of the road, which made encounters with smoking six-wheeled steam-powered transporters harrowing.

Still, we escaped mishap, and, on the morning of our fifth day of travel after crossing the river, crested a hill and saw, spread out below us, the city of Quercus.

It was a city of straight roads and low brick buildings and lots of trees, very neat and organized. I saw parks and fountains and public buildings with the Greco-Roman facades common to old, important buildings in my own world. Unlike the Free City of Phileas, Quercus did not have a defensive wall, except around the many-pillared white-marble palace atop the Acropolis-like hill that rose on the far side of the city from us, with no apparent geological reason for existence other than that Robur had wanted his palace on a hill, one that offered both a view over his city and, on the far side, over the ocean—for our journey had indeed brought us back to the coast. I looked out over the sparkling blue sea and wondered where the *Narwhal* was. Had anyone returned to the submarine to tell Captain Hatteras what had happened? Had he already reported to Prince Dakkar?

I thought of Belinda and felt a new wave of guilt and regret.

Robur seemed to have decided the best way to keep his capital looking pretty was to make sure his industry stayed elsewhere. Off to my left I saw smoking smoke-stacks and hulking factories, but nothing of that sort sullied Quercus itself.

We rolled down the hill toward the town, and my pulse picked up. By the time we were in the streets of the city, it was almost racing, and I had to wipe my damp palms on my green cotton trousers (I'd found other clothes in the days since I'd joined the troupe, but the ones I'd first pulled from the bench in Athelia's wagon remained my favorite, so I'd chosen them for today). It wasn't that there was anything threatening about the surroundings: the people I saw seemed happy and prosperous, certainly not giving off oppressed-and-in-fear-for-their-lives vibes. Everything was just as lovely and tranquil as it had appeared from the hill.

The palace loomed larger from below than it had from on high, though. Elegant and reserved, it lacked the phallic towers the prince's palace had (appropriately, based on my interactions with him) boasted so prominently. Only one flag flapped from the peak of the topmost roof: the golden sun on a black background I had first seen on the *Albatross,* moments after I'd arrived in this world.

The gate of the wall at the base of the hill stood open, revealing terraced gardens of carefully landscaped flowerbeds, dotted here and there with bushes cleverly trimmed into the shapes of animals. Fountains plashed, and birdsong filled the air. Families moved among the flowers, children laughing and running among the animal-bushes.

The wagons did not enter the palace grounds. Instead, we rolled up in front of the gate, and Athelia and I dismounted. One of the twins came to take the reins of Athelia's wagon—I was feeling too nervous to do the mental work to determine which one it was—and then the Worldshapers Theatrical Troupe rolled away, parallel to the palace wall, the actors I had been performing with just the night before waving goodbye.

I wondered whether I would ever saw them again.

Athelia led the way through the gate and along a long walk of crushed white gravel, lined by slender green trees and graceful statues of men and women in flowing robes. The path led to broad stone steps, the beginning of the ascent to the palace. Two men stood guard, wearing black uniforms with Robur's golden sunburst on their chests. They did not challenge us. Quite the contrary: they saluted as Athelia approached and held that salute until we were past.

So it went, up five levels. On each beautifully landscaped terrace (each unique—fruit trees on one, more statuary on another, fountains and pools on another), we had to walk part of the way around the hill to get to the next set of stairs. By the time we reached the topmost level, we were on the west side of the hill, facing the ocean, on a promenade above a sheer drop to surf-pounded rocks far below. On the north side of the palace, I now saw—it had been invisible from below—a huge flat expanse, paved in white stone, easily two hundred yards long and perhaps fifty wide, stretching toward the ocean and ending at the cliff's edge. A large building with a rounded roof stood at the inland end, huge closed doors facing the sea.

At the main entrance to the palace, up a flight of broad stairs, twelve guards stood at attention, Buckingham-Palace style, eyes fixed on the ocean horizon. Only the two nearest the big black doors (emblazoned with the sunburst in what I was pretty sure this time was solid gold) moved as we approached. Like those farther down, they saluted Athelia, who this time stopped and returned the salute properly. Then they moved to the center of the doors and swung them inward.

I half expected Robur to be standing there, ready to greet us, but all that lay beyond was a long marble hallway, with tall doors opening to left and right and a staircase sweeping up to the second floor right in front of us. It looked pretty much the way I might have expected it to, but it certainly *felt* different: the air was pleasantly cool and dry, unlike the near-equatorial oceanside humidity outside the door. "Air-conditioning?" I blurted.

"I don't know what that is," Athelia said.

"The air," I said. "It's cool."

"Oh! Frigifiltering, you mean."

"Frigifiltering?" I almost laughed. "Really?

Athelia shot me a puzzled look. "Yes, really."

People crossed the hallway in front of us, moving from room to room, some carrying papers and briefcases (presumably government officials), others carrying mops and brooms and wearing black and white (presumably servants, but unlike in Prince Dakkar's palace, the women here wore simple blouses and skirts). We garnered curious glances, but no one approached us. It seemed clear that here, everyone knew Athelia's true rank.

We climbed the staircase. At the top, hallways stretched left and right, but we went straight ahead, down a short, pillared corridor to the door at its end—black, of course (polished ebony, by the look of it), inset with another pure-gold sunburst.

Athelia knocked.

"Enter," said a voice.

I steeled myself to meet Robur, but when Athelia opened the door, the man beyond, balding and fiftyish, was clearly just a secretary of some kind, ensconced behind a massive desk, a grim fortress guarding yet another black-and-gold door behind him. "General Richelot," he greeted Athelia. "The Master is expecting you. Please go on in." He reached beneath the desk. I heard a click, then the inner door swung silently open.

I swallowed hard. Then I stepped forward to finally come face-to-face with the Shaper of this world.

TWENTY-TWO

IN THE OVAL office beyond (*of course it would be an oval office,* I thought), a man stood with his back to us, hands clasped behind him, looking out a tall window over the rooftops of Quercus, far below. In the distance, I saw the blue line of the ridge from which we had first done the same. "Hello, Shawna," the man said. Only then did he turn around and, grinning, come around the desk of black wood (far smaller than the intimidating one in the outer office). "Long time, no see." He held out his hand.

I took it by reflex and looked him over as he shook it, his grip warm and dry. I don't know what I'd expected. A bearded giant, maybe, like Michelangelo's Sistine-Chapel version of God, or possibly a greasy fat dude, a dead ringer for Comic Book Guy on *The Simpsons.* Instead, Robur was . . . pretty ordinary, smooth-shaven, with brown skin and black hair, dark-brown eyes, and a rather dashing goatee. He had three inches and maybe ten years on me—older, but not old, by any means.

"I've *never* seen you," I said, releasing his hand.

He laughed. "I should be hurt, but I guess it's not surprising you don't remember. You were only . . . what? Ten, I think?" He touched his beard. "And I didn't have this, then."

There was a strange roaring sound. For a minute, I thought it was something outside the window—then I realized it was only in my ears. "You . . . knew me? For real? In the First World?"

"Of course! At Madame Ygrair's Preparatory School.

'Shaping the minds that shape the world.' Her little joke, *almost* telling the truth in that slogan."

"Like your joke in naming Athelia's acting troupe Worldshapers," I said.

"Pretty much. Please, sit—we have a lot to talk about, I think." He indicated two comfortable-looking leather chairs pulled up to the hearth in the wall to my left. Between them stood a low, oval table, of the same black wood as the desk but with an ivory top. The air-conditioned . . . um, frigifiltered . . . air was cool enough I was actually glad when he touched something under his desk and the fireplace—gas, obviously—flickered to life.

I followed him to the chairs. The moment we were seated, a side door hidden in the wall next to the fireplace opened, and two servants came in, one carrying a tray of cheeses, breads, meats, and olives, the other a tray with two carafes of wine—one red, one white—plus two glasses. Only two: Athelia, it appeared, was not invited to partake.

Glancing over my shoulder, I saw her quietly take a seat on the chaise longue against the opposite wall. I was about to protest her lack of refreshment when a third servant came in and set a tray bearing a coffeepot, a cup, and cream and sugar on the table in front of her, twin to the one between Robur and me. Athelia saw me looking at her, winked, and leaned forward to pour.

I turned back to Robur as he said, "White or red? Both very nice, I assure you."

"White," I said.

One of the servants poured white for me, then red for Robur, then all three servants bowed and left, closing the hidden door behind them. I sipped the wine—a Viognier, I thought—then set it down again. *No more. Keep your head clear.* I didn't touch the food. The butterflies in my stomach had intensified.

"Well," Robur said, lifting his own glass and taking a good-sized swallow, "let's get right to the big question. How on Earth—*any* Earth—did you manage to open a passageway from your world to mine?"

"I didn't," I said.

Robur blinked. "Come again?"

"I didn't open it."

"Then who did?"

"Have you ever heard of Karl Yatsar?"

Robur frowned. "No. Should I have?"

"He's a friend of Ygrair's."

"Ygrair had no friends that I ever saw. You know how she was."

My stomach clenched. "No," I said. "I don't."

Robur's eyebrows knitted. "What?"

"I don't remember Ygrair's school," I said. "I don't remember the First World. All my memories . . . *all* of them, from toddlerhood to last week . . . are from my world. My *Shaped* world."

Robur looked blank. "That's impossible."

"It's also true."

He set down his wineglass and leaned forward. "But . . . to do that . . . you'd have to Shape yourself. Ygrair said we *couldn't* Shape ourselves. 'Shape your world to suit yourself, because you can't Shape yourself to suit your world.' I don't know how many times I heard her say that."

"Did she? I don't remember."

"If that's true—"

"It is."

"—how did you even find out you were a Shaper?"

"That's where Karl Yatsar came in." I told Robur the story, in brief. He listened, taking occasional sips of wine, but disbelief grew on his face with every word.

"Oh, come on," he said, when I started talking about how the Adversary planned to seize control of world after world, and eventually all of the Labyrinth. "This sounds like a bad fantasy novel. This 'Adversary'—why not just call him the 'dark lord'?—is taking over entire Shaped worlds? Stealing the *hokhmah* from their Shapers and then killing them? Surely Ygrair would have warned us if such a threat existed."

"It didn't exist, until the Adversary came along." I suddenly thought of something else. "You say you knew me as a child."

"Briefly," Robur said. "You arrived at the school the year I graduated."

"Then you might have known the Adversary, too."

Robur raised an eyebrow. "Really. And what does this 'Adversary' look like?"

I tried to remember. I'd only seen him once, in the coffee shop . . . right after his cadre had killed Aesha. My mind shied away from that part of the memory. "Unremarkable," I had to admit. "Caucasian. Brown hair, brown eyes. Average height, average build."

"Doesn't ring a bell," Robur said dryly. His glass was empty; he refilled it from the carafe of red. Clearly, *he* wasn't worried about keeping a clear head. My own wine sat largely untouched. "Or, rather, it rings too many bells," he continued, sitting back. "There were easily two hundred students there the year I graduated. Several of them could have been fairly described as 'average-looking.' Including me."

Two *hundred*? Two hundred *Shapers*? Two hundred Shaped *worlds*? And that was only a few years' worth of students?

My guess, based on his complete unfamiliarity with any pop-culture reference later than about the First World War, was that Karl—somehow—had met Ygrair in the nineteenth century. If she had been training Shapers that long, how many thousands of Shaped worlds were there by now? And I was supposed to go to all of them, one by one, gather their *hokhmah,* and take it to Ygrair? I'd been in Robur's world for . . . what? Three weeks? . . . and almost died enough times to lose count. *This quest isn't just Quixotic, it's positively Sisyphusian.*

"Your real name can't be Robur," I said, thinking maybe if I heard what it really was, it would jog my mysteriously missing memory.

"Nothing so exotic, no," Robur said. "At school I was plain old Michael Hartshore, an orphan from Kansas City."

"Orphan?"

"A lot of us were orphans . . . or kidnapped as babies,

for all I know," Robur said. "Most didn't know anything about our families. The few who did didn't seem to miss them. Or be missed by them."

And me? I wondered, and would have asked, but Robur had carried on, in a musing voice. "As I grew older, I often wondered why the school was never investigated by authorities. All those children, and no family entanglements to worry about. Never mind the fact that when the children graduated, they simply vanished. But somehow, no one ever seemed to find that suspicious. My best guess is Ygrair, unlike any of the rest of us, had power to Shape, or at least influence, people in the First World."

That's because she's really an alien, I thought, but didn't say. I wasn't giving away everything I knew to this man who, as far as I was concerned, I'd just met and, having seen how he'd chosen to Shape his world, didn't much trust, either.

"When Ygrair asked us to choose what our Shaped worlds would be like, I decided to go with a Verneian theme," he carried on. "That being the case, what better character to assume than the Master of the World?" He helped himself to an olive.

"You didn't want to be Captain Nemo?"

He spat the olive pit into his hand and dropped it into a bowl provided for the purpose. "I thought about it. But Robur seemed fresher. And I prefer air travel to submarines." He picked up his wineglass again and waved it around as he spoke. "Back to the point. You emerged into my world on a strange island, which promptly disintegrated. What was on your side?"

"An even stranger island," I said. I told him about it. I even described some of the disturbing statuary that had graced its monster-haunted halls, and how, to open the Portal, we'd been forced to make a blood sacrifice on an altar in an arena populated by shadow-people . . . and other things. "Karl thought it was a mingling of our subconsciouses, stuff from your nightmares and mine, all jumbled up together."

Robur laughed. "Actually, it sounds like stuff from

my dungeon. Mingled with a bit of *Indiana Jones and the Temple of Doom.*"

I glanced down at the palace floor. "Dungeon?"

He laughed again. "Not a literal one. My *Dungeons and Dragons* dungeon. I used to play at school. A form of worldshaping, really, although it only involved graph paper and dice. A lot of us were into it." He gestured at the food. "Please eat. And you're not drinking your wine."

I put a piece of hard yellow cheese on a seed-covered cracker and popped the makeshift hors d'oeuvre into my mouth while I thought. I'd played *Dungeons and Dragons*. And now that I thought about it, that made perfect sense of the island . . . underground tunnels, monsters, traps. *No wonder Karl wasn't sure what to make of it. D&D came around decades after he was active in the First World.*

I swallowed. "I suppose I should be thankful you didn't model your whole world after it." Deciding to risk another sip of wine, I lifted my glass.

"No, that was Thomas Falkenberg's plan," Robur said cheerfully, as he put salami and cheese and a dab of brown mustard on a bun. "I've often wondered if he actually did it." He bit into his mini-sandwich.

Another name. It meant no more to me than "Michael Hartshore." Apparently, my memory was not as easily jogged as all that.

"But if the Mysterious Island in my world was your subconscious leaking in," I said, "That would imply your Mysterious Island came from mine. But I didn't recognize . . ." I stopped. "Wait. Were there any large animals on the island?"

"As a matter of fact, yes," Robur said. "It struck Captain Smith-Harding as odd, so he included it in his initial report. A rather beautiful black horse . . . a stallion, he thought. Finest he'd ever seen."

I felt a pang of regret. I'd been on an island from one of my favorite children's books, and it had crumbled away . . . presumably taking the black stallion with it . . .

before I'd even realized where I was. "Was that why you found the island mysterious?"

"Not really," Robur said. "What made it mysterious . . . infuriating, in fact . . . was the fact I hadn't Shaped it. It just appeared. I didn't realize it was where your world and mine . . ." he smiled, ". . . rubbed up against each other."

"Our worlds had always touched there," I said. "So, why did these islands suddenly pop into existence? Even Karl didn't understand it."

"That's easy," Robur said. He sipped more wine. He was halfway through his second glass. I took a third swallow from my first. "The Mysterious Island formed five weeks ago. From what you told me . . ."

I sat up straight in sudden excitement. "That was when I started Shaping again! When I reset time!"

"Exactly," Robur said. "That was a huge surge of Shaping power that affected your entire world. It hit the thin spot between our worlds and forced its way through the . . . call it a membrane . . . into mine, Shaping something from your subconscious, something appropriate to where it emerged: the middle of the ocean."

"If that's why my subconscious island appeared in your world," I said, "why did that monstrosity of yours appear in mine?"

"Monstrosity?" He put a hand on his chest in mock dismay. "I'm hurt. I had many an exciting adventure in the dungeon that inspired that island."

"I had a few exciting adventures in it myself," I said. "Ones I could have done without. But why did it even appear, if it takes a huge surge of Shaping power to push Shaping from one world into another?"

"You bragged of kicking time back three hours," Robur said.

I hadn't *bragged* about it, but I nodded, just the same. "What's that got to do with it?"

"That's an impressive trick, and very few Shapers could do it."

"That's what Karl said."

"Did he say *only* you could have done it?"

"Not exactly."

"Good, because he would have been wrong."

I frowned. "Are you saying *you* could have done it?"

"You saw the ruins on your way here?"

I nodded.

He grinned at me. "I've rebooted this world, from scratch, seven times, wiping away *years,* not just hours."

I think my mouth fell open. *"What?"*

He spread his arms, wineglass still in his right hand. "I was fully trained by Ygrair. I Shaped and tested and discarded many practice worlds in the Sandbox before graduating and being granted access to the Labyrinth. I'm far more powerful in my world than you were in yours, it sounds like—not surprising, when you consider I scored higher in Shaping ability than anyone else in my class, anyone else in the history of the school." He seemed to rediscover the wineglass in his hand as he brought his arms back in and took another sip. "And I have very carefully husbanded my power over the years, never using enough to burn myself out completely, saving it for when I really need it.

"Those ruins you saw are from two versions ago. There are some on Dakkar's island from . . . let me think . . . four reboots ago, almost fifteen years now. It takes a lot of Shaping power to reboot, so sometimes I conserve it by not bothering to clean up every little reminder of the last time around. The ruins add character to the landscape, and it takes me months to recharge as it is." Another sip of wine. "That's why things are so peaceful right now. I've barely begun to replenish my power since the last reboot."

"Peaceful?" I remembered the attack on the *Albatross,* the deaths in the firefights in the Free City, the bullet through Anthony's skull.

Anthony, whom you lied to and led to his death . . .

"Relatively," Robur said. "Oh, there are always skirmishes, but there haven't been any major battles. Of course, that will change once I'm back to full strength. I'm planning a huge air-sea engagement this winter, somewhere up north, so the weather will be a major factor. That's always fun."

I'd guessed Robur saw his world as a kind of war-game, but to hear him put it in such coldblooded terms, in that amused and self-satisfied tone of voice, was shocking . . . and infuriating. "These are real people you're playing with! Real people you're *killing.*"

"Real people?" Robur looked at me as if I'd lost my mind. "Don't be silly. They're nothing of the kind."

I twisted around in my chair to look at Athelia, astonished he would say such things in front of her . . . and she, lowering the coffee cup from which she'd just taken a serene sip, smiled at me.

"You thought Athelia would be shocked?" Robur said, as I turned to glare at him again. "You under-estimate how carefully I have Shaped this world. Those in my closest circle are utterly loyal to me. I could tell Athelia to jump off the cliff into the ocean and she would do it without question. Wouldn't you, Athelia?"

"The Master's wish is my command," she said instantly.

I felt sick. "You've stolen their free will!" *As did you in your own world, in order to escape,* my conscience reminded me. *You sure you belong up on that high horse?*

But I didn't do it systematically. I didn't take it from everyone.

No, only the people you could use. *That's better . . . how?*

"Nonsense," Robur said calmly. "They still have free will in everything but the roles they play in my grand entertainment." He shook his head. "I wasn't sure you were telling the truth about having forgotten everything Ygrair taught you, but if you think the Shaped are real people, as real as those of the First World, you really *must* have amnesia. Ygrair made it quite clear they are not."

"This world's holy book is *The Word of the Shaper.* And you make them call you Master!"

"It amuses me, and it's appropriate to the world I've Shaped. Not just because of the Jules Verne novel, but because of . . ."

"*Doctor Who,*" I supplied. "You think you are so su-perior you can use them however you want, as if you were a Time Lord and they were just ordinary humans."

"I'm pleased you get the reference."

Robur refilled his wineglass. I was beginning to think the Master of the World had a drinking problem. *Maybe he drinks to salve his conscience,* I thought, but I didn't really believe it. I wasn't sure he *had* a conscience.

"It did enter my mind," he went on. "I *am* a kind of Time Lord, only instead of regenerating *myself,* I regenerate the whole world, and make everyone forget about the wars they have already fought. The survivors, of course. The dead, I don't have to worry about." He took a swallow from his full-again glass.

"So, to you, everyone in your world except yourself is a . . . a non-player character?" I demanded.

"An NPC. Yes." He leaned forward, examining the food tray again.

I turned toward Athelia again. She seemed as unperturbed as Robur did. I looked back at him. "And you've made all of Prince Dakkar's followers as ludicrously loyal to him as yours are to you?"

"It's not *all,* on either side." Robur plucked a pickled asparagus from the plate and bit off the end. "That would be boring," he said as he chewed. "There are . . . wild cards, I guess you could call them . . . to allow for espionage. On Dakkar's side, they can crop up at any level—that's how I knew he had sent you with an escort to the Free City." He shoved the rest of the asparagus stalk into his mouth. "On mine, I don't allow it in my closest associates, like Athelia over there, but at lower levels, even I can be undermined by moles. It makes it all more exciting. And, of course, the farther out you go from the inner circle, the less the level of loyalty to which people are Shaped. Farmers and shopkeepers are free to love or hate me as they wish—although, should they attempt rebellion, they will, of course, be crushed." He pushed the food plate toward me. "Please, have more of the charcuterie."

I ignored it. "But you can never be defeated. Not really."

"Sure, I can," Robur said. For the first time, he sounded a little irritated. "What would be the fun if I couldn't?

Where do you think those ruins you saw up the road came from? Two versions ago, Dakkar talked his satellite countries into contributing forces to an enormous army—first time he'd ever done *that*!—and successfully launched an invasion of the Republic, staging it through the Free City. Vicious fighting, hand-to-hand combat, artillery bombardments, sieges . . . it was great. And I lost."

"But survived."

Robur snorted. "The world's not going to let its Shaper die."

I blinked at that. It seemed to me my world had given me ample opportunities to die in the last couple of weeks I'd been in it. On the other hand, . . . my world was only ten years old, according to Karl Yatsar. In the last decade, had I suffered any serious harm?

I had not. Perhaps my world had been protecting me without my being any more aware of it than I was of the fact I was its Shaper. Perhaps I'd only become vulnerable to real harm when the Adversary had burst into my world and stolen my *hokhmah*.

"Did Ygrair *tell* you your world protects you?" I said.

"Not in so many words. But it only makes sense, doesn't it? I made this world, for me. How can it possibly continue to exist without me?" He looked at his empty-for-the-second-time wineglass. For a second, I was sure he'd pour himself a third one, but instead he sighed and put it down on the table.

I left mine where it was and leaned forward. "You said the ruins came from two versions ago. But the undergrowth has barely started reclaiming them. So, you must have rebooted again since then. What happened?"

Robur chuckled. *"You* happened."

I blinked. "What?"

"The Mysterious Island, not to put too fine a point on it, freaked me out. I hadn't put it there. I hadn't Shaped it. It came from outside. It felt like the beginning of an invasion . . . or a cancerous tumor that, left unchecked, might fatally metastasize. I thought—hoped—that if I rebooted the whole world, the island would vanish."

"But it didn't."

"No, it didn't. Not until after you came through the Portal. Instead, it sounds like my resetting of my world thrust a matching Mysterious Island into your world." He smirked. "Although my subconscious clearly came up with something way more interesting than yours did."

I ignored the jibe. "So, you sent the *Albatross* to see if the island had vanished?"

"I sent it to investigate the *first* appearance of the island," Robur corrected. "I simply kept it there after the reboot. Oh, and Shaped Prince Dakkar's *Narwhal* to be close by."

"What?" I thought of tumbling helicopters and falling bodies. *"Why?"*

"Whether the island disappeared or remained, I thought the encounter of the two opposing forces would be amusing."

Amusing? I glared at him; he didn't seem to notice.

"I admit, I didn't expect you," he went on. "I felt this 'Portal' of yours open, of course, and I felt it vanish . . . and I *definitely* felt you arrive—someone not of this world, someone I did not Shape and could not Shape. A *real* person, in other words.

"I could not contact the *Albatross* directly and tell Captain Harding-Smith to search for you—although the *Albatross* is capable of wireless communication, I have only allowed a primitive level of such technology in my world, and the island was so remote the *Albatross* was out of range. Had I not just carried out a reboot, I could have used my Shaping power to communicate my orders—but I didn't have that power, either." He sighed. "A lack of foresight on my part. I may be the Shaper, but I admit I'm not quite as omniscient as the version of me described in holy writ."

Again, I shot a glance at Athelia: she didn't seem troubled by such blasphemy. *Can a god commit blasphemy against himself?* I wondered.

"I could only hope that Captain Harding-Smith would dutifully follow his orders and maintain constant surveillance of the island, if the reboot had not destroyed it," Robur continued. "Fortunately, he did, or you would not have been seen and rescued and we would not be having this conversation."

I remembered the way the island, in the wake of the destruction of the Portal, had crumbled away beneath me as I was hoisted aboard the *Albatross*. "Very fortunate."

"My impetuous decision to place the *Narwhal* near the spot was less fortunate," Robur admitted. "Your kidnapping and everything that came after was not what I would have planned for you if I'd had any notion you were going to pop into my world. But it all worked out, and it was certainly exciting along the way, wasn't it?"

"One word for it."

"My spies in Dakkar's palace told me you were there, and that you were headed to Phileas. I ordered Captain Zoof to watch for your arrival and sent Athelia to retrieve you." He grimaced. "I knew Zoof was a fool, but I didn't think he was enough of a fool to hire a bunch of local toughs to try to capture you, which not only risked getting you killed, it exposed our operations to the Free City Guardsman . . . well. He'll be punished." He made a gesture like he was shooing away a mosquito. "My fear, when I felt you open and then close a new Portal in the Free City . . ."

"Wait!" I interrupted. "You felt that?"

"Of course, I felt it," he said. "When the last one opened . . . if the Mysterious Island was a tumor, the Portal was like an open sore. They feel *wrong*."

I remembered my reaction to the one in Snakebite Mine and had to agree.

He leaned forward again. "I was afraid you had left my world without my getting a chance to talk to you. That would have been a disappointment, since I was anxious to find out who you were and why you were here, and a worry, because how could I be sure more interlopers wouldn't come charging into my world if one had? I felt great relief when Athelia sent word she had you. I take it the Free City Portal did not lead back to your world and this Karl Yatsar?"

"No," I said. "It leads to the next world. And I'm not ready to go there yet. Not without Karl." I didn't mention the apparent werewolf.

"Ah, yes, Karl." Robur's gaze sharpened. "So, tell me, Shawna Keys. If it took Karl to open a Portal from your world to mine . . . how were you able to open one from my world to the next?"

I opened my mouth . . . then closed it again. I did not want to tell Robur the truth, that the ability to open Portals arose from alien technology that I'd apparently picked up by coming into contact with Karl's blood. Robur struck me as a man who would not hesitate to take some of my blood to see if it would have the same effect on me, even if I was the first "real person" he'd seen in years. Whether that would give him the ability to open Portals or not I did not know, but based on what I'd seen of his world, I also didn't want to find out.

"He taught you how to do it, didn't he?" Robur's gaze sharpened. "And that means you can teach me."

TWENTY-THREE

I CONSIDERED MY next words very carefully, triply glad I hadn't drunk much of the wine. "No," I said at last. "Only Karl can do that."

"Why?" Robur demanded.

"He . . . I don't know how to explain it . . ." (*mainly because I'm lying*) ". . . shared the knowledge with me nonverbally." *Okay, that was kind of true.* "Telepathically or something." *Definitely* not *true.*

"Like some kind of Vulcan mind meld?"

Despite the perilous path onto which the conversation had swerved, I grinned inwardly. *At last! Someone else who makes* Star Trek *references!* Outwardly, I remained impassive. "I guess. The point is, I don't know how to pass it on to you. Only Karl can do that. And I don't think he will."

"Why not?" Robur pressed.

"Because if you knew how to do it," I improvised, "the Adversary could take the knowledge from you if he succeeds in entering your world and stealing your *hokhmah*. He gave me the knowledge after I'd already lost sole control of my *hokhmah*."

Robur laughed. "Oh, right. I almost forgot. There's a big bad 'Adversary' out there planning to come into my world and take it away from me."

"Robur . . ."

He waved off my objections. "Don't sweat it, Shawna. Keep your secret. I really don't care. It's not like I have any desire to leave this world. Why would I? I like it. I

Shaped it so I *would* like it, so that's hardly surprising. And if I decide I don't like it, I'll just reShape it." He studied me. "Why don't you just go back to Phileas and go through the Portal there? Athelia will take you. I know who you are now—that quiet little girl, all grown up—and why you came, and what the Mysterious Island was. Since I'm not about to give you my *hokhmah,* this quest of yours has already failed. There's really no reason for you to stay in this world any longer, and if you leave, you'll be one step ahead of this 'Adversary' you're so worried about. Karl will have no trouble finding me once he enters this world. I will point him in the right direction and facilitate his travel, and then you'll both be out of my hair."

I stared at him. Hadn't he paid *any* attention to what I'd told him? "You have to give me your *hokhmah* before I can leave," I said. I admit I may have emphasized each word, as though I were talking to a particularly dense child. "If you don't, the Adversary will take it from you whenever he shows up, and then he'll kill you to cement his control and seize your world just like he's seized mine."

"Tell me," he said. "If I give you my *hokhmah,* will I still be Shaper?"

"I don't know that for certain," I said. "Maybe we'll share it."

His mouth quirked for some reason. "Shared *hokhmah* . . . but I don't want to share."

"Michael . . ." I said, trying for a real-person-to-real-person moment.

"Robur," he corrected. "Michael Hartshore doesn't exist anymore. And I don't fear this Adversary of yours. I already told you, I'm a more powerful Shaper than you. If he gets through, I'll stop him in his tracks. *If* he gets through. He has to follow this Yatsar guy, right?"

I nodded.

"And Yatsar can completely destroy the Portal if he has the Shaper's help?"

I nodded again.

"So, if Yatsar comes through ahead of the Adversary, I'll help him destroy the Portal. Then you and he can go on and save the Labyrinth, if that's really what you're doing. And I can carry on with my wargames."

Games? In my mind's eye, I again saw Anthony dying. I also saw red. But I held my temper (not without some difficulty). "You'll know when the Portal opens. But you still have to get there. The Adversary could come through and have hours or days to act before you can do anything—and if he leaves the Portal open behind him, he'll have enough power flowing in to enable him to Shape individuals to his side even if you still have your *hokhmah*. That's what he did in my world. He turned it against me even though I was still in it!"

"Again, I'm far more powerful than you are . . ."

I opened my mouth to protest; he held up his hands to forestall me.

". . . and even if you're right, and I'm not powerful *enough,* it won't matter as long as we're there when the Portal opens, waiting to welcome Karl Yatsar with open arms. Then we can destroy the Portal before the Adversary shows up." He folded his arms. 'So, tell me, Shawna Keys: where will that be?"

"What? I don't know."

"Don't you? You knew where you could open a Portal in Phileas."

I opened my mouth and closed it again. He was right, and I should have already wondered if I could pull off that potential-Portal-finding trick again. Robur might be an egotistical jerk, but he was—most annoyingly—a very *smart* egotistical jerk.

"Prince Dakkar showed me a globe," I said, somewhat grudgingly. "Somehow, I was able to sense it on there."

"A globe?" Robur said. "Nothing could be simpler."

He got up, went to a cabinet next to the fireplace, opened it, and took out a globe, twin to the one Dakkar had showed me, except the colors of the countries were different. He moved the barely touched charcuterie plate out of the way and put the globe on the ivory-topped table. He scooted his chair around the end of the table until he was sitting right next to me. "We're here," he said, pointing to the coast of Verne's Land. "Raj is currently here."

He indicated a spot in the ocean to the northwest. "Here's the Free City." He indicated its isthmus. He gave me an expectant look. "Well?"

I hardly heard him. I sensed . . . something.

I reached out and turned the globe. Another land-mass came into my view, about where Easter Island would have been if Verne's Land was South America, though far larger—if not Australia-sized, at least New Zealand-sized. "Tsalal" read the label. Its interior, like most of the world, was marked "Unexplored," although there were a few named settlements along the eastern coast. My fingers reached for it of their own accord. "Here," I said, pointing to a spot in the blank space deep inside Tsalal. "That's where Karl will open the Portal."

I knew it with absolute certainty, and that was seri-ously weird. It felt like a thought had been implanted in my brain from something outside me, although I guessed it had really come from the Shurak technology inside me. *Yuck.*

Robur looked where I was pointing and laughed. "How appropriate," he said, though he didn't say why. "Then that's where we have to go. It's a considerable distance."

I pulled my hand back. "How do we get there? The *Albatross*?"

Robur shook his head. "The *Albatross,* I'm afraid, is currently in the far north, at a secret base in the ice. The prince's helicopters inflicted severe damage when they forced it down in order to kidnap you. Although its re-pairs are essentially complete, it is too far away to do us any good. And my smaller airships . . . blimps, really . . . are far too slow. No, we will take the *Terror.*"

I frowned. "That's the . . . surface/air/underwater thing, right?"

"Inelegantly put, but yes. One of Verne's more in-triguing creations."

"What is it with you and Verne, anyway?" I said.

He shrugged. "I like his stories, I like the steampunk aesthetic, I liked the idea of playing his supervillains . . . or heroes, depending on how you feel about their reasons for doing what they do . . . against each other. So I made it the basis of the world."

"Right down to names."

"Some of them. Others just kind of . . . boil up from the Verneian underpinnings. My world is an homage, not a copy."

"Can you really journey to the center of the Earth from a volcano in the far north? Dakkar said something about it."

Robur grinned. "Indeed, you can. That's why I have a base up there, though Dakkar knows nothing about it, or the fact there are explorers down in the caves as we speak. I'm thinking of having them bring a dinosaur to the surface and throw a little *Jurassic Park* into my world mix. Would you like to take a side trip to see it?"

"No," I said. *I'm not here as a tourist,* I thought irritably. Then I thought of something else I'd wanted to ask since I'd boarded the *Albatross* and been threatened with sudden expulsion from it. "Also, what's with the witches?"

"You heard about them? Just a bit of spice. They have no actual magical ability, of course. Bunch of mumbo jumbo."

"You made them all redheads."

"I had a redheaded girlfriend once. It ended badly. I hold a grudge." He lifted his palms. "So sue me. I'm human."

"So are the people who live here! The people whose lives you play with! How many redheaded girls have suffered because, just for fun, you decided to associate red hair with witchcraft?"

He sighed. "They are *not* human. They're Shaped. Just copies. We've been over this . . ."

"This is their world. The only one they know."

"Until Dakkar fires off his moon cannon," Robur said. "Which will actually work in this world. How cool is that?"

"It's not funny!" I said, with considerably more heat and volume than I'd realized I was going to use. I stopped and took a breath to calm down. "It's not," I said more quietly. "Maybe they're not humans from the First

World. Yes, they're Shaped. But they still live and love and hurt and grieve . . . and you couldn't care less."

"That's not true, and I'm hurt you should think it is," Robur said. "Of course, I care. I'd be devastated if anything happened to Athelia," he gestured in her direction, "or any of the others who have become my friends and colleagues. I've wept many times at the death of commanders and operatives, the senseless destruction of the things I've Shaped. I feel it all very deeply and personally."

"Then why not stop it?" I cried. "You can still Shape this world, more than most Shapers, if what Karl told me was true. Why not Shape it to be peaceful? You and Dakkar could build instead of destroy!"

"*SimCity* instead of *World at War*?" Robur said. "I might get there, a few iterations down the road, if my power holds out. But not yet. This," he spread his arms, encompassing the palace in which we stood and, I guessed, the entire world outside its walls, "is everything I've ever dreamed of."

He leaned forward, eyes locked on mine. "Don't you get it? When you came to the school, you practically lived inside books as I remember it. So did I when I was a kid. Now it's like I'm *literally* living inside the kind of novel I loved. I'll live out the rest of my life in it. I'm not putting away my toys until I'm good and ready. And even if I did get together with Dakkar and we built a utopia . . . utopias are boring. I'd blow it all up, or maybe Shape a nice deadly plague, and then start over with a fresh round of fighting in short order."

He must have decided he'd waited long enough since finishing his last glass of wine. He reached for the carafe, poured himself a third glass, took a sip, then indicated my glass, still half full. "You're not drinking. Doesn't it agree with you? I'd say try the red, but," he laughed, "there's not a lot of it left."

I glared at him. "You're fucking insane!"

Athelia suddenly appeared at my side. "Hold your tongue!" she snapped. "You cannot speak to the Master that way."

Robur waved her away. "It's all right, Athelia." Reluctantly, she returned to the other side of the room, but she didn't sit down.

"Of course, I'm insane," he said cheerfully to me. "We all are, in one way or another. All the Shapers. None of us fit in where we came from. That's how Ygrair found us. She looked for the misfits, the kids who were troublemakers because they were bored, the class clowns, the ones who spent all their time making up stories. She looked for the ones whose parents were at their wits' ends, whose schools were on the verge of expelling them. The ones who wouldn't be missed when they dropped out of the world entirely . . . and, like I said, I think she had the power to make *sure* they wouldn't be missed, altering memories and minds and even official records.

"Somehow, once we were in her school, the outside world mattered less and less. All that mattered was our inner worlds, the ones we built in here," he tapped his head, "and then, after graduation, in the Labyrinth.

"Ygrair found me in an orphanage. I hated the orphanage, I hated the school they sent me to, I hated all the other kids. She rescued me, gave me a new home, with friends, with a purpose. She gave me this." He spread his hands and turned his head, looking in turn at the gilded walls, the thick carpet, the decorated ceiling, the high glass windows overlooking the city, and me. He lowered his arms and picked up his wine again. "Yes, I'm nuts. Or at least I was *going* nuts. But now I have my own World, and nobody gets to tell me what to do with it."

"The Adversary will," I said.

"Let him try." Suddenly, he leaned forward and put his hand on my knee. I flinched back, but his grip tightened, holding me there. "I don't know your story, Shawna," he said softly. "You were still little when you came to the school. But you know what I remember? You were quiet. Very, very quiet. Hardly said a word. Wouldn't look at anyone. Lived in your books. Always had your nose in one. You must have blossomed, because you're not exactly the retiring type now," his hand moved a little farther up my leg, "but there was something wrong with you. Something bad in your background, maybe, someone who hurt you. Maybe that's why you chose not to remember your real life. Maybe part of your ideal world was never *having* to remember."

My breath caught in my throat. "What else do you know about me?"

He gave my leg a final squeeze, then, to my relief, straightened and leaned back again. "Nothing. I don't even *know* that much." He sipped his wine before he continued. "But it seems likely, doesn't it? We both had reasons to Shape our worlds the way we did. So, let's make a deal: you don't psychoanalyze me, I don't psychoanalyze you. And tomorrow, we get in the *Terror* and go see if we can find this Karl Yatsar of yours. What do you say?"

I lifted my glass to my lips. To my annoyance, it trembled. I took a sip and set it down on the table again. "Deal."

Because however much of an asshole Robur, aka Michael Hartshore, might be, he was the Shaper of this world. I had to get his *hokhmah* if I was going to save his world from the Adversary and begin my quest to save the Labyrinth. Only Karl could tell me how to do that, and Robur was the only one who could get me to where Karl might finally make an appearance. Without Karl, my quest was already over.

It wasn't quite a deal with the devil, but when I thought of all the death Robur had visited upon the Shaped citizens of his world, I thought it might be close.

TWENTY-FOUR

"BEHOLD THE *TERROR*!" Robur said pretentiously the next morning (I'd come to realize he said pretty much *everything* pretentiously) as two ensigns pulled open the steel doors of the building with the rounded roof I'd noted the day before at the east end of the flat, paved space north of the palace entrance, which I now knew to be a runway.

Inside the building, brilliantly lit by electric light, the *Terror* glittered like a jewel on a snow-white floor. More people in the black-with-golden-sunburst uniforms of the Republic of Weldon bustled around it.

I remembered the *Terror* from the Verne book, *Master of the World*. I didn't remember the precise description, only that it was said to be capable of traveling through air, on and below water, and on the ground. I also remembered thinking, as I was reading the book, that it wasn't all that large. This version, I was pretty sure, had been upscaled.

It looked to be about eighty feet long, and perhaps fifteen wide—any cabins inside it had to be strung out like beads on a string. Unlike the *Albatross,* with its ship-like hull, the *Terror,* made of shiny metal—aluminum, maybe?—had the rounded cigar-shape of a submarine. Folded against both flanks were enormous translucent wings, attached to the hull by huge, complex mechanisms.

Thick portholes dotted the sides. A flat deck ran about half the length of the hull, from the bow aft. At the front of that was a cockpit, screened with glass like the helm of the *Albatross* had been—and, just like on the *Albatross,* a ship's wheel stood there. However, a glass window also curved around the bulbous bow, where it stuck out below the cockpit.

Two enormous screws thrust out of the stern, and the whole thing rested on four massive pneumatic tires, set on wheels with broad, bladelike spokes that extended well past the edges of the tires, probably to serve as paddlewheels when the thing was above or below the waves.

It was magnificently improbable and impractical and unworkable, just like the *Albatross.* It clearly could not possibly fly, or swim, and yet, presumably, it did . . . not surprising in a world Shaped so that even Jules Verne's cannon-to-the-moon was an actual thing.

"It really flies?" I said, walking around it.

"Flies, rolls, swims, floats," Robur said. "As advertised in *Master of the World.* My version, however, is about twice as long as the one in the book; his would have been unbearably cramped."

"What's to keep Prince Dakkar's mini-helicopters from blasting it out of the sky?"

"They'd have to catch it first, and there's nothing else in my world as fast as the *Terror.*"

"But if they do? It looks unarmed."

"Steam-powered machine guns can be shipped above-deck as required, on those pylons fore and aft." He pointed to them; I'd wondered what they were for. "And although you can't see them, there are fore and aft torpedo tubes on the lower decks, and an aft cannon, as well, behind a watertight port, for surface action."

"Just an aft cannon? Not one in front?"

"Any ship we're shooting at will be chasing us," Robur said confidently. "Besides, there's no place for a bow cannon—it would have to go where the control room is." He put his hand on my shoulder and squeezed in what he probably meant to be a reassuring fashion . . . or something. "Don't worry, Shawna. The *Terror* will get us safely to where the Portal into your world can be opened . . . where this 'Karl Yatsar' has to appear, if he's going to appear anywhere."

"With the Adversary potentially hard on his heels," I said. I wanted to shrug off his hand but endured it instead—to a certain extent, I was at his mercy. No need to antagonize him.

"We'll have enough firepower to take care of any unwanted visitors." He gave my shoulder another squeeze and then dropped his hand at last.

Clearly, nothing I could say could penetrate Robur's impressive shields of obliviousness and ego. *And it's not as if The Adversary can bring tanks and jets through the Portal,* I thought. *It's not big enough for that.*

Or is it?

I realized I didn't know. One more thing to ask Karl, if he ever showed up.

If he wasn't dead.

If the answer to the question wasn't actually *seeing* tanks and jets bursting through the Portal. *I'll bet an F-35 would make short work of the* Terror.

Think positively, I ordered myself, and I continued to tell myself that as I followed Robur up a folded-down ladder onto the vessel's deck, an aluminum grid with a sawtoothed upper side for grip. There, Robur introduced me to Captain Daniel Sullivan, a surprisingly jolly-looking gent. "We'll endeavor to provide a smooth ride, ma'am," Captain Sullivan said, extending his hand.

I shook it. "Smooth would be nice, although even a little turbulence is fine as long as we arrive in one piece."

Captain Sullivan laughed. "Aye, ma'am. Any landing you can walk away from is a good one, as they say."

"Has General Richelot come aboard?" Robur asked the captain. It took me a moment to remember he meant Athelia.

"Not yet, Master."

"Strange." Robur looked back at the open hangar doors, frowning. "It's most unlike her to be late." The frown smoothed. "Well, it gives me time to give you the tour of the vessel. This way." He held out his hand to me. Trying to mask my reluctance, I took it.

It wasn't like I would have gotten lost without taking it. "This way" was down a ladder through a hatch at the aft end of the deck, so his hand-in-mine guidance consisted of a dozen steps, tops. Then he released my hand so he could put his hands on my waist to help steady me as I stepped down onto the ladder. *What's he up to?* I thought.

Okay, I knew what he was up to. The question was, why?

I stepped off the ladder at one end of a narrow cabin with four double bunks, eight beds in all, with barely enough room to walk between them. Robur pointed toward the stern hatch, right beside us. "There's a small chamber beyond that with a gangway to the lower deck. Beyond it is the passenger cabin you and Athelia will share. The crew is forbidden to enter it. They—eight in all—bunk in here. Past your cabin are the galley and wardroom, and aft of that, food storage, and then the head: not a lot of water ballast aboard, obviously, so no showers. Sponge baths only. Aft of the head on this deck is the rear cannon that I told you about, and another gangway to the lower deck. The crew will use it to access the wardroom, so they don't have to come through your cabin."

He turned the other way, leading me forward. The next cabin, though the same size as the crew cabin, had only one bed in it, paneled walls, two portholes, a bookcase, a writing table, a small love-seat-sized sofa, and, of all things, a wine cabinet. "My cabin," Robur said, unnecessarily. He smiled at me, waiting. It took a moment for me to realize he wanted me to comment on it.

"Very nice," I said. "Cozy."

"It is, isn't it?" he said. "It reminds me of my dorm room at school . . . well, except for the wine cabinet." He grinned, turned, and carried on toward the bow.

We next passed through a smaller space, with two beds. "Captain's cabin, with an extra bed for the relief helmsman." Forward of that, we passed between a series of cabinets. "Forward storage—replacement parts, mostly." Finally, we emerged into the interior control room, behind the big bow window. Through it, I saw the hangar, the runway, and a few fluffy clouds.

A ship's wheel, though an odd one, set in a slot so it

could move forward and back like the wheel of an airplane, stood at the room's center. To the left of it was a black-leather seat atop a cylindrical pedestal. A control panel, dotted with dials and buttons and mysterious lights, curved around in front of the wheel and the seat. A crewman knelt in front of that panel, head twisted to look up into it, fiddling with something. He glanced our way as we entered, then straightened so suddenly he banged his head on the bottom of the control panel. Wincing, he jumped to his feet and saluted.

"At ease," said Robur. "Everything okay?"

"Just adjusting the air pressure indicator, Master," the crewman said. He rubbed his bumped head. "Last flight a hose came loose, and it dropped to zero on the panel. Captain said he didn't think we'd flown *quite* that high."

Robur laughed. "Not yet," he said. "Carry on."

In front of the control panel, between it and the window, an open hatch in the floor revealed another ladder leading down. "The forward torpedo room is on the lower deck," Robur said, pointing to it. "Ammo room right behind it." He indicated a tube hanging from the ceiling, with handles folded against it. "Periscope." Against the starboard wall of the room, below the window on that side, stood a wooden console covered with dials and switches, centered by a telegraph key and a pair of headphones on a stand. "Wireless," Robur said.

"Very impressive," I admitted.

"Thank you," Robur said. "That means a lot, coming from another Shaper."

I blinked. Had the real Robur been kidnapped, and this was a double? *That would explain all the touchy-feely stuff.*

At the back of the control room, a hatch I hadn't noticed until then (although the ladder rungs leading up to it on the aft bulkhead should have been a clue) suddenly swung upward. Captain Sullivan looked down at us, framed by two of the giant electric bulbs in metal cages that dangled high above from the hangar's girder-spanned ceiling. "Master," the captain said, "General Richelot is aboard. She has an urgent message for you."

"Coming," said Robur. "Rest of the crew?"

"Completing walkaround inspection, Master. They'll stand by on the ground for the rollout and then come aboard."

"Very good. Continue preparations."

Captain Sullivan disappeared. Robur climbed up to and out through the hatch; I followed, only to be surprised by him kneeling and reaching down, offering me his hand in assistance. Wishing I could refuse, I took it.

When we reached the deck, Robur's hand lingering in mine just a little too long, we found the captain had disappeared, presumably down to the ground to finish his own inspection. Instead, Athelia stood there.

She no longer looked like the theatrical impresario who had escorted me to Quercus. Now she wore a military uniform, with several gold stripes on her sleeves to complement the golden sunburst on her breast, and two stars on her black beret, one on either side of another iteration of the golden sunburst. She snapped a crisp salute. "Master," she said. "News." She glanced at me.

"Speak freely," Robur said. "Shawna is not a security risk."

I felt a little insulted. Maybe I was. How did he know?

"Yes, sir," said Athelia. "It seems that Prince Dakkar's spies in the Free City registered the departure of Captain Zoof and his men. They contacted *Narwhal* by wireless. In defiance of treaty, Rajian helicopters attacked Zoof's small force in concert with surviving members of Shawna's escort, who managed to slip out of the city. Most of Zoof's men were killed."

"Including Zoof, I hope?" Robur growled.

"Unfortunately, no," Athelia said. "He was among those taken prisoner and interrogated."

"Pity," Robur said.

"Master," said Athelia, sounding almost angry, "I'm not sure you grasp what this could mean. Dakkar's men should have spent days or weeks trying to figure out what happened to Shawna, especially since they knew she had intended to leave the Free City through a Portal—to vanish into thin air. But now that they know the truth . . .

we know Dakkar has spies here, and the departure of the *Terror* will not escape notice. Those spies will message Dakkar that Shawna is aboard. We may be attacked."

"Dakkar has nothing that can keep up with the *Terror*," Robur said dismissively.

"Yes, sir, but that does not mean we could not be intercepted," Athelia said.

"And your alternative is . . . ?"

"Launch the *Terror* as planned, but without Shawna aboard. Place her, instead, secretly on board one of the surface ships we use for clandestine transport—the rice carrier *Jasmine,* perhaps. Have the surface ship rendezvous with one of our small airships at sea to pick her up and complete the journey."

"And if a Rajian sub decides to torpedo the *Jasmine*?"

"There have been no merchant attacks in months," Athelia said.

"That does not mean there won't be one tomorrow," Robur replied.

"Master—"

"No, Athelia. There's no time for all that skullduggery. We must get to our target location before the new Portal opens and Karl Yatsar—and possibly this 'Adversary' Shawna seems so concerned about—enters our world. As for the Rajians intercepting us . . . I think you overestimate their chances."

I shot him a sharp look. Was he *aware* he'd just quoted Grand Moff Tarkin from *Star Wars* . . . right before the Death Star blew up?

If he was, he didn't give any sign of it. "This will only backfire on Dakkar," he went on. "He violated the treaty, launching an air attack within the Free City's claimed borders. Phileas will almost certainly initiate a boycott. He has many merchants who trade with the Free City or use it as a neutral place to meet and negotiate with our merchants. His economy will suffer. All the better for when we launch our own air/sea attack on Raj this winter." He waved his hand dismissively. "Thank you for your report, Athelia, but the mission will continue as planned."

Turning his back on her, he went to the rail and shouted over the side, "Ready for rollout, Captain?"

"Ready, sir," came the captain's voice, though he was out of sight from where I stood. I walked over to Athelia, who did *not* look happy.

"Those helicopters that attacked Zoof . . . I know who commands them," I said.

"So do I," Athelia said shortly. "Lieutenant Commander Belinda Hatteras, daughter of Captain John Hatteras of the *Narwhal*."

"Anthony—the man who helped me escape and was shot by the Phileasians Zoof hired—was her second-in-command. By now she knows he's dead." *And knows he died helping me,* I thought uneasily. *And possibly— probably—that he first shot Colonel Everest, and to what can she possibly attribute that bit of treason except my corrupting influence, as well?* "I don't think she'll be very happy with me."

Understatement of the year. *I* wasn't happy with me, even though everything I had done had been aimed at getting me where I was right now, in the company of the Shaper, about to embark on a journey to the place where Karl Yatsar would appear (if he was going to appear anywhere, as Robur had realistically but worryingly noted).

I'd lectured Robur about his cavalier use of the Shaped citizens of his world to achieve his own ends . . . yet was I any better? I wasn't even the Shaper of this world, but I'd managed to turn Anthony against his own mates, to the extent of murdering one of them.

"Lieutenant Commander Hatteras is tenacious," Athelia said. "I wouldn't want her for my enemy . . . well, my personal enemy. In a way, of course, she's already my enemy."

"How do you know about her?"

"I've followed her career more closely than I normally would concern myself with someone of her rank, because she's one of the few female commanders in Dakkar's forces. They are far more primitive about such things than we are in the Republic."

"Tenacious is the right word for her," I said. "She won't give up trying to find me."

"And Prince Dakkar is likely to use that tenacity by ordering her to do just that," Athelia said. "From her report, he'll know you lied to him, that you had no intention of bringing support for his cause back through the Portal from your world. He'll be furious. Which is what gave rise to the concerns I expressed to the Master about you traveling aboard *Terror*." She glanced at Robur. Captain Sullivan had come back aboard, and the two men were engaged in deep conversation on the aft part of the deck, their words lost to us in the noise of the hangar. "This is a very fast vessel, but it is lightly armed and armored, due to weight considerations. It is far from invulnerable."

And neither is Robur, I thought, remembering what he had said about being far under his full strength due to the recent "reboot" of his world. *But he thinks his world protects him from serious harm, so he figures nothing can happen to him on board the* Terror. I hoped he was right, since I was going to be on board the *Terror,* too.

Athelia sighed. I could almost see her throwing away her doubts, as if she were heaving them over the side. "But the Master has knowledge I do not. The decision is his, and he has made it."

"And you trust it's the right one?" I said.

She gave me a sharp look. "Trust in the Master is a given."

The deck jerked beneath our feet, hard enough I had to reach out a hand to grab the thin metal railing. We started to roll. I tilted my head to look past the tail fin and saw that we were being towed out of the hangar by . . .

I blinked, then looked at Athelia. "A mule? The most advanced machine in the world is being rolled out by a *mule*?"

Athelia seemed puzzled by my bemusement. "That's Francis. Everyone loves Francis."

"Francis?" I glanced at Robur, who, still standing

with the captain, had his back to us, watching Francis and the soldier guiding him. "He doesn't talk, does he?"

"What?" Athelia's puzzled look deepened. "Mules don't talk. Not in our world. Do they in yours?"

"No. I was just . . . wondering." There was no way "Francis the Mule" wasn't a deliberate joke on Robur's part (he'd clearly watched some of the same old movies I had—maybe Ygrair had showed them at the school), but apparently, he'd decided against twisting the natural order quite far enough to create talking animals.

But he could have, couldn't he? I thought. *Does that mean there's a Narnia somewhere among the Shaped worlds? Or some other anthropomorphic-animal paradise?* I felt a thrill. *That would be so cool!*

But then I thought, *If I think that would be cool, why didn't I Shape my world to be like that?* And again, I had no answer.

You were very quiet, Robur had told me.

What memories had I hated so much that I had blotted them out—even though Ygrair had apparently told her students Shaping themselves was impossible?

We were out of the hangar, facing tailfirst down the long white runway to the sheer drop into the ocean. Francis' driver (skinner? Weren't mule drivers called, for some inexplicable reason, skinners?) now had the mule pull the tail around, repositioning us for takeoff. Once that was done, he unhitched Francis and led him away.

Several uniformed men had been strolling alongside the *Terror* on both sides, watching closely. Now they swarmed up the port and starboard ladders onto the deck: our crew, apparently. Each man saluted the captain and Robur before disappearing into the vessel through the midship hatch down which Robur had led me when I'd first come aboard.

The captain came forward, nodded to me and Athelia, and descended into the control room. Robur came over to us. "Time to go inside," he said, putting his arm around my waist to propel me gently toward the hatch. I kept my elbow where it was instead of driving it into this stomach.

One after the other—Athelia, me, then Robur—we clambered down the ladder. The captain sat in the chair I had noticed earlier, secured by seatbelts. The crewman who had previously been fixing the barometer dial now stood at the wheel, his feet locked into what looked like stirrups. A stout line went from a hook on his belt to the base of the wheel.

It was crowded in there with five people, but Athelia immediately excused herself and made her way aft. I started to follow her, but Robur put his hand on my arm. "Wouldn't you rather watch takeoff from up here?" he said, smiling. "I think you'll find it exciting."

I looked at the abrupt end of the runway, not all that far away, it seemed to me, and had a feeling he was absolutely right, and that I might be just as happy not experiencing that excitement. But, "Sure!" I said staunchly.

"We'll just step to the aft bulkhead," Robur told the captain.

Captain Sullivan nodded, then pulled an extendable speaking tube from the control panel. "All hands secure for takeoff," he said into the mouthpiece.

I glanced at Robur. "Hang on to the ladder rungs," he then said to me, and I gripped one tightly. He put his hand on the same one, just touching mine. "The crew strap in for takeoff—there are assigned spots for them around the ship—but we'll be fine here."

"Sure," I said again.

The captain let the speaking tube retract back into the panel, then said to the crewman, "Please extend the wings, Mr. Pazik."

"Aye, aye, sir," Pazik said. He touched a button, and I heard a clanking, ratcheting sound, though the wings were too far back for me to see anything of them out our portholes.

"Start engines," Captain Sullivan said.

"Start engines, aye, sir," said Pazik. He twisted two knobs, and the *Terror* started thrumming, a deep bass note like a droning Tibetan monk.

"Powered by electricity, like Dakkar's submarines?" I said to Robur.

"Of course," he said. "I Shaped battery technology here to be far more advanced than in the First World."

"Full ahead," said the captain.

"Full ahead. Aye, sir." Pazik pushed at a throttle. The hum intensified. We began to roll down the runway, faster and faster, the sharp cutoff of the white pavement at the end now rushing toward us. Beyond it, I could see only sky and clouds . . . and an instant later, we charged off the end of the runway into the abyss beyond. My stomach leaped up and my hand tightened to a death grip on the rung. For a moment we glided. The nose dropped, and I saw the sparkling ocean, two toylike sailing ships cutting across the scene, trailing long white wakes.

"Engage wings," the captain said. Pazik pushed a button.

THUMP. The first powerful downbeat made me stagger as the deck leaped up beneath me. THUMP. The nose lifted; I could no longer see the sailing ships. THUMP. Now we were flying, heading out to sea. THUMP. Each boom through the fuselage was like the beat of a powerful heart . . . one I really, really, hoped didn't develop any fatal arrhythmias.

I looked at Robur, who was grinning like a little boy on Christmas morning who'd just discovered Santa Claus had brought him a puppy. "Isn't this amazing?" he crowed. "It's my favorite Verne-thing of them all!"

"But it doesn't make any sense!" I protested. "You know about fixed-wing aircraft. Jets, even. Why Shape something as utterly nonsensical as a craft that flies by beating its wings?"

"Because Verne described it."

"You made other changes. You could have changed this."

"But why? It's *cool.* This whole world is what I think is *cool.* Haven't you figured that out yet?"

Boys and their toys. I'd thought it before, when Anthony had bragged about the Rajians' "Leniebroek Mark VII" rifles. I just hadn't applied it to the whole fricking world until now.

I wondered what had taken me so long.

I sighed. "Now what?"

"Breakfast, perhaps?"

The mention of it made my stomach growl. No food had been offered when I'd gotten up that morning in the lavish guest suite I'd been provided overnight. At least there had been coffee, or I might have murdered someone. "Yes, please!"

Robur led me back through the captain's cabin, his own, and the crew cabin—all of which I'd already seen. Aft of the crew cabin was a small interstitial space which included a gangway to a lower level. I glanced down. "Batteries, engines, that sort of thing," Robur said. "That's where the rest of the crew is right now."

Past that was the passenger cabin I was to share with Athelia: a tiny thing, no longer than the two bunk beds it contained, one on each side—four beds in all, with two storage drawers under each set. There was a porthole on each side between the bunks: I resolved to sleep on the bottom so I could look out.

We entered the wardroom next, just four sets of narrow tables and benches, two on each side, built into the walls. Athelia sat at one of the tables, poring over a stack of paper: reports of some kind, I assumed. She glanced up as we came in. "Breakfast," I explained.

"Had mine," she said and returned her focus to her paperwork.

The wardroom boasted four portholes, two on each side, through which I could see the wings beating, flashing iridescent in the sun with every sweep. THUMP. THUMP. At the aft end of the wardroom the passageway shifted to the port, to bypass the galley, visible over a countertop. A crewman was at work in there, and I smelled the most wonderful smell anyone can smell in the morning: bacon. (Okay, second-most wonderful smell: coffee is the *most* wonderful smell—and I smelled that, too—but I'd already *had* coffee. What I had not yet had was *bacon.*)

Both soon appeared, along with eggs and toast and orange juice. It was an utterly mundane breakfast that just happened to be served inside an improbable flying machine whose mighty wing thumps shook the table once a second.

"There are a few safety rules for flying aboard the *Terror*," Robur said. Rather to my surprise, he had joined me at the table, on the other side of the wardroom from the work-engrossed Athelia. Between mouthfuls of egg, he explained that they mostly boiled down to strapping in during takeoffs and landings, "or if we go to battle stations."

He'd told me earlier that the crew had assigned posts. Now he twisted around and pointed at four folding seats, currently pushed up against the bulkhead at the forward end of the wardroom. "Fold one of those down, fasten the seatbelts, hang on," he said. "There. That's your safety lecture."

"What about getting out of the ship in an emergency?" I said uneasily.

He laughed. "There won't be one. But if there were, I'm afraid there's nowhere to go if we're in the air or under the water. If we happened to be on the surface or on the ground, well, you've already seen the available exits. One hatch in the control room, one amidships."

"Lifeboats?"

"Inflatables, tucked under the edges of the deck." He leaned forward and put his hand on mine, startling me. "Relax, Shawna. The *Terror* is safe as houses. Safer. You're with the Shaper of this world. And as I told you, it won't let anything happen to me . . . it can't."

You also told me Ygrair never actually said that was true, I thought about pointing out but didn't.

Robur's hand squeezed mine, then he released it and stood, although he'd only eaten half his food. "I should be getting back to the control room. I want to consult with the captain about our course."

"Of course," I said. "Thank you for the tour." I dredged up a smile. "It's . . . quite a vessel."

"Quite a Shaping," he corrected. "Wouldn't you agree?"

"Absolutely," I said. "No question."

He beamed, then turned and went forward.

I glanced at Athelia; she didn't appear to have been paying any attention. I returned my own attention to the breakfast, putting the puzzle of how unsettlingly friendly Robur had become out of my mind. My immediate future, after all, was entirely in his hands, so better he flirt with me than throw me in a cell or over the side—either of which he could do anytime he wanted.

For the moment, I had no control, no decisions to make. It made a nice change.

TWENTY-FIVE

I COULDN'T REMEMBER how fast the *Terror* could fly, and I didn't really know how far we had to go, so I had no idea how long our journey would be. I quickly discovered that pretty much any length of time flying in the *Terror* was too long. The constant thumping of the wings was intrusive in a way the roar of jet engines—or even the thunder of turboprops—was not in my own world.

Robur, who, after all, had a kingdom—sorry, "republic"—to run, spent very little time outside of the control room, where he used the wireless to issue orders and receive reports and do whatever else it was the very model of a Verne-inspired dictator did. (I actually spent a considerable amount of time trying to compose a Gilbert-and-Sullivan-inspired patter song along those lines, but didn't get much beyond, "I am the very model of a Verne-inspired dictator, my *Albatross* and *Terror* make me better than Darth Va-a-der," and decided to cut my losses and leave it at that.) I was rather surprised to find I missed his company, and not just because I would have liked to have picked his brain more about what he remembered from knowing me in the First World.

I spent most of my first few hours aboard the *Terror* in the tiny wardroom by the galley, chatting with Athelia, who, since her cover had been managing a traveling theatrical troupe, was fascinated by what I could tell her of theater in my own world. She was familiar with opera, but musical theater was new to her (even operetta had never developed in this Shaped world). She flatly refused to believe that anything such as *Cats* could possibly exist, never mind the more recent (in my world, at least; perhaps in the First World they'd never attempted to make a musical starring a giant puppet monster) *Godzilla*.

I was trying to explain method acting to her when bells suddenly started jangling at an earsplitting volume. Athelia jumped up. "That's battle stations!"

I jumped up, too, intending to run to the seats folded up against the forward bulkhead that Robur had shown me, but I'd only taken a step when the *Terror* banked so sharply and suddenly that I staggered across the floor and had to slap my hands against the curved starboard wall to catch myself. Since I was there anyway, I edged over to look through the thick glass of the porthole. Athelia was doing the same at the second porthole, farther forward. There was nothing to see but water, rushing up at us as we dove as well as turned.

A moment later, alarm bells still ringing, we leveled out.

I started toward the safety seats again, but almost at the same moment Athelia, still by the porthole, shouted, "Rocket!"—and something hit us.

The impact, accompanied by a terrible sound of rending metal, drove me to the floor. An instant later I had to grab a leg of the nearest table to keep from sliding all the way to the port wall again as we rotated so far that I thought we were going to flip over.

The thumping of the wings stopped. We nosed down. With agonizing slowness, the *Terror* began righting itself. But I remembered the water I had seen outside the starboard porthole, the water that had been rushing toward us. How much altitude did we have to . . . ?

Not much.

We hit the water, accompanied by an enormous crashing in the galley as pots and pans and dishes—all metal, I'd noted earlier, probably in case of just such an event—banged together, even though they were secured inside locked cabinets. My arms were almost pulled from my sockets as we bounced off the surface, came down, bounced again, and again, each impact less and coming sooner. For a moment we were afloat . . . and then a klaxon cut through the ringing of the bells and we nosed down and dove beneath the waves.

The light outside the porthole went from white to green in an instant, and quickly darkened. Shakily, I let go of the table and scrambled to my feet. Athelia, who had grabbed the table next to mine, also got up. "What just happened?" I cried.

"Rockets, launched from a submarine," she said grimly. "A barrage of them, across our path. I saw them just before they hit. I'd say one damaged our port wing. Must have frozen it but not taken it off, or we wouldn't have been able to glide in."

I took a deep breath. "So, Robur was wrong, and you were right."

Athelia's expression went cold. "Master Robur was not wrong. He is Master of the World. He has knowledge I do not. I had concerns, I expressed them, he listened, he made his decision. His decision was correct. I do not question it."

I opened my mouth. Closed it again. *Shaped,* I thought, and felt another surge of anger that Robur had given the smart, skilled woman who had spirited me out of the Free City, whose company I had been enjoying for days, this one enormous blind spot.

Irrational belief in the infallibility of leaders has been the recipe for disaster throughout most of human history, I thought. *And Robur decided to bake it into his world.*

As if on cue, the forward hatch opened, and a crewman stuck his head in, having apparently been given special dispensation to pass through our cabin, which was supposed to be off-limits. "Master Robur wants to see you both," he said curtly. Not, I noted, "Master Robur requests that you attend him in his cabin at your earliest convenience" or any of the other archaic (from my point of view) circumlocutions I might have expected.

Well, I thought, *I want to see him, too.*

We made our way forward. Things had been pretty well stowed—with its flapping wings, the *Terror* wasn't the steadiest of platforms at the best of times—so there didn't seem to be too much detritus from broken this-that-and-the-other-thing lying about. Some lights were out. I was primarily happy (and impressed) that there was no sign of our aircraft-turned-submarine leaking.

At least, as far as I could tell. What might be going on down on the lower deck . . .

I really wished I hadn't thought about that.

Still, both the klaxon and the bells had cut off once we'd dived. I figured if we were in imminent danger of sinking there'd be some other horrific alarm going off, so perhaps we weren't going to drown just yet.

Robur, when we reached his cabin, looked furious. He was sitting on his bed and had a bloody cut just above his right eyebrow, which he kept dabbing at with a handkerchief. "How did Dakkar know our flight path?" he demanded of Athelia without preamble, as we stood in front of him.

"A particularly skilled spy, how else?" Athelia said. "Just our bad luck Dakkar had a submarine in position to make use of the intelligence. May I tend that wound, sir?"

"Go ahead."

Athelia went to a white box attached to the wall next to the the aft hatch. I'd noticed similar boxes elsewhere but hadn't thought to wonder what was in them. Now she opened it, revealing a neat array of bandages, bottles, and other first-aid paraphernalia.

"I know you blew most of your power on the reset a few days ago," I said to Robur, "but don't you have enough by now to fix the *Terror* and get us back in the air?"

He shook his head. "No. I wasn't quite at full power even when I did the reset. I've drained myself more than I ever have before."

Athelia returned to the bed with a small brown bottle, a roll of gauze, another of tape, a container of cotton balls, and a pair of scissors. She unscrewed the top of the bottle, then upended it over a cotton ball.

"I won't be good for much of anything for another couple of weeks," Robur went on, eyeing Athelia warily. "Ow!" He jerked his head back as she daubed the dampened cotton ball onto his wound.

"Sorry, Master," she said. She put down the ball and

picked up the gauze. She cut a square of it with the scissors, then applied it to the cut. "If you'd hold that, Master?" Robur put up a hand to keep the bandage in place while she applied the tape. "It's fairly small. It should heal quickly."

"Athelia, doesn't all this talk about the world being reset bother you?" I said to her.

"Of course not," she said. "Robur is the Master." She stowed the supplies back in the box.

I returned my gaze to Robur. "And it doesn't bother *you* that you've Shaped her mind so much she won't even question what sounds like total impossibilities?"

"Of course not," he said, echoing Athelia. "I'm the Master, as she said. This is my world. I can do whatever I want with it."

"Is that what Ygrair taught you?"

He laughed. He seemed calmer now. "It's what she taught you, too, you know. It's what she taught all of us."

"You know I don't remember."

Athelia turned from the first-aid box and stood at parade rest by the hatch.

"Ygrair," Robur said, "taught us how to Shape, but when it came to Shaping our worlds, she gave us only one rule, the 'Law of Thelema.'" He paused, looking at me with an expectant smile.

"Thelema?"

He sighed. "Aleister Crowley?"

I frowned. "That sounds . . . familiar. He was some sort of . . . weird occultist guy, right?"

"Close enough. And his 'Law of Thelema' is, 'Do what thou wilt shall be the whole of the Law.'"

Well, that's chilling, I thought. "She put no restrictions on you . . ."

"On *us*," he corrected.

". . . on us, at all?"

"No, she did not. What would have been the point? She couldn't have enforced them if she had. She didn't accompany me into the Labyrinth. When I stepped onto the vast, empty, featureless plain of this, my soon-to-be world, I was quite alone. As were you, when you stepped into yours. And so, in accordance with the law I had been given, I did what I willed. This was the result." His gesture took in his cabin, the *Terror,* Athelia, and by extension, everything else. He gave me a grin. "I think it turned out rather well."

"Rather well?" I looked at Athelia. "Your followers are robots."

"Shawna, you're being silly," he said, patiently, as if I were a petulant teenager. "They're nothing of the sort. I already told you, within the bounds of her loyalty to me, Athelia is also free to do whatever *she* wills . . . although, of course, she is as subject to both natural and government-imposed law as we once were in the First World. Doing what you will sometimes results in unfortunate consequences." He grimaced. "As Captain Zoof recently proved."

"You know my goal is to reach Ygrair," I said. "To reach her and bring the *hokhmah* of as many worlds as I can to her, so she can protect the Labyrinth against the Adversary."

He gave me an indulgent smile. "So you keep telling me. Over and over."

I let that go. "If I take your *hokhmah* to her . . ."

"I won't let you have it, so you won't," he said. "But carry on."

". . . do you think she would approve of your Shaping?"

"I would say," he said, "that nothing she ever taught us or said during the years I was in her school indicated otherwise."

I had no response. I had clung to some hope that Robur's approach to his world was an anomaly, that most of the Shaped Worlds I entered would at least be . . . well, moral, I guess; worlds where right and wrong existed and were within spitting distance of the right and wrong I knew. But if Robur were right . . . and he had memories of Ygrair's school and I didn't . . . I could find myself in worlds where right and wrong were inverted or simply didn't exist: where the Law of Thelema, "do what thou wilt," would apply to *every* person who lived there, without restraint. What kind of anarchic hellhole would that be?

And when I accepted the *hokhmah* of another Shaper into my mind, would I internalize, not just the knowledge of how the World was Shaped, but *why*? Would I find the beliefs . . . not to mention the failings and perversions . . . of the original Shaper infiltrating my soul?

No, I tried to convince myself. *If it worked like that, the Adversary would have internalized my sense of morality when he stole my* hokhmah *from me. He would have become our ally, not our enemy.*

Except, an unhelpful part of my mind reminded me, *he's not really human, is he? It might work differently for him.*

"Don't look so horrified," Robur said. "And quit looming. Here. Sit down." He scooted over to make more room on the bed. Somewhat reluctantly, I joined him, and he turned toward me and put his hand on my knee. I did my best not to squirm. Athelia looked straight ahead. "When I knew you at the school, you were just a kid. You must have been there another decade. You would have learned how to Shape just like I did . . . which means you, too, learned that Ygrair had not the slightest interest in imposing any outmoded notions of right and wrong on the Shapers she trained. And yet you remained. You didn't drop out."

"People actually did that?" I said, startled. "Dropped out?"

"Several, every year."

"And Ygrair let them leave?"

"Of course. I saw them go."

But did you see what happened to them after they were out of your sight? I wondered.

"The point is," he went on, "you stayed, so clearly what you were being taught didn't bother you any more than it did me. As I've told you, Ygrair was focused entirely on liberty: on allowing individuals to 'do what they will.'"

I was getting tired of that phrase. "Even to the point of hurting others?" I looked at Athelia again. She was following the conversation with detached interest, as if it were just an intellectual exercise with no bearing on the real world.

"I told you," Robur said. "I keep telling you. How many times do I *have* to tell you? *The Shaped are not real people.* They're just figments of my imagination, given flesh and blood."

"Flesh and blood, desires and hopes, pleasure and pain," I shot back. "They don't think of themselves as figments of anything."

"Well, of course they don't," Robur said. "The world wouldn't *work* if they did."

I wanted to slap him. Instead, I clenched my fists. "This is getting us nowhere," I said. "So, you don't have the power to fix the *Terror*. Where does that leave us?"

"Right where we are now," he said. "Riding in comfort. We cannot fly, which will certainly slow our journey, but all other functions of the vessel remain intact. The damaged wing was folded successfully back against the hull, so we are as streamlined as we should be, and are making excellent time underwater. Once we are safely out of range of whichever of Dakkar's submarines managed to intercept us, we will ascend and continue our journey on the surface."

"What if his submarine catches us?"

Robur laughed. "There are no other vessels in the world as fast as the *Terror,* in whatever configuration she is in. Verne decreed it, and so have I." He touched the bandage on his head and looked at Athelia. "I neglected to thank you for tending to this, General."

"It is my pleasure to serve you, Master."

"Do you still think your world is protecting you?" I said. "We could have all have been killed—including you—when that rocket hit. You're lucky that cut is all that happened."

"Nonsense," he said decisively. "The world knows its Shaper. Minor injuries are one thing, but killed? Never. In fact, I believe it was the world that insured that the rocket that hit us only damaged a wing rather than, say, struck us amidships and broke us in two."

"But you said Ygrair never actually said your world would protect you."

"No, she never 'actually said your world would protect

you,'" he said, mimicking me. But then he smiled, as if to ease the sting. "But she didn't say it wouldn't, either. In fact, when we asked her directly, she said she didn't know."

That startled me. *Ygrair* didn't know all the rules of the Labyrinth?

"But we students talked about it a lot," Robur continued, "and we concluded . . ."

"Concluded? You mean you just decided to believe it?"

"Because it's the only thing that makes sense!" Robur spread his hands. "How could this world possibly continue if I cease to exist? It's all just something I've imagined. Imaginary people, imaginary technology, imaginary landmasses, even imaginary stars in the sky. My Shaping made them real, after a fashion, but they'll vanish the instant I am not here to imagine them anymore."

"No," I said. "They won't." Because I'd suddenly remembered that I knew the answer to this question.

"What do you know about it?" he said, with a touch a scorn. "You don't remember Ygrair's teaching at all."

"I don't have to. The world the other side of mine, the Shakespearean world Karl emerged from, did not cease to exist when the Adversary killed the Shaper of it, nor did the Adversary's world cease to exist when he left it to start chasing Karl. My world did not cease to exist when I left it, and it would have gone on had he killed me, too."

I looked into his eyes, willing him to believe me. "Robur, you may have imagined this world, but it exists outside of your imagination. It has to, or how could I be here?" *That's a good point,* I thought, though I'd just then thought of it. "And that means, when you tell me the people who live here aren't real people—no matter how many times you tell me that—you're wrong. They will live on after you die. And *that* means there is no reason at all to think that this world will protect you, unless you are actively Shaping it to do so. Let your guard down . . . or run out of power, like you have . . . and you are as vulnerable to the vagaries of chance as anyone else within it. The fact we're all alive right now, after that rocket attack, is pure luck."

Listen to yourself, I thought. *"Vulnerable to the vagaries of chance." Not bad.*

It didn't impress Robur, though. He shook his head vigorously. "No, Shawna," he said, "you're wrong. I am as confident of my essential invulnerability within this world as I have ever been of anything. Do you think I would have risked myself on this journey, bereft of power as I currently am, if I thought there was the slightest chance I could actually be killed?"

"If you're right, why would your world even allow you to be hurt?" I pointed at the cut on his head. "What if that got infected, or you suffered a fatal blood clot after the blow to your head, or . . ."

He touched the bandage. "Because minor injuries make the game more interesting," he said, sounding irritated. "A small amount of risk spices things up. But nothing like this will ever kill me." He took a breath, as though calming himself, patted me on the knee again, then stood. "I've enjoyed discussing this with you, Shawna . . . it reminds me of school. I must speak to the captain now, but if you'd care to join me here for supper in an hour, we can continue our chat . . . and getting to know each other." He smiled. "I've remembered a few more things about you from when you were a kid. You might find them amusing."

I was a little ashamed of how much I wanted to hear those "few more things." Throw in a nice dinner, and it actually sounded like a pleasant evening. "Of course," I said.

Robur went forward.

I looked at Athelia. "None of that bothered you?"

"No," she said staunchly. But she wasn't looking at me, she was looking after Robur . . . and for just a moment, I thought I saw a flicker of doubt cross her face.

TWENTY-SIX

DINNER (SOME VERY nice steaks, accompanied by asparagus and roast potatoes) came and went. Despite his
stated willingness to continue our earlier conversation,
Robur at first refused to talk further about Shaping or
Ygrair, except to tell me the "few things" he remembered about me as a kid, which were few indeed: besides
my love of books, he remembered I had liked chocolate,
enjoyed playing with the cats and dogs that lived at the
school, had a nice singing voice . . . and that was about it.

Mostly, we reminisced about movies and TV shows
and music and books we both remembered (since my
Shaped world was apparently identical to the First World
through the date of his departure from it, and presumably through mine).

I discovered I enjoyed talking to someone with whom
I didn't have to pretend to be anyone other than who I
was, and I discovered that Robur, for all I had a low
opinion of his Shaping of this world, was pleasant enough
company—pleasant enough that I let him refill my
wineglass . . . more than once.

"You don't know how wonderful it is for me to have
the chance to talk to a real person," Robur said, putting
his hand on my knee (again). "Especially in this world.
I sometimes wish I'd Shaped something closer to the
First World, as you did, just so I would have more in
common with the people around me."

"I didn't know that was what I'd done," I pointed out.

"But you chose to do it originally," he said. He squeezed my knee, then sat back. "Smart girl."

I found myself thinking maybe he wasn't so bad after all. He had to be lonely, setting himself up in a world like this. Maybe he'd made a mistake, and he was just beginning to realize it. *Maybe he'll change things for the better after this,* I thought, and took another sip of wine.

After we finished a bottle of a Pinot Noir ("We don't call it that," Robur said, "but that's what it is"), we moved to the little couch that took up one corner of his cabin, a second bottle open on the table in front of us, to continue our conversation. I tried to get him to tell me more about what he had learned about Shaping and I hadn't (or, at least, couldn't remember), but he seemed reluctant. "At least tell me if Ygrair said anything about one Shaper sharing her *hokhmah* with another," I said. "I understand you don't want to give me yours, but at least give me a clue, if you have it, how I can get it from the next Shaper." *In that world with the werewolf guarding the Portal,* I thought. Remembering the beast galloping toward me through the moonlit night, I shivered a little.

Robur must have felt it because he put his arm around me. And maybe . . . probably . . . okay, *definitely* because I'd drunk too much wine, I let him.

"There is one thing," he said, leaning close, dark eyes peering into mine from inches away. "But I don't know how helpful it will be."

"Tell me."

He dropped his voice to a murmur. "Two people can share *hokhmah* if they're . . . intimate."

My heart quickened. "Lovers?"

He nodded.

I swallowed. "How do you know?"

"There were couples," he said. "At the school. Ygrair sent them into the Labyrinth together. She said they'd be able to Shape a world between them. Together. Like Adam and Eve."

"Naked?"

He laughed. I liked the sound. "She didn't send them

that way, no. What they chose after they got there, I don't know. She didn't send a serpent with them, either."

"Did they . . . develop that ability when they . . . became intimate?" I almost whispered.

"Yes," Robur said. "So, if you want my *hokhmah* . . ."

And then, without any warning at all, he leaned in and kissed me.

And I, with even less warning, kissed him back.

There was no thought in it. The truth was, for the first time since I'd entered this world, I'd let myself drink enough I didn't have much thought left in my head. His arms went around me, and my arms went around him. It felt good. It had been a while. Brent was lost to me. I pressed close . . .

. . . and then I felt it. Like a worm, trying to get inside me. (No, not *that*.) It was in my head, nibbling at the corners of my brain. At the corners of my *hokhmah*. Tugging at it. Trying . . .

He was trying to steal my *hokhmah*—not to share it, but to take it from me!

Fury blazed up in me, and with it, power, energy, not Shaping power, but the power I'd felt when I'd opened the Portal on my own in Phileas. I sensed it as a flash of blue light, but I don't know if I really saw it with my eyes or not. All I know is that Robur stiffened, his eyes rolled up in his head, and he collapsed limply onto my lap.

I scrambled out from under him and off the couch, pressing my back against the forward bulkhead. Had I killed him?

No, he was breathing. He even moaned a little, but he didn't wake up.

Almost without thinking about it, by instinct, I stepped forward and put his wineglass right under his fingertips, as they dangled down from the couch, toppling the glass so the last of the red ran onto the floor. Maybe, when he woke up, he'd think he'd passed out from drinking too much.

Then, my own head spinning, my insides in turmoil, I went out through the back hatch. Two men snored in their bunks in the crew quarters; they didn't seem to notice as I passed through.

I don't really remember getting to my own bunk and falling asleep. I woke to a splitting headache and a queasy stomach, and the realization that honest sunlight was streaming through the porthole . . . and that the room was swaying, the circle of light moving back and forth across the deck plates. Athelia still slept. We were on the surface, clearly, and I . . .

And I, clearly, really, really needed to throw up.

I made it to the head just in time, emerged into the bacon-scented miasma lingering in the otherwise empty wardroom from the crew's long-past breakfast, and had to duck back inside the head again. When at last I made my way back to our tiny quarters, Athelia was awake, stretched out on her bunk, reading. "I didn't expect to see you here last night," she said.

I stared at her. *Was that . . . ?* "Are you . . . jealous?"

"No, of course not," she said, her eyes on her book, but the spots of red in each cheek belied her statement.

"Athelia," I said, "trust me. We didn't . . . I didn't . . ."

"It is the Master's concern," she said. "Not mine. Whatever the Master chooses to do is right." She closed the book, got up, and went aft, into the wardroom.

I stayed on my bed, fuming. *"He didn't want me, he wanted my* hokhmah!*"* I wanted to shout after her. Anger swelled in me again as I remembered that . . . invasion. He knew how to take my *hokhmah,* he'd always known. He'd just needed me to lower my guard. Maybe all he'd really needed was for me to give him permission, to let him in . . . but he'd known he'd never get that, so instead he'd gone for subterfuge. The flirting (the "casual" touches, which had begun almost the moment we met—he'd planned this from the beginning!), the easy conversation, the confession he was lonely, and especially, the wine (and boy, had I confirmed I shouldn't drink when I needed my wits about me) had all been calculated to get me to that kiss, that close, extended physical contact, when I was supposed to be focused entirely on him.

If I hadn't had the Shurak technology I'd apparently absorbed from Karl's blood, he might have succeeded.

But what did he want with my *hokhmah*? That part I couldn't figure out. My *hokhmah* was useless. He couldn't honestly think he could go back into my world and face down the Adversary and claim it for his own, a second world to play games in . . . could he?

Yes, he could, I thought. *He totally could. Because he thinks he's the most powerful Shaper there's ever been. He doesn't really believe in the Adversary, or at least doesn't believe he's any sort of real threat.*

But there was more to it than that, and after a moment, I knew what it was. *He thinks if he steals my* hokhmah, *he'll learn how to open Portals! And since he knows how to take* hokhmah *from another Shaper, he probably thinks he can take other worlds, if he wants them. He believes his own press releases. He thinks he's master, not just of this world, but of any world he wants. More worlds to play games in. More Shaped people to use as pawns.*

The defining quality of Robur's personality was, without a doubt, ego.

"Whatever the Master chooses to do is right," Athelia had said before she left me. I felt sorry for her, thinking that, sorry she had been *forced* to think that . . . sorry, and angry, all over again and at an even deeper level, not only at Robur, but at Ygrair. "Do what thou wilt," indeed. What more monstrous philosophy could exist? Individual freedom, taken to its *reductio ad absurdum*.

Don't get me wrong, I'm a big fan of freedom and liberty. But if everyone does just what they want, then they'll inevitably hurt others. "Do what thou wilt" means power is all-important, because only by being powerful can you truly do what you want. "Do what thou wilt" means imposing *your* will on others, denying them the right to do what *they* "wilt," and again, the only way to do that is to be powerful . . .

. . . to be, in fact, Master of the World.

Robur had tried, and failed, to steal my *hokhmah,* but my task, set by Ygrair, remained. I was supposed to take *his hokhmah,* his knowledge, his reasons and methods of Shaping this world, into myself. It would be like swallowing sewer water . . . and yet, I had to do it.

What would that mean to me? What would that mean to my quest, going forward?

I jumped up, suddenly not wanting to be alone with my thoughts anymore, and went into the wardroom. Athelia sat by one of the portholes with a cup of coffee, staring out. I got my own cup of coffee and joined her. "So, we're on the surface," I said, after the silence had stretched a little too long.

Athelia nodded without looking at me. "We must have left that Rajian submarine far behind." She turned to me at last. "Breakfast?"

I blanched. "God, no," I said. "The coffee is all I want right now."

She went aft to the galley, returning with porridge, left hot in a pot for anyone who needed something between breakfast and lunch. Yesterday, we'd been tossed around the wardroom during the rocket attack. Today, we were tossed around more gently, swaying as we sat at a table, me nursing my coffee and Athelia eating her porridge. My throwing up, I was relieved to realize, had had nothing to do with being seasick—it had been caused by the wine and, I think, a delayed reaction to what had happened the night before, to Robur's violation of my mind. My stomach had settled now. Even though I'd been prone to motion sickness all my life, I'd lost the urge to upchuck during the terror-filled hours I'd spent aboard the sailboat *Amazon* in my own world, and it looked like it hadn't come back.

Alternatively, of course, I'd never *really* been subject to seasickness and my tendency to it was just another of the fake memories I'd apparently somehow implanted in myself when I was thrown into the Labyrinth.

I found Robur's callous disregard of the Shaped people in this world, people like Athelia, horrifying. It offended me. But did it offend the *real* me, the girl who had spent years at Ygrair's school, apparently never worrying about the ethics of Shaping entire populations? Or did it just offend this fake version of me, crafted from false memories that came from what-or-who-knew-where?

Maybe I didn't implant them, I thought suddenly. *Maybe Ygrair did. But why?*

And then I thought, *How can I even be certain what kind of person I am when I can't trust my memories of the kind of person I've been?*

I had no answer.

The hatch to our cabin opened and the same crewman who'd summoned us to Robur's cabin the evening before announced, "Master Robur's compliments, and would the two of you care to come on deck?"

Well, that was a lot more polite than last night's summons. I wondered what Robur remembered from our almost-amorous encounter. What had that strange surge of energy from the Shurak technology felt like to him? He hadn't locked me up yet, so maybe he thought he'd just passed out from too much wine. *I guess I'm about to find out.*

We went through our cabin and through the forward hatch into the crew cabin, then up the midship ladder to the deck. At the bow, Captain Sullivan stood at the wheel in the cockpit, glass surrounding him on three sides. Robur stood to his left with his binoculars raised.

"Did that glass stay in place while we were underwater?" I asked Athelia.

"No," she said. "It's hinged at the bottom. It folds down, one piece over the other, automatically when we submerge."

We were cutting through whitecapped sea toward a dark coastline, beneath gray skies. Spray cascaded up and over the bows of the *Terror* with every intersection of a wave, though we were high enough it only spattered us a little. It was cold, though.

Robur had told me when I first came aboard that steam-powered machine guns could be mounted on the deck pylons. They were there now, long-barreled, with big ammunition drums attached to them and metal-clad hoses connected to outlets in the deck: one to port, one to starboard, and one at the aft end of the deck that appeared to be capable of being swung a full 360 degrees, to fire in any direction. A crewman stood ready at each. Since the aft one, if it fired forward, could conceivably fire right through where I stood, I hoped the crewman manning it was very, very good at his job.

I looked to port, at the wing crippled by the rocket. It was more-or-less folded into place, but the beating mechanism was buckled and blackened. We clearly weren't going anywhere in the air without some major repair work, which seemed unlikely to be accomplished anywhere but back in Quercus . . . unless Robur regained enough Shaping ability to effect it.

Robur lowered the binoculars and turned toward us. "Shawna," he said. "General. Please join me."

We made our swaying way to the cockpit. "Land ho!" I said, pointing past him.

"I had noticed, yes," he said. He had a sour expression on his face. I wondered if it were because of me. But he said nothing about what had happened, leaving me to continue wondering how much he remembered. "Navigation is somewhat compromised by our inability to get a clear shot of the sun in this cloud cover, but we should be very close to where we intended to cross the shore. Since we can no longer fly, however, landing may prove difficult."

The land had grown appreciably clearer in the few moments we'd been on deck. It did not look hospitable: towering forests, gray rocks against which the waves broke in vast explosions of spray; not a friendly boat landing or even a flat bit of beach to be seen.

Something squealed. Captain Sullivan lifted a speaking tube attached to the pedestal of the wheel. "Report," he said into it, then put it to his ear. I couldn't hear the conversation, but he nodded. "Thank you, Mr. Pazik," he said into the tube, then hung it on the pedestal again and pulled back on a lever atop a second pedestal to his right. The thrumming of the engines slowed, and so did we. "Getting into shallower water, Master Robur," Sullivan said. "Any sign of a landing place?"

Robur scanned the coast with his binoculars again.

"I'm afraid not, Captain Sullivan." He lowered the glasses. "If we're where we think we are, though, the terrain changes a few miles north. We might find a place there. I suggest we parallel the coast in that direction."

"Aye, aye, Master," said the captain. He spun the wheel, and the *Terror* turned to starboard.

I stared at the coast passing by. "Looks untamed," I said. "I noticed most of your maps are marked 'Unexplored.'"

"Wilderness is a playground for adventure," Robur said. "I like to keep a lot of it around in case I need it."

Something nagged at me, had been nagging at me for a while. I'd put it down to the aftereffects of the night before, but now . . .

Oh! I thought.

I concentrated and . . . yes. That wasn't a hangover: it was the potential Portal. I could sense it, somewhere inland. Definitely not open. We still had time.

Maybe all the time in the world. If something had happened to Karl in my world, and he never showed up in this one . . .

I thought about that as the dark forests and surf-pounded rocks slipped by. If I stood where I could open a Portal back into my own world, the world I'd thought was the *only* world, which I hadn't even dreamed I'd Shaped, until an achingly short while ago . . . would I be able to leave it closed?

I remembered Aesha, dying in front of me in a hail of bullets, murdered by the cadre loyal to the Adversary, Shaped to be as loyal to him as Robur had Shaped his inner circle of followers to be loyal to him.

It's not my world anymore, I told myself.

But I still didn't know if I would be able to resist the temptation.

Which led to another unsettling thought. Would it be *better* if Karl Yatsar had died in my world? When I'd last seen him, he was on my version of the Mysterious Island, trapped with members of the Adversary's cadre. Had he escaped the island? Had it suffered the same fate as the one in this world, and he'd fallen into the ocean, as I would have if the *Albatross* hadn't been standing by?

If Karl is dead, if he doesn't open this potential Portal, and I don't open it, either . . . then is the Adversary trapped? Does that mean I don't have to worry about my quest?

No. Sure, I'd been mostly focused on staying ahead of the Adversary, but that wasn't the real quest at all. According to Karl, Ygrair was the cornerstone of the Labyrinth. All the worlds within it were connected, touching each other (which was why you could make Portals between them), but also, all of them were connected to her . . . and she'd been hurt in an attack. According to Karl, she was weakening, losing her connection to the many worlds of the Labyrinth. She needed someone . . . me, apparently . . . to collect the *hokhmah* of as many worlds as possible and bring it to her. Somehow, she could use that gathered *hokhmah* to reforge her connection to the Shaped worlds, strengthening the fabric of the Labyrinth. If she did not do that, it would collapse, taking with it all the billions of individuals living in all the only-Ygrair-knew-how-many Shaped worlds—the individuals I'd been so strenuously insisting to the skeptical Robur were real people, as real as us. How could I let that happen?

Karl failing to show up might mean I didn't have to worry about the Adversary, at least not for a while—though there was no guarantee that, given time, he couldn't *learn* to open Portals—but it would not change what I had to do. And not having to worry about the Adversary wouldn't, as my adventures in *this* world had proven, keep me from having to worry about being killed. Although this was a dangerous place . . . I glanced at the wreckage of the *Terror's* port wing again . . . it might not be—hell, it almost certainly *wasn't*—anywhere near the *most* dangerous of the worlds I would have to visit.

A certain werewolf came to mind.

So, Karl failing to show up was not something to be hoped for, especially when I considered I still didn't know how to get the *hokhmah* from another Shaper. Robur knew—as I'd discovered so embarrassingly and infuriatingly last night—but he seemed unlikely to teach me, and he certainly didn't intend to just hand his over. Karl might be able to instruct me . . . but I had to find him first.

"General Richelot," Robur said, breaking into my thoughts. "What do we know about Tsalal?"

"Very little, Master," Athelia said. "There are only a few coastal settlements and a single road connecting them—somewhere just beyond that initial stand of forest, I would say," she added, pointing. "They are nominally under the protection of Prince Dakkar, but they are of no strategic importance to him—or to us, either. It is possible Dakkar has a small garrison here, but it is difficult to see why he would. Some exploration has taken place in search of mineral resources, but nothing has been found that would justify the immense investment it would take to extract and transport them."

"What about indigenous people?" I said.

Athelia blinked at me. "What kind of people?"

"She means primitive tribes," Robur explained. "None in Tsalal," he said to me. "I gave them the run of one of the other continents."

"Let me guess," I said. "For future games."

"Exactly! And because Verne had savages in his books."

"I remember that," I said. "I also remember Nemo commenting that the 'savages' he met were no more savage than the 'civilized' men he met elsewhere."

"Nemo had a sour disposition," Robur said.

"In any event," Athelia said, "there are no primitive tribes *here*."

"There is some interesting wildlife, however, as I recall," Robur said. "Giant herds of enormous bison, saber-toothed cats, dire wolves, that kind of thing. And some fascinating landmarks. One of which, I believe, is our destination."

Fascinating landmarks? What did *that* mean?

We plowed on. The coast slipped by, changing little. But after a time, a noise impinged on my consciousness, a strange, chopping noise. I looked out to sea. Something moved out there, close to the surface of the water, but not on it. I was still trying to figure out what it was, and where I'd heard that noise before, when one of the gunners shouted, "Helicopter to starboard!"

Robur spun, lifted his glasses, took one look, and snapped, "Can we dive, Captain?"

"Not enough depth, sir!" Captain Sullivan said. "And no time to clear the deck if there were." He picked up the speaking tube. "Surface battle stations!"

Bells rang. The starboard and midships gunners swung their weapons toward the helicopter. I waited tensely for the firing to start, but the 'copter came no closer. It swung around and vanished to the north.

Robur watched it go with his binoculars. "Reconnaissance flight," he said as he finally lowered them. "Someone knows we're here."

"The sub that shot us down?" I said.

"Maybe. Or the helicopter could be land-based." He took a deep breath. "No matter. Those things have very little range. Once we're far enough inland, they won't even be able to look for us." He turned to Captain Sullivan. "We need to find a way ashore, Captain. Or we may find ourselves under attack."

"Agreed, Master." The captain shoved the throttle ahead a notch, and the thrumming of the electric motors intensified again as we leaped forward through the waves. He picked up the speaking tube. "Keep a sharp eye on those depth readings, Mr. Pazik."

The wild coast slipped past faster than before, but I looked back out to sea, wondering who had been at the controls of that helicopter.

TWENTY-SEVEN

TWO HOURS CRAWLED by. The helicopter did not return. It occurred to me that meant little, since the 'copter could have been based aboard a submarine that might have dived and was now paralleling us, out to sea—or perhaps had us in its sights at that very moment, and our next hint of its presence would be a torpedo . . .

But no torpedo struck. Instead, we saw the coastline begin to change. The rocks receded, the forest dwindled, and soon we were instead looking into scrubland—near-desert, judging by the sere vegetation. A dirt road ran through it, parallel to the coast, just as Athelia had said, but we saw no movement on it. "Wherever you think best, Captain," Robur said.

Captain Sullivan nodded. "All stop," he said, suiting actions to words and pulling the lever by his right hand to its center position. What seemed a deep silence descended as the hum of the engines faded. The rocking of the *Terror* in the waves immediately became more severe, so that I had to grab on to the handrail to keep from stumbling. Captain Sullivan didn't seem to notice. He picked up the speaking tube. "Mr. Pazik," he said, "disengage screws and engage wheels, if you'd be so kind."

With the engines stopped, I could hear Mr. Pazik's tinny reply. "Aye, aye, sir."

I turned and looked out to sea. If the prince's forces were going to make a last-ditch attempt to stop us going ashore, it would be now. But no specks appeared in the sky, no bug-eyed submarine surfaced. The sea rolled in, uncaring, as it had for millions of years . . .

As it *hadn't* for millions of years. Maybe twenty? I remembered reading a Creationist argument once that the apparent age of the universe was not the evidence atheists thought for the nonexistence of a Creator. "Just as God created Adam a grown man, so he created the world a grown world, the universe a grown universe," the argument went. "The universe appeared to be billions of years old in the very instant it sprang into existence."

It was, of course, the kind of argument you couldn't refute because it couldn't be falsified. That premise, or a variation of it, could counter any evidence of the universe's great age you threw at it. I'd discounted it when I encountered it. Little had I known I lived in a world where that argument was literally true—and that I was the Creator in question. The ocean I had sailed in my world, the stars that had looked down on me, the moon on which nations of the world had permanent settlements, none had been more than ten years old.

It was mind-boggling, and I was getting really tired of my mind being boggled.

The captain pushed the throttle ahead maybe a half-inch. With a *whump!,* the wheels, with their paddle-like spokes, began to spin—or so I assumed, from the foam generated on the surface. We crept forward at a snail's pace. The captain turned the wheel, and the bow followed, until we were aiming at the beach, covered with millions of flat rocks that had been beaten down by the constant surf. He pushed the throttle ahead a little more. The beach neared.

And, suddenly, we weren't on a boat anymore. I felt the moment the front wheels touched ground; some spark seemed to go out of the *Terror,* some almost life-like energy. We rolled forward, foot by foot, until the entire massive vehicle, water running from it in sheets, had cleared the surf and was no longer any kind of boat or aircraft. Now, it was a . . .

Car? Truck? Tank? There wasn't really a word for it . . . except, I guess, *Terror.*

We paused as the captain lifted his speaking tube. "All hands," he said. "Rig for land travel."

I looked around the deck, wondering what that entailed, and saw the gunners going down into the crew quarters. They emerged a minute later carrying bundles that turned out to be leather jackets, leather helmets, and goggles, in grand First-World-War-flying-ace tradition. It seemed odd, since we were now on the ground.

All the same, I took a jacket, helmet, and goggles when they were passed up to me by Mr. Pazik through the control room hatch. Athelia, the captain, and Robur all donned them as well. "Now, Captain," Robur said when that was done. "Take us inland at best possible speed. Let's get away from the shoreline and that road." He pointed west, and at the horizon, I saw a thin line of blue beneath the gray clouds. "Clearer skies ahead. We should be able to get a fix on our position this evening."

"Aye, aye, Master," said the captain. He pushed the throttle forward, the electric motors began to thrum, and we rolled into the scrubland. We crossed the road—just a rutted track running in both directions—and kept going, accelerating.

The reason for the protective gear quickly became apparent. Within two or three minutes we were tearing across the desert at something approaching what I would have called highway speed, the wind plucking at us even though Athelia, Robur, and I were all crowded in behind the windscreen surrounding the helm (the gunners could only hunker down in place). Despite the resemblance between the surrounding terrain and the Arizona desert, it was a chill wind, too. (Not Montana-winter cold, but still . . . chilly.) The journey was surprisingly smooth, the *Terror* obviously boasting a top-notch off-road suspension system.

At times, the captain slowed to a relative crawl, when he didn't like the looks of the terrain. I heartily approved: suddenly plunging into a ravine seemed like a really good way to break the necks of everyone on board— especially those of us on deck. Even if Robur were right about being invulnerable, I wasn't.

After a short time, Athelia announced she was going inside. "Despite the distance separating me from my office," she said, "I still have paperwork to attend to."

"I'll come with you, if I may, General Richelot," Robur said. "I'd like a word with you about a small matter."

"Of course, Master," Athelia said.

Robur wasn't gone long; he soon rejoined me. "You can go below whenever you want, you know," he shouted to me when he noticed me hugging myself.

"And miss this breathtaking tour of the hinterlands of your world?" I shouted back. "I wouldn't dream of it."

He shrugged. "Suit yourself."

Of course, I did go below a couple of times during that long day, to eat and use the head, but mostly, I just stood and watched the scenery roll by. Initially, I could still see forest to the south, the same forest we had seen from the water, but it receded bit by bit until it was below the horizon. Even the scrub we initially crunched our way through dwindled away, leaving only the occasional bush to vary an otherwise endless spread of desert: Nevada on stilts. The promised wildlife stayed well clear of us, which wasn't too surprising, although once I was thrilled to see, far in the distance, three huge, hairy beasts making tracks away from us: living, breathing mammoths. (Or maybe mastodons. I've never been entirely clear on the difference.)

And ahead of us, growing closer all the time, now almost glowing in my mind, was the place where this world touched mine, the "thin place" where a new Portal could be made.

It occurred to me that Robur had never asked me to confirm we were headed in the right direction. Could he sense it, too?

But, no. He'd seemed to recognize the spot when I'd pointed to it on the globe. "How appropriate," he'd said then, and he'd mentioned before we came ashore that he thought one of this region's "fascinating landmarks" was our destination. I still didn't know what he'd meant by that, but he was clearly navigating to it, and as long as the direction seemed correct to me, I wouldn't interfere.

If it seemed we were off-course a little, I'd say something.

When I had been in my world and Robur had been in his and never the twain had yet met, the burst of my Shaping power when I'd reset my world by three hours had apparently forced the Mysterious Island into existence in his world. His rebooting of his world in an attempt to get rid of it had apparently forced the Mysterious Island into existence in my world. But that wouldn't happen this time. So in what kind of space would the Portal form, when it opened? The one Karl and I had destroyed in Snakebite Mine hid behind an already existing door. So had the one I'd opened in Phileas. Did that mean there would be a building of some sort out here in the middle of nowhere? Was that the "fascinating landmark" Captain Sullivan was driving us to?

It appeared I wouldn't find out today. All day, ahead of us, the gap of clear sky grew, and maybe an hour before sunset, the sun suddenly appeared in it, directly in front of us, blinding, but already beginning to turn orange. It lit up the desert around us in spectacular fashion, turning what had been rather nondescript sand into a glittering expanse of gold, sending dramatic fingers of shadow stretching out from every upthrust rock or lonely bush.

When I turned and looked behind us, I saw our shadow stretching out—and our tracks, marking the desert as far as I could see, a clear path for any pursuers to follow. I pointed them out to Robur. He glanced at them, then at me. "What pursuers?" he yelled above the wind. "Even if the submarine chasing us put men ashore where we came out of the water, they cannot catch the *Terror*. And we're beyond the range of their helicopters."

"How fast are we going?" I shouted back.

He leaned over and checked a dial in front of the captain, then straightened. "Currently, sixty miles an hour! Less than half of what the *Terror* can do on a paved road!"

"Don't suppose you could Shape one?"

He frowned. "No. I told you. I'm used up."

I knew that, but I'd hoped his power might have

regenerated at least a little. I wasn't thinking a paved road would be nice just as a way to hide our tracks, though it would do that, too, of course; I was thinking that we might need to flee along it at all possible speed if the Portal opened and the Adversary came through it instead of Karl, especially if it was large enough he could come through it with some kind of armed vehicle.

I didn't say that to Robur. He was supremely confident of his invulnerability, and supremely dismissive of everything I had told him about the Adversary, and nothing I could say seemed likely to change that. And, truth be told, I'd be perfectly happy if he proved to be right and the Adversary posed no threat to his world at all. I'd be thrilled if we reached the incipient Portal, it opened, Karl appeared, he not just closed but destroyed the Portal (as he could, with Robur's help), and the Adversary was trapped forever in the world that once belonged to me. Then Karl and I could, at our leisure, travel from world to world until we reached Ygrair and helped her save and preserve the Labyrinth.

It could happen, I thought.

And sure, it *could*—but recent experience did not incline me toward hope.

The sun set, and it got even colder. A light blazed to life on the nose of the *Terror,* casting a stark-white pathway ahead of us. The captain slowed the vehicle to perhaps a third of its previous speed, but there would be no stopping overnight.

I decided to go below and get something to eat. Robur showed no sign of moving. The captain remained in place, too. He'd been relieved a few times by Mr. Pazik, but for the last hour, as the sun set, had been back at the wheel.

The interior of the *Terror* seemed almost stifling after the *extremely* fresh air of the deck. I made my way to the cabin I shared with Athelia, shedding my coat and helmet and goggles as I went. I tossed all of them on the bed, and then went into the wardroom. Four crewmen were eating stew at one table, tearing chunks of brown bread from a shared loaf. Athelia sat by herself with her own bowl of stew; I went to the galley and received mine, along with a fresh loaf, and took both to the table, where a water pitcher and glasses already waited. I poured myself a glass of water, drank deeply, and then looked doubtfully at the stew. The glistening lumps in the dark broth looked back at me.

"What is this, exactly?" I said, reaching for a spoon.

"Better not to ask."

I took a tentative bite; it was actually pretty good, beefy and savory, and I suddenly realized I was hungry. Apparently, my body had interpreted standing on the deck of an ungainly vehicle bumping across an uncharted desert at high speed as hard work. Go figure.

I dug in. "Robur's still up there," I commented as I ate.

"Waiting for nautical twilight," Athelia said.

"But the sun's been down for more than half an hour."

"Nautical twilight starts around an hour after sunset," Athelia explained. "Enough light so you can see the horizon, but dark enough you can see the stars. You need to be able to see both to take a star sight with a sextant."

"Ah," I said. I knew what a sextant looked like, and I knew they were used in navigation, but I had no idea how they worked. Nor did I care all that much, so I changed the subject. "Did you get your paperwork done?"

"Yes," she said.

"What exactly did you have to do?" I was just making conversation.

She shrugged. "Usual stuff. Transfers, promotions, executions."

I paused, a piece of stew-soaked bread halfway to my mouth. "Executions?"

"Traitors and Rajian spies."

I put down the bread, feeling a little ill. "How . . . ?"

"Firing squad for traitors. Spies, we hang. Publicly, in both cases."

"And you . . . give those orders?"

"I command the Secret Service. Who else?" She frowned at me. "What's wrong?"

I shook my head and pushed my bowl away. "I keep getting blindsided by this world," I said. "It's a violent place."

"Is it?" Athelia considered the question. "I suppose. And yours isn't?"

I opened my mouth to say, "No, not like that," but something held me back. It was true the world had gotten more peaceful in the past few years . . . but that might have been—hell, almost certainly *was*—due to my Shaping. The history of the world before that, which was presumably also the history of the First World, was choked with bloodshed.

At least I tried *to Shape my world into a more peaceful place,* I thought. I hadn't succeeded entirely—violent crime and even war continued to occur—but things were, in general, better. Robur, though—Robur had *deliberately* set up his world to be violent. He wanted to play at being a ruler in a world constantly at war. He hadn't had to. He could have Shaped any kind of world, but he'd Shaped this one, a world where part of Athelia's routine paperwork was approving executions.

So what? I could almost hear him say. *They're not real people.*

"If you're not going to finish that," Athelia said, pointing at my stew, "can I have it?"

"Be my guest." Suddenly feeling very tired, I got up and went back to our cabin, where I stretched out on the bunk. I thought the rumble and rocking of the *Terror* would keep me awake, but I figured at least I could lie there with my eyes closed and worry. Which I did, until, sometime later, the worry turned into troubled dreams involving chases and gunfights and exploding heads, and then a dream in which I was on the deck of the *Terror,* rolling through the night, and on the horizon I saw a bright light, which turned into a giant flying saucer, all colored lights and weird sticky-out metal booms . . .

And then the dream gave way to hands on my arms, shaking me. "Begging your pardon, ma'am," said the same crewman who always seemed to be coming to get me, "but Master Robur requests your presence on deck. He said to tell you—"

"—we're getting close," I finished for him, because I could feel it. That light on the horizon, which in my dream had been a flying saucer—that was the thin place between this world and mine, the place where a new Portal could be opened. But why had I dreamed it as a UFO? *Brains are weird,* I thought.

That sense of the nearness of the potential Portal chased the sleep from my mind and limbs with pretty much the same effectiveness as a bucket of ice water in the face. I scrambled up and, feeling grungy (a feeling that had been growing with each day of not bathing or changing clothes, and wasn't helped by the general miasma of *many* people not bathing or changing clothes), hurried forward.

Up the midship ladder, through the hatch, and back onto the deck. The sun wasn't up yet, but enough light filled the sky to show me that a night's travel had not improved the scenery to any noticeable degree.

Then suddenly the still-hidden-but-rising sun lit the top of something on the horizon—something so familiar, and yet so out of place and unexpected, I actually laughed out loud. "You're kidding me!"

"You see why I thought this such an appropriate location," Robur said. "What better place for visitors from another world to appear?"

"But . . . what's it doing *here*?" I stared around at the otherwise blank landscape.

He shrugged. "I had a fondness for a number of famous landmarks of the First World, so I copied them and scattered them here and there around the planet: things like the pyramids, Niagara Falls, Stonehenge, the Grand Canyon . . . and this." He glanced at me. "I told you how much I liked this movie."

It was the first time he'd mentioned the evening in his cabin. I waited for him to say something more, but he'd already turned his attention forward again.

Well, that probably explains the UFO in my dream, I thought.

Because there, on the horizon, the sun creeping down its deeply incised sides, stood an exact copy of Devil's Tower, Wyoming.

"Re, mi, do, do, so," I sang.

TWENTY-EIGHT

KARL SPLASHED THROUGH black water, mud sucking at his feet beneath the murky surface. Bare-chested, he clutched his wadded-up shirt to his left shoulder with his right hand, pressing hard to contain the bleeding from the gash caused by his fall against the sagging ruins of a galvanized-steel fishing shack twenty minutes before, when the rickety pier to which he'd tied *Amazon*'s inflatable dinghy had collapsed under his weight.

Bad luck at any time; worse luck now. By now, the Adversary knew he had been located at last. If they weren't already on the beach, the Adversary and his remaining cadre members would be at any moment: the Adversary certainly wouldn't be averse to the profligate use of power necessary to instantly transport whatever force he deemed necessary to ensure Karl's capture.

Karl pressed his shirt harder against the wound. He couldn't afford to bleed, not here, not now, not with the Adversary so near. He didn't know how much blood the Adversary needed to clone the nanomites he carried. He *did* know that if the Adversary ever obtained that blood, and the nanomites in it were still active, his quest was doomed. If the Adversary gained the ability to open Portals, he would bull his way through world after world. He would steal the *hokhmah* of the Shapers, killing them to cement his power over their worlds. He would Shape each world to his authoritarian version of utopia. He would leave the Portals open between the worlds, so power would flow to him from those he had conquered, so he would have more and more Shaping ability as he stormed through the Labyrinth . . . so that, when he finally faced Ygrair, he could crush her, destroy all the Shaped worlds, and close the Labyrinth forever.

Karl didn't know exactly where he was—somewhere along the coast of Mexico, he thought. Knowing another storm might capsize or even sink the damaged *Amazon,* he'd intended to sail straight back to land after the Mysterious Island dissolved, but the wind had failed him and the engines, too, leaving him becalmed for days in gray, foggy seas, the aftermath of the enormous Shaping of the ocean Shawna had performed that had helped them escape the Adversary, but had also almost sent them to the bottom in a storm that was nearly hurricane force. He used the time to make what repairs he could on the little yacht.

By the time the wind returned, and the sky cleared, he'd felt the call of the new place where what had once been Shawna's world touched the next world over, the one into which she had disappeared without him. For almost two weeks he had sailed south and slightly east, with favorable winds and only one storm—a mere squall, fortunately. The only vessels and aircraft he saw were in the far distance and seemingly uninterested in him.

He'd come into shore when he'd deemed he could get no closer to the potential Portal by water—and that was when his luck had failed. A coastal patrol aircraft flying over had circled around to get a better look at his vessel, and kept circling, clearly reporting the sighting. Then he'd fallen and cut himself, hurried inland, and now . . . here he was.

Mist curled around the trunks of the giant trees rising from the flooded landscape through which he struggled. He didn't know what kind of trees they were, nor what might be lurking below the surface of the muddy water. *Poisonous snakes,* his brain suggested. *Possibly crocodiles.* But so far nothing had bitten him, and there was nothing he could do to prevent it if anything tried. He was not a Shaper. He could have been, once, and he might yet be again, if he returned triumphantly to Ygrair with Shawna, the Labyrinth secured . . . but here and now, he had no power at all.

He clutched his wounded shoulder more tightly and struggled on toward the thin spot between the worlds, which was glowing brighter in his mind with each splashing step.

Ahead, the land rose at last, and the trees thinned. Something bulked above them, rising high over the canopy, something he hadn't been able to see before: a pyramidal pile of stone.

A temple of some kind, ancient. *Nobody builds a temple in a swamp,* he thought. But perhaps the temple had been built in the First World from which so much of this world was copied before the swamp claimed the surrounding land.

The place where he could open a new Portal into the world where Shawna had vanished was close, now. Very close.

Then he heard shouts behind him.

Just not, perhaps, close enough.

We trundled up to the base of Devil's Tower. When we could get no closer, the captain halted the *Terror.* While he and the crew secured the vehicle, Robur and Athelia and I climbed down onto the ground. Robur and Athelia both wore sidearms. Nobody had offered me one.

We stared up at the massive stone pillar. By now the sun had risen, lighting the whole thing dramatically.

The tower stood on top of a hill of tumbled rock. In my own world, I remembered from pictures, there were trees around the base. There were no trees here. But it was still clearly Devil's Tower: the deep indentations in its flanks, like some giant bear had been sharpening its claws on it, were unmistakable.

"This is where the Portal will open?" Robur said to me. I nodded.

"Where, precisely?"

I reached for my sense of that thin spot between the

worlds. "All I can tell is . . . up there, somewhere." I gestured at the tower. "I think we have to get closer."

"Very well." Robur started climbing. I followed him. Athelia followed me.

It wasn't a long climb, but it was steep, and the jumbled rocks made it difficult going. After twenty minutes we stopped to rest, and I looked down at the *Terror,* which seemed like a toy far below us. I looked ahead again, took a deep breath, and resumed climbing.

At the base of the tower, I consulted my inner compass again. "That way," I said, pointing left.

"Perhaps you should lead," Robur said. He waved down at the *Terror.* The tiny figure of Captain Sullivan, standing in the cockpit, waved back. Robur turned back to me. "I instructed Captain Sullivan to follow us around the tower as we circumnavigate it, and to keep all weapons manned," he explained. "Just in case."

"Good idea," I said.

I moved to the front of our little column and focused on the increasingly powerful sense of the place where this world rubbed up against mine, drawing nearer with every step.

We picked our way through the rocks for a few hundred feet. The *Terror* rolled slowly along below us, keeping us in sight, as we moved around the tower's base . . .

. . . and then, suddenly, we were there.

I stared into a cave, no more than thirty feet deep; even from the mouth, I could see the back of it. It contained nothing but dirt and rocks—and the thin space between the worlds.

I entered, Robur beside me, Athelia behind us. I reached the back wall and touched the stone.

To my fingers, it felt solid—but to my mind, it felt like a sheet of rice paper, a barrier I could tear down in an instant, joining this world and the one that used to be mine. It was so thin I could sense something on the other side . . .

No, some *one*!

I straightened, jerking back my hand. "Karl!"

Robur looked around. "Where?"

"Not here. Not yet. But just the other side . . . he's close. I can feel him." I stared at the stone wall. It remained a stone wall. I couldn't see through it with my eyes . . . but with my mind, I almost could.

"Then all we have to do is wait," Robur said.

"I guess so."

"How long?" Athelia asked.

"No idea. But if he's close . . . it shouldn't be long."

"Excellent," Robur said. He nodded to Athelia, who stepped forward—and pointed her pistol at me.

My eyes widened in shock. *"What?"*

Athelia said nothing. In the gray light of the cave, her face might have been carved out of the same stone as its walls.

"I'd hoped not to do it this way," Robur said conversationally, "but after that night in my cabin, I'm afraid I have no choice."

I stared at him. He'd given little indication he remembered what had happened in his cabin. Clearly, he did. "You tried to seduce me! You tried to steal my *hokhmah*."

"Not steal," he corrected. "Share." I noticed he didn't deny the seduction part. "I'm afraid I wasn't entirely honest with you. Ygrair taught all of us—you, too, presumably, though unfortunately for you, you've forgotten—how to share *hokhmah* with one another. It wasn't something just lovers could do—another small fib on my part—although it does require prolonged contact, and what more pleasurable form of prolonged contact is there than sex?"

"Why would she teach that?" I demanded.

He shrugged. "So that, if we chose, we could enter the Labyrinth in the company of someone else and Shape a world together. She also warned us, though, to only attempt it with Shapers of our same level, because a strong Shaper could potentially strip the *hokhmah* from a much weaker Shaper completely."

He leaned casually against the wall of the cave. "I didn't think I could strip your *hokhmah* from you since you were strong enough to manage at least a minor reset of your world, but I did think—since you didn't even know it was possible—I'd be able to share your *hokhmah* without you even being aware of it if I kept you . . . distracted."

"You were using sex to get what you wanted," I growled. "How cliché is that?"

"It wasn't just to get your *hokhmah,*" he protested. "I really do like you, Shawna, and everything I said about how wonderful it was to talk to a real person after so long . . . that was all true. I am lonely sometimes. I would have enjoyed our lovemaking immensely, had you let things proceed."

"I'm sure you would have." I grimaced. "And speaking of clichés, 'I feel so used.'" I glanced at Athelia, in whom I'd thought I'd detected jealousy the day before, but her face remained impassive, though her eyes flicked back and forth between us.

"Unfortunately," Robur continued, "you detected what I was doing . . . somehow . . . and rebuffed me . . . somehow. I admit the details are hazy, although that may be largely the fault of the wine. In any event, when I woke up and discovered that you were gone and it hadn't worked, I moved on to Plan B." He indicated Athelia and her raised pistol.

I looked at her. She looked back. "Which is?"

"Hold you hostage. When your friend Karl comes through the Portal, I'll threaten to have you shot if he doesn't teach me to open Portals the same way he taught you."

Doubly glad I hadn't told Robur that it was the alien technology in my blood that made Portal-opening possible, I kept my eyes on Athelia. "You wouldn't shoot me," I said. It was in response to Robur, but I said it to both of them.

"I wouldn't," Robur said. "But General Richelot will if I order her to. Won't you, Athelia?"

"I obey the Master without question," Athelia said.

I looked for any sign of doubt in her face and saw none. I turned back to Robur. "Karl won't cooperate."

"Then I'll have Athelia shoot you and threaten to do the same to him unless he complies."

My heart hammered in my chest. "You won't shoot me or have me shot," I said again. "You're bluffing. You said it yourself; you like me. I'm the first 'real person' you've seen in years." I tried a smile. It wasn't very successful. "There's no one else here you can talk with about *Goonies*."

Robur straightened. "Don't flatter yourself, Shawna," he said, his voice suddenly cold. "My interactions with you have been amusing . . . and could have been highly pleasurable for both of us . . . but in truth, talking to you has made me realize I can be just as happy interacting with Shaped people. Maybe more so, since they don't talk back."

"Even if you shoot me and threaten Karl, he won't cooperate."

"Of course, he will," Robur said contemptuously. "He believes the fate of the entire Labyrinth rests on him. He'll *have* to cooperate with me so he can continue his quest. He just has to teach me to open Portals. Once I've picked up a couple of extra worlds to play with, I'll let him carry on. I'm sure, in some other world, he'll eventually find someone to replace you."

And there it was. I'd guessed right about why he wanted my *hokhmah*. He thought if he had it, he'd know how to open Portals and take over worlds for himself . . . just like the Adversary.

He went on. "I'm far stronger than most Shapers. The odds are that if I can open Portals to the other worlds, I can outright strip the *hokhmah* from the Shapers I find there. Having more worlds to play with entices me. Much as I like mine, I'm beginning to think it may bore me, given long enough . . . and here's something else you may not remember, Shawna: Shapers live a long, long time."

I tried a different tack. "The Adversary—"

"You said we could seal the Portal, Karl and I. So, we'll seal it before the Adversary arrives. It's a win-win . . . well, for everyone except you, I suppose, if I have you shot. If Karl gives in immediately, though, even better: Karl tells me how to open Portals and you two can go on your merry way, leaving me to 'do as I will' with the worlds I will claim for myself. You save the Labyrinth, I continue enjoying myself, and I don't have the weight of your death on my conscience. Win-win-win, in that case."

"You don't have a conscience," I snarled.

"Not much of one," he agreed cheerfully. "Terribly inconvenient things, consciences. Pinocchio should have stepped on Jiminy Cricket the minute he turned up."

He really does think he's invulnerable, I thought, staring at him. *He doesn't think the Adversary, or anyone else, can possibly pose any kind of real threat.*

I didn't believe in his invulnerability for a moment. Even if his *world* wouldn't hurt him . . . he wouldn't get struck by lightning or perish in an avalanche . . . that didn't mean he was safe from what might come through the Portal from my world alongside the Adversary. It seemed unlikely I could convince him of that, however.

"Shortly," Robur said, "two crewmen armed with Leyden rifles will join us here. Once they are in place, with orders to stun anyone who comes through the Portal, we will return to the *Terror* to await the arrival of your friend in comfort. General Richelot will personally guard you at all times. I would prefer to have you alive when Karl appears, but the fact is, menacing Karl directly is quite certain to work, so you're not entirely necessary. Don't try anything stupid that will get you shot.

"And if all of this seems massively unfair," he added, "remember that I offered you the opportunity to quietly go on to the next world. I would have awaited Karl's inevitable arrival at my palace and threatened him directly, without involving you at all. You made the bed you are now lying in." He glanced at Athelia. "You understand your orders, General?"

"Yes, Master," she said.

"The let's all go outside into the fresh air," Robur said.

The three of us emerged blinking into the morning sunlight. Robur glanced back at the cave. "I confess, I am excited to see this Portal," he said, "although I know I will find its presence . . . sickening. I'd love to visit your world, so much like the First World up until you took over . . ."

"It's not that world anymore."

"Right. The Adversary." Robur said it indulgently, like he was humoring a small child. "Well, I suppose I will bow to your judgment of his power, and not risk facing him directly. I'm sure there are more interesting worlds to explore down the road, anyway."

"Which you'll destroy."

"What?" He put his hand on his chest. "You wound me. Nothing of the sort. I'll just . . . alter them. To make them more fun."

"For you."

"Of course. Who else?"

"What about the people who live in them?" I looked at Athelia. "People like her."

"What about them?" He sighed. "We've been over this, Shawna. Over and over it. They aren't real."

"They think they are."

"I'm sure they do. But so what?"

I had no arguments that would change his mind, that much was clear. I fell silent. I could still sense Karl, somewhere on the other side of the potential Portal. I couldn't tell if he was getting closer, but I knew he was there, and still alive.

I sat on a boulder. Athelia sat next to me, weapon at the ready. Robur sat some distance away, looking down at the *Terror,* though he occasionally glanced back at the cave.

In short order, two crewmen came laboring up the slope to us, one a skinny, balding black guy, the other blond and stockier, both armed with weird-looking weapons that had what looked like compressed-air tanks hung underneath them, and two magazines of ammunition sticking up above. Robur went to meet them.

"So, those are Leyden rifles?" I said to Athelia.

She nodded. Her pistol never wavered. "Loaded with stun charges, but they can be switched to lethal charges with the flick of a lever."

Memories of *20,000 Leagues Under the Sea* surfaced. "Right . . . they use compressed air to fire glass balls that deliver a massive electric shock on contact."

She raised an eyebrow at me. "Very impressive, considering their existence and manufacture is one of the most closely held secrets in the Republic."

"Why?"

"They're the ultimate spy weapon," Athelia said. "I and my operatives love them. Their operation is almost silent, and the bullets shatter on impact, leaving nothing but shards of glass and metal that so far, at least, Prince Dakkar's investigators have been unable to make heads or tails of."

In the book, as I recalled, the weapons had been used for an undersea big-game hunt, and the bullets were said to be able to kill any creature, no matter how large. Aim wasn't important, as long as you made contact. I decided to say well away from any possible line of fire.

Not that I would have planned to be in the line of fire even if they'd been armed with "ordinary" weapons. Not that I wanted there to *be* any fire. What I had wanted, as the three of us had left the *Terror,* had been for Karl to step through the Portal, for him and me and Robur to destroy the Portal, trapping the Adversary in my old world, and then for Robur to nicely give me the *hokhmah* of his world, under Karl's guidance. Then Karl and I would have taken a leisurely and scenic ride back to the Free City, where we would pass through the Portal I'd already opened into the next world, leaving this one to Robur forever.

Unfortunately, Robur had revealed he had very different plans.

I looked over at him; he was still issuing orders to the crewmen. "You've heard Robur say the people of this world aren't really real to him," I said. "I know you have."

"Yes."

"Doesn't it bother you?"

She shrugged. "It must be true because the Master says it. But I admit I have a hard time believing it. I feel like a real person. I experience pain and pleasure. I bleed."

"'If you prick us, do we not bleed? If you tickle us, do we not laugh?'" I murmured.

"What?"

"A line from a play in my world. A very old play."

"From that playwright you mentioned . . . Shakelock? Shyspear?"

I laughed, despite the fact the woman I'd thought was a friend had a pistol aimed at me. "*Shakespeare*. He had a character named Shylock. Yeah, him."

"Well," she said. "If you prick us . . . Shaped people . . . do we not bleed? If you tickle us, do we not laugh?" She raised a warning hand. "But don't try tickling me. I'd have to shoot you in self-defense, right here and now."

I leaned toward her. "You are most definitely real, Athelia," I said in a low voice. "Whatever the Master says."

Her face closed. "Please don't say things like that."

I straightened and glanced at Robur again. It was clear he would not change. My arrival hadn't changed him; the arrival of Karl wouldn't change him. *He'll just keep resetting his pieces, fighting his wars, letting—no, making—people die, altering the lives of everyone else, including Athelia, over and over and over again. And if he gets control of other worlds, he'll do it there, too.*

I thought about what he had said about Karl having to cooperate with him. The scary thing was, I thought he was right. Karl *would* have to cooperate with him, or at least pretend to, because Karl *did* see himself as the Labyrinth's only hope. Karl himself had told me that if something happened to me, he would simply carry on, in the hope of finding another Shaper powerful enough to carry out the quest of gathering the *hokhmahs* of as many Shaped worlds as possible and conveying them to Ygrair.

Powerful enough. Like Robur?

The thought made me sick. Robur certainly wouldn't leave well enough alone if *he* started gathering the *hokhmah* of other worlds. He'd Shape them, without regard to the original Shapers' wishes, or the wishes of those who lived within them, or Karl's wishes, or Ygrair's wishes.

The question was, what could I do about it?

I needed to know what else the alien technology

within me could do. It could find potential Portals and open and close them. It had protected me from Robur's attempt to steal my *hokhmah*. But did it have offensive capability? Could I use it to steal Robur's *hokhmah* from him, even against his will, powerful as he was?

And if I did . . . did I have the right, or even the responsibility, to Shape his world differently?

I knew what Karl would say. My only goal should be to get the *hokhmah* and get out. I should think of this world the way Robur did, as a game, the people in it nothing more than non-player characters.

But then I glanced at Athelia, aiming a pistol at her friend because she had been Shaped to be blindly loyal to the Shaper, and knew I couldn't.

The question was currently moot in any event. I did not have Robur's *hokhmah,* and right now it seemed unlikely I ever would.

Robur came toward us with the two crewmen. "Foley," Athelia said to the black guy by way of greeting. "Urrican," she said to the blond. They nodded back, then moved on to the cave mouth, standing in front of it with their weapons aimed into the interior.

"If the Adversary comes through first, or his cadre does, with modern weapons, those two don't stand a chance," I said to Robur.

"They're just our early warning system," he said. "The Terror will make short work of anyone who comes out, guns blazing. But is that really likely? This Adversary of yours has no reason to suspect anyone on this side might be waiting for him, except you. And from what you tell me, surely Karl will come through first, since only he can open the Portal. And for a single man, two Foley rifles will be more than sufficient. Overkill, in fact. They will stun him and bring him to us on the *Terror,* and then negotiations can begin in earnest." He gestured downslope. "And speaking of the *Terror,* shall we . . . ?"

Then he stiffened, as the battle stations bells began to ring on the vessel. "An attack?" He stared out over the desert. Nothing moved. "From what?"

Suddenly, I heard a new sound mixed in with the clangor, a "whup-whup-whup" sound. I whipped around and stared up at Devil's Tower.

Around its shoulder came a single tiny helicopter. It banked, close to the wall, and headed straight for us. Even at that distance, I could see that the pilot wore bright-red leathers.

Belinda!

TWENTY-NINE

IT DIDN'T SEEM likely Belinda just wanted to catch up on what I'd been up to since I'd left the *Narwhal,* and since what I'd been up to included betraying my promise to her prince and getting Anthony killed, I hadn't been much looking forward to filling her in, anyway. I wondered if she recognized Robur as she came hurtling toward us, but I only gave it a passing thought, since by then I was sprinting down the slope, toward the *Terror,* in terror, and in Robur's wake, as Belinda started firing the guns on either side of her seat, bullets stitching a line of dust-geysers and splintered stone shards across the tumbled boulders.

Athelia passed me. I didn't know what Foley and Urrican were doing, but I hoped they'd taken cover. Their Leyden rifles didn't have much hope of hitting a helicopter.

I've really *got to work out more,* I thought inanely as I charged downhill, risking a broken ankle (or leg, or neck) with every step. *It's beginning to look like I'll be running for my life for the rest of my life.*Which might not be very long, so there was that.

The guns stopped. Belinda whup-whup-whupped directly overhead. I looked up at the underside of her 'copter, to which I had been strapped just . . . what? Three weeks ago?

There would have been no room for me there at the moment, because she was carrying a rocket, bigger than the ones I remembered seeing on the little 'copters when they'd attacked the *Albatross,* an evil-looking thing with stubby wings and a bulbous nose.

The steam-guns on the *Terror* opened up below us, spraying bullets in the general direction of the 'copter as it raced away, but not, so far as I could see from the tracers included in the rounds, coming even close to hitting it. I had mixed feelings. I didn't want Belinda killed, but I really didn't want her killing me, either.

Clouds of vapor drifted across the *Terror*'s deck, almost hiding the gunners from sight. In a moment Belinda was out of their range, turning, far out over the desert, presumably to make another pass.

Robur reached the *Terror* and raced up the ladder, Athelia on his heels. I was close . . . well, relatively close . . . behind her. Robur dashed up to Captain Sullivan. "How is that thing even here?" he demanded. "It doesn't have the range."

"No idea, Master," said the captain. He turned to the gunners. "It's coming back!" he roared. "Don't miss again!"

I stared up at the approaching helicopter as the gunners resumed fire. This time the tracers converged on it. A huge gout of white smoke erupted. *She's going down!* I thought . . .

. . . and then realized my mistake. The smoke came from the rocket she'd just dropped and ignited. It screamed toward us, riding a tail of flame as Belinda banked hard right, her rotors stuttering.

By instinct, I flung myself on the deck. Athelia crashed down beside me. Robur stayed upright next to Captain Sullivan. "Idiot!" he screamed at Belinda, though she couldn't possibly have heard him. "My world won't let me be—"

The rocket ripped into the ground well short of the *Terror*—and exploded.

The enormity of the sound, the pressure of the blast, wiped every thought from my head. I didn't lose consciousness, but I couldn't feel or think or react. I felt the deck lift underneath me, felt myself flung from it, felt the impact with the ground, felt myself roll over and over, saw smoking pieces of metal slam down around me, felt the suck of air rushing over me back toward the *Terror*. For a moment, I saw myself from above, lying on the ground, staring blankly up into the sky.

Then everything snapped back into place. I was inside my body again—my aching, bruised body. My ears rang and felt stuffed with cotton, but at least I could hear. I knew I could hear because I heard someone moaning.

I rolled over. Much to my surprise, nothing seemed to be broken, sliced open, or missing. Athelia lay not far away, motionless but breathing. The moaning wasn't coming from her.

I turned my head. Another body lay on blood-soaked ground just a few feet away. I crawled toward it. Beyond it, I could see what remained of the *Terror,* on its side, split almost in two, crackling flames in its interior sending up a tower of black smoke, its wings no longer tucked up against it but splayed on the ground, crumpled and bent like those of a stepped-on dragonfly.

I was practically on top of the moaning body before I recognized it as Robur . . . and even then, it was a near thing.

His right eye and right ear and most of the skin on that side of his face were gone. So were his right hand, and his right leg below the knee. A long piece of metal— part of the *Terror*'s handrail, I thought numbly—pinned him to the ground through the abdomen, like a badly mounted butterfly.

His remaining eye turned toward me. His mouth opened, releasing a gush of blood. "This . . . can't . . . be . . . happening," he choked out in a crackling, bubbling whisper. "This . . . isn't . . . happening . . ."

It was the same thing I had said when Aesha had died, when I'd turned back time to save myself. But he had already reset his world, less than a month ago, far, far more completely than I had in the coffee shop. At that moment, he was barely the Shaper at all.

His remaining eye widened; he sucked in air and blood, and then he choked and arched his back . . .

. . . and died.

And I was hit by a second overwhelming blast of force.

This one wasn't physical. This one slammed into my mind, tore it open, plunged inside, and buried itself there. For an instant, I grasped everything about Robur's world. I knew the shapes of the continents, the depths of the oceans, the wildlife, the people, the nations, the politics, the technology, everything he had set in place when he'd first Shaped the World. It was all there. In that instant, I could have reShaped everything . . .

. . . and then the instant passed.

The knowledge, the *hokhmah,* remained inside me. I could feel it, but I could no longer access it consciously. It had buried itself somewhere deep inside my mind, or my soul, or some specialized organ that only Shapers had. It occupied the same place as the *hokhmah* of my own world, without crowding it.

I can do this, I thought in wonder. *I can absorb the* hokhmah *of as many worlds as I can reach, from as many Shapers as I can find, and carry all of it to Ygrair. I won't fill up or burst like an overinflated balloon. I can do this!*

And then that rush, too, passed, and the aches and pains returned. I groaned out loud and rolled over onto my back.

"Hurting?" said a voice. "Good."

I raised my head.

Belinda came limping toward me across the debris-scattered desert. She stepped around another body, or part of one. I saw gold braid on one bloody, outstretched sleeve (though the hand that should have extended from it was missing) and realized it must be Captain Sullivan.

Belinda held a pistol in her right hand. Her other arm hung awkwardly at her side—broken, or at least dislocated. Blood ran down her face and soaked her uniform from a gash in the calf of her left leg, the one she was favoring.

"Belinda," I croaked. "Why . . . ?"

"I could say I'm just doing my duty." She glanced at Robur's body. "I've just done the prince a great service, after all. Robur the Conqueror is no more. Without him, how long can his evil Republic last? Prince Dakkar will triumph. War will end. Peace will reign." She turned her bloody gaze back to me. "But that wasn't why I did it. That wasn't why I stole a fulgurator from the *Narwhal*'s armory after we shot you down at sea and followed you to the coast, or had my crew load it aboard my 'copter in the dead of night and help me launch. They'll face court-martials, but they did it anyway, and they weren't doing it for the prince, either. Duty wasn't why I comman-deered a freight transporter rolling along the coast road, loaded my copter onto it, and followed your tracks out here, either."

Fulgurator? "You came out here to kill me. *Me,* spe-cifically."

"Smart girl." Belinda stood directly in front of me now, just a few feet away. I thought about leaping to my feet and trying to wrestle the pistol from her, but the way my body felt, "leaping to my feet" would take me a couple of minutes of groaning, after which I would prob-ably fall over and possibly pass out. "I thought the ful-gurator would do for you, but those damn steam-guns must have damaged the steering vanes at the same time they tore up my tail rotor. The bloody thing hit the ground, so the bulk of the *Terror* protected you, since you had the sense to throw yourself on the deck. But only because the fulgurator is still experimental. There's a new warhead coming. With one of those, even that wouldn't have saved you."

· She shook her head, grimaced, and swiped blood from her face with the back of her sleeve, which meant for a moment she wasn't pointing a pistol at me. If I were James Bond, I would have leaped to my feet and tried to grab it. But I'm not, and I didn't, and in a second, it was aimed at my head again. "I'm babbling. Hard landing. Nasty jolt. Not as nasty as you took, though. And now I'm glad the fulgurator fell short. I'm glad you're still alive, because now I can look you in the eyes as I put a bullet in your brain."

I tried to swallow, but my mouth had gone dry. *Shape her,* I thought suddenly. *You have this world's* hokhmah!

"You don't want to do that, Belinda," I said. I put every possible ounce of conviction I had into it . . .

. . . and failed miserably. Nothing happened. I had the world's *hokhmah,* but I had no power.

Robur's was exhausted, I thought. *Maybe that's the reason.*

Not that the reason mattered, with a pistol aimed at my head.

"Yes, I do," Belinda said conversationally. "And do you know why?"

I started to say, no, I didn't . . . but the words died in my throat, because, once I thought about it, the why was obvious, and I had been blind and stupid not to see it before. "You loved him," I whispered. "You loved Anthony."

"And he loved me," she said, voice tight. "Oh, it was all platonic, of course. I was his superior officer. There could be nothing between us, not while we served. But our service wouldn't last forever. Once it was over . . ." She took a deep, shuddering breath. "You stole that from us. From *me.* Bishop was one of the few members of your escort who survived. He told me how you seduced Anthony, twisted his mind, somehow tricked him into shooting the colonel—a hanging offense right there— and then, as if you hadn't already sentenced him to death, arranged to have him executed by one of your Weldonian friends who attacked the inn."

"That's not—"

"Shut up." She took a step closer. The barrel of the pistol trembled, but I didn't think for a second she would miss. "All of it was a ruse, all of it, from the very beginning. You somehow convinced my father you weren't a spy—but you were, weren't you? You even convinced the prince to believe you, convinced him to escort you to the Free City. Then you made your bloody escape and off to Quercus you went, to tell Robur's engineers everything you had learned about the *Narwhal* and the defenses of Raj. You didn't care how many bodies you left in your wake, did you? We weren't ever real to you—just enemies to be duped."

"You're wrong," I said. "Belinda, you're wrong. I never meant for all those people to die. I never meant for Anthony or the colonel to die. I told the truth. I really am from another world . . ."

"Then where are the forces you promised the prince? Where's the Portal you promised to open in the Free City?"

"There *is* a Portal there," I said, hoping she'd listen, hoping she'd let me keep talking, hoping . . . all right, *praying,* to God or Ygrair or whoever or whatever would listen, that my Shaping power would suddenly manifest itself. "But it's to the wrong world. The real Portal back to my world will open here, up the slope. There's a cave . . ."

And two armed crewmen, I suddenly remembered. *Foley and Urrican. Where are they now? Are they watching this? Are they coming? If I can keep her talking until they get in range . . .*

. . . they'll kill her.

I didn't want her to die. But I didn't want to die, either. If Karl were right, I might be the only hope for this world and countless others. I *had* to survive, had to live to take the *hokhmah* of this world and as many more as I could to Ygrair. Given the stakes, wasn't it better if Belinda died here and now, struck down by a Leyden bullet, than if I died with a bullet through my brain?

A Leyden bullet. Fired by compressed air. Not exactly a long-range weapon. Even if Foley and Urrican see what's going on, they'll never get close enough to shoot her without her seeing them. And one quick convulsion of her right hand, and I'm . . .

"I don't care," Belinda said. "I don't care if you were telling the truth about being from another world. I don't care if you were telling the truth about the Portal. I don't care if you were telling the prince the truth when you promised him help." Another step closer, as if she wanted to be absolutely certain she wouldn't miss. "All I want," she finished, "is to see you die. Goodbye, Shawna—"

And in that instant, that last possible instant, the Portal opened.

It was the third enormous blast of energy to tear

through me, different from the explosion that had hurled me from the *Terror,* different again from the spiritual (for want of a better term) force that had filled me when Robur died and his *hokhmah* became mine. This felt like . . . like the moment when you take a deep breath as you enter the hallway of your mother's house after a long, cold trip home at Christmas, and you smell ginger-bread and woodsmoke, and your mother comes out of the kitchen, wiping her hands on her apron. . . .

It felt like I was *home,* and that warm, welcoming feeling filled me up in a way the cold blast of Robur's *hokhmah* had not. It filled me with power, a power I'd hardly realized I'd been missing, but recognized at once, the power I'd just begun to get used to in the days before I left my own world forever: the power of the Shaper.

I don't think Belinda felt a thing. Why would she? She was a Shaped denizen of Robur's world. If she had tried to enter mine, she would have ceased to exist, so how could she possibly sense it?

Time slowed almost to a stop. Almost imperceptibly, her finger tightened on the trigger. But now I could not only feel Robur's *hokhmah,* I could use it. In that moment, I could do anything . . .

. . . and so I did.

I did not Shape Belinda to suddenly think of me as a friend, or to forget Anthony (my mind recoiled at the thought), or to become loyal to the Republic of Weldon instead of the Principality of Raj. I was sick of manipulating people, twisting their minds, turning them inside out.

Instead, I simply Shaped her . . . away. Far away, back to the *Narwhal,* where she would suddenly find herself in the surgeon's sick bay, to get the medical attention she needed . . . and face the wrath of her father and captain. She vanished, with an earsplitting thunder crack.

Even in that moment, I wished I'd had just enough time to point out to her that she had made the fatal flaw of every villain in every B movie. She'd talked too long, explained too much. If she'd just pulled the trigger the moment she saw me . . .

Well, I thought, *she was shaken up by her crash landing, not thinking clearly.*

I realized I wasn't thinking all that clearly myself. That Shaping had been enormous, and I could already feel the power that had flowed into me from my world waning, almost as quickly as it had come. Perhaps my use of it had prevented it from creating a storm like the opening of the Portal into my world back at Snakebite Mine had. But I couldn't let it slip away entirely. Not yet.

We'll need a way out of here . . .

Only one idea presented itself to my desperate mind. Scrabbling for the vanishing power, I performed one more Shaping, even greater than the one that had removed Belinda. And then my power was gone again. I could do nothing more . . .

. . . and I did not know if I'd succeeded. I could see no sign that I had. But succeed or fail, I was drained of my Shaping ability. Just like on *Amazon,* before we reached the Mysterious Island, I was burned out . . . temporarily, perhaps, but burned out just the same. Whatever needed to be done next would have to be done without Shaping.

And what had to be done next was get up to the open Portal and see if Karl had come through . . . and who else might have come through with him.

Groaning, I sat up. Then I heard a moan and turned to see Athelia sitting up, as well. "What . . . what hit me?" she said a little fuzzily, hand to her temple.

"Something called a fulgurator, apparently," I said.

Her eyes widened as she turned her head toward me. "They exist?"

I glanced at the smoking wreckage of the *Terror.* "They exist."

"Then we're lucky to be alive."

"Not all of us are," I said gently, and nodded toward Robur's corpse.

She looked. Her eyes widened. "Oh, no," she whispered. "No . . ." She crawled over to him on her hands and knees. "No!"

She sounded so heartbroken, so forlorn, that I felt my own eyes well with tears . . . but the sorrow switched to anger in a moment. Robur had had no business forcing himself into someone's life like that, making himself as central to her being as a god.

I wanted to comfort her, but what could I say? I had no idea how it felt to have someone you had been Shaped to serve with absolute loyalty suddenly lie dead in front of you. But I also didn't have time to worry about it. "You're in command, General Richelot," I said harshly. "Ranking officer. Captain Sullivan is dead, too." I twisted around and at last saw, running toward us, Foley and Urrican. "We need to get back up to the Portal. It's open. Karl must be up there, but the Adversary may be close behind. Karl and I have to close the Portal."

"I'm . . . ?" Athelia blinked at me. For a moment she looked far younger than I knew her to be, and lost, like a child whose father had died. But then the light came back into her eyes and her face hardened. "Right," she said. "Right." She clambered to her feet, swaying a little. "Foley! Urrican!" she shouted. "Hold there! We'll come to you."

She limped over to me and pulled me onto my feet. The world only seesawed once and twirled twice, then settled down, although I couldn't repress a groan. "I'll help you secure this Portal of yours," Athelia said. "Then we'll deal with everything else."

"Thank you." I looked up the slope toward the cave. Nothing moved. No sign of Karl.

I wanted to dash back up the slope, but my body said, "No way." Settling instead for a quick . . . relatively quick . . . hobble, I headed for the doorway back into my world—and, I hoped, my only guide to the Labyrinth and my impossible quest.

THIRTY

THE PORTAL BURNED in my consciousness brighter and brighter with every step I took toward it, but the sensation was very different from the first time I had approached one, back in Snakebite Mine. There, the Portal through which both Karl and the Adversary and his murderous cadre had entered my world had felt wrong, evil, an obscene gash in the fabric of my universe. This one didn't feel like that at all. It was simply a doorway to another place that was as much mine as this one.

My original world, after all, still nestled inside me. I had not lost the *hokhmah* of it when I entered this one or when Robur's slammed into me. I could still pass into it, still Shape it . . .

. . . or could I? If I went back, *I* would be the interloper. The Adversary had had weeks now to solidify his control. I could no longer run and hide. He'd know where I was and kill me before I could even look around.

I knew that. And yet, there was still a part of me that wondered if maybe, just maybe, I could set things right, get back my old life, my mother, Brent, my pottery studio, the Human Bean . . .

I shoved that useless longing away. "This slope is a damn sight longer going up than it was going down," I growled to Athelia.

"There's no one shooting at us to provide motivation," she pointed out.

The cave mouth gaped in front of us at last, just another

fifty yards or so up the slope. I glanced back down at the burning wreckage of the *Terror.* I thought I saw movement. Had there been other survivors after all?

Then I looked back at the sky. It remained empty. Had my last, desperate Shaping failed?

Belinda said she brought her 'copter out here on a transport vehicle, I thought. I wondered where it was. Somewhere over the horizon, presumably: otherwise, the crew of the *Terror* would have seen it approaching. *Maybe we can find it, drive it back to the coast, and . . .*

. . . and what? Hand ourselves over to Prince Dakkar's forces? Flag down the *Narwhal?* I didn't think Captain Hatteras would welcome us with open arms. Belinda certainly wouldn't. Maybe by then I'd have regained enough Shaping power to sway both of them to our side. Maybe not. Maybe the captain would have us shot on sight. Or maybe it would be the brig for all of us and a very unpleasant interrogation for General Athelia Richelot, Commander of the Secret Service of the Republic of Weldon . . .

A man staggered out of the cave mouth. He wore jeans and boots, but no shirt. Blood streaked his lean torso from a gash in his left shoulder. He had long black hair pulled back into an untidy ponytail.

I blinked, then filled my lungs and yelled, "Karl!" at the top of my voice.

His head swung, focused on me. "Shawna!" he shouted. "The Adversary's cadre . . ."

Light flashed in the dark mouth of the cave as a shot rang out, shockingly loud. Karl yelped and collapsed, clutching his leg. Foley and Urrican flung themselves behind rocks. I started to run to Karl, but Athelia tackled me. I went down hard and swung my head toward her angrily. "What are you doing? That's—"

"Quiet!" she whispered.

"That's Karl! He's hurt! We have to—"

"Wait!" She turned her head to the crewmen. "Are we in range? Can you make shots from here?"

The nearest man, Foley, now lay prone, his Leyden rifle aimed at the cave. "Yes," he said, without taking his eyes from the sights. Beyond him, Urrican crouched behind a boulder, his own weapon aimed and steadied.

Athelia peered over top of the rock she had pulled me behind. I raised my head, too. I still wanted to jump up and run to Karl's aid . . . but my common sense had finally returned enough to clobber me on the side of the head for being an idiot, telling me that whoever had shot Karl in the leg must be in the cave . . .

And here he came. Or, rather, *they* came.

Two of them. Two of the Adversary's cadre, wearing the head-to-toe black I remembered all too well from the attack on the Human Bean, automatic rifles at the ready. I was surprised by the surge of hatred their appearance provoked in me. I reached inside, hoping some modicum of Shaping power might have returned . . . but still, there was nothing.

The men took a quick look around. I scrunched down behind the rock for a second, then peeked again. While one kept his weapon ready, scanning the surroundings, the other slung his over his shoulder and started to kneel down beside Karl . . .

There was a soft "pfft!" from Foley's Leyden rifle. Blue light flashed on the shoulder of the kneeling man, who went rigid, then toppled without a sound, twitching, right across Karl, who cried out in pain. After a moment the twitching stopped.

Athelia pulled me down again as bullets sprayed the rocks. Foley had already rolled away from his rifle into better cover. Urrican, much farther to our left, stayed put, aimed, and fired.

Another "pfft." The second cadre soldier stiffened and fell backward, gun still firing, expending its entire magazine into the empty sky before his convulsing body, like that of his comrade, went still.

I swallowed. "Nasty weapons," I said. "I thought you said they were probably loaded with stun charges."

Foley looked over at me and grinned fiercely. "We switched them out when the 'copter attacked."

I started to get up; Athelia grabbed my arm. "Wait," she said. "To be sure there are no more . . ."

"We can't wait," I said. "The Adversary himself could come through next. And Karl could be bleeding to death!" I shrugged her off, got up, and finally ran to Karl's side.

The body of the cadre member lying across him stank of burned meat and voided bowels. Almost gagging, I dragged the corpse off Karl. Despite the horror of the man's death, I felt no guilt—not this time.

Karl's eyes opened as I knelt beside him. "Shawna," he rasped. "It is good to see you."

"Not quite the way I imagined our reunion," I said. "You've been shot."

"Yes, but very carefully," he said, faintly. "Flesh wound in the calf, if I'm judging it right. Missed the artery. Bind it . . ." His eyes fluttered.

The only thing I had to bind it with was my shirt, light white cotton from the *Terror*'s uniform stores. I tore it off and ripped it apart. Karl's jeans fit loosely enough I was able to roll up the leg almost to the knee to get at the wound. It looked nasty, but it wasn't pumping blood, and the bullet had gone clean through. The cadre members must have been under orders not to kill him, and fortunately had had the skill to make a shot that wouldn't.

I wrapped the wound. Blood soaked through the cloth almost immediately, but it didn't keep oozing through. "Ouch," Karl said faintly.

The (surprisingly modern) bra I wore, which I had found in the costume stores in Athelia's caravan, covered me well enough, so I didn't give modesty a thought, except to wish it was warmer. I twisted around to look at Athelia, Foley, and Urrican, who had come up the slope behind me. "He'll live," I said. "But more may come through. Urrican, watch that hole at the back of the cave."

"Pistol," Athelia put in. "No room for the Leyden rifle."

The big blond man nodded. He set the Leyden rifle by the entrance, then disappeared inside.

I turned back to Karl. "I have this world's *hokhmah*," I told him. "Once I have more power, I can heal you . . ."

He shook his head. "No, you can't," he said, and even in that moment, managed to sound disappointed and annoyed that I didn't already know that . . . a tone of voice I realized I had, surprisingly, missed. "You can't Shape me. I'm from the First World. I'll have to heal the old-fashioned way." He turned his head toward Foley, who still had his Leyden rifle. "Judging by the weapons, old-fashioned is all that is available here."

"It's a Jules Verne-inspired world," I said.

"Ah," Karl said. "Interesting. Then perhaps not as low-tech as all that."

"Steampunk," I said.

He frowned. "An odd term."

I grinned. I had my guide back, complete with his weird lack of knowledge of anything after about 1910. "We have to destroy the Portal," I told him.

"The Portal. Right." Karl, wincing, sat up, but then clutched at me. "Ah," he said. "Weaker than I thought." He twisted around to look into the cave. "You know what destroying a Portal did to me before, in your world. And I was not wounded then. I do not think I even have the power to seal it . . . not that that is worth the effort, since The Adversary can unseal it at will."

"How close is he?" I said, staring into the darkness.

"I would suspect he is already on the other side of it, simply waiting for the two cadre members he sent through to return from their hunt, dragging their prey."

"You."

"Indeed. He wants the technology I carry within me, so he can rampage through the Shaped worlds unimpeded, without having to follow me from Portal to Portal."

"And when the two cadre members he sent through don't return?"

"He will come through himself, with as much force as he can bring. Which, even though only hand-held weapons can pass the Portal, will be immense, coming from your world."

"Then we *have* to destroy the Portal," I said. "If we destroy it, he'll be trapped in my world. Maybe forever."

"I told you," Karl said, sounding exasperated. "I do not have the power."

"Maybe I do," I said.

"No, you do *not*," he said. "The only reason I was able to destroy the Portal in Snakebite Mine was because of the technology Ygrair implanted in me. Just as I am the only one who can open a Portal, so am I the only one . . ."

"But you aren't," I said.

He blinked. "Aren't what?"

"The only one who can open a Portal." I shrugged, striving to look modest. "I've already opened the Portal to the next world. And closed it again, but it's waiting for us, as soon as we're ready to move on."

He stared at me. I waited for him to say, "I don't believe you," or, "That's impossible," Or even, "But how . . . ?" But in fact, as his momentary expression of confusion cleared, all he said was, "Ah. The altar. I bled on it. You must have touched my blood."

"I put my hand in a puddle of it," I said. "Yuck, by the way."

"And it was still very fresh. You must have had a cut on your hand, as well."

"I had minor scrapes."

"All it would take. That kind of transmission of the nanomites . . ."

"Nanomites?"

"Cell-sized, or smaller, robots, with powerful, net-worked quantum computers built in," Karl said. "Or so they were described to me. Though I am not entirely sure what 'quantum' means."

"Yuck," I said again. In truth, I'd thought it must be something like that, but Karl had never called it anything but "implanted technology" until now.

"That kind of transmission," he continued, "can only occur when the blood is very fresh and enters directly into your bloodstream. If you have the nanomites, then you might be able to *seal* the Portal, but not destroy it. To do that, you still need the Shaper of this world."

"I told you," I said. "*I* am the Shaper of this world. I have its *hokhmah*."

"Perhaps, but as powerful as this world's Shaper must be, I doubt it is entirely yours—he must still be sharing it. That means you will need his or her cooperation to . . ."

"He's dead."

"What?" Suddenly Karl looked more alert. "Truly?"

No, I'm just pulling your leg, I wanted to say. *The one with the gunshot wound in it, preferably, so it will hurt.* "Truly."

"Then it might be possible after all!" he breathed. He struggled to a sitting position. "Get me up. Now!"

"I'll help," said Athelia. "Foley, you get in there with Urrican. Put down your Leyden rifle, too. Pistols."

"Aye, aye, General," Foley said, suiting actions to words.

With Athelia's help, I got Karl to his feet, not without a fair amount of groaning on both our parts. "That's a nasty cut on your shoulder," I said. "There's blood all over your chest and side and back."

"I took a stupid fall. I used my shirt to . . ." He suddenly stiffened. "My shirt. Do you see it?"

"You weren't carrying it when you came out of the cave."

"Damn it!"

"What?"

He shook his head. "Never mind. Maybe it's inside. Let's hurry."

The slowness of our approach to the Portal, I would have liked to have pointed out, was not the fault of Athelia and me, since, bruised and battered though we were, *we* were not the ones limping along on a leg with a gunshot wound, but again, I refrained from saying anything. Apparently, unlike what I've been led to believe my entire life, I *can* learn to keep my mouth shut.

"You were very quiet," I suddenly remembered Robur saying. *Doesn't sound like me at all.*

Inside the cave, the back wall had vanished, the stone replaced by a sheet of pure blackness, like a pool of crude oil (minus the reflections) somehow made vertical. Urrican stood next to it, holding his pistol trained on that disconcerting nothingness.

"It's gone all *2001* monolith," I said. "Why can't I see through it?"

"Because the Portals between this world and your world are very strange," he said. "Unique, in my experience in the Labyrinth thus far. Although at least this time there is no arena full of bloodthirsty ghosts or an altar requiring a human sacrifice."

"What *is* on the other side?"

"An ancient stone temple in a Mexican mangrove swamp," Karl said. He had his head down, searching the floor of the cave in the dim light. "Damn it," he said again, but with more feeling.

"Karl," I said. "Focus. How do I do this, exactly?" We had reached the weird black wall.

His head came up. "First, put your hand on the Portal, so you know what it feels like."

"There's nothing there."

"Do it."

I put my hand out . . . and I *did* feel it. The *potential* Portal had felt like rice paper separating the worlds, something I could tear a hole through. The *open* Portal felt like a soap bubble I could simply walk through if I chose to.

I chose not to. I pulled my hand back. "All right, I know what it feels like. So, I touch it, and then . . . ?"

"It's like Shaping. You have to will it into oblivion, Shape it into nonexistence—Shape it to never have existed at all."

"Like what I did in the Human Bean after the Adversary's attack."

"Something like that, I suppose."

I closed my eyes, took a deep breath. "How will I know if it's working?"

"Because," he said. "It will hurt."

I remembered him screaming in Snakebite Mine.

"Right." I swallowed, prepared myself, pushed my hand into that darkness—

—and a hand shot through from the other direction, grabbed my wrist, and started pulling.

THIRTY-ONE

I SCREAMED. WHO wouldn't?

Fortunately, Athelia, for one. In one swift movement she drew her naval saber and slashed. It cut cleanly through the wrist of the hand pulling at me. The stub, spurting blood, disappeared into the darkness of the Portal. The hand dropped from my sleeve and fell to the stone floor.

And then Athelia dropped her saber and slammed into me and Karl, wrapping her arms around both of us and driving us to the side of the black opening that marked the Portal. "Foley! Urrican! To the sides!" she shouted.

Just in time! Gunfire erupted through the Portal, shattering the ceiling and floor, sending shards of stone spraying toward the entrance.

The gunfire stopped. I stood with my back pressed to the cave wall, panting, ears ringing.

"Return fire!" Athelia ordered.

The crewmen stepped back in front of the Portal, dropped to their knees, emptied their pistols through it, and then fell back, reloading.

"That should give them something to think about," Athelia said.

Karl, white-faced, sat slumped against the cavern wall. "Near thing," he panted. "I should have realized..."

"How did you know?" I said to Athelia, more than a little shaken myself.

"It's what I would have done."

"The next thing through might be a hand grenade," Karl pointed out. "Shawna. You have to seal it. Now."

I took a deep breath. "Right. But maybe not standing right in front of it this time." I looked at Athelia. "I'll lie down, reach out to it. If Foley and Urrican provide covering fire . . ."

"Good idea." She glanced at the crewmen. "Reloaded?"

"Yes, ma'am," Foley said.

"Great," I said. My heart pounded. "Well, no time like the present . . ." I got onto my hands and knees, then onto my belly, and crawled forward.

Foley and Urrican fired over my head into the Portal. I tried to ignore it, and my own aching body, and my ringing ears, and the fact I didn't *really* know what I was doing. I touched the Portal again. It felt . . . alive. The other Portals I'd seen joined worlds that did not want to be joined, that found it . . . offensive. This Portal was happy to exist: the *hokhmah* of my old world, and this, my new world, were pleased to be mingling.

But I had to put a stop to it.

I concentrated. I knew what it felt like to Shape things now. I'd done it many times in my own world and had just done it here, sending Belinda away, although the other Shaping I had attempted seemed to have failed. I'd worried that I'd used up all my energy, but now, with my hand in the Portal, I discovered it could give me all I needed. It brimmed with power, the massive amount of energy from both worlds required to bridge the gap . . . physical, magical, interdimensional, whatever it was . . . packed into that infinitesimally thin interface.

I pulled that energy into myself, held it close, and imagined the Portal closed . . . not just closed but gone. Vanished. Never existed. Never *could* exist. I felt the Shaping begin . . .

And then I screamed again because it felt like I'd just poured gasoline over myself and lit a match.

I tried to jerk free of the Portal, pull my hand back, desperate to escape that agony, but I couldn't move; I was frozen there, as if I'd seized a high-voltage line and all my muscles had spasmed tight. Brilliant blue light streamed from my body . . . and for the first time, the Portal became transparent.

I saw a stone chamber, pillars, an archway, beyond it, giant trees. Two black-clad men lay crumpled in front of the Portal, Foley and Urrican's work. A woman sat cross-legged against a pillar, clutching the bloody stump where her hand had been.

And then I saw another man, off to one side, a man I'd only seen in person once, an ordinary-looking man who, nevertheless, I could never forget—because the *first* time I had seen him had been seconds after my best friend, Aesha, had been gunned down. He had touched my forehead and stolen my *hokhmah,* though I hadn't understood that at the time, and then, as he had aimed his pistol at my head to shoot me dead, had called my name.

The Adversary.

He saw me. His eyes narrowed. He drew his pistol and strode forward, keeping to one side, out of any possible line of fire from Foley and Urrican. Fury on his face, he lifted the pistol amd aimed it at my head, just like he had in the Human Bean, when he'd stolen my world from me, when Aesha had died . . .

My own fury rose like bile in my throat. It poured out in choked words, the same words I had used in the Human Bean when I had rejected what I was seeing, what had happened, and what was about to happen. "This . . . isn't . . . happening!"

In the Human Bean, it had reset time by three hours, though it had not brought the dead back to life—nothing could do that. But here, now . . .

The Portal flashed white, blindingly, atomic-explosiony white. A blast lifted me from the ground, threw me backward through the air.

Hand grenade, I thought. Then all thought vanished.

I didn't feel myself hit the ground.

The Adversary stared at the place where, a moment before, the Portal into the next world, the next step in his long journey to bring Ygrair to justice, had stood open, where Shawna Keys had been lying on the ground, eyes wide as he stepped forward to finally, finally, put an end to her. And then . . .

She'd shouted something. There had been a flash, a sound like a crash of thunder, a great rush of wind past him, through the chamber, and into the Portal—and she and the Portal had simply vanished. Now there was only a wall of stone blocks.

Shawna Keys, the only Shaper who had ever escaped him, had escaped him again . . . and taken with her his only way out of the world he had stolen from her.

He holstered his useless pistol. He glanced at the wounded woman from his cadre. She had slumped to one side now, face pale, eyes half-shut, blood pooled around her, arms limp, no longer even holding the stump where her right hand had been. He Shaped her whole. She blinked, then scrambled to her feet. "Sir," she said, "I—"

"Quiet," the Adversary snapped. She, of course, obeyed.

The Adversary glared at the wall where the Portal had been, frustration boiling inside him. Then he saw something to one side of it, in the shadows, a pale lump. He strode over, knelt down, and picked it up.

It was a shirt. An ordinary, white shirt . . .

. . . stained with blood.

The Adversary smiled. Then, holding the bloody shirt, he Shaped himself and the surviving member of his cadre far, far away.

Karl Yatsar, bare and bloody back pressed against the cold stone of the cave wall, watched Shawna Keys crawl forward, lie prostrate, and reach out her hand to the Portal, as the two men armed with pistols fired over her head. He saw the flare of blue light, saw the Portal's blackness thin, saw the chamber of the temple in which the Portal had appeared in Shawna's world, saw beyond it the trees of the swamp through which he had struggled, saw two bodies on the ground . . . and saw the Adversary step into view, pistol aimed at Shawna's head.

He opened his mouth to cry a warning, tried to struggle up—but then the world seemed to explode in a flash of blinding light. The blast slammed him back against the wall, sent Shawna flying up and backward to crash down almost at the mouth of the cave. Ears ringing, he crawled to her on his hands and knees, reaching her moments before Athelia did. He put his ear against her chest. "She's alive," he said and felt enormous relief.

"Back away," Athelia snapped. Karl did so. He felt something liquid on his lips, licked it, tasted salty copper, and realized his nose was bleeding. So was Athelia's. He glanced around and saw the other two men . . . Foley and Urrican, was that it? . . . picking themselves up, shaking their heads.

Athelia examined Shawna carefully, peeling back an eyelid, taking her pulse, running her hands over her body. "Nothing seriously damaged that I can see," she said, sitting back on her heels. "Could have cracked ribs or something, though. And I can't rule out internal injuries."

Karl twisted around to look at the Portal, through which, seconds before, he had been able to see into Shawna's world. Now, there was nothing but blank rock. More importantly, his mind . . . or rather, the nanomites in his blood . . . *registered* it as nothing but blank rock. He felt another surge of relief. "She did it! She destroyed the Portal!"

Then he heard a rumble above them . . . and his relief turned to renewed terror. "We have to get out of here!" he cried.

Athelia stared at him. "We shouldn't move her . . ."

The ground shook. "That blast, when Shawna sealed the Portal, released a lot of Shaping energy," Karl said urgently. "When Portals are destroyed, things around them tend to get unstable."

A huge crack suddenly opened in the back wall, right where the Portal had been, releasing a flood of dirt and loose rocks. "Very unstable!" he cried, perhaps unnecessarily.

Athelia jumped to her feet. "Urrican! Take Shawna! Foley! Help me with Karl!"

Urrican hurried over, and with a grunt, picked Shawna up, then shifted her into a fireman's carry. She remained limp. Foley and Athelia hauled Karl to his feet, the wound in his leg stabbing him. With one on either side of him, helping to support his weight, he was able to limp from the cave.

Devil's Tower shook and rumbled. A boulder the size of a horse slammed into the ground thirty feet from them, the impact making them stagger. Karl choked on the dust it raised. He remembered how the Mysterious Island had melted away beneath him, becoming spongy. That wasn't what was happening here. The masses of stone dropping from the tower were very solid. They would squash them all like bugs if they didn't get away.

In the end, Foley and Athelia had to pull Karl down the slope with his legs dragging, bouncing off rocks, each impact driving a dagger into his calf. Despite Shawna's shirt bandaging his wound, he knew he was leaving a trail of blood, but for once, he didn't have to worry about it: the Adversary would not be coming through the Portal.

Not this one. Not yet.

Although . . .

Well, enough time to worry about *that* when and if they survived *this*.

They reached the floor of the desert. The wreckage of the *Terror,* bodies strewn around it, still poured smoke into the air. They staggered on another hundred yards, then stopped and looked back.

The entire near side of Devil's Tower had collapsed, burying the cave in which they'd been moments before beneath tons of rock. Boulders continued to bounce down the sides. One slammed into the *Terror.* Dust hung in the air, making them cough.

But the rumbling and crashing of stones had subsided. Devil's Tower still stood, but it was a sad, truncated, and mutilated version of its former self.

And then, from around its shattered sides, an improbable airship came flying toward them, held up by dozens of whirling blades on masts on the deck of what otherwise looked like a ship, larger propellers fore and aft providing propulsion, stubby wings aiding control. Karl had no idea where it had come from, or how long it had been there: the bulk of the Tower had hidden it entirely until moments before.

He felt Athelia stiffen. "That's the *Albatross*! But that's impossible! She's half the world away."

"Not anymore," Karl said, pointing out the obvious.

"How . . . ?"

A weak voice spoke from Karl's right. "I called for it. Didn't think it worked. Glad it did."

A fresh wave of relief poured through Karl. Shawna Keys was alive and well. The Portal had been destroyed. The Adversary could not follow.

Despite the gash in his shoulder and the bullet wound in his leg, it had turned out to be a good day.

Since my adventures began, I've woken up in some pretty weird places. Slung over the shoulders of a sweating man was a new one, though. While I could imagine circumstances in which it might be exciting, these were not those. "Put me down," I said, and Urrican knelt and let me off.

I stood up, then had to grab his shoulder to keep from falling over as my head swam. Also, I hurt, in too many places to list. Even my teeth hurt. And my ears still rang, though at least I could hear, so I guessed they'd recover eventually.

Apparently, I'd successfully destroyed the Portal because here I was, here was everyone else, there was Devil's Tower . . . somewhat the worse for wear . . . and here came the *Albatross* to rescue me, that last enormous Shaping I had attempted before I ran out of oomph apparently having worked after all. *I must have just Shaped it too far away and on the wrong side of the Tower,* I thought.

Karl looked pale. The blood on his shoulder and torso and the blood on his wounded leg were now fetchingly complemented by a smear of blood across his face below his nose. Athelia had one of those, too, as did Foley and Urrican, evidence of the force of the blast that had thrown me backward when the Portal closed. I wiped my hand across my own nose, and it, too, came away red. Apparently, we all matched.

The Adversary had been very close to the Portal, back in my old world. I wondered if he'd taken the force of that blast in the teeth.

I hoped so.

I reached inside myself to see if by some miracle I now had unlimited Shaping power, in which case I was totally going to Shape us all back to Robur's palace and myself into the longest, hottest bath I could imagine.

Unfortunately, I had nothing. I was as empty of power as I had been before I'd reached the Mysterious Island on my world, after conjuring a fog and fighting a hurricane, as empty of power as I'd been for the entire time I'd been in Robur's world, until his sudden demise poured its *hokhmah* into me. It would come back . . . I hoped . . . with rest and recuperation, but for the moment, we were at the mercy of the *Albatross*.

Which now was settling down to land, not far away—not far away enough, since the wind of its rotors drove dust and grit into our faces. The rotors continued to whirl while stabilizing legs, to keep the vessel level, were run over the sides. Then they chop-chop-chopped down to silence at last. A ladder dropped. Four armed crewmen descended, then waited, rifles ready—not Leyden rifles, but the old-fashioned kind (whatever that meant in a world with this one's weirdly mixed-up levels of technology). For all that three of us wore the same uniform as they did (and the other two of us were shirtless), they clearly were not taking any chances.

A fifth man came over the side of the *Albatross,* a big man, dark-skinned, with a gold hoop in one ear (I could see it glinting even from that distance): Captain Nebuchadnezzar Harding-Smith, who had welcomed me to this world (and then promptly accused me of being either a spy or a witch and threatened to throw me over the side of his flying ship, but I was willing to let bygones be bygones).

The *Albatross* still bore scars from the attack Belinda had led against it, when I had been spirited away on her helicopter, in the form of holes in the hull that had been patched but not yet painted. But it clearly flew, and that was important, since it was our only way out of this desert.

The captain came closer, his armed guard with him. Urrican snapped to attention and saluted. Foley did the best he could but was hampered by the fact that he still had one arm around Karl.

Athelia did not salute. Captain Harding-Smith, stopping in front of us, frowned at her. "Who are you, sailor?" he rumbled.

"Sneffels Yoculis," Athelia replied.

For a second, I thought she'd had a stroke, but the captain's eyes widened. "Twenty-two," he replied.

"What's going—" I began, but Athelia silenced me with a quick downward stroke of her hand.

She frowned, clearly concentrating. "Saknussemm," she said at last.

Sneffels . . . Saknussemm . . . I recognized the first. Sneffels was the volcano, at least in the English translation I'd read, which was probably the same one Robur had read, into which the heroes of *A Journey to the Center of the Earth* descended to start their adventures. I didn't remember Saknussemm, but it certainly sounded Icelandic, so it was probably from the same story.

How the two were linked by the number twenty-two I had no idea, but Athelia's response had clearly satisfied Harding-Smith. "So, you are an intelligence officer," he said. "May I ask your name and rank?"

"You may," Athelia said. "I am General Athelia Richelot, commander of the Secret Service of the Republic of Weldon."

Captain Harding-Smith's eyes widened. Then it was his turn to stiffen and snap a salute. "Ma'am!"

"At ease, Captain," Athelia said.

He relaxed, but kept his eyes locked on her. "Ma'am, can you explain how I and the *Albatross* suddenly came to be here?" He glanced back at the *Terror.* "And what that wreckage belongs to?"

Athelia took a deep breath, as if she were shouldering a great burden, far greater than I had been on Urrican's broad shoulders. "That is the wreckage of the *Terror,* Captain," she said softly. "And lying next to it, I regret to inform you, is the body of your master and mine."

The captain paled. One of the men with him cried out. The others looked stunned. Their rifles drooped. "Ma'am," the captain said in a choked voice. "You can't mean . . ."

"I do, Captain," Athelia said. "Robur, Master of the World . . . is dead."

THIRTY-TWO

I'VE HEARD THE expression "there shall be weeping and gnashing of teeth" my whole life (Sunday School, remember?), but I'd never really seen it in action until then. Captain Harding-Smith held his composure, but two of his escorts dropped to their knees, faces contorted, and screamed their grief to the sky. The other two wept openly. It was both unsettling and infuriating. Robur was dead, but the selfish Shaping of the inhabitants of his world continued to cause misery.

If I'd had the ability, I would have Shaped them myself, right then, to relieve them from the burden of horror Robur's Shaping had placed on them, but I was still in a Shape-free zone, not even a hint of ability to be found in any crevice of my mind.

Athelia, however, stiffened as the men collapsed. "Get up!" she snapped. "That's an order!"

"You heard the general!" the captain shouted.

To my surprise, they managed to pull themselves together, though tears still streaked their faces—as they streaked the captain's. As, indeed, they streaked Athelia's.

"Captain Harding-Smith," she said. "You will send a party to the wreckage of the *Terror* to look for wounded, bury the dead, and salvage whatever may be salvageable. Then you will place demolition charges to ensure that Prince Dakkar's forces, which will undoubtedly find their way here in fairly short order, gain no useful information about the *Terror*'s technology." She turned and looked across the desert. "Somewhere in the vicinity, there is a large transport vehicle . . ."

"Yes, ma'am," Captain Harding-Smith said. "We saw it. It was below us when we . . . appeared here."

"Destroy it."

"Yes, ma'am."

"We'll need quarters aboard *Albatross* and fresh clothing," Athelia said. "And food and drink."

"Of course, ma'am," the captain said. "I will escort you myself." He turned and gave brisk instructions to his escort to set in motion the execution of Alethia's orders, then led us to the *Albatross,* which looked ungainly—and very, very large—on the ground. I'd never been happier to see anything. Athelia was undoubtedly right. Dakkar's forces from the *Narwhal* or from elsewhere in Tsalal must even now be converging on this site. I did not want to end up back in the prince's clutches, not after the way I had lied to him and manipulated him to get to the Free City—at least, not until I had my Shaping ability back . . .

And already, I'm thinking of how I can twist the people of this world, just like Robur did. Am I really any better?

The fact I was currently wearing only a bra above my trousers, the remnants of my shirt having kept Karl from bleeding out through his leg wound, might have been a problem, climbing aboard what was, despite its flying ability, essentially a sailing vessel full of sailors a long time between ports—if not for the fact Athelia was piped aboard as General Richelot, Commander of the Secret Service, and if not for the fact that Urrican glared murder at everyone staring at us as we climbed up the ladder, as if daring them to so much as draw a breath in response to my half-clad state.

Said state didn't last long, in any event. Soon enough, I found myself back in the same cabin I had been placed in when I'd first been hauled aboard the *Albatross.* Athelia had insisted on joining me there, while Karl was next door. Fresh clothing—generic Weldonian military uniforms, but clean and warm—had been obtained for us.

We went up onto the deck once we had changed. A

work party was busy by the wreck of the *Terror*. Another group, I saw, was toiling across the desert to a black speck in the distance—presumably, the transporter on which Belinda had brought her helicopter.

Athelia inquired after the party sent to the *Terror* and learned that three crewmen from that vehicle had survived the attack: Mr. Pazik and two others, whom he had led a short distance away in case of further explosions. Clearly, that had been the movement I'd glimpsed when I'd looked back as we'd climbed toward the Portal. I was happy Mr. Pazik had survived, and very sorry that Captain Sullivan had not. The three survivors were being treated for burns and lacerations and broken bones but would recover.

The members of the *Albatross*' crew, having been informed of Robur's demise, all wore stunned expressions. I saw one piratical sailor, every square inch of exposed skin covered in tattoos, gold rings in his earlobes, sobbing quietly in the middle of the deck, his back against one of the rotor masts. Athelia did not reprimand him.

Like the survivors of the *Terror,* Karl had been turned over to the ship's surgeon, whose sick bay was in the bow. We went that way but were told at the door that we were not allowed to see Karl until the surgeon had completed his repairs. That left us with nothing to do but find food, which we did in the officers' mess, midship. Sliced meat, fresh bread, apples, cheese, and a glass of beer later, we returned to the sick bay to find Karl sitting up, still shirtless, and apparently pantsless, too, since his bare, wounded leg extended out from under the sheet draped across his middle. Both the cut in his shoulder and the bullet wound in his leg had been bandaged. Someone had also cleaned the blood from his upper body.

The survivors from the *Terror* all slept, sedated, in beds nearby. Mr. Pazik's head was bandaged; it looked like he might be missing an ear.

There was a bandage around Karl's head, too. I didn't remember him having a wound there, but I'd been a little busy. He looked odd in some other way, though it took me a minute to figure it out: his hair had been cut.

The long ponytail that had made me think of him as an aging hippie the first time I saw him was gone. "What happened to your hair?" I blurted out.

He touched the bandage on his head. "There was a cut I didn't even know I had, back of my skull. They had to cut off my hair to get at it." He sighed. "I have had long hair for a great many years. I feel somewhat naked."

I looked at the rest of him, of which I could see quite a bit, and raised an eyebrow.

He laughed. "Yes, I know. Yet it is the lack of hair rather than clothing that makes me feel exposed."

"We have not been properly introduced," Athelia said, stepping forward. "I am General Athelia Richelot, Commander of the Secret Service of the Republic of Weldon."

He inclined his head a little. "Karl Yatsar," he said. "I serve Ygrair. She is . . ."

"I've told Athelia everything you told me," I said. "She knows about the Labyrinth."

"Indeed?" It was Karl's turn to raise an eyebrow. "And believes in it?"

"The Master told me about the Labyrinth, and the Shaped worlds, before Shawna did," she said, which startled him enough his other eyebrow rose, too. "Shawna told me about you, and your quest."

"As I told Robur," I said.

"And he brought you out here to further your quest?" Karl said. "Admirable. You must have done an excellent job of explaining the situation."

"He didn't bring me out here to further my quest," I corrected. "He refused to even consider sharing his *hokhmah* with me. He lied and said he didn't know how to do so, or if it was even possible . . . and then tried to steal it from me. He didn't seem to fear the Adversary. He intended to hold me at gunpoint to force you to teach him how to open Portals."

I didn't mention that it been specifically at the point of Athelia's gun that I was to have been held hostage. I couldn't blame her. Robur had Shaped her so that she didn't have a choice.

"And did you tell him that would not work?" Karl said.

"No," I said. "I didn't think telling him about the Shurak technology was a good idea. He might have decided to see if he could . . . extract it."

"It sounds like that was a wise decision." He glanced at Athelia. "I am surprised Robur told you the truth. In my travels in the Labyrinth, I have never encountered another Shaper who did that. I am even more surprised you believed him."

"Of course, I believed him," Athelia said. "He was the Master."

"Robur Shaped his inner circle to be absolutely faithful to him," I told Karl.

"I see," Karl said. He looked at Athelia thoughtfully. "Now that your Master is dead, and his *hokhmah* dwells in Shawna, your world will turn more and more to her as its Shaper. Given time, *she* will be Master of the World. If nothing changes, your absolute loyalty will shift to her."

I gaped at him, horrified. "No!" I said. "I don't want that."

"It does not matter what you want. That is the way of it. You are now Shaper of this world. Once your power returns, you will be able to do with it as you will."

I hated the thought . . .

. . . didn't I?

I suddenly didn't want to be there, with Karl sizing me up with his cold blue eyes, with Athelia staring at me with an intense gaze in which I imagined I already saw the beginning of the unthinking, compulsory devotion Robur had engendered in her and others. "I'm going for a walk," I said, and turned, and went out on deck, down the ladder, and out into the desert, alone.

It was still before noon, the day that had started so early and in which so much had happened still only a few hours old. The chill that had troubled me when I was shirtless had largely disappeared, though it still wasn't hot.

I wandered maybe half a mile, found a rock, sat on it, and then turned and looked back at the *Albatross,* and the shattered remnants of Devil's Tower beyond. I remembered when I had first seen the airship, as the Mysterious

Island dissolved beneath me and it hauled me up into the sky. I'd known nothing about this world then. Now, I knew too much, every detail that Robur had imposed on it. And the one thing I knew, the one thing I was certain of, was that I could not leave it the way it was.

Robur, self-centered, concerned only about his own enjoyment, had Shaped this world to be locked in endless combat. He had crafted Prince Dakkar—his version of Captain Nemo—as his nemesis, given him loyal followers, given himself equally loyal followers, set up a certain level of technology inspired by Jules Verne, and then started . . . playing. Because that was all this world had been to him, a giant game, a virtual reality game, a place where everything looked real but wasn't real, at least not to him.

Soldiers died? That was their job.

Civilians suffered? So what? They were non-player characters, NPCs, existing only to flesh out the world, make it seem more real.

Men and women devoted themselves blindly to him, were willing to take any risk, suffer any consequences, in order to serve him? Well, you couldn't win the game if you didn't have a powerful team on your side.

And it didn't even matter if he won or lost because he always had a reset button handy. He'd build up his Shaping ability, hoard it, and use it, really, for only one thing: to restart the game when it went badly, or simply when he was tired of it. And then everything went back to the way he'd Shaped it to begin with, with a few modifications to make the new game more fun. All the sacrifices and death, all of the people who had given up everything to help him defeat Dakkar, or Dakkar to defeat him, convinced that they were doing what had to be done, that they were trying to make the world a better place for their children and grandchildren, that somehow, they were working toward peace . . . he wiped that all away. Those who had died remained dead, but their deaths had been meaningless, as meaningless as the disappearance of pixels on a computer screen when a kid shuts off the system.

He'd wanted my ability to open Portals so he could

have a couple of more worlds to play with. Given the opportunity, he'd have taken over *my* old world.

He was no better than the Adversary, I thought. And then, *Well, he's better in one way. He's dead.*

I wouldn't let his world continue the way he'd Shaped it. I couldn't. It belonged to me now, which made the people within it my responsibility. *And when I leave it,* I vowed, *I will leave it better than when I entered it.*

With a new sense of duty, I jumped off the rock and hurried back to the *Albatross.* I needed to talk to Karl.

When I got back to the sick bay, Athelia had left, so I had him to myself—well, except for the still-sleeping Mr. Pazik and the two other survivors of the *Terror.*

I sat on Karl's bedside. "I have to fix this world," I said, without preamble. "I can't just leave it as it is. The war will continue, and without Robur, I think the Republic of Weldon will eventually lose to the Principality of Raj . . . and Dakkar will be a tyrant."

Karl studied me a moment. "What do you propose?" he said at last.

"I want to Shape the people of this world one last time," I said. "I'd . . . I'd like to teach the world to sing in perfect harmony." (I know, I know, but I couldn't resist. At least I didn't *sing* it. Anyway, Karl wouldn't get the reference.)

"You can't," he said.

"Why not?" I demanded. "This world is now a sole proprietorship, and I'm the proprietor. I have the holy *hokhmah.* Me, and no one else. It's safe from the Adversary. I've done my job. Before I leave, I want to fix what Robur messed up."

"You . . . can . . . not," Karl repeated, emphasizing each word.

Anger flared in me. "And how, exactly, do you plan to stop me?"

He sighed. "Grammar matters," he said, which was pretty much the last thing I expected him to say. "I did not say, 'You may not,' as I would have if I were refusing to grant you permission. I said, 'You cannot,' as in, you are not capable of it."

"Why not?" I demanded for the second time.

"Because the Shaped individuals, for all that they have only existed in absolute terms for as long as the world has existed, for all that they are, in essence, copies—significantly altered, but still copies—of real people in the First World, for all that they are not human beings in the same way you and I are, still have the thing that is both humanity's greatest glory and its fatal flaw: free will. You do not—no one has—the Shaping ability to completely eliminate that."

"Robur—"

"From what you have told me, Robur Shaped a relative handful of people to be absolutely loyal to the two leaders he established, himself and Prince Dakkar. Another, larger number of people were no doubt placed in an initial state of trust, but not one impervious to the vagaries of circumstance. And still others, the 'peasants' or 'hoi polloi' or however he thought of them—"

"The non-player characters," I muttered.

Karl frowned. "Not a term I am familiar with, but if you say so . . . the 'non-player characters' simply exist, their memories Shaped by the Labyrinth itself to give them a history in this world. Those memories, and their own individual proclivities, as inherited from their originals in the First World, are their starting point. After that, they develop and act and make decisions as would any other human being, because that is what they are— human beings, at least of a sort."

I let that "of a sort" go by and thought about what he'd said. It made sense. Once I'd learned about my own power, I'd Shaped people to do what I needed done. The consequences had often been unexpected, and occasionally deadly—proof that Shaping a human being was indeed fraught with potential complications. Perhaps even those Robur had Shaped to be loyal to himself, like Athelia, had had the capacity to act in an unexpected fashion. Perhaps, had it come to it, she *wouldn't* have pulled the trigger when she'd held me at gunpoint. And as for those who *hadn't* been Shaped to be loyal to him . . . well, they might fire a rocket at his aircraft, even knowing he was aboard. Or *especially* knowing he was aboard.

"But Robur was able to reset them all, erase all their memories . . ." I said, thinking out loud.

"Return them to their initial condition within the world, yes," Karl said. "An extremely impressive act of Shaping. As I said to you in your own world, when we realized that elements of this world had leaked into it, Robur might well have been more powerful than you—powerful enough to carry out the quest you have undertaken for Ygrair. I am sorry I did not meet him."

I gave him a narrow look. "You're sorry you didn't meet him? That sounds like you might have thrown me over for him, if you had."

"I apologize if I gave offense."

Which was not the same thing as saying the thought hadn't crossed his mind. *Why did I try so hard to save this guy?* I asked myself.

Because he knows stuff you need to know.

But is he my friend? I'd thought so. Then I wasn't sure. Then I'd thought so again. And now, once more, I wasn't sure . . .

"So," I said. "It's impossible to Shape everyone so they just . . . get along."

"Since that has never happened in the First World, I would say yes," Karl said. "At least in any world with a large population. If, somewhere, a Shaper has limited him or herself to just a few dozen people . . . perhaps. But even then, I doubt it."

"I'll just have to come up with something else, then."

"Why not leave well enough alone?" Karl said. "The people of this world are now free in a way they have never been free before, and once you leave this world, there will be no one here who can Shape it. In fact, if we seal the Portal through which we leave, I don't believe anyone will ever be able to even enter this world again. Why not let them make their own decisions, live their own lives? That is, after all, Ygrair's ideal."

"I will," I said. "But right now, everything is warped because of Robur's initial conditions."

"I just told you, you can't . . ."

"I *will* find a way to make this world better before I leave it!"

He looked at me silently for a moment. "Then all I can say is, 'Good luck.'"

THIRTY-THREE

THE FLIGHT FROM what was left of Devil's Tower back across the desert and sea to Quercus took two days. Karl was allowed up on the second day, to limp through the corridors beneath the deck. Buffeted by the manmade hurricane winds of the rotors, abovedeck was not a good place for a man on crutches. (When I went on deck, I wore a leather jacket, helmet, and goggles, as I had on the deck of the *Terror* during our drive across the desert. I had no *need* to go up there—I just got a kick out of the whole steampunk aesthetic.) We dined with the captain, with whom Athelia consulted on the best way to announce the terrible news to the citizens of the Republic of Weldon. Karl and I mostly listened quietly. In private, Karl occasionally asked me if I had decided what I would do.

I had, but I didn't tell him.

We arrived at Quercus early on a clear morning, landing on the same runway from which *Terror* had departed. Athelia had sent coded wireless messages ahead, so the awful truth was known to those who needed to know it. The bodies we had brought with us—Robur's and Captain Sullivan's, which had been kept in the "frigifiltered" cold room belowdecks where perishable foods were likewise stored—were spirited away. Robur's would be cleaned up and prettified and eventually would lie in state, once Athelia announced the news.

And it *would* be Athelia. Because as I had watched her talking to the captain, thought about all my experiences with her, and thought about what I could do to set this world on a better course, I had decided she was the one in whom to put my faith.

I told her as much, in our shared cabin, the night before we landed at the palace.

"You know I'm now the Master of the World," I said to her. (I felt silly saying it, but I seemed to be stuck with the title.)

"Mistress, surely?" Athelia said, with a sardonic smile.

I laughed. "Sure." I let the merriment die. "You can feel it, too, can't you?"

She nodded. "Yes. It feels . . . I remember my loyalty to Robur, but it feels distant. A memory. I know that whatever you tell me is true and right. Which makes no sense because I only met you a few days ago."

"Well," I said. "You won't have to fret about it for long."

Her eyes narrowed. "What do you mean?"

"I mean," I said, "that I'm going to do one last Shaping before Karl and I leave this world for the next. I'm going to make *you* Master . . . or, if you prefer, Mistress . . . of the World."

"What?" She straightened suddenly. "I'm no Shaper."

"No," I said. "You're not. Once I leave, there'll be no Shaper. Because of that, Karl thinks that, once we leave and close the Portal behind us, this world will be cut off from the Labyrinth forever. Neither my world—the one holding the Adversary—or the next will touch it any longer, which means no Portal can ever again connect it to another world. It will be left to make its own way under the direction of those who live here . . . and God, I guess, if you believe in God."

"There are heathen, those who reject *The Word of the Shaper,* who profess belief in other gods," Athelia said thoughtfully. "Perhaps they are closer to the truth than we."

I had nothing to say to that. "I'm getting stronger," I went on. "This world is adjusting to me, and I'm starting to get my Shaping power back. The question is, what do I do with it? Karl tells me I can't Shape everyone any more than Robur could. You're head of intelligence, so you know that, even in the Republic, not everyone was perfectly loyal. Am I right?"

She smiled. "Extremely right."

"But," I continued, "I can Shape a few people. So, here's what I plan to do . . ."

I told her. She resisted a little, but only a little; guilty though it made me feel, I took advantage of the loyalty that had been transplanted from Robur to me with his death to win her to my side.

And so, upon our landing, General Athelia Richelot, Commander of the Secret Service, asked the Speaker for permission to address the Citizens' Assembly, the putatively democratically elected legislature of the Republic of Weldon, which Robur had created primarily (so far as I could tell) so he didn't have to deal with the minutiae of governing—collecting taxes, recruiting soldiers, keeping the peace, all that kind of thing.

Within the high-vaulted Gothic confines of the House of Assembly, as Athelia was recognized by the Speaker and rose to address the gathered delegates, I sat in the public gallery alongside Karl, took a deep breath . . . and Shaped everyone there.

It almost drained me again, but I knew at once I had succeeded, because as Athelia, who had never missed a step, mounted the dais, the members of the Assembly rose as one and applauded her.

She took her place at the podium. "Friends, delegates, countrymen," she said, her voice ringing out across the hushed gathering, "I come not to praise Robur, but to bury him . . ."

Karl shot me a look. "Really?" he said in a low voice as, below us, Athelia continued to lay out her vision for the future of the Republic of Weldon, now that the Master of the World was no more.

"Not my doing," I said, and it wasn't. I was as startled as he to hear that echo of Shakespeare, who, after all, hadn't existed in this world. Presumably, his words had somehow bled into this one from the First World. *Well,* I thought, *he was a kind of Shaper of worlds . . .*

By the end of that session, Athelia had been unanimously acclaimed, by members from all four of the Republic's political parties, Interim President. And by the end of that day, I'd recovered enough strength to Shape one more person, from afar.

The fruit of that Shaping ripened four days later when, trailing long white banners, a flight of Rajian helicopters flew in over the sea cliff and landed on the white-paved runway. Safely out of sight in the shadowed interior of one of the rooms overlooking the scene, with Karl at my side, I watched Belinda and three airmen stand at attention as Prince Dakkar, Captain Nemo himself, unbuckled from the 'copter he had been flying, saluted the Weldonian honor guard there to greet him, and then shook Athelia's hand, before walking with her (and a gaggle of advisers and aides) into the palace proper.

"Well done," Karl said. "I do not know if peace can truly take hold on this world, but you have given it, I think, the best possible opportunity."

"I hope so," I said. I looked down at Belinda as she passed below me, following her prince. *One more little touch of Shaping,* I thought, *just a tiny touch, and she'll forgive me . . .*

Instead, I let her go, out of my sight. I didn't deserve forgiveness for Anthony's death, and I wouldn't tamper with Belinda's grief.

"Come on," I said to Karl. "We have a caravan to join."

For five days we retraced the roads that had brought me to Quercus from the Free City, once more among the company of the Worldshapers Theatrical Troupe. Each night, for old times' sake, I sang "The Sound of Music," broke a ship, and ate a puppet-sailor in *Twelve Angry Sailors,* and donned my donkey costume for *Cymbalella.* One night, after having enjoyed (by his own admission) perhaps a little too much wine, Karl offered a surprisingly good rendition of "I Am the Very Model of a Modern Major-General."

At journey's end, we stood in the dead-end alley in front of the Portal I had opened, and then sealed. "Show me," Karl said.

"Sure," I said. I remembered exactly how it had felt, opening this Portal. I reached out, light flashed, and the door swung open. No moon shone in the cloudy skies above the Free City, where it was well after midnight, but a full one, bright and white, greeted us in the skies of the next world. What seemed to be missing was the werewolf—if that was really what it was—that had greeted me last time. I didn't miss it.

The *hokhmah* I had taken from Robur cringed at this hole in its reality, hating it—a far cry from how comfortable and welcoming the Portal back into my own world had felt (not counting the bullets flying out of it). I couldn't wait to close this Portal again . . . but I wouldn't do it from this side.

"Impressive," Karl said.

"Now that we're back together," I said, "I can hopefully avoid having quite as many 'adventures' as I had in this world." I put on an English accent. "'Adventures? Nasty, disturbing, uncomfortable things. Make you late for dinner!'"

Not surprisingly, Bilbo Baggins' oft-quoted maxim went right over Karl's head. "Perhaps," he said. "Although every world holds its own."

"At least we won't have to worry about the Adversary," I said.

"Perhaps," Karl said again.

I raised an eyebrow at him. "Perhaps?"

"You'll recall that when I came through the Portal into this world, I was shirtless."

"I did notice, yes."

"And I had a gash in my shoulder."

"Noticed that, too . . . how is it, by the way?"

"Still aches, but much better, as is my leg." He glanced at me. "I was not wearing a shirt because I had taken it off and wadded it up to press against the cut."

"To stop the bleeding," I said. "Makes sense."

"To stop the bleeding, but also to ensure I did not

leave any blood behind. Remember how you gained the power to do . . . this." He nodded at the open Portal.

"The blood on the altar." I suddenly realized where this was going. "You mean, if the Adversary got hold of your blood . . ."

"He could gain the ability to make his own Portals between worlds, as you have, instead of merely following in my steps."

"Good thing you had that shirt, then."

"It was," Karl said. "But when you saw me, I did not have it. Nor was it in the cave."

I stared at him. "You think . . ."

"I fear that I left it in your world."

"Then the Adversary . . ."

"Might not have found it," Karl said. "It could have sunk into the water in the mangrove swamp. Even if he did find it, the blood would not be fresh, as when you touched it. The nanomites break down rapidly. It might only provide him with hints of the ancient Shurak technology Ygrair brought to Earth that allows for opening Portals. But it does not do to underestimate the Adversary. He is brilliant, and focused, and relentless . . . and not human. Even hints might be enough to eventually provide him with the means to travel from world to world on his own."

I felt a chill. "If he gains that ability . . . will he come through this world?"

"Not if I am right, and the complete absence of a Shaper means that, once you leave, no Portal can ever again be opened into it."

"But you're not certain about that."

"No. But even if I'm wrong, and the Adversary does, someday, enter this world, he will not be able to Shape it or anyone who lives here: you are taking its *hokhmah* with you. He could bring, at most, a dozen cadre members—once he has replaced the ones who have died, itself a long, drawn-out process: they must be Shaped over and over again, like a blacksmith forging the steel of a sword, before they can pass through Portals without winking out of existence. Even with a full cadre, he would have to be furtive in crossing from Portal to Portal—he could not fight against all the might of this world, even with modern weapons, not with just twelve soldiers, limited to what they can carry with them. No, this world is safe from his depredations. But that does not mean we will not see him again."

"He may never find that blood-soaked shirt."

"He may not," Karl said.

"I'm going to hope for that, then." I turned and looked behind us, down the short alleyway into the dark street beyond. "Even if we do have to face him again, if this world is safe . . . then I've done something right."

"I would say," Karl said, "that you have done a great deal right."

I raised a Spockian eyebrow at him. "Why, Karl. That's the nicest thing you've ever said to me." I didn't give him an opportunity to respond; he probably would have spoiled the moment. "Let's get out of here," I said instead, and walked into another world.

I found myself on a hilltop, once again looking along a pale path winding down into a deep, pine-filled valley. Once again, I saw a castle on a crag on the far side of the valley. Tonight, more than just a single light glowed there. The castle blazed with light, every window illuminated, as though for a great festival.

I turned and looked behind me, as Karl stepped through the Portal. On this side, it had appeared in the side door of an old, run-down barn, empty of animals. The ruins of a small cottage stood nearby, one wall tumbled, half its thatched roof missing.

"Not the high-rent district," I said. I turned back to face the castle. "I guess that's where we're headed . . ."

Something flew over the moon, something with batwings, but far too large to be a bat. An unearthly, chilling wail echoed through the valley.

"In the morning?" I said, with a mouth that had suddenly gone dry.

"In the morning," Karl agreed.

I turned, closed, and sealed the Portal, a flash of blue light briefly lighting the ruins and tree trunks. The instant

I did so, I felt the Portal vanish entirely, winking out of existence as though it had never been. Karl had been right: no Shaper would ever trouble Athelia's world again.

Then Karl and I repaired to the cottage. Beneath the intact portion of the roof, we sat with our backs to a still-standing section of wall and looked out past tumbled stone toward that distant, inviting castle, waiting for the sun to rise on the second new world I had entered.

I glanced at Karl. This time, at least, I wasn't alone.

The weird wailing of the winged thing in the sky echoed across the dark valley.

AVAILABLE SEPTEMBER 2020 FROM DAW,
THE THRILLING SEQUEL TO
MASTER OF THE WORLD
BY EDWARD WILLETT

THE MOONLIT
WORLD

READ ON FOR A SPECIAL PREVIEW.

THE NEW EXPERIENCES travel offers are said to broaden the mind. I'd had rather more new experiences (and more mind-broadening) than I really cared for since exiting my own world, pursued not by a bear but by the Adversary, and I'd just added a new one I could have done without: being shaken awake in the dark inside a ruined thatched-roof cottage and told, "An armed party is heading this way from the castle."

I admit, I didn't immediately know a) who the person shaking me awake was, b) why I was lying fully dressed between far-too-thin blankets on a cold wooden floor, or c) what castle? But it all came rushing back in a moment. In order, a) was Karl Yatsar, the mysterious stranger who first revealed to me that the world I used to live in was one I'd Shaped into existence (though I didn't remember doing it) and told me I had to flee it due to the encroachment of the aforementioned Adversary (who killed my best friend and would have killed me if I hadn't instinctively re-Shaped the world to save myself); b) was because, a few hours ago, we had entered this world from the Jules Verne-inspired one we had just left, sealing the Portal behind us, and this cottage had been close at hand and offered at least a modicum of shelter; and c) was the castle across the valley, around whose towers we had seen mysterious winged things flying. An armed party leaving that castle and heading in our direction seemed unlikely to be good news.

Unless . . .

"Is the Shaper in the castle?" I asked Karl. "Maybe we should just let ourselves be captured."

I couldn't really see Karl in the dimness: he was just a darker shape bending over me, outlined against the stars shining through the hole in the roof behind his head. He straightened and turned away—I could see that much—and said, "I do not know."

It was so rare for Karl to admit he didn't know something I almost stammered my response. "You . . . you don't know if . . . if we should let them capture us, or you don't . . . ?"

"I do not know if the Shaper is in the castle." His silhouette against the stars changed shape as he turned back toward me. "I cannot tell."

"I thought you said you could always sense the Shaper's whereabouts when you entered a new world."

"I always *have*. This time . . . I cannot."

I sat up, emitting only a minor, ladylike groan. "So what does that mean?"

"I do not know."

Two times in a single conversation. Utterly amazing.

"So . . . you think we should avoid them?"

"Until we know what is transpiring, yes," Karl said.

"How long until they get here?"

"They are on foot. We might have, at most, forty-five minutes. Probably less."

"Do they know we're here?"

"I do not believe so," Karl said. "I think there would be more urgency in their movements if so."

"Right, then." I got to my feet. I hadn't slept nearly enough, soundly enough, on a soft-enough surface, or with enough covers. But I'd slept, and we'd taken our time during the journey to the Portal in the world we had just left, so I felt like I could function. I quickly rolled up my bedroll and tied it to the top of the backpack I'd brought with me from the last world. (It was nice to enter a world with clean clothes, food, and water, not to mention a good sharp knife and, at the very bottom of the pack, a pistol and extra ammunition for it, instead of arriving with nothing, like I had in the last one.)

We hurried out of the cottage. The road to the castle, covered with crushed, pale-white stone, shone in the moonlight.

Wait. What? I blinked up at said moon. It hung, full, and bright, in exactly the same spot in the sky it had been when we'd first entered this world, hours ago. *That's weird . . .*

And that wasn't the only thing that was weird. That moon was *huge*. Way bigger than it should have been. The way the moon looks when it's rising or setting, except that's an optical illusion. This one looked that big even though it wasn't too far off the zenith.

"We must not stay on the road," Karl said. "They will see us for sure."

The overgrown fields associated with the cottage lay on the side toward the castle. In the direction we turned rose a ridge, covered with a forest of towering pines whose tops glimmered in the moonlight, but at whose roots pooled darkness, into which the white road plunged and vanished.

The forest did *not* look like the sort of place I wanted to be forcing my way through in the middle of the night. "If we leave the road, we'll be lost in no time," I pointed out.

"Are you saying we are not lost now?" Karl said. "Do *you* know where we are?"

A fair point. I sighed. "All right," I said. "I guess the forest it is."

Fortunately, it wasn't as dark in the forest as it had looked before we entered it. The moon, shining between the spindly trunks, painted the needle-strewn floor with long streaks of silvery light, enough to show us our way. And although it's true we didn't know *exactly* where we were going, the direction we needed to take was abundantly clear—away from whomever had come out of the castle.

The ridge, though not terribly steep, was not *not* steep, either. I concentrated on putting one foot in front of the other and not turning my ankle on one of the fallen branches or loose, flat stones that littered our path, hearing Karl's steady breathing behind me. I remembered how much more out of breath than him I'd been while climbing a mountain pass back in my own world. Clearly, a few weeks of healthy outdoor activities like running for my life and being shot at had toughened me up. (Which is not to say I wasn't out of breath, because I was: I just didn't feel like my heart and lungs would explode any time soon.)

I'd had no way of knowing, when we'd begun our journey, what time it was. "Middle of the night" seemed to cover it. But clearly it was more like "very early morning," because almost without my being aware of it, the forest became less black around us, the first hint of the coming dawn—though that full moon continued to shine, in exactly the same place in the sky.

It doesn't move, I thought. *Which means it has to be in a geostationary orbit.*

Which made no sense, for something the size of the moon. What would that do to tides?

Unless, in this Shaped world, the moon was much smaller . . . say, the size of the Death Star. Or something. (I had no idea off the top of my head just how big the Death Star was supposed to be or how big it would look if it were in geostationary orbit. Once again, I missed the internet.) But even then, weren't geostationary orbits only possible at the equator? Were we at the equator? Since I was distinctly chilled, I thought not. But this wasn't the real world, it was a Shaped world. So anything was possible . . . wasn't it?

A world lit by an extra-large moon hanging motionless in the sky sounded crazy. But so did the idea of a world based on the works of Jules Verne—a world where you could literally journey to the moon in a spacecraft launched from a giant cannon—and I'd just come from such a place.

The trees thinned and the light continued to slowly wax as we approached the top of the ridge. By unspoken agreement, we paused and looked back down the way we had come. The riders from the castle had just reached the ruined cottage we had fled, and enough light now finally filled the sky that I could see them: though it was taking its own sweet time about making an appearance, dawn couldn't be far off.

As if on cue, the snowy peaks on the far side of the valley to the west suddenly turned bright orange, as though set on fire. The sun had touched them, but it still had to crawl down them and across the valley floor before it rose above the peaks shadowing us to the east.

Two of our pursuers entered the cottage. They emerged again. A discussion ensued. Pale faces looked toward the sunlit peaks across the valley, then turned in our direction, staring up the ridge. *They can't see us*, I told myself. *Not in this light. We're too low down on the ridge to be silhouetted against the sky.*

But I still got chills. "They can't see us, right?" I asked Karl, seeking reassurance.

"Not if they are human," he said, which didn't exactly provide it.

"What do you mean, not if they're human?" I demanded. "Can Shapers Shape intelligent non-humans?"

"I told you about the elves and dwarves I have encountered," he said. "Of course they can."

Of course they can. I stared down at the group of riders. "They *look* human."

"Humanoid," he corrected. "Remember the giant wolf you saw when you first opened the Portal."

I wasn't likely to forget that monster with red, glowing eyes running toward me along the white-stone road . . .

"It wasn't humanoid," I said.

"But you thought it was a werewolf."

I had. Did that mean . . . ? "Are you saying those riders down there might be *werewolves*?"

He shrugged.

"But the thing I saw looked like a wolf. Those things down there look like humans. And they came out of the castle while it was still dark. If they were werewolves, shouldn't they have been in wolf-form?"

"A fair point," Karl conceded. "Nevertheless, if within this world there is one non-human, intelligent race—werewolves—there may very well be . . ." His voice trailed off. It didn't matter, because even if he had kept speaking

I wouldn't have heard him. Like his, my attention was suddenly entirely focused on one of the dismounted riders, who broke into a run in our general direction, let his long black cloak fall, revealing, to my startlement, he was naked beneath it . . . and then leaped into the air, body reshaping itself in an instant into something bat-like, with spread black wings, that arrowed up the slope toward us.

"Run," suggested Karl, and I didn't argue.

When we had entered this world the night before, we had sought shelter immediately in part because of a weird, winged thing in the sky, whose chilling, wailing cry had echoed across the valley. Now we heard that cry again, from the weird, winged thing pursuing us, and that keening call stabbed itself into my brainstem, the limbic system, the "lizard brain," and would have sent me scrambling away and up the slope even without Karl's urging.

I knew the instant the thing flew overhead. We were screened from the sky by trees, but I still felt the chill of its passing. We could not see it, and yet I had the uncanny sense that it knew exactly where we were, that the skein of branches above us could not hide us from it. If this world had seemed more Tolkienish, I would have guessed it was a Nazgûl.

And then . . . it was gone. The sky felt empty . . . clean. "Why didn't it land and attack?" I gasped out to Karl as we hurried on through the forest. "And what was it?"

"I do not know," he said.

That, I thought, *is becoming tiresome.*

We topped another ridge. Looking back, I could see the distant towers of the castle, but not the cottage where we had spent the night, the winged creature, or the riders. The sun chose that moment to touch the topmost tower of the castle, limning it in gold. "Maybe it's the sun," I said. "Maybe they don't like the light." I paused. "Whoa," I said. "Winged things that don't like the light, in a world where werewolves are real . . . are you thinking what I'm thinking?"

"I am not a mind-reader," Karl said.

"I'm thinking vampires," I said.

He shrugged. "Anything is possible." He turned away from the castle. "In any event, since whatever they are, they do not seem to like the sun, I suggest we make the most of the day, and get as far away from the castle and whatever those were as we can while the sun shines."

"We have to find the Shaper," I said. "Can you tell where she or he is yet?"

"No," Karl said shortly. "I cannot sense anything."

"Why not?"

"I do not know," he said . . . again. "Nor do I have a clue *why* I do not know."

He started down the slope. I followed a few steps behind, staring at the back of his head. *Great*, I thought. *Last world I entered, my all-knowing guide was missing. This time I've got him with me . . . and it turns out he's not all-knowing after all.*

"I've got a bad feeling about this," I muttered.

Edward Willett

"*Marseguro* won Canada's prestigious Prix Aurora, while *Terra Insegura* was a finalist for that award a year later.... The characters are well defined with emotion, purpose. ambition. and revenge. The action is relentless and violent. Mr. Willet has crafted an incredible world on Marseguro."
—Outworlder Reviews

"The pieces all come together nicely to tell a good story of the man who created a new race of amphibious humans, and the results of his efforts to protect them from the growing threat of religious zealots...steamrolling to an inevitable, but satisfying and enjoyable conclusion."   —SFScope

The Helix War

Marseguro   978-0-7564-0464-2
Terra Insegura   978-0-7564-0553-3

And don't miss:
Lost in Translation
978-0-7564-0340-9

To Order Call: 1-800-788-6262
www.dawbooks.com

DAW 177

Edward Willett
The Cityborn

"Willett wraps his capable new adult science fiction adventure around the fate of a mysterious many-tiered city and its inhabitants.... [*The Cityborn*'s] spunky protagonists and colorful world will entertain SF adventure fans."
—*Publishers Weekly*

"Set in a metal city at the center of the mountain ringed Heartland, *The Cityborn* is sprawling space opera centering on Alania, born to the City's privileged caste, and Danyl, a lowborn scavenger.... This is one suspenseful sci-fi thriller not to be missed." —Unbound Worlds

"Willett brings J.G. Ballard's *High-Rise* into the distant space age in this dystopian tale of class, power and freedom that will entertain devotees and non-genre fans alike. The worldbuilding in this book is impressive, creating an atmosphere that is both fascinating and oppressive, and characters who are magnificently complex." —*RT Reviews*

ISBN: 978-0-7564-1178-7

To Order Call: 1-800-788-6262
www.dawbooks.com

DAW 174

Violette Malan

The Novels of Dhulyn and Parno:

"Believable characters and graceful storytelling."
—*Library Journal*

"Fantasy fans should brace themselves:
the world is about to discover Violette Malan."
—*The Barnes & Noble Review*

THE SLEEPING GOD
978-0-7564-0484-0

THE SOLDIER KING
978-0-7564-0569-4

THE STORM WITCH
978-0-7564-0574-8

and

PATH OF THE SUN
978-0-7564-0680-6

To Order Call: 1-800-788-6262
www.dawbooks.com

E. C. Blake
The Masks of Aygrima

"Brilliant world-building combined with can't-put-down storytelling, *Masks* reveals its dark truths through the eyes of a girl who must learn to wield unthinkable power or watch her people succumb to evil. Bring on the next in this highly original series!"

—Julie E. Czerneda

"Mara's personal growth is a delight to follow. Sharp characterization, a fast-moving plot, and a steady unveiling of a bigger picture make this a welcome addition to the genre."

—*Publishers Weekly*

"*Masks* is simply impossible to put down."

—*RT Book Reviews*

MASKS
978-0-7564-0947-0

SHADOWS
978-0-7564-0963-0

FACES
978-0-7564-0940-1

To Order Call: 1-800-788-6262
www.dawbooks.com

DAW 191